JOHNNY

AND

GRACE

Christopher Morosoff

A special thank you to the amazing artist, Jason Hunt, for his cover
artwork. www.jasonhuntdrawings.com

Printed in the United States of America

First Printing, 2017

ISBN 978-0-9909543-1-6

Dedication

This novel is dedicated to my parents. Your love story is an inspiration to all.

It is also dedicated to Anatole and Sonia Morosoff, whose perseverance and love, made our family what it is today.

Destiny Calling - Albert Joseph Poe

Out of the darkness, from a brutal start, in a life soaked in pain, as his world tore apart

Being told all was hopeless, surrounded by darkness and stench, lives all decaying, stuck inside life's trench

But he had a vision, of a much better life, of escaping this place, which had caused him much strife

The sins of the past, he wanted to put away, and look to a bright future, and a much better day

But his dream was realized, when he did meet the one, she was the love of his life, and she shone like the sun

She was a singular vision, that he had many years, someone perfect and sweet; he could put away all his fears

She was beautiful and kind, and she loved him for real, even with the scars and the baggage, together their future was sealed

Now all that he dreamed, it had finally come true, no matter what happened in life, together they'd always get through

© Albert Joseph Poe 2017

Chapter One

THE TRUCK REEKED with the smells of fear and sweat. With a gun being held to his head, Petrov followed the soldier's orders and stripped naked.

"Look at these fools. Puppets! They will do whatever we tell them to," laughed the Red Army soldier.

Full of naked bodies, the soldiers drove the trucks from one town to the next. Filling truck after truck with scared Russian peasants, artists, and gentle souls, these poor men no longer felt like men. Their hearts, minds and souls had been robbed by sadistic exterminators, gun bearing barbarians.

"Are you willing to die?" barked the soldier.

"Do what you must, but strip naked? I will not!" yelled Anatole.

"Just do it," begged Christopher.

"No, don't shoot them! Those who won't listen, let's take them to dig their own graves. They will bury themselves. All while we laugh at their pathetic souls."

The naked men, huddled flesh that quivered as masses of humiliation, would do anything at this point. Covering their private areas with their hands, they were thrown about as the trucks came to a screeching halt.

"Those who have followed orders, you are sheep, but you will live. At least for a little while longer. Get out! You are not men, but cowards! But you shall at least live to see tomorrow."

The emasculated males, at gunpoint, jumped from the back of the truck into the cold and raw fields. These shamed souls ran for any cover they could find. Perhaps a bullet would have been better after all.

Those who dared to be shot, who refused to follow orders, were driven deep into the woods. Driving through the very rough terrain, they were unable to hear their own thoughts, the noise was so immense as the truck swerved before stopping in a barren and lonely looking field. Swirling clouds of dust covered the trucks.

"Out! Now!" barked a soldier.

As angry as he looked, a trace of an evil smile could be seen within the soldier's demeanor. Barbaric control over others made him feel bigger; his true inner cowardice was camouflaged, for another moment at least.

"Line up! You've chosen to die. Let's see how brave you are now!"

Stretched over several hundred feet, the clothed but soon to be dead men, wondered if they should not have just followed orders, and stripped naked of their clothes, of their dignity.

Sweating profusely, Anatole couldn't bear to lift another shovelful of dirt. To dig a trench for six hours straight was brutal enough, but to dig one's own grave?

"Keep digging! I can shoot you right now if you prefer," the soldier barked at Anatole and his friends.

The abrasive sounds of gravel and dirt, scraping the large rusty shovels, created a symphony of impending doom.

"I can't do this anymore. If they're gonna shoot us anyway, let them do it now and just be done with it," said Christopher.

Anatole thought back to his past, to a simpler, more innocent time. Childhood was joyous and in no way, could prepare one for the harsh and often brutal ways of life. As he kept digging, Anatole's mind drifted back through time…

Christopher was Anatole's best friend. Growing up together in the small town of Lesnoy, Russia, they had become the best of friends, at the age of seven. These pleasant memories would last for mere seconds as the sounds of the screaming soldiers filled Anatole's ears as well as mind.

"No, listen to me! I have a plan," said Anatole. "Just do as I do."

"Okay, Anatole, but I think you've lost your mind!"

"Keep digging!"

The soldier was looking directly towards Anatole this time.

"They don't want to listen? Okay, that's enough!"

"These fools have just dug their own graves. Pathetic sheep!" said a second soldier.

"Get out of the trenches. Now! Line up! Stand up! Throw the shovels into the pit and stand up!"

The sounds of hundreds of shovels, all hitting the pit of death was horrific. Metal on metal screamed out, crying in fear, fear with no hope.

"Listen to me Christopher, when they start to shoot…"

As Anatole started to divulge his plan to his best friend Christopher, the horrifying sounds of screaming started to multiply. Down the line the soldiers went, shooting the men, as well as boys, some as young as ten years old. Hundreds lined the huge trench, a grave that they had just dug. A grave that would bury them, for eternity.

"What do I do?" asked Christopher.

"When they get close to us…."

As Anatole was explaining to his best friend what his plan was, the shots were getting closer and closer. As the poor victims fell, Anatole grabbed ahold of Christopher's shirt. Seconds before the bullets reached them, they would jump.

"Now!" yelled Anatole.

As the two friends jumped into the mass grave, it seemed as if life had slowed down. Everything moved, but in slowest motion. His mind's eye could see clearly now. His trip backwards in time was as vivid as a movie.

As Anatole's mind slowly drifted back through time, it found its peaceful place. Anatole was just seven years old. He never did want to move. Leaving behind all his friends, Anatole cried himself to sleep, night after night.

"I'll never make new friends."

Anatole's dad, Sergei, was a calm and understanding man.

"Anatole, of course you will. Look at all the boys outside. Go ahead son. Your ice skates are unpacked. Go on. Go skate with the boys," said Sergei.

"I don't want to. I'll never have friends again! I hate you, and I hate Mamma also."

"No son, trust me. Just go outside. Be yourself. The boys will love you."

Anatole was a very talented, but shy little boy. Having moved from the much larger city of Saratov, Anatole's parents had wanted a quieter life, a slower pace. Going into his new bedroom, Anatole emerged later, skates in hand.

"I'm ready, Poppa."

"That's my boy, Anatole."

"I'll try, but I am nervous."

"That's only normal, son."

Bundling up, Anatole carried his skates with him. Walking the hundred feet or so to the frozen pond that neighbors let all the children skate and play hockey on, Anatole just sat off to the side, skates draped over his shoulder.

"Hey, kid."

"My name is Anatole. Not kid."

"Okay, Kid Anatole. I'm Christopher. I see you're not skating today, huh? Me either. Twisted my ankle. Still swollen up."

Anatole immediately felt at ease with Christopher. Maybe Poppa was right after all.

"Let's take a walk," said Christopher.

"But your ankle?" asked Anatole.

"Ohhhh, I guess I really didn't hurt it. But don't tell my Momma. I just didn't wanna go to school. Tests. I didn't study," smiled Christopher.

"Okay. I won't say a word," said Anatole.

The boy's started to walk. As they walked, they talked about everything. Anatole wanted to know about school. He was nervous about public school. His parents had money, why couldn't he just continue with his private studies? After all, public school wouldn't understand his love for drawing and painting. Sketching was his passion.

"It's all good, kid. Don't worry so much. All of my friends are automatically your friends now as well. It's the law," said Christopher.

"Really? It's the law?" asked Anatole.

"No! Haha, you are something else, my friend. I was just kidding, but seriously, you will have many friends by this time tomorrow. I guarantee you," said Christopher.

"It's getting dark. I better get home. My dad is understanding but my mom has a temper. I don't like to cross her," said Anatole.

The boys made their way back to the pond. Everyone was now gone. Anatole could see his mother in the front window of their new home.

"Uh ohh, I'm in for it now," said Anatole.

"Why? What's wrong?"

"Just walk with me to my front door. If Momma sees that I made a friend, I think she'll calm down."

"Okay, kid, let's do it."

Chapter Two

THE BLOOD SPRAYED all over Anatole and Christopher.

"Jump! Now!" screamed Anatole.

Taking no chances, Anatole grabbed and pulled his best friend by the shirt. Falling the ten feet or so into the mass gravesite, the two friends covered their heads and faces. The bodies fell on top of them. Blood flowed downwards, covering them within minutes.

"Anatole!"

"Shhhhh! Do not speak! Do not make a sound!" said Anatole in a hushed tone.

As the two friends lay at the bottom of the pit, they heard the sickening and gut wrenching sounds of moaning and pain. Death was all around them. Death was now a wish for those that were still alive. The sounds of agony consumed the mass grave.

Soon all was quiet except for the sounds of laughter. The soldiers were admiring their handiwork.

"Fools. Cowards. They dug their own graves and like pathetic children, waited for their own death. Not an ounce of fight in any of them," laughed the soldier.

Light, filtered by blood and death, made its way through the mass of quivering flesh. It was getting dark.

"We must still be quiet. They must not hear us, Christopher," whispered Anatole.

"I am sick. I am going to vomit."

"You can't! We mustn't make a sound," said Anatole.

Anatole's mind, full of pain and anguish, sorted through his life. Fear, pain, and anger consumed him but his mind, once again, returned to his childhood.

"Anatole, it's time to wake up son!"

"Oh, Momma. Five more minutes. Please, Momma?"

"Now, Anatole!"

Anatole knew that when Momma had *that* voice, that he better not push things. Popping out of bed, Anatole was no longer nervous about his first day at his new school. After all, he had already made a new friend. Things would be okay.

"Anatole, sit down and eat your breakfast," said Momma.

"But I'm not hungry, Momma."

"Eat!" said Momma.

As Anatole started to eat, there was a knock at the door. It was Christopher. Grabbing his heavy winter coat, Anatole hugged his mother good-bye and raced out the front door.

"Anatole!"

It was too late. As Momma looked out the front window, she saw the two boys laughing as they walked. Perhaps things were going to be alright after all.

Chapter 3

THE BLACKNESS WAS suffocating. The stench of death consumed every bit of their existence. The moaning had stopped. At least within several feet of the two friends, it had. Anatole figured that five hundred bodies had fallen into this grave.

The smells were horrific. The smell of death, sweat and fear. With literally hundreds of pounds of death upon them, the friends could no longer lay still. Unsure of whether they had slept or not, all had been silent for several hours now.

"Gently," said Anatole. "We must make our move now. But be respectful. We wear our friends as homes wear their roofs."

Anatole and Christopher pushed their way upwards. With their heavy boots slipping on blood soaked death, the sounds of dead bodies serving as steps, became louder and louder. Christopher gagged as blood from one of the bodies dripped into his mouth.

"Shhh! They may still be here. Try, Christopher, just a little more. Silently, please."

The early morning light was a welcome sight. Full of grayness and holding an early day's dew, the scene would normally have been a depressing one. But for now, it was the most welcoming sight that Anatole had even witnessed.

Anatole climbed out of the pit of death and extended his bloody hand to his friend. Spitting someone else's blood and looking as he was close to passing out, Christopher exhaled as he emerged from the pit.

"Tell me Anatole, tell me we're going to be okay."

"We will be, my friend. I've looked in every direction and I see no one. But we still must move quickly and quietly."

"Okay, my friend. I'm so glad you're with me. I could not do this alone. I love you, Anatole."

As Christopher looked in all directions, a sense of relief came over him.

"Thank you, Anatole! Anatole, we made it!"

As Anatole turned his head to reply and comfort his best friend, a shot rang out. The blast created a frightening echo.

"Christopher!"

As Anatole called to his friend, he saw the most painful, as well as gruesome sight yet. The right side of Christopher's head, had been blown off. Hearing soldiers in the nearby woods, Anatole ran. He ran as fast as he could and for as long as he could.

Anatole's clothing, soaked in blood, the blood of his friends, had started to dry. Running behind some bushes, he tried to slow down and quiet his breathing. Slowly putting his hand into a very deep pocket of his pants, Anatole was relieved. The money was still there.

Anatole's parents were very wealthy. The family had owned a series of grain mills until tiring of the hectic lifestyle. When Anatole's father sold the business and properties, they literally had more money than they could ever spend.

Fearing something like this could happen someday, Anatole's father had insisted that he never leave home without enough money to escape. Escape his country, Russia. Sensing the impending communist takeover, his father tried to plan for his son, his family.

His destination would depend on several things. Both his mother and father had encouraged him to head to Hungary. They had some connections there, and the government was somewhat stable and conducive to the lifestyle that Anatole truly wanted.

Nearly twenty years old now, Anatole had done his share of traveling during his short lifetime. When he was barely a teenager, Anatole's parents sent him to France to study under the most acclaimed instructors in the world at The Royal Academies of Art. Painting and sketching since he was old enough to walk, Anatole had a passion for expressing himself this way. It was all he could think of. But right now, he could only think of one thing—his escape.

Hearing shots in the distance, Anatole resumed his running, this time he would not stop until he reached true safety. He just knew that if he ran far enough, there were farms, farms that had been customers of his family, purchasing grains, and at a very fair price as well.

Realizing that the farms were not too far from Georgia, Anatole thought this would be the perfect place to hide for a while. From Georgia, he would just need to get to the coastal region where he would try and get aboard a ship headed for Turkey.

Coming to a summit, Anatole peered over the grassy hilltop and into the valley below. There were in fact, several small cottages set an acre or so apart. Hiking down the hillside, Anatole realized that his appearance would be frightening, but he had to find help. Approaching the first cottage he came to, he knocked at the front door.

Chapter Four

A STOUT LOOKING man, Boris was a gentle soul. He and his wife lived alone and they liked it best that way.

"How may I help you, son?"

Anatole, looking disheveled as well as scared, just stood there nervously.

"Come in."

"Thank you, sir."

"Son, you look a mess. My God, you are covered in blood! I imagine that you're hungry as well. Why don't get you a bath and then something to eat."

Boris brought clean clothing for Anatole to change into after he was done bathing. They served him a filling hot meal. Although tremendously thankful, Anatole was still shaking from his recent ordeal.

"Thank you, sir. I think I should be going."

"Please friend, stay the night. It will be very cold tonight. Stay, warm up and then you can leave in the morning," said Boris.

"Thank you, my friend, but I must keep moving. Thank you for everything."

"If you change your mind, you are welcome to come back. Be careful."

Anatole shook Boris' hand and took off. The cold wind hit him in the face like a slap.

As Anatole walked, he thought of his best friend, Christopher, and the day when he had first met him. Anatole was overcome with sadness. He would never see him again, or his own parents for that matter. But he had no choice. The sooner he could make his way to Turkey, the safer and hopefully happier, he would be. Anatole kept walking. The terrain was rough but there had been no signs of soldiers so at least he felt safe. Resting only occasionally, Anatole was becoming tired. His legs ached and his feet felt as though they were on fire.

I must keep pushing. I must escape.

It was now approaching nightfall, and the temperatures were rapidly dropping. He should have listened to Boris. It would have been wiser to leave in the brightness and warmer temperatures of the morning. He figured that he was about a day's walk from the coastal region of Georgia.

Looking for the first safe place to huddle up for the night, Anatole came upon an old horse barn. The large and heavy wooden doors took some effort to open and the barn was empty inside. At least it would offer some shelter from the elements, a little warmth and safety, and some privacy. Anatole fashioned himself a makeshift bed with some old straw and a few loose boards that he found. He would have no problems sleeping tonight.

The morning sun streamed into the barn through the cracks in its walls. Creating a strange sight, the light held up the small particles of hay that had been stirred by Anatole's movements. Lying perfectly still, Anatole's mind drifted. Where would this journey lead him? Before heading out, Anatole relieved himself in the corner of the barn. Better this way, he thought, then needing to go when there was no place to hide. He had been lucky. Lucky to have survived, to have escaped, and to have the money on him to get to Turkey.

After walking several hours, Anatole had crossed the border and came upon the business areas of Georgia. Asking a few of the locals, it seemed that the docks were not far from him at all.

This was the first time however that he had seen soldiers and it frightened him. Trying to just blend in, Anatole walked casually in the direction of the docks. A small café was the first thing he saw as he entered the outer edge of the docks.

Taking a seat, Anatole positioned himself next to people that had luggage with them. He listened intently and identified a family that was on its way to Hungary. Feeling a bit more relaxed now, Anatole had a cup of coffee and made sure to leave and to follow the family with the same destination that he had.

Watching their movements intently, he observed that they entered the ship at about the midway point of the large blue vessel. But there was one problem. Soldiers lined the entrance ramp to the ship. Without a government signed and sealed travel permit, he would be going nowhere. Except to jail. And that was if he was lucky.

Hiding behind some large oak barrels, Anatole tried to think of a way to get aboard. He couldn't even bribe anyone as there was only one way on and those soldiers were still there. The large smoke stack of the ship emitted a thunderous roar as well as a blast of white smoke as the ship started to slowly move. The soldiers stood about as the ramp was pulled upwards towards the ship.

Becoming frantic, Anatole realized that every second spent on Russian soil meant the chances of ever escaping became less and less likely. As he scanned the ship, Anatole saw a shipmate all alone. He was towards the rear of the vessel and was just calmly standing there looking out to sea. Anatole looked towards the soldiers and realized that they were very engrossed in each other's trivial tales. This was his chance. Maybe his only chance.

Grabbing some cash from his pocket, he quickly sprinted towards the direction of this lonely looking shipmate. Waving the cash frantically, he finally caught his attention.

"And you! What do you want?"

"Shhhh!" said Anatole as he held a finger to his lips.

Pointing at the money and then the shipmate time after time, Anatole finally made his point. The ship was now about five feet away from its docking position. Anatole watched as a very small ramp was let down.

"Now! You come now!"

Anatole didn't have to be told twice. Looking directly towards the soldiers, Anatole jumped towards the ramp. Picking himself up, he heard shots ring out. He had been spotted. The soldiers were yelling and the shooting continued. With the ship now really picking up speed, Anatole leapt on board, tumbling to a stop at the shipmate's feet.

The shots grew distant before they finally stopped. The soldiers were done for the day and really cared about one thing and one thing only. Vodka. They were already heading to the bars to drink all the rest of the day and night.

"My name is Vasily. You pay me now or I throw you overboard," the shipmate snapped harshly.

"Okay, my friend, how much do you want?"

Anatole paid Vasily and the two briefly and quietly spoke.

Anatole would sleep in the boiler room. In fact, he would stay there the entire two days it would take to reach Turkey. He would stay warm but it was smoky and very noisy. He must keep quiet. Vasily would sneak him one meal per day.

Anatole appreciated the warmth and after what he had been through, the noise wouldn't bother him. There were plenty of sounds still deep within his mind. He missed his mother and father. He heard their comforting voices. The screams of pain and dying, were horrific and he heard them in his mind's eye, clearly and painfully. And he still heard Christopher. Poor Christopher.

As darkness approached, Anatole closed his eyes. Huddled up against some sort of motor, he wanted to forget. Forget all the pain. The fear. Anatole cried.

Chapter Five

THE BOAT'S THUNDEROUS roar signaled that they were just about there. How would he get off, Anatole thought? Praying that he would see Vasily, he knew of only one way to get off. If he stayed on too long, he would surely be found and thrown in jail.

There was no sign of Vasily. Slowly opening the boiler room door, Anatole looked in all directions. He walked towards the center of the ship and after observing a line that had formed, he casually got in it. As he got closer and closer to exiting, he saw that a certificate needed to be shown. As his turn came up, he would either run or try a gentle explanation. Nervous and unsure of himself, he quietly explained that he had unintentionally ruined his papers by washing his clothing in his room without removing them from his pocket.

"Okay, over here. You must wait and we will deal with you after everyone is off."

"Yes sir, of course," said Anatole.

After waiting some time, and never taking his eyes off the two men who were letting passengers through, Anatole started to walk slowly away. He quickly blended into a crowd that was walking. No one had noticed.

Reaching the newer looking boardwalk, Anatole observed the fine craftsmanship in every detail. He liked this. Casually walking into town, he finally started to relax. Perhaps he would someday see his wonderful parents. For now, though, Anatole would need to start a life of his own. He had a running start with the money from his parents, but after getting a place to stay, hopefully a small but clean apartment, he wanted to paint.

From what he could see, the scenery was amazing. After having some lunch, Anatole found a driver. Not sure of exactly where to go, Anatole decided to head to Tokat. The small, beautiful town was lightly populated but friendly, and his horse and buggy driver told him that the scenery would be stunning. They took several stops to rest and water the horses, before Anatole had reached Tokat.

After paying and thanking the driver, Anatole roamed the streets. So many scenes to sketch. He would need to find supplies. He would need to find an apartment, and right away.

Perhaps his luck was beginning to change. The people of Tokat were indeed friendly. An older man suggested an apartment right down the road. After meeting with the manager, Anatole agreed on a rental amount. He would pay each month.

The view from the second story window of his new apartment was fabulous. While there were no ocean views, there was in fact a lake. Trees and birds and charming cobblestone streets would all be great for him to sketch.

The one room apartment had a small cot, a table and three wooden chairs, as well as a small couch. It was clean. The windows were wide and tall, extending from floor to ceiling. This would be perfect for sketching the activities of the quaint little town.

With the sun setting, Anatole ran out and bought a bottle of vodka, as well as some drinking glasses. Getting back to his new home, he arrived just in time to watch the most glorious sunset he'd ever witnessed. Words at times fail to really explain God's creations but a talented artist could. This is what Anatole loved so much about painting. His own interpretation, yes, but also a replication of the splendor that that his eyes bore witness to.

Anatole continued to sip on his vodka. Not nearly as good as the genuine Russian vodka that his father had introduced him to as a young boy, it would do the job tonight. Anything to dull his senses, senses that held a heavy burden laden with pain. Pain and death. Anatole was, in his heart, a gentle soul, but we all have our primitive sides and Anatole drank to suppress the rage that was coming to the surface. It frightened him. It was all too real.

Before he knew it, Anatole had finished the bottle and was very sleepy. Finding a few blankets, he lay down on the small but comfortable couch. This was his couch now. The realization suddenly hit him. He was on his own. All alone. Anatole cried softly as he passed out, waiting for the sunlight of tomorrow. As the sun rose,

Anatole's fears would be seen much more clearly. For now though, sleep was a welcome escape from reality.

Chapter Six

TOKAT WAS A peaceful town. Anatole had left the window open all night. Too drunk to remember to close it, the apartment was cold. The rising sun would lend some warmth to his chilly bones. Anatole was hungry and hungover; he didn't want to move but his growling stomach ordered him to rise.

Washing up, Anatole realized that he must hide his money. Finding a loose wooden floorboard, he wrapped his monies in some newspaper he found and replaced the boards. Keeping enough for what he may need today, Anatole planned his day. He would need to buy some food, perhaps some more vodka, a pillow and most importantly, his art supplies.

Anatole used many of the mediums that he learned about in art school. He loved to sketch and charcoal sketching, while not easy, was his favorite.

As the weeks passed, Anatole became more and more familiar with his new home of Tokat. He made some friends but mostly he spent his days alone, sketching and thinking. He missed his stern, but loving mother, his gentle soul of a father, and his friends. He often spent time thinking of his best friend, Christopher. He also felt a sense of guilt, after all, Christopher's last words were *"Anatole, we've made it."*

Having plenty of money still, Anatole realized that it wouldn't last a lifetime. In the corner of his little apartment, he had canvas upon canvas leaning against each other. No one had yet seen his works but Anatole decided to put his fears aside and try and sell them, his expressions of the life that now surrounded him.

Within a block or so was a small café. Anatole would often stop in after a day of painting and have a bite to eat. He became friendly with the owner who had encouraged him to sell some of his works. Anatole spoke to him and asked if he could set up an art display on the sidewalk in front of the café. The café owner said yes, but there was a condition. Anatole was to split the profits with him fifty-fifty. Not being very business savvy, Anatole did not negotiate, but simply said yes.

On Saturday morning, a display was set up and Anatole displayed thirty-one sketches as well as paintings. He got a lot of interest and sold a few paintings but it had now been hours since he'd even gotten a look.

A commotion of sorts, about a block or so away, got Anatole's attention. There seemed to be one man who was in charge. He ordered the people around him to complete various tasks and within minutes he had made his way to Anatole's display.

"So, young man, are you the artist?"

"Well, yes, sir, I am," said Anatole.

"These are excellent. How much?"

"For which one, sir?"

"All of them," said the very fast-talking and aggressive stranger.

"Well, I don't know. How much would you like to give me?" said a nervous Anatole.

Accepting the first offer made, it was again apparent that Anatole was not the most seasoned of business people. He didn't have the heart for it but he surely had the talent.

"Listen, son. I am a businessman. I build things. My company builds offices, apartments, and more. When I see something of quality and I like it, I will buy it. Do you realize just how talented you are, son? Your works are amazing."

"Why thank you, sir," said Anatole.

"No more calling me sir. My name is Mr. Hoover. Mr. Herbert Hoover. Listen, have you ever been to America?"

"No, sir, I mean…Mr. Hoover, I have not. I am from Russia and have just recently moved to Hungary. I would love to go some day."

"Okay, then you will do so! I will have my man draw you up a letter of recommendation. I am well known and respected in America and you will have no problems entering. Now, package my purchases up and have them shipped to the address that my man will leave you with."

"Thank you, Mr. Hoover, thank you so much."

Anatole spent the rest of the day packaging up his entire collection and set about learning how to ship his works to Mr. Herbert Hoover. In the United States of America.

Chapter Seven

AS THE MONTHS passed, Anatole continued to paint and his works were selling. Never actually getting close to what they were most likely worth, his passion was mostly to do the work and not so much the business part of things.

Not very outgoing, Anatole managed to make friends. Quiet and still a bit shy, he was very likeable and had a big heart.

Years slowly passed by and Anatole had now been living on his own in Turkey for close to six years. He had met a very special friend. She was a tall and slim brunette and her name was Sonia. As they grew closer and closer, they eventually fell in love. Sonia was a writer and supported herself by selling her stories and poems. She was an amazing woman. Sweet and caring. She loved Anatole and would do anything for him.

Quite the talented writer, her expressions of loves, fears and passions were easily put to paper.

"Anatole, I would love to someday move to America. I hear that the opportunities are limitless," said Sonia.

"America?"

"Yes. Why, do you also want to move to America?" said Sonia.

"I have been thinking more and more about such a move."

Anatole explained to Sonia about the letter of recommendation he had received from Mr. Hoover.

"Mr. Hoover? I have talked about him with friends. He is an engineer," said Sonia.

"Really? He was a very aggressive businessman when I met him."

"Yes, he is that as well. I hear he has political aspirations also."

Over the next few months, Sonia and Anatole made plans. Plans to marry, plans to move, and even spoke of plans to have children. Two children. They both agreed that two children would be perfect.

It was now the summer of 1923. It was almost time to start their long journey to America. They had secured tickets aboard an ocean liner and would travel as third class passengers. This would save money as well as allow them travel "as they were." First and second class travel required fancy clothes and such, and neither Sonia or Anatole had any interest.

On a quiet Saturday morning, Sonia and Anatole were married. A few of their closest friends were in attendance and it was a quick and simple ceremony. Mr. and Mrs. Anatole Rostov, newlyweds, would be traveling to America. Both excited as well as nervous, they were ready. At this point, they had no choice. There was no turning back now.

Third class accommodations weren't bad at all. Sonia spent much of her time writing. Using her experiences of the trip as a source of ideas, Sonia observed people, observed families. So many stories could be written this way. Sonia had a vivid imagination.

For Anatole, the trip to America also provided a means to be exposed to many sights, new ones daily, to use as material for sketching. He even sold some while aboard the ship, as many wealthy first and second class passengers would walk the entire ship, sometimes looking down their noses at the lower level guests.

When they arrived at America, they would need to get through customs. Being advised by those much smarter than he was, Anatole was reassured that his letter of recommendation from Mr. Herbert Hoover as well as a certificate of marriage would assure entry into the land of opportunity for both Sonia and himself.

Once on shore, they had made plans to move to Brighton Beach, as they were told that many Russians had already taken up residence there, and safety in numbers gave him a sense of comfort. Not speaking much English at all, this would help them to slowly learn the language with many Russian speaking people around them.

Standing in line, waiting to go through customs, Anatole and Sonia witnessed many people that were rejected. No amount of arguing seemed to do much good, even when the immigrants could speak English.

Nervous, they handed the letter of recommendation to the immigration officer and he slowly read it.

"Who is this Herbert Hoover? I don't know this guy! Get outta here. Wherever you came from, take your girlfriend and go on back."

Anatole was intimidated as well as confused. Mr. Hoover had promised that this letter was sufficient and lawyers in Turkey had agreed as well as assuring them that a marriage certificate would then guarantee Sonia's admission as well.

Anatole and Sonia just stood there, not knowing what to do or say.

"Go on now! You people are all stupid. Go on, before I have you both arrested."

Having no idea what the immigration officer had just said, Anatole knew that they better get off the line. Walking about, they passed an official that was checking in on each station.

"Over there, you two," he said, talking to Anatole and Sonia. "No, no. No good."

Anatole was doing his best to communicate. Sonia grabbed the letter and put it in the officials' face; he had no choice but to read it.

"Okay, follow me," he told the two foreigners.

Walking away and gesturing for them to follow, the official led them to a small office. Sonia then gave him the marriage certificate as well.

Smack! Smack! Anatole jumped as the loud sounds of the official stamping "approved for admittance" onto their papers had startled him. Sonia remained calm. As the papers were handed back to Anatole, Sonia grabbed them and put them in her bag.

Pulling their heavy luggage behind them, Sonia told Anatole to wait for her as she approached person after person and finally found someone whom spoke Russian.

"We must go over there Anatole. Outside there is a ferry boat that will take us to the shore of New York."

The ride was very short and after reaching shore, the exhausted couple found their way to Brighton Beach and the apartment that had been held for them. It was a good thing that they made these plans while still in Hungary.

A simple but clean, three-bedroom dwelling, they pre-paid six months' rent. Not broke by any definition, the money was certainly declining. They would need to start to work almost immediately.

Chapter Eight

"OVER HERE. HEY you! Set up your stuff over here."

The fast-talking and not too friendly man instructed Anatole and his friend Alexei to set up the artwork on the sidewalk outside of the Department store.

With some forty paintings, as well as sketches, Anatole knew he would need the help, as well as someone to advise him on getting paid and such, so he brought Alexei along.

Anatole had met Alexei at a small market while buying groceries. Anatole found himself laughing as he watched Alexei trying to negotiate the price of fruit. Seeing his laughter, Alexei approached Anatole and they immediately struck up a conversation. Alexei was very good with matters of money, and a more aggressive sort.

Over the next ten hours, all forty paintings had sold and for far more than Anatole had ever dreamed of.

"My friend, I like you. Here is what I will do for you. I will take all the money. All of it and we will establish a partnership. I am wise to the ways of Americans. I will be your manager. I will set up a bank account. I will pay the bills, your rent, art supplies and I will negotiate everything. You leave it all to me. You paint. I do all the business my friend. Because I like you."

"Okay, but how much will I pay you?" asked Anatole.

"Don't worry. For you, because I like you so much...We split everything. I will do all the work and all you do is what you love. Paint."

"Okay, Alexei, thank you."

Over the next year, things would work out wonderfully. Anatole would paint and sketch. There were very diverse areas to choose from. From the industrial factories to the scenic wonders of Central Park, New York had it all. Alexei did a great job also. He booked art exhibits, made the agreements as far as monies to be paid and even had the newspapers come to evaluate his work. Someone even wrote an article about Anatole. The rent was paid every month and Alexei gave Sonia enough cash to buy groceries and household needs.

"Anatole! Anatole! Come here please. This man is saying that our rent hasn't been paid in four months and we need to get out! I knew your friend couldn't be trusted. I never liked him. He's a crook Anatole and he stole from us!"

"Calm yourself, Sonia. We will find out where the mistake has happened. I will pay a visit to Alexei right now and we will straighten this right out."

After explaining to the landlord, Anatole was told that if he didn't pay everything due in twenty-four hours, that they would be evicted. Almost all the money from his parents was gone. There just had to be an explanation.

"Alexei! Alexei!"

Anatole continued to knock loudly and yell Alexi's name but no one was home.

"He's not here anymore. The bastard stiffed me four months' rent and just took off! You know this criminal?" asked Alexei's landlord.

"I thought I did," said Anatole.

Talking to friends, the only very low cost rent apartments that were available, were in a place called Brownsville. A place was available right then but they needed to put money down.

"It will take every penny we have, Anatole," explained Sonia.

"No, I will go after him! I will get back our money. This is my fault Sonia!"

"We can't live on the streets Anatole. Besides…I think I'm pregnant."

"What, Sonia. You kid me? I am much happy. For both us. I love you. We can do this together.

Brownsville was a tough town. Without fully realizing it, Sonia and Anatole had moved to one of the roughest and most dangerous parts of New York. Directly across the street was a candy store, Meyers. Meyers was a perfectly legitimate eatery but also the home of Murder Incorporated. As the name implied, Murder

Incorporated was a group of dangerous murderers. Murderers for hire. Gangsters were in and out of the store all day.

The brains of the operation were the tough, but smart, Jews. Italians also were part of the scene, but were mostly relegated to carrying out hits, murdering on the orders from their Jewish bosses.

On top of being incredibly dangerous, Brownsville was also very depressing. Old and filthy looking brick buildings lined the street. Anatole and Sonia simply couldn't believe that this would be their new home. The apartment was on the fourth floor. After putting their last money down for rent and getting two keys, Anatole and Sonia climbed the dirty stairs, each step creating a loud echo in the filthy and barren hallways.

Opening the door to their new home, they were both startled by two enormous rats that scampered in different directions.

"Don't worry, Sonia, this is my fault. I will kill them."

Searching the hallways for something to use, Anatole just didn't have the heart. Sonia knew this and planned to just shoo them towards the front door and chase them out.

Continuing to paint, Anatole's works were better than ever. However, he had gotten no better at the business end. He was constantly being ripped off. Sonia sold a few books and now eight months pregnant was not feeling well.

"Anatole! It's my stomach. I have the pain. The baby, it's coming I think."

"I will get Anna right away."

Anna was Sonia's friend and had experience with birthing children.

Anatole paced the hallways of the grungy apartment building and even when he was quite a distance away, could still hear Sonia's cries. They just knew it was going to be a boy. In fact, they had only picked out one name. They wanted him to fit into America, so they picked a simple and very American name. John. John Rostov would be their pride and joy.

The cries soon subsided and Anatole, nervous, went back to his apartment.

"Anna, is Sonia and baby boy okay?"

"And how do you know that it is a boy? Artists are now magicians too? Yes, the boy and Sonia are good," said an amused Anna.

John was a tiny baby and was often sick. Anatole did his best to sell his paintings and Sonia, becoming depressed, was having a hard time writing. Everything she wrote was deep and dark. John was growing but was very thin. He was full of so much energy that Sonia was convinced that he was indeed healthy.

"Sonia, I am doing my best. It is 1932 and the depression has been with us for more than two years now. We're not the only ones that struggle."

"Yes, but real men get real jobs."

"This is what I do. Sonia, you know this!"

"Yes, but you must get a real job, Anatole. We have responsibilities for more than just ourselves now."

John was a good baby, sick more than his share of the time but always had a pleasant disposition. As he grew, John became healthier and had a thick head of beautiful, jet black hair.

Now five years old, John Rostov was far more independent than many kids his age. Sonia would leave to go shopping, and Anatole to a place to paint, and John would be left to fend for himself. Both of his parents worried about this but there were times that it was the only way.

"John, you make sure you stay inside. Don't answer the door for anyone, okay? John, are you listening? Stay inside." said Sonia.

"Okay, Mom, I'll be good."

As soon as his parents left. John would look out the window of their fourth-floor apartment. Waiting until they were out of sight, John would let himself out. Walking quickly down the lonely looking hallway, he ran down the stairs as fast as he could. It was fun.

Barely able to push open the heavy, creaking door that led to the streets, John would walk up and down the block.

"Hey kid. What's your name?"

"John. What's your name?"

"Jimmy. Listen, we can't call you John. From now on, your name is Johnny boy, okay?"

"Okay, I guess."

"You have any other friends, Johnny boy?"

"No, just you."

"Let's go get into some trouble," said Jimmy.

Running across the street, Jimmy just waved for John to follow. A bit nervous, he stopped and started many times, it was scary with all the oncoming cars.

"Just run right through, they have to stop for us. We own this block. Just do like I do, Johnny boy."

The boys made their way across the street and Jimmy took John aside and said "Listen to me. They have awesome candy here. Just watch me and if I say run, then you run! Whatever way I run, you run the other way, okay?"

"Okay."

Entering the candy store, Johnny boy just stood there in amazement. He had never seen so much candy in his entire life. There were packs of spearmint gum, snaps, three musketeer's bars, Boston baked beans and more. But what really had John fixated were the big men that went in and out of the candy store.

Wearing long coats, John could see that they were wearing guns! There were ladies with them also. These guys looked mean and they scared John.

"Hey kid, what's your name?" asked one of these men.

"He's Johnny boy," said Jimmy.

"Kid can't talk?"

"Yeah, I'm Johnny boy. I can talk."

"A regular wise guy, huh?" said the man.

As Johnny boy stood there talking to this stranger, Jimmy returned to filling his pockets with candies.

"Now Johnny boy, run!" said Jimmy.

"Look at this, it's a robbery!" laughed the stranger.

The clerk behind the counter ran around and was headed right towards Johnny boy. As he was about to grab him, the stranger interceded.

"Woah there. Look, how much does the kid owe?" asked the stranger.

"I'm gonna give this one a beatin'. He was part of it."

"Nobody's gettin' a beatin' around here unless I'm givin' it, you hear?"

"Okay Al. But money is tight. You know that."

"Listen Abe, here, you take this. Two bucks. That'll pay for ten times what the kid took. Even more. Okay?"

Johnny boy walked outside with the tall stranger.

"Listen Johnny boy, you wanna make some real money?"

"Sure."

"Take this package and bring it next door. Give it to the man behind the counter. When you get back, I'll pay you. Okay?"

"Pay me now," said Johnny boy.

The stranger just started to laugh.

"Okay kid, here's a dollar. Now take this package and bring it next door, you hear?"

"Okay."

Johnny boy did as he was told. Stuffing the dollar bill into his pants he opened the door and brought the package to the man behind the counter.

"Thanks, kid," said the man.

"No way. Al told me you have to pay me a dollar first," said Johnny boy.

"What? I oughtta slap you," he said.

"No, you won't, I'll run and you'll never catch me, you won't get nuthin'."

"Okay, kid. You win. Here's your buck. Now gimme the damn package."

Johnny boy waited until he could grab the dollar from the counter. Standing on his toes and reaching as far as he could, he barely reached it. He then gave the package to the clerk.

"Go on. Get outta here you little con man. Whatta scammer!"

Stuffing the second dollar into his pants, Johnny boy went outside.

"Hey, Johnny boy!"

It was Jimmy.

"Hey Jimmy. I've been looking for you."

"What's with the package, Johnny boy?"

"Oh, nothin'. That man in there paid for the candy so I brought the package over for him."

"That's all?"

"Yeah."

"I gotta go home before my parents get back, Johnny boy."

"Me too."

As Jimmy went down the block, Johnny boy was left to cross the street all by himself now. Feeling somewhat brazen, he started walking. Trying to look tough like Jimmy did, he almost fell over from fear as the car horns blared. Johnny boy ran the rest of the way.

Pushing open the large heavy door, Johnny boy started his way up the stairs. Realizing he had to pee, he started to run. Reaching the fourth floor, Johnny boy frantically tried to open his apartment door. It was locked! Knocking and knocking, he knew that no one was home yet. Drenched with sweat, Johnny boy ran down the hallway and when he reached the end, he unzipped his pants and started to pee.

"Hey you! What you do? You no piss in my hallway!" yelled an old lady who had just opened her hallway door. "You pee in toilet! Go on damn roof if you need," she added.

Johnny boy went back to his apartment and waited. Sitting down in front of his door, he knew he had to wait until his parents got home. Fighting to keep his eyes open, Johnny boy drifted off to sleep.

Chapter Nine

"JOHN ROSTOV! WHAT are you doing in the hallway?"

"I'm sorry, Mom. Here's what happened—I heard a kitty cat crying and I opened the door. I looked both ways and the door closed behind me. I need to go to the bathroom, Mom."

Johnny boy looked down the hallway and saw the old lady coming.

"Hurry, Mom. I need to pee really bad."

After going into the bathroom and just standing there for a few minutes, Johnny boy flushed the toilet. Sitting down on the small couch, Johnny boy figured he would do something so that his mom wouldn't get mad at him.

"John, what are you doing?"

"I'm practicing. Reading. Just like you have been teaching me. You said it was important, right, Mom?"

"Yes, John," said Sonia, as she turned the book the correct way so that Johnny boy could actually read from it.

Sonia smiled as she knew what her son was up to. As Johnny boy continued to read, his father got home. Carrying a canvas and a pouch containing his art supplies, Anatole greeted both Sonia and Johnny boy.

"So, John, what did you do today?"

"Nothing much. I tried to save a cat, dad."

"Really? That is good," said Anatole.

"Sonia, I think that I have a buyer interested in my paintings."

"That's good Anatole. You keep saying that but nothing ever happens. At least that bum Alexei found you buyers."

Anatole felt hurt but couldn't argue. He was barely selling anything and they were close to losing this apartment now.

"Dad, do you need some money?"

"Why, John?"

"Well, I found some money in the hallway."

Johnny boy handed his father the two dollar bills that he had stuffed into his pockets.

"This is a lot of money John! We must find out who lost it!"

"No, it was all crumpled up and old. Wherever it came from, it was there for a long time."

Johnny boy could see the expression on his father's face relax. He couldn't understand why this made his dad so much more relaxed.

Over the years, Sonia continued to write, Anatole continued to paint and they all continued to struggle. That is, except for Johnny boy. Almost nine years old, Johnny boy continued to get to know Al and his friends that hung out at the candy store.

Now in third grade, Johnny boy was happy that school was out and summer was here.

"Johnny boy. Where's Jimmy and the rest of your friends?"

"Don't know, they sometimes need to do homework."

"Homework won't make them any money, right kid?"

"That's right, Al."

"Here, take this envelope and bring it around the corner to Grossman's. Now listen, I'm on to you. I pay you and then you scam your way into getting paid again."

"No way, Al."

"Look kid, you think I'm stupid? Don't get me wrong, you're a smart kid but don't pull that shit with me. You treat me right and my customers, okay? You just do things the right way and there'll always be something in it for you. Okay, kid?"

Johnny boy knew the drill. He'd run around the corner to Grossman's deli and hand the envelope to Sol. When he got back, he'd get paid. Sometimes a dime. Sometimes a quarter and if Al was feeling generous, fifty cents. He still remembered that day a long time ago when he made two bucks.

"You know, I used to make more when I was a kid."

"A kid? Hahahaah, listen to this guy. Here, take your fifty cents and say thank you."

Johnny boy walked outside and looked up and down the block. He knew that Jimmy would soon be here and probably the rest of the guys too. There was Mickey and Danny and the new kid, Jackie.

Waiting outside of the candy store and leaning against the brick exterior, Johnny boy fumbled through his pockets and pulled out half a cigarette.

"Hey, you gotta light?" Johnny boy asked a woman passing buy.

She was beautiful. Tall, blonde, with red lips, Johnny boy was in love. He wanted to marry her.

"Here, kid," said the blonde, as she lit his cigarette for him.

As she walked into the candy store, Johnny boy watched her ass sway from side to side.

"Hey, Johnny boy. Who was that? Man, you see the tits on her?"

"Yeah, I sure did. Jimmy, I'm gonna be grabbin' those tits someday."

"Yeah, whatever. You wouldn't know what to do with them," said Jimmy.

Johnny boy's mind wandered. He thought back to when he was just about six years old and there was a new girl that had moved into his building. She lived right above him and they could always hear her father and mother yelling and screaming. It sounded scary and Johnny boy's dad was going to go up and talk to them. But he never did.

Her name was Roxanne and she took a liking to Johnny boy. They played together and one day, went up to the fifth floor. The hallway was a filthy place but there was no one around.

"Wanna play doctor?" said Johnny boy.

"What's that?"

"Well, we make sure that we're not sick," said Johnny boy.

"Okay, what do we do?"

"Well, first we pull our pants down and then we look at each other. Something like that, but then we know we're okay."

"I'm not sure about this," said Roxanne.

"Here, it's easy. I'll go first."

Johnny boy pulled down his worn and tattered pants. Three sizes too big, Sonia had tied a rope around them so they didn't fall off.

"There, now you go," said Johnny boy.

Roxanne laughed and laughed.

"What's so funny?"

"You have a little PP," said Roxanne.

As she stopped laughing, Roxanne pulled down her pants as well.

"All the way down. To the floor," said Johnny boy.

Johnny boy looked. And looked. He didn't know what he was looking at but it sure wasn't a PP. He did like what he saw though. He just didn't know why.

"Turn around so I can see your butt," said Johnny boy.

Johnny boy was confused. He really liked looking at Roxanne but he wasn't sure why. He knew that babies came out of a hole and that men put their PP's in a lady's hole. But which one?

"Hey fella's. What's up?"

Snapping out of his trip down his own memory lane, Johnny boy was back to the hustle and bustle of Christopher Street.

Danny was a little bit older than the other boys. About eleven, he was the crazy one. If you dared Danny to do something, he'd do it. No matter what.

"Ahh, nuthin'. Where is everybody?"

"I seen Mickey and Jackie playin' with the wino's head down the block. They was tryin' to talk him into givin' them his change and they was gonna get him some wine."

As the boys stood around just hanging out, they looked for cigarette butts on the sidewalk. Finding a few, they used Johnny boy's lit one to get them all puffing away.

"Okay, fellas, where we off to?" said Mickey.

Mickey was about ten years old, just like Johnny and Jimmy.

Jackie, just having turned nine years old was the youngest of the group, and in more than one way. All the boys had pretty much grown up on the tough streets of Brownsville. Even lifelong residents of Brooklyn avoided Brownsville.

Everything about Brownsville was tough. If you couldn't protect yourself, you were pretty much dead, and Johnny boy and his group of friends learned that early on. That is, except for Jackie.

Smaller for his age and slightly overweight, Jackie was a softer kid. Having just moved to Brownsville from the country area of Orange, Connecticut, Jackie's parents split up. Well, more like his dad just took off. Lost his job and couldn't deal with things.

The economy was terrible and jobs were scarce, so Jackie's mom moved in with her sister and that's what brought Jackie to Brownsville.

"Look at this kid, will ya? Come on fatso, move it," said Jimmy.

"Oh, leave him alone Jimmy."

"What, are you in charge now, Johnny boy?"

"Well since you asked me, I was thinkin' we should organize, fella's. There's money to be made and we stick together, we'll never have any problems with the niggers or Jews. I should be the leader. I'm in charge. I'm good at bein' in charge. Jimmy, you take care of all the money that comes in. We'll figure the rest out from there. But the rest of you guys are just as important," said Johnny boy.

Johnny boy noticed that Jackie's head was slumped a bit and he was looking sad.

"What's wrong, Jackie?"

"I don't know. I know I don't belong with you guys. I couldn't blame you guys if you just left me out."

Johnny boy glanced around at the other boys and nodded a bit.

"No way Jackie."

"What, are you kiddin'?"

"Listen, without you I'm out Jackie. In fact, we're all out, right fella's?"

All the boys nodded and slapped Jackie on his pudgy back. The boys all liked Jackie. A lot. They did however, worry that when it came to fighting, he'd get hurt and maybe even get one of them hurt.

"Okay, and I'm gonna lose weight and learn how to fight. Cause' I wanna be like you guys."

The boys all took off down the block. Walking five across, they could be intimidating. Although they were young, they still would scare people. Especially ladies. With pocketbooks.

"Jimmy. I'll sweet talk her and you grab the purse. We split up and meet at the alley in fifteen minutes. Go!"

As Johnny boy walked directly towards the pretty, middle aged woman, Johnny looped around behind her. Johnny boy, quite the actor, had tears welling up in his eyes and was stuttering.

"It's my m-m-mom. She's hurt. She fell really bad."

The pleasant looking woman felt terrible and as she started to console Johnny boy, Jimmy snatched her purse and ran. All five boys took off and followed.

"Come back here! You little asses. If my husband gets you, he'll beat you all!"

Chapter Ten

THE ALLEY WAS a special meeting place for the boys. Whenever they were in trouble, they took off to the alley. No one ever found them there and there was only one window on one of the old brick buildings, and that was the first-floor bathroom for Mrs. Williams.

Mrs. Williams was hot. She had huge tits and if you timed it right and the angle was just perfect, you could see her ample round ass.

"Open it up," said Johnny boy.

"Okay, okay! Calm down."

As Jimmy was searching through the lady's purse, the boys could hear the plodding and heavy breathing approaching. It was Jackie.

"What did I miss guys?"

"Nothing, Jackie," said Johnny boy.

"We're just opening the purse now."

"Holy shit. This lady has money, guys," said Jimmy.

"How much, how much?" asked Danny.

"I'm adding, I'm adding! Let's see. Sixty-four dollars! We're rich!"

"Well Jimmy, do your job. Split it up. Whatever you say, goes," said Johnny boy.

"Okay fellas, here's five bucks each. The rest is thirty-nine bucks. We put that in a box in my room and we save it for us all."

"What? That's it? Why do you get the money?"

Danny, Mickey, and Jackie all wanted to know why Jimmy kept the rest of the money.

"Look, I'm in charge here and Jimmy runs the money part. You know what fella's? We need to have a name. We'll save money and buy those cool jackets and we'll get the name put on it. On the front and the back. People will know it's us and they'll fear us. We won't take any shit."

"I don't wanna be a gang though. We should be 'Some kind of Boys'," said Jackie.

"What the fuck is he talking about?" said Danny.

"No, he's right. I get it. I know. We'll call ourselves 'The Money Boys,'" said Johnny boy.

"I was thinking 'The Donut Boys,'" said Jackie.

The whole group of boys cracked up. It figured that Jackie thought of food. The boys also decided that they needed a clubhouse. Having no idea where, Johnny boy assured them that he'd come up with something.

It was getting dark now and the boys split up and went in different directions to their homes.

Coming close to his place, Johnny boy couldn't help but think that it had been a good day. He almost felt the tits of a gangster's lady, they stole some money, became a real official bunch, and had plans for the future.

"Hey, Johnny boy."

"Hey, Roxanne. I haven't seen you in a while. Must be most of the summer. How are you? You look different."

As Johnny boy said that, Roxanne, with her hands on her hips, pushed out her still girlish chest. Eleven years old now, she was just starting to develop. She was no Mrs. Williams, but she would do.

"Wow Roxanne. They look…I mean, you look great!"

"Johnny boy? Remember when we were little and we played doctor? Wanna play again?"

"Sure. Let's go in my room. Oh man! My parents aren't home yet."

"Well, that's good then."

"No! I don't have a key!"

"Johnny boy? Let's go on the roof," said Roxanne.

"The roof? Okay, but let's go now. It's getting dark."

As Roxanne and Johnny boy made their way up to the roof, they wedged a piece of wood in the door jamb. Just in case the door closed on its own, they wouldn't be stuck up there.

Hiding behind a tall vent stack, Johnny boy put his hand under Roxanne's thin summer shirt. Her belly was flat. He wasn't sure why, but he liked that. He moved his hand rapidly to Roxanne's small sized bra and squeezed. Evidently, too hard.

"Johnny boy! Ouch! You're supposed to be nice to them. Gentle."

Johnny boy was getting excited. Feeling himself harden in his tattered jeans, Johnny boy went back to work. Sliding his hand up Roxanne's slender back, Johnny boy was determined to unhook her tiny bra. He just knew he could do it. Maybe two hands? He had seen his mother's monstrous sized bra hanging in the bathroom but this one was stubborn.

Sensing Johnny boy's frustration, Roxanne pulled the straps down and off of her arms. Awkwardly, she slid the part that attached, around to her front and quickly unhooked herself.

Johnny boy let his hands explore. Boy, that bra sure did make her seem bigger, Johnny thought. Jackie may have had more tits than this girl did.

After about ten minutes of playing with Roxanne's tits, Johnny boy stopped. Just stopped.

"So, what's next? Can I see your butt again?"

"No! We're not little kids anymore Johnny boy. Here, let me loosen your pants a little."

Johnny boy was breathing hard now and that wasn't the only thing that was hard.

"Wow. You have a big one! I mean, I've never seen one before but yours is a giant," said Roxanne.

Roxanne pushed her hand down Johnny boy's pants until she reached what she was looking for. Starting to pull on it, slowly at first and then harder, and faster, it was hurting him a little but it felt too good to ask her to change anything.

"I feel something happening Roxanne. I feel like, like I'm gonna…pee!"

"What? Don't pee on me!"

Johnny boy grabbed his dick and spun around, a huge semi-circle of pee following his movement.

"No! Johnny boy! You peed all over me!" said Roxanne.

Shaking his drained member off a few times, Johnny boy stuffed it back into his pants. Taking a deep breath and exhaling slowly, he turned to face Roxanne.

With a huge grin on his face, Johnny boy took Roxanne's hand and started heading to the entry door to get back inside.

"Ewwww! Don't touch me. You have pee on your hand!"

"No I don't. I wiped it on my shirt!"

"But you had your thing in your hand," said Roxanne.

"So did you. You were jerking it!"

"Just leave me alone!"

With that, Roxanne slammed the door shut leaving Johnny boy on the roof.

"Roxanne! Come back! The door is locked. I'm locked up here now!"

It was too late. In fact, it was late already. They had been on the roof a long time and Johnny boy just knew that his father and mother would be mad.

Looking over the edge of the roof, Johnny boy daydreamed. He thought of all the places that his dad had described that he had painted when he was in Europe. Johnny boy was getting tired now and slowly but surely, he drifted off to sleep.

"John! John Rostov!"

The light of an approaching new day was making its way from the grip of the large clouds overhead. Johnny boy had been sleeping a long time.

"Dad! I knew that you would find me. I'm sorry, Dad!"

With that, Johnny boy's father slapped him. Hard. Right in the face. Stunned, Johnny boy was hurting. From the slaps, yes, but emotionally, he hurt. How could his dad hurt him like that? It got worse, much worse.

"Dad. Please stop! I didn't do it on purpose!"

Slap! Slap! Johnny boys face was reddened but that wasn't enough for the angry Russian. Johnny boy was really scared now as his father's anger was increasing. He could smell the alcohol on his breath.

The painful slaps had now become heavy, brutal heavy punches. With Johnny boy's eyes swollen and almost closed, his father unleashed one final blow and split his lip wide open. Blood spurted everywhere. But it was over. For the moment, at least.

Chapter Eleven

JOHNNY BOY WAS usually up bright and early, eager to find his friends and play some baseball, or more often, just get into some trouble.

But not this morning. Johnny boy barely slept. He was too angry to sleep. Sure, he had messed up and he knew that his parents had been worried and angry, but to get a severe beating like that from his own father?

Lying in bed and waiting for the house to become silent, Johnny boy slowly got out of bed. Barely able to see, his eyes both swollen almost all the way shut, he went to the bathroom to take a leak. Looking at the cracked mirror hanging directly over the sink, Johnny boy saw for the first time what his beaten face really looked like.

There was no way that he could admit to anyone what had really happened. Johnny boy slowly dressed and made his way down the four flights of steps. Gingerly walking across the street to the candy store, he saw Al coming out the front door. Feeling embarrassed, Johnny boy had his head down.

"Hey, kid. Whoa! What the fuck happened to you?"

"Ahhhh nuthin'. Got into a fight, I'm okay."

"A fight? With what, a whole gang of niggers?"

"Well, it was about three niggers. I'm gonna get them back."

"Kid, listen. You want me to send some boys down and take care of these clowns?"

Johnny boy thought for a second.

"No. I wanna take care of this. Al, where can I get a gun?"

"A gun? Listen kid, I could get you one right now but you'd probably shoot your own fuckin' baby-sized balls off! You ever shoot a gun?"

"No. But I learn fast."

Thinking for a few seconds, Al shook his head in agreement, almost as if he was agreeing with his own thoughts.

"Follow me kid. Hey Abe, me and the kid need some privacy. No one in the backroom, okay?"

"Okay, Al," said Abe from behind the front counter.

Johnny boy followed Al to a small back office. Reaching behind a small wooden desk, Al pulled out a small hand gun.

"Come here. Watch me. I'm gonna show you how to load it, clean it, and shoot it. This here gun is special. Special for killin' niggers," said Al.

Al and Johnny boy spent almost two hours in that back room. Al gave him bullets and everything he would need. He even explained how he should never keep a bullet in the first chamber. That way if it ever went off by mistake, he wouldn't blow his own fuckin' dick off.

Johnny boy had other ideas though. No one was home yet and Johnny boy still didn't have a key, so he headed up to the roof. He'd hide the gun up there until someone got home. He'd then go back and get it, but he'd keep it right with him. Anyone ever tried to hurt him again, he'd blow their fucking head off.

Reaching the roof, Johnny boy made sure to wedge the door open. Finding a good hiding spot, Johnny boy crouched down to hide his new best friend. As he got closer to the roof's hot metal flooring, he could see blood stains. It was his own blood from the night before and only served to make him even angrier. The level of rage that he felt inside scared him. The uncertainty of not knowing what he may be capable of was extremely frightening to him.

Heading back to the door, Johnny boy's stomach was growling. He knew what it was. He squeezed his ass tight but it wasn't gonna work. He had to shit and he had to shit right then!

Loosening the rope that held his hobo-like pants up, Johnny boy pulled them off and his boxers as well. Finding a spot behind a large metal stack, he squatted. In pain and angrier than he ever knew he could be, Johnny boy started to laugh. And laugh. The shit was so big that he was afraid it was gonna crawl right back up his ass! And if it did, that shit would find more still coming out to meet it. Finally, this monster was done. Johnny stood there for a moment, unsure of what to do. Using his boxers to wipe his dirty ass, Johnny boy pulled on his pants and tightened the rope. Still laughing hysterically, Johnny boy could smell his own shit and there was nothing funny about it. It was a pile of hot, brown, steaming death.

Grabbing his shitty boxers, Johnny boy walked to the roofs edge. Peering down, he tried to time it perfectly. A group of about five guys were hanging out, smoking cigarettes. Johnny boy dropped the shit laden boxers over the edge of the roof and watched as they floated their way down. Like a shit passenger parachute, the shorts almost seemed to move in slow motion. Finally finding their resting spot, Johnny boy cracked up as he saw the boxers land on some guy's head. Startled, the guy grabbed the shorts from atop his head and flung them to the sidewalk.

Johnny boy could barely hear him but he was screaming about shit being all over his head and his hands. Deciding against leaving his gun on the roof, Johnny boy picked it up and stuck it in the back of his pants just as he'd seen the tough guys across the street do so many times.

Taking the piece of wood out of the door jamb, Johnny boy made his way back into his apartment building. Walking down the empty staircase, he reached the fourth floor, and as he approached her door, the old, scary lady opened it as she was sweeping dirt and dust into the hallway.

"You no pee in my hallway!" she said.

"No, but I did shit all over the roof," Johnny boy said as he ran towards his apartment.

Barely able to contain his laughter, he picked up speed.

"Come here. You nasty boy! I speak to your mamma. Your mamma know you shit like monster on my roof?"

Knocking on his apartment door, his mom opened and hugged Johnny boy. Not usually very affectionate, she didn't say a word but hugged him very tightly. Pulling away a bit, she stepped back and looked at Johnny boy's face. Johnny boy could see tears welling up in his mother's eyes.

"Forgive him, he was drinking, but he was so scared that something happen to you. He loves you."

"I know, Mom, it's okay," Johnny boy lied.

Going into his bedroom and closing and locking the door behind him, Johnny boy hid his gun under his bed.

No one will ever fuck with me again. I'll blow their fucking heads off. Dad too. Especially Dad, Johnny boy thought.

It was dark outside and Anatole hadn't come home yet. Sonia was worried as it was unlike him to be so late. A few minutes went by and Johnny boy could hear the lock turning on the front door. Dad was home. Johnny boy felt a tightness in his belly as anger welled up inside of him.

"Anatole, you're late. Is everything okay?"

"Yes Sonia, I'm sorry if I worried you. I had a bad day and stopped to drink some vodka before coming home."

"Vodka? We don't have money enough for rent and there is barely anything to eat! Anatole, we have a son, we have a responsibility to feed him. There is no food!"

"I'm sorry, Sonia. I have a few dollars. Should I go buy food?"

"No! I go!"

Johnny boy didn't like this. If his loving mom left, he'd be alone with his father. Although this was the first time he'd ever hit him, Johnny boy was not going to let it happen again. Looking at his father's gentle eyes, Johnny boy couldn't believe this was the same man who was so violent, just one day before.

I will never trust him. I will never forgive him. I hope he dies! thought Johnny boy.

"Dad, I'm not hungry, I'm so tired. I'll just go to sleep now."

"Okay. John? I am sorry."

Anatole's voice trailed off to barely a whisper as his son shut his door.

Johnny boy reached under his small bed and lay his gun down. After pausing for a moment, he pulled it back out. Checking it, he made sure that there was no bullet in the first chamber.

That's ok. I'll just pull the trigger twice, he said to himself.

Lying in his bed, Johnny boy pulled the single sheet over his wiry body. Staring intently at his bedroom's doorknob, Johnny boy with his gun in hand, drifted off to sleep.

"John, wake up."

The knocking at the door startled and angered Johnny boy.

"Okay, I'm getting up, Mom."

Putting his gun under the bed, Johnny boy cautiously opened his bedroom door. Seeing that his father's art supply bag and easel were gone, he breathed a sigh of relief.

Staggering into the bathroom, he splashed some cold water on his face and rinsed his mouth. His face still hurt but at least his eyes, bruised and discolored, had opened again.

Johnny boy was feeling better and with that, his appetite was returning. Looking into the closet, there was no food, save some stale and crusty bread. It would have to do. He inhaled the outdated bread and scooping up the crumbs, devouring them as well.

Johnny boy decided it was time to face the world again. After all, no one would need to know the truth. As he bound down the stairs, he wondered how he could in fact love his father, but also want to kill him.

Opening the heavy front door and bouncing down the street, he felt more and more like himself. That swagger was starting to return.

The clouds darkened as it looked like the impending rains could hold off no longer. At first a mist, them a warm drizzle, the skies suddenly exploded with a torrent of rain. Looking across the street, Johnny boy couldn't believe his eyes as the sun was shining. He was soaked in the wetness from above but across the street the sun was out. Stopping in his tracks to observe this dreamlike phenomenon, Johnny boy wasn't paying attention to the human traffic that surrounded him.

"Hey, you little fucker! Watch where you're going!" yelled a thuggish looking stranger.

"Fuck you! And fuck your mother!" yelled Johnny boy as he reached for his gun that was tucked into the back of his filthy pants.

"Johnny boy! Get down, get down!"

Quickly looking around, Johnny boy spotted Jackie. As Jackie was getting closer, he had seen what was about to happen and warned his friend to hit the ground.

Out of the corner of Johnny boy's eye and almost in slow motion, the black cars windows slowly descended. With the long barrels of several shotguns pointed towards the rain soaked side of the street, the barrage of bullets started.

Johnny boy, quick as a rat being chased by a baseball bat, ducked behind the metal garbage cans, as low as he could get. Pulling his gun from the small of his back, Johnny boy tried to focus his still bruised and swollen eyes on the murderous scene unfolding before him.

The strangers that Johnny boy had bumped into, pulled their own guns out and fired back at the slow-moving black car.

Blood sprayed everywhere as the accurate shots from the car, mowed down their intended targets. As the cars picked up speed, Johnny boy could see the guns recede back into the gangster's car, and the windows come upwards again.

Instead of being scared, Johnny boy came out from his sheltered hiding spot and walking up to the bleeding and shaking thugs, spit at them.

"Don't ever bump into me again. The Money Boys don't take that shit!"

"Johnny boy, are you okay?" asked Jackie.

"Yeah, I'm okay. But let's get the fuck outta here, Jackie. The cops will be here soon."

"Okay. Hey, what happened to your face?"

"Nothing. Some niggers got cute, but I have a new friend."

"A new friend?"

"Yeah. I'll show you. In the alley," said Johnny boy.

Walking the six or so blocks to the alley, Johnny boy checked the bathroom window for Mrs. Williams' tits. No such luck. Those damn tit monsters had been in hiding.

"Come here, Jackie. I'm gonna show you something, but you can't say a word to anyone. Okay? Promise?"

As Jackie nodded his head up and down, Johnny boy reached behind to the back of his pants. Pulling out his new best friend, Jackie turned away.

"What? I'm not pulling out my dick! My dick's not in my ass, you want it in yours?"

Bringing the gun into focus, Jackie just stared at it. Jackie had never seen a real gun up so very close. I mean, just minutes ago, he did see the guns slowly escape from the long black car and start shooting up anything in their way, but that was almost like a dream. Jackie just remembered the sounds. Could sounds be heard in motion so slow, so incredibly slow that you could see them, feel them, wear them?

"What's the matter? A little fucking gun scaring you? You really are a fucking pussy, aren't you? Come on, Jackie, it's not like I'm gonna shoot you!"

"Where'd you get that, Johnny boy? Guns are dangerous. You saw what they just did."

"Yeah, and they can also protect you from assholes, no matter who they are or how tough they are, they can't beat up a bullet, Jackie. There's always someone bigger, stronger, and tougher. This just evens out the fuck'n' odds a little. Know what I mean?"

"Where's everyone else, Johnny boy?"

"I don't know, but I've been thinking, and Jackie, you're gonna be my right-hand man."

"What? Me? No, Johnny boy. I'm fat, I'm slow, and I can't even fight."

"That's okay, Jackie. We're gonna get you to lose some weight. In fact, it kinda looks like you've lost some already."

"I have? Thanks, Johnny boy."

Jackie slowly started to smile. That made him feel really good. Confidence was not a feeling that came easily to Jackie. Without even knowing it, Johnny boy was good at this.

"So, anyway, when I have an idea or something important to do, I need you to help me make up my mind. Okay? You got that, Jackie? It's important! You're the man for the job."

"Yes! Thank you, Johnny boy!"

"So, Jackie, I've been thinking, we need a clubhouse. We need somewhere to go, to meet up, hide shit, fuck girls, you know what I mean?"

"Yeah, I know. I need someplace to fuck girls," said Jackie.

Holding back a laugh, Johnny boy was really trying to help Jackie. Underneath that soft belly and scared exterior could be a tough guy. It just needed to be coaxed out a bit. Johnny boy just knew it. Some guys just took a little longer to have their balls drop. It was probably having no father at home. Johnny boy was gonna change all that though. Before he knew it, both balls were gonna drop, just like that shit flying parachute did.

"Hey, Johnny boy. You know what?"

"What, Jackie?"

"Would it be a good thing or a bad thing to have our place to fuck girls, close, or farther away?"

"Why, close, I guess," said Johnny boy.

"Cause I was thinkin', right under Mrs. Williams' tits, there's like a half basement. It's pretty empty too, I think."

"What? Where is this place and how do you know about it, Jackie?"

"There's no windows but it has a few lights. I was being chased by some spics and they were really gonna fuck me up. I found this door at the end of the alley. Right over there. I opened it and locked it from the inside I'm not sure the lock even worked. I turned around and went down the stairs and there it was. It's kinda dirty but no one would ever find us," explained Jackie.

"Come on, Jackie, let's check it out."

Walking to the end of the dreary looking alley, the boys made a left and the door was right there. There wasn't even a doorknob, just a cut-out where the knob used to be. Walking down about ten filthy steps, the boys had one more door to contend with. Turning the handle, it was in fact open.

"We'll have to get a pad-lock, Johnny boy."

"See, that's why I picked you, Jackie, you have the brains. See what I mean? I know this shit"

"Jackie, hold that door open. Man, it's totally black down here! Are there any lights?"

Johnny boy looked around and saw a string hanging from the wooden-beamed ceiling. Pulling on it, a dim light flickered on and off briefly. Johnny boy had seen enough though. It was gonna take a lot of work, but the boys now had their own place. Now they'd just have to think of a name for it.

Chapter Twelve

DINNER WAS THE best time of the day for Johnny boy. Both of his parents were home from work and his dad was tired. Less chance of him becoming angry when he was tired.

"So John, would you like to come with me tomorrow when I sketch and paint?"

"I don't know."

"Okay, well let me know. We will leave early. I plan on going to Sunset Park. The landscapes are beautiful now at this time of the year," said Anatole.

"Sure, okay," said an emotionless Johnny boy.

Johnny boy slept with his gun that night. Should he bring it with him in the morning? Probably not. He was still very angry, as well as scared but was starting to trust his dad a little more these days. He wasn't certain if he'd ever fully trust him again but for now, he'd just try and avoid him as much as possible. Tomorrow would be different however.

For the first time in a while, Johnny boy slept pretty well. He still kept that gun tight against him though. He was dreaming of a woman. She was blonde. And had huge tits.

"John! Let's go. Time to get up. Your father would like to leave soon," said Sonia.

"Okay, Mom. Just a minute."

"Now please, son." she said softly.

It only took Johnny boy a few minutes to wash up and get ready. There wasn't much to eat, but he did find an apple and a few bananas.

"How are we getting there, Dad?" asked Johnny boy.

"The BMT, John. I would like you to help me carry my supplies. How about this bag? Too heavy?"

Johnny grabbed the bag and acted as if was light. The added weight made his plodding steps that much louder as he made his way down the dusty old steps.

Walking the few blocks to the subway, Johnny boy and his dad went down the hard metal stairs to get to the subway train. Getting to the turnstiles, Anatole gave him two nickels.

"Be careful. It is so expensive, the subway."

"But why do I need two, Dad?"

"Just in case. Put one in your shoe for safe keeping."

The subway car was pretty empty. The wheels would screech very loudly when going through a curve. Johnny boy liked this but it seemed to agitate his dad.

"These engineers don't know what they're doing, John. I could have designed a much better system."

"I know, Dad. I see you fixing things all of the time," said Johnny boy, with just a trace of pride and a bit of a smile. "Dad, how did you learn to fix everything?"

"In Russia, when I was quite young, my father, he teach to me. He could fix anything. Make anything. He was amazing man."

"Can we go see him?"

Anatole turned his head abruptly and just glared at his son. There was that look again.

After about a thirty-minute train ride, the two Rostov's arrived at the park. Well, they were almost there.

"It's just a short walk," explained Anatole.

"Dad, I'm hungry. Thirsty too."

"John, we're just getting there. We will try to get some water and a sandwich later."

The park was beautiful. Strong looking oak trees looked like senior citizens guarding the next up and coming generation of smaller and younger trees. There was a small lake that glistened as the sun's rays just started to kiss the water's top. In the distance, one could see the outline of skyscrapers. It was beauty outlined by concrete. A city's heart and soul, all laid out before their eyes.

"Right here, Dad! This place is great," said Johnny boy.

"No, son. I must capture the correct light. I need to make certain that the shadows don't interfere with what I start now as well as what it will look like hours from now."

Setting up his easel, Anatole moved it several times before settling on the perfect spot.

Johnny boy didn't understand all of it as no one bought his dad's stuff anyway.

"Dad, when are you gonna get a real job? You know, like most dads?"

"This is a real job!" yelled his father.

Johnny boy was starting to question himself for not bringing that gun along after all.

Johnny boy sat on the grass, several feet away from his father. His dad pulled out a knife and carefully sharpened a few charcoal pencils that he used to sketch with. At times, he would just leave them as such, but most of the time he would fill everything in with his paint colors.

As time went on, Johnny boy was getting bored. Constantly pacing, stretching and yawning, he was driving his father crazy.

"John! What is the matter with you? Can't you sit still?"

"No. Can I just go for a walk all around and come back before it gets dark?" said Johnny boy.

"No! You're too young."

If his dad only knew. He was feeling up titties, shitting on roofs, and stealing whatever he needed, almost daily now.

Anatole thought for a moment.

"Okay, John. But be back in maybe two hours?"

"Okay, Dad, I will."

Johnny boy was on a mission. There must be pretty girls somewhere in this old park. And they probably had tits. Big tits. Walking around the lake, he just wanted to get away. In a way, it was nice to get away from the mean and dirty streets of Brownsville. There would be no shootings or robberies here. Soaking in the beauty, the peace, the tranquility, he wished that he could somehow live here. Or a place like this.

As Johnny boy wandered around, circling the lake, he was now out of sight from his father. He had no idea how he'd know when two hours was up, but he'd figure it out.

"Hey! Gimme some money."

A tall and thin man, shabbily dressed, had yelled from the woods. Woods that mimicked the shape of the lake. As the man approached, Johnny boy could see that he was not alone. He looked to be in his thirties and the stranger had a young boy with him. He was most likely a bit younger than Johnny boy, probably around eight or so. Unshaven, the man's eyes gave away his soul, which was kind and unthreatening.

"Don't worry, I mean you no harm. Do you have some change? We haven't eaten in days," said the stranger. "My name is Fred and this is my boy Ernie. We've been living in this tent that we made. That is, until the cops chased us. We were over at 'Tent City' in Central Park, but it's real dangerous there."

"Yeah, I'm Johnny boy, I have about seven cents, I guess I could give you that."

With that, Johnny boy reached into his pocket and grabbed all the change he had and handed it over to Fred.

"Thank you, Johnny boy. Appreciate that so much. Go on Ernie," said Fred.

"Thank you," said Ernie.

"No problem, I didn't have much."

"What you doin' out here all alone?" said Fred, as his nervous eyes twitched a bit.

"Oh, I'm not. My dad is an artist and he's over there, doing some painting," said Johnny boy.

"An artist, huh? They make pretty good money I guess, huh?" asked Fred.

"Maybe, but no one buys his stuff anyway. We never even have food. He doesn't have a real job like most dads."

"Well Johnny boy, thanks so much again. Little bit more and we can get something to eat."

With that, Fred and Ernie took off walking. Johnny boy kept an eye on them before turning his back. Continuing his walk, Johnny boy started to appreciate even more, the beauty of the lake as well as the surrounding woods. Maybe he was starting to understand why his father painted. Maybe he wasn't. The water was beautiful and he figured that he had walked about a mile or so. Maybe his dad's paintings were a way for him to memorize beauty. But if that was the case, he should really be painting his mother, thought Johnny. Johnny loved his mother so much. Sitting down by the water's edge, he rested and just let his mind wander. He really did love his father. He was just so angry, as well as scared of him. After sitting and thinking for a while, Johnny boy started to feel drowsy. Fighting it as his head kept falling, he soon drifted off to sleep.

As Johnny boy opened his heavy eyelids, he didn't recognize anything. Suddenly a panic overcame him. It was almost completely dark out. Remembering how angry his father had become when he was missing last time, Johnny boy shook his head a bit to clear out the cobwebs and took off running. Approaching the area where he remembered his father setting up to paint, Johnny boy was confused. No one was there. Walking a bit farther, Johnny boy saw his father's supply bag and easel on the ground.

"John. John!" came a voice from about twenty feet into the woods.

"Dad?"

Johnny boy walked into the woods and saw his father lying against a tree. His pants were very badly ripped and his face and mouth were bleeding. Johnny boy's anger towards his dad quickly vanished and was replaced with fear and concern.

"What happened, Dad?"

"Some guy with a kid came up to me. They wanted money and said that you said I had lots of it. They knocked me to the ground and while the kid went through my pockets, his father kicked me in the face."

"Are you okay, Dad? I'm so sorry, I fell asleep. I didn't mean to. And I never said that to those guys," said Johnny boy.

"I know son. It's okay, I'm not mad. But John, I need you to help me. I need you to go home and get me a pair of pants. I can't possibly go. My pants are shredded. I tried to fight them off but the pants split and just got worse and worse as I struggled. You have that extra nickel and when you get home, have Mom give you some change so you will have enough. She will know how much."

"Okay, Dad. I will go as fast as I can. And I know the way to the subway."

With that, Johnny boy took off. Running as fast as he could, he ran and ran, never stopping until he got to the subway. Now pitch black outside, Johnny boy was breathing heavily. He approached the subway's turnstile. Putting his hand in his pocket, Johnny boy searched for his nickel. His father sure was smart getting an extra one. His father really did know a lot of things.

Johnny boy started to panic as he couldn't find the nickel. Wait! He had grabbed all of the change in his pocket for that miserable and lying son of a bitch Fred, and handed him all of it. His dad had told him to put the extra nickel in his shoe for safe keeping but he didn't listen. Looking all around him, Johnny boy didn't see any cops.

He quickly scampered under the turnstile. A train had just pulled up, screeching and squealing, loud as can be.

"Hey, you son of a bitch little fucker. Get your ass over here or I'll shoot you dead," screamed a cop.

Where had he come from? Johnny boy took off running, running faster than he ever had in his life. Timing it just perfectly, he jumped into an open door and a moment later, the closing door sealed itself tight. *That was close,* Johnny boy thought. Taking a seat in the mostly empty subway car, he deeply exhaled. Checking out his surroundings, Johnny boy saw exactly what he didn't wanna see. The cop had made it on board. Looking between cars, the cop was looking everywhere for him and was now in the adjacent car, gun drawn. Johnny boy just had to get away, get home. His father was alone and he was counting on him.

Taking off running towards the opposite end of the car, Johnny boy opened the door that lead to the next subway car. Ducking down and trying to hide under a seat, he strained his neck while try to see where his copper friend was. There seemed to be about three more stops left and Johnny boy's was the last one. Knowing that he never could stay away from the cop for that long, he decided he'd exit the next time those doors opened. The timing was perfect as the wheels, starting to scream that it was coming to a stop, brought the train to a complete halt seconds later. As the doors opened, Jonny boy waited. Waiting until they started to close, he sprang upwards and like a shot, ran for the closing doors. Barely making it, Johnny boy realized that his friend with the gun had made it also. Was he serious? Never thinking that the cop would chase him this far, Johnny boy took off running, once again. Flying down the metal steps two and three at a time, Johnny boy was soon on the streets. Where was he though? He took off running once again.

Flying down the street, he fully expected to be shot at any moment. Was it gonna hurt? After a few more minutes of full out sprinting, Johnny boy reasoned that he had 'lost' his friend the cop. Coming to an abrupt stop, he hid behind a large, green support beam that held up the tracks over- head as the subway had taken to the open spaces. Starting to recognize his surroundings a bit, Johnny boy really regretted not having his gun with him. As bad as Johnny boy's block, Christopher Street was, this area was even worse. Much worse. There was nothing he could do about it now, he was gonna run and run until he made it home. His lungs aching and his heart racing faster than his legs that were carrying him, Johnny boy realized he was pretty close now.

"Hey, white boy! You in the wrong section of town. Come here. Bring 'yo little white ass over here. I got somethin' for yo white ass! Whatsa matta, you no like niggas?" yelled a middle-aged black man.

Veering off to a side road, Johnny boy, at the point of exhaustion, used every ounce of strength that he had left and hopped a fence. As he continued his frenzied dash home, he heard what sounded like a vicious dog chasing him. Glancing behind him, the wolf-like dog's teeth were showing. Rapidly approaching the end of the empty space, he came upon yet another fence and he leapt, latching onto the fence at full speed.

A few more blocks, a few more blocks, I can do this. I have to do this! an exhausted Johnny boy thought.

Crossing a dark, unlit alley, he transitioned onto Christopher Street. Opening the heavy front door to his apartment building, Johnny boy flew up the steps and started to frantically knock at his front door.

"Who is it?" came a voice from inside.

"Mom, it's me. Hurry up! Open the door please!"

As the apartment's door opened, an out of breath Johnny boy explained to his mother, what had happened.

"Please, Mom, give me the nickels for me to get back to the park and then Dad and I to get home. Also, a pair of pants for dad!"

"Don't worry, I have some change and a few nickels hidden," said his mom.

As Johnny boy's mom went to get the nickels, he shot into his bedroom and reached under his bed. Grabbing his gun, he stuck it under the back of his pants making sure his shirt covered it.

Grabbing the money, Johnny boy started to run for the apartment's door. Spinning around, he kissed his mom on her cheek.

"Be careful, John. I love you."

Johnny boy took off running again. He knew that he had lost some time by having to exit the train early, but he would make it up somehow.

The trip back was much easier and as he approached the last stop, Johnny boy had to decide what to do if that same cop was there. As the doors opened, Johnny boy slowly exited. Looking around, everything seemed to be clear. Reaching the streets, he took off running. Everything ached and hurt but he kept going. He was really worried about his dad now. Not that he would be angry, but he just hoped he was okay.

Approaching the park, Johnny boy made his way, in complete darkness to where he had left his dad.

"Dad!"

"Over here, John."

Johnny handed his dad the pair of pants as well as two nickels. Changing quickly, his dad noticed that his son was totally drenched in sweat.

"Why are you sweating so much, John?"

"The train was so hot. And I ran as fast as I could to get back here as quickly as I could, dad."

"Thank you, John. Please help me gather up what's left of my things. These thieves destroyed most of it though."

As Johnny boy and his dad walked to the subway, they talked. His father felt badly as he was not providing for his son.

"Perhaps I should get a real job, son."

"No. You already have a real job, Dad."

Chapter Thirteen

GOVERNEMENT CHEESE WASN'T so bad. When you got used to it, it wasn't even okay for breakfast. Cutting off a small piece from the large block of cheese, Johnny boy knew that this cheese had to last. Washing up and quickly brushing his teeth, Johnny boy, after grabbing his gun, headed out to the streets. Almost the end of August now, school would soon be starting up again and Johnny boy would be entering the sixth grade. Maybe some of the girls had grown tits over the summer. At least bigger tits than Roxanne's, Johnny boy hoped.

Walking down Christopher Street, he noticed Jackie coming his way.

"Hey. You startin' to lose weight, Jackie?"

"I think so. Not much to eat lately anyway."

"You hungry? Did you eat today yet?" asked Johnny boy.

"Yeah, I had some bread and we had a little oatmeal that my mom cooked for me, but I'm still kinda hungry."

"Let's walk. They should be setting up the carts. We should be able to steal some apples at least. Just like we did last time. You distract them, talk to the guy and tell him that you want some stuff for your mother and I'll grab what I can and run. When they start after me, you just walk away, real slow like. Then meet me at the alley, okay?"

"You sure? Okay, no problem."

The boys got there just as the carts were being pushed out in front of the grocery stores. Apples were expensive now, some places had them for four cents apiece. Johnny boy walked up first, and the guy asked what he wanted. Johnny boy just shook his head no and walked away. Jackie then got his attention and told him that his mom wanted some apples, bananas, and some vegetables. As the man was asking Jackie how much money he had and to show it to him, Johnny boy came racing in and targeted the apples. Fast as anything, he grabbed four apples and flew down the block like lightening.

"Hey, you. Come back here, you thief!" yelled the man with a heavy accent.

As he ran a few steps, he quickly realized that he'd never catch him and turned back towards his cart. Jackie, thinking that he'd give chase for a longer while, figured he'd help himself to some free fruit as well. The only thing was that Jackie really couldn't run very well.

"Get back here, you fat bastard. Thief! I will slap the shit out of your face!" screamed the man.

Running barely ten feet, Jackie felt himself being shoved to the hard cement walkway. Turning him over and grabbing back the apples, the proprietor proceeded to follow through on his promise and smacked Jackie with all his might, time after time, right across his face. Jackie burst out crying and begged the man to please stop. Now mocking Jackie, the man started to laugh.

"Some tough guy. He cry for his momma."

Letting the sobbing Jackie get up, the man continued to laugh at him.

Backpedaling, Jackie yelled and cursed the man.

"Fuck you. I'll come back and shoot you in the balls, you motherfucker!"

With that, Jackie ran. Stopping after a few moments to catch his breath, Jackie made his way back to the alley to meet up with Johnny boy.

"Hey, you made it. Here's two apples for you. Wait! What the fuck happened to you?"

"The guy beat the shit outta me," answered Jackie.

"Let's go, Jackie!"

"Where to?"

"I wanna go back. I'm gonna shoot this fucker right between his eyes," said Johnny boy.

"No! No, not now. It was my fault. Please," pleaded Jackie.

Jackies chubby cheeks were turning a bright red. Soon his face looked like the apples that Johnny boy was holding.

"Look, Jackie. You're my main guy and we stick together. If anyone, and I mean anyone, fucks with one of us? We all get them back. Understood?" asked Johnny boy.

"Okay, but this time…Just don't shoot him, okay?"

A hesitant and pissed off Johnny boy told his friend that he would in fact do nothing, but Johnny boy wasn't done with the situation yet. He'd get him back. He always got everyone back. This guy would be sorry that he ever laid a hand on his friend Jackie.

Jackie and Johnny boy walked towards the boy's new hangout, stopping to see if Mrs. Williams' tits were there for their viewing. Johnny stood on his toes, elevating as high as he could. He needed some new sights to jerkoff to. There would be no such luck, so they proceeded down to their club.

"Okay, so we're gonna need a desk, some chairs, a radio, and a couch. We'll also need a box to hide our money in," explained Johnny boy.

"I say that Jimmy, Mickey, and Danny need to do that," suggested Jackie.

"Agreed."

"Let's go find the boys. You tell 'em what they have to get," said Johnny boy.

"Okay."

Crossing Christopher Street, the boys went down an alley and headed towards Jimmy, Mickey, and Danny's apartments.

"There they are," said Jackie.

"What's up guys?" asked Mickey

Mickey was a tough Irish kid. His father, once a boxer, was really hard on him. But he did teach him how to fight. Whenever there was a problem or a fight, Mickey could always take care of himself, and more.

"Nothing much. Listen, we found a perfect place for a clubhouse. The alley right over by me. You pass Mrs. Williams' tits on the left and go around back. It's dirty, with no locks yet and we need some stuff…" said Johnny boy, before Jackie cut in.

"Look, Mickey, Danny, and Jimmy, we need you guys to get a couch, a few chairs, a table and…and…oh yeah, a box for hiding the money," said Jackie.

"So, who made you the fuckin' boss?" asked Jimmy.

Jimmy was a wiry little guy but tough as nails. Even Johnny boy would never want to go up against Jimmy. He had a temper and sometimes didn't really think things out before doing them. Jimmy was smart in school. One of the few kids that had both of his parents working, Jimmy may not last long in the broken- down apartments of Brownsville. If Jimmy was telling the truth, his parents were looking to get out, move to a nicer, cleaner, as well as safer, area.

"I did," answered Johnny boy.

No one said a word. Danny kicked a small can that was just sitting by the curb.

"What? You gotta problem now?" asked Johnny boy.

"No, I mean, one minute he's a fat kid that we have to watch out for, and now all the sudden, he's giving orders? What the fuck?" said Danny.

"Wait a minute, look at him, he's losing weight and I'm gonna teach him how to kick ass. He don't have a dad to teach him that shit. Remember? I'll tell you what though, he's smarter than all of you's jerkoffs put together," said Johnny boy.

"Oh yeah? He's so smart, why's his face all red and bruised?"

"Don't worry about it! Listen Danny, just do what he says, okay?"

"Okay fellas, let's all go check out the clubhouse," said Johnny boy.

With that, Johnny boy gave Jackie a bit of a nod telling him to lead the way. Out of breath after just a little ways, Jackie kept looking towards Johnny boy, who wouldn't relent. He was gonna keep pushing Jackie, toughen him up a bit, make a man of him.

"Okay fellas, right here, down the alley and around to the left," instructed Jackie.

Jackie opened the outside door, and had a problem with the next one. Old and warped, the door was wedged tight.

"Here, let me do it," said Danny.

"No, I got it," said Jackie.

With Johnny boy nodding his approval, Jackie proceeded to put his weight into things a bit and blasted the door open. The boys let out a bit of a cheer and slapped Jackie on the back. Jackie was feeling better about himself. Just the way Johnny boy had planned.

"Shit, this place is cool. Man, we can get lots of broads down here," said Jimmy.

"Yeah, but we also have a place to hide our money. And fellas, the way I have things planned in my mind? We'll have a lot to hide!" exclaimed Johnny boy.

Turning on the several lonely looking bulbs by pulling the attached strings, Johnny boy shed some light on the boy's new place.

"Okay, Mickey, Danny, and Jimmy, we need you guys to get a couch, some chairs, a table, and a box for hiding the money," said Jackie.

Even though Jackie had already told the boys what they needed, his orders were no longer resented. The boys were buying in. They could see what Johnny boy was doing. They understood that they'd only be as strong as the weakest among them.

"Let's go fellas. I have some idea's where we can steal…I mean get, most of this stuff," said Mickey.

The boys all took off, leaving just Johnny boy and Jackie there in the clubhouse.

"So, whatta you think, Jackie? The Money Boys?"

"What," said Jackie.

"You know, the name of our gang!"

"Oh yeah, I like it, it's perfect," said Jackie.

"Listen, I wanted to wait until the rest of the guys left. I'm gonna tell you something. But no one and I mean no one, can know! Okay?"

"Definitely!"

"I'm gonna go back and get that mother fucker with the carts and I'm gonna do it tomorrow morning, Jackie," said Johnny boy.

"Wait, you promised you weren't gonna shoot him," reminded Jackie.

"I know, I know! Listen! I'm gonna set his carts on fire. He's got two, right? I'm gonna burn both to the fucking ground! I always get them back, Jackie. Always."

Jackie looked scared but just nodded. Inside, he was happy. While he was gaining confidence and getting braver, he was still scared of fighting.

The last days of summer were winding down. In a way, Johnny boy sort of looked forward to it. He hated school, what boy didn't, but it got him away from home, somewhere quiet, somewhere safe.

But tomorrow, he had a job to do. Nobody fucked with The Money Boys.

"Let me come with you, Johnny boy," pleaded Jackie.

"No, no way. Not for this. This is dangerous, Jackie. I don't want you getting mixed up in this."

"But come on. I'm the one who got the snot smacked outta me, lemme help."

"Look, Jackie. I need you to be my second guy. You know, right after me. I'm the boss, but if there's ever a problem that I can't deal with? It's all you. Okay?"

"Oh, alright. But no guns, right? You promised me, Johnny boy."

"Alright! Yes, I promise. Go home Jackie. I gotta go too. I don't wanna get in trouble again with my dad or I'll have to …"

Johnny boy's voice trailed off. He knew what was in his mind and he better just keep it there. No one was gonna fuck with him.

That would start very soon. Tomorrow morning in fact.

Chapter Fourteen

"JOHN, TIME TO wake up. You are going with your father to watch him paint today."

Johnny boy stirred and then his mother's words clicked in his still sleepy mind. No way. He had other plans for this morning.

"No, Mom. I can't do that this morning. I promised Danny that I would help his mom fix some things around their apartment," Johnny boy lied.

"What things?"

"Danny's dad is very sick. They need to move a bed so that…"

"Okay, John, you better not be lying to me!"

"Never, Mom."

Johnny boy knew that his mom didn't believe him. But he wasn't lying when he said that he had something else to do.

Lying in bed and pretending to be asleep, Johnny boy waited until the house was quiet and he was certain that both of his parents were gone. He knew that is dad had cleaning solutions that he used to clean his brushes with and that they were extremely flammable. His dad had told him over and over to never touch them.

Looking in his father's closet, Johnny boy located the cleaning fluid, and some matches. His father was a heavy cigarette smoker and there were always those little wooden matches all over the apartment. The cleaning fluid was in one of those small little metal cans and you take the little tip off it and just squeeze a little fluid on a rag. There was only one can so his father was going to notice it was gone.

The little can fit perfectly in his well-worn and tattered jeans. The matches fit in his other pocket. Johnny boy looked around the kitchen for some food. His mom had made pasta but that never lasted long. So, it was a slice of government cheese, a piece of stale bread, and some water.

Running down the stairs, Johnny boy was going much faster than usual. Not afraid at all, he was a little anxious. He could feel his heart beating. But why? He wasn't planning on killing anyone.

It was still early but the streets were already busy. As Johnny boy walked down the block, heading towards the pushcarts, he rehearsed just how this was gonna go. He was early enough that he should get there just as the old man was setting up his two carts. Johnny boy would walk past them and then walk slowly back. Just a few drops around the wooden base and maybe a little more on the old and worn out canopy. That should do it. He figured the old man would go into a panic and Johnny boy would just walk away. He'd never know what happened or who did it. As he waited, he looked around for any cops. He had to have a little luck this morning. This was important.

Johnny boy saw his intended target. That short, fat bastard would pay. No one fucked with the Money Boys! Johnny boy was working himself into a rage! As he planned, he walked past the carts, then slowly walked back to them. Shielded by plenty of people, Johnny boy reached into his pocket and got his father's small can of cleaning fluid. Pulling out the matches he then squirted the green wooden base of the cart as well as the canopy. Maybe this was too much. Oh, fuck it. This bastard wasn't gonna feel so tough anymore. He'd pay for slapping Jackie around! Putting the can back in his pocket, Johnny boy quickly lit a match and tossed it at just the base. The wood must have been very old and dry, as it ignited instantly. The flames were really growing tall now and before he knew it, the canopy was a roaring blanket of orange heat.

"Hey! What the fuck! What happen? Oh my God! No!" yelled the panicky cart owner.

The heat was incredible. Johnny boys face stung. Backing away slowly, his eyes locked with the old man.

"You again! I kill you. You no good fucker!"

As the old man started to go after Johnny boy, his white apron brushed against the flaming inferno. Flames burned rapidly up his apron. Within seconds the old man's entire body was consumed with a raging and deadly flame. Johnny boy looked in the old man's eyes. He could smell his flesh burning. The smells were horrific. As he came out of his frozen stance, Johnny boy started to backpedal. Still looking at the charred old man, he saw something that he may never forget for the rest of his life. Both of the old man's eyes exploded from the intensity of the flames. Blood was gushing out of both, now empty sockets. Soon, there would be no more agonizing screams of unbearable pain. The old man was dead. He continued to burn as Johnny boy finally started to turn away. Now running, he heard the panicked crown of people start to scream. The screaming became less and less as Johnny boy got farther and farther away. Not wanting to draw any attention to himself, Johnny boy soon slowed to a casual walk. Taking a longer way home and looking all around first, he dumped the cleaning fluid in an old metal trash can. Figuring he'd just put back his dad's matches when he got home, he held on to them. Several blocks away, Johnny boy could still see smoke, as well as hear the sirens of either the police, fire department, or maybe even both.

As he walked aimlessly around his neighborhood, Johnny boy couldn't get the sight of the old cart-man's eyes exploding, out of his memory. *The bastard deserved it,* he reasoned! There was no reason to slap Jackie around and even worse, to humiliate him. Fuck that. No one would ever get away with hurting Johnny boy again, and the same applied to any of the Money Boys.

As Johnny boy approached his apartment, he glanced down the alley. Maybe Mrs. Williams' tits would be out? If ever there was a time he needed her tits, it was now. Looking towards the end of the alley, Johnny boy could see a couch being dragged and rounding the corner. Johnny boy made his way to the clubhouse door and saw that

Jimmy, Mickey, and Danny had just about dragged the couch down into the clubhouse. Maybe Jackie did have things under control?

"Hey! Good job. Where'd you guys get that? Oh shit, a table, chairs and you even got that wooden box to put all our money in," said Johnny boy.

"Yeah, we did good. They was throwin' stuff out," said Jimmy.

"I don't think so. Sometimes when the rent ain't paid, they open your door and take everything out. Well, we can't put it back," said Johnny boy.

"Hey, you see the fire down by Cartville, Johnny boy?" asked Mickey.

"Shit, it's probably still burning. It smelled terrible too," added Jimmy.

"I did see smoke," said Johnny boy.

"You know how it happened?" asked Jimmy.

"Naaahhh, I heard some people saying it was an accident. Probably a cigarette or somethin'."

Johnny boy and his cohorts proceeded to set up the hangout. Putting the couch against a wall, they realized that it would be perfect for screwing girls. They talked over getting more light down there and saw there were a few more spots to screw in light bulbs.

"Hey fellas. We need some light bulbs. See if you guys can get some. We'll need a lock as well," said Johnny boy.

"I know how to put in a locking door handle, my dad showed me. I can get one with a few keys also," said Mickey.

"Great. This is gonna come together. But no one can say a single word to anyone, okay," said Johnny boy.

"You sure you don't wanna run that by your boss over there, Johnny boy?" said Danny, as he pointed to Jackie.

"Shut the fuck up," answered Johnny boy.

"Let's go fellas. We need to make some money. Pocketbooks today? I wanna wait 'till dark to break into cars. Let's go," said Johnny boy.

"Not today, I can't. I promised my mom that I'd be back early. She has to sew up my clothes seein' that school starts soon," said Jimmy.

"Okay, the hell with it. Tomorrow though. We need to start saving," Johnny boy mentioned.

The boys all cleared out and Johnny boy headed home. He ran up the four flights of stairs to get his shoe shine kit. He'd go down to the subway, and as men were getting home soon from work, he'd hustle up some work. Morning was usually the best time as they wanted to look good for work but he'd make a little bit of money at least.

After getting his shoeshine kit, Johnny boy started his walk towards the subway. There were three benches set up right at the bottom of the metal stairs, and he took a seat.

"Mister, shoe shine? Just a nickel," said Johnny boy.

"Hey kid, how much for a shine?" asked a well-dressed man.

Johnny smiled and again said that it was just a nickel. Was this guy a moron?

"The best shine you can find, Mister. I don't just shine 'em, I clean 'em and polish 'em," said Johnny boy.

Johnny boy's dad could make anything or fix anything. Not being able to afford a shoe shine kit, his dad made one from scraps of wood and whatever else he could find. He got the cleaner and polishes for free from his art supply friends. Even though Johnny boy knew that he could give a better shine, he also would out-hustle the other guys out there.

"Okay, kid. Let's go."

Johnny boy had the wealthy looking man sit down on the bench. Taking out the cleaner and a cleaning cloth, he proceeded to wipe and remove all the dirt and dust from the nice pair of shoes. Looking at the shoes color, he determined them to be a dark brown, almost black. Johnny boy was good. Really good! He blended in a little black polish with the brown. He learned all of this from his dad. Having conflicted feelings, anger as well as adoration and love, Johnny boy really did idolize his father. His dad blended colors to obtain unique shades. Johnny boy applied these lessons to his shoe shine business.

"Here kid, I have a quarter, you have change?"

It was too late, Johnny boy grabbed the quarter and took off. The well to-do customer just shook his head. He couldn't help but laugh. He was ripped off by some hustling kid.

Johnny boy went down a few blocks and set up again.

"Hey, what the fuck are you doing here? This is my place, asshole."

"Maybe it was, but it's mine now," responded Johnny boy.

It was on. The big kid went at Johnny boy. Lightning quick, Johnny boy pulled out his gun, aiming it squarely at the charging shoe shine boy.

"Whoa, okay, okay. I was just kidding. Easy now."

"Bullshit. Easy, nothing. Get the fuck outta here. I'm not playin'," said Johnny boy.

Backing up, the kid retreated. Johnny boy kept the gun aimed square at his face. Slowly but surely, the kid backed away and disappeared. Johnny boy was hungry and wanted to help his mom and dad as well.

Chapter Fifteen

"OKAY, JOHN, IT'S time to eat," called Johnny boy's mom.

"Wait, Dad isn't home yet."

"I know; he went to apply for a job."

"Like a real job, Mom?"

"John, your father works very hard. Times are difficult. He is doing the best that he can, son. His art is a real job. Go wash up John. What happened to you today? Trouble everyday now. What is that all over your face and hands?"

"I was working a real job. Shining shoes. I made eighty cents today, Mom," bragged Johnny boy.

"Wash and sit!"

"I want to give the money to you, Mom."

"Okay, John. We need it. But I want you to keep some. We talk this over later. Now eat."

Johnny boy sure was hungry. Washing all the stubborn shoe polish from his face was another 'real job.'

Johnny boy took the old bar of Lava soap and rubbed it directly on his face. Getting soap in his eyes, Johnny boy started to curse.

"John! I hear this. Do not speak such language in our home!"

Rinsing and drying off his face, Johnny boy looked like a new kid.

"Now sit. Eat," said his mom.

As Johnny boy sat down to eat, his mother brought a small pot of macaroni and cheese and a glass of water to him. Digging in, he started to feel that tenseness in his belly as the apartments door handle started to turn.

"Anatole, you are home. Did you apply for job?"

"Yes, Sonia, they have two positions for guard at the museum. Many men are there. I feel embarrassed as my writing and English is not too good. I write down my name and they say to check back next month."

"Okay, Anatole, that is good. You should not feel embarrassment. You are an amazing artist but to sell art in these times is very difficult."

"I do feel like failure. Sonia, I never expect this. I thought I would sell many expensive paintings. Perhaps I get this job. Security is good job. Much hours they said."

"Sit ,Anatole, eat," said Sonia.

Seeing that there was little left in the pot, Anatole lied and said that he had eaten already.

"They had some food there that we ate."

Sonia stared at her husband.

"You have a very good heart when you do not drink too much of the vodka, Anatole," said Sonia.

With his stomach still feeling nervous, Johnny boy finished his meal.

"May I be excused please?"

"John, please sit for a little longer. Drink your water. I never have much of a chance to speak with you," said Anatole.

As Johnny boy's dad talked, he separated his young mind from the words coming from his father's mouth. As his eyes traveled around the apartment, he noticed just how darkened the white walls had become.

"If you are such a great painter, how come our walls look like shit?"

"John Rostov! Don't you ever speak to your father like that! Do you understand?" said Johnny boy's mom.

"I'm sorry. I'm sorry to the both of you. I talk like that with my friends on the street and I forget where I am. Am I in trouble?"

"No. But please no speak this way," said Sonia.

Johnny boy really did feel badly. He wasn't being a wise ass at all. He just had made a mistake. He was sure that he was gonna get it again! If his father beat him, he was just gonna run. As far away as he could. He was growing up now. He could make it on his own. He'd almost had sex, was a leader, and he'd even killed someone. No one was going to mess with him!

"John, it is okay. I have made mistakes too in my life. I disrespect my own father. I pay the price. You no worry. It okay."

Johnny boy's dad had really surprised him. Anatole had a very calm and even tone to his words. He understood. Johnny boy really was confused now. He loved his dad. When he was like this, at least.

"So, John, what do you think you want to be when you grow?"

"I'm not sure dad. I want to have money. I like to play baseball. Maybe a ballplayer. I was talking to the boys and I was thinking maybe a soldier?"

"Money is good. Baseball too. But not a soldier, John. I have feelings that we will be in war soon. You don't want to fight in war. I have seen this in Russia. Someday, I tell you of how I get to America. Not easy. Soldiers must sometimes do things they not wanting to do. Also, some want to at times," explained Johnny boy's dad.

This was different. Johnny boy so wanted to open his heart once again. He had loved and trusted his father so much. However, he didn't trust him now. He would never beat him again. No one would. Ever.

"John, please help with the dishes. We need to wash some of your clothes as well," said his mom. "Wash up and brush teeth first," she added.

Sonia Rostov was a loving woman. Normally a gentle approach with Johnny boy was her way, she would occasionally become frustrated with him but that was because she worried about him.

Living on the third floor wasn't so bad. The people above had always been quiet. In fact, the apartment above them had been empty for a few months. But new tenants were now moving in. They sure did seem loud. But then again, moving in was always loud.

"Stop your mind from wandering. John! Wash yourself and brush teeth and help me."

As Johnny boy washed his hands and face, he kicked closed the bathroom door. Staring into the mirror, he determined that he was a really, good looking guy. He was gonna screw lots of girls, and soon. In fact, as soon as they did a little more work to the hangout across the alley, he would screw Roxanne. And she would like it.

The sharp knocks at the bathroom door were impatient.

"Now, John!"

"It's okay, Sonia. He is a boy. A boy's mind goes on trips. He thinks of many things. This is normal. He thinks of girls…"

As Anatole continued to explain these things to his wife, she suddenly interrupted him.

"No! He is a young boy Anatole! He is but eleven!"

"Okay, Sonia. You are right. But his mind thinks of many things and it takes a while to focus his thinking again. Be patient. He is good boy."

Johnny boy could hear all of this back and forth between his parents. Feeling a bit emotional, he was becoming more and more aware of just how much he indeed loved his dad. He just wished that he wouldn't drink. Ever.

Continuing to stare at the mirror, Johnny boy took off his tee shirt. Making muscle poses, he admired his lean but wiry frame. He'd started doing pushups to get even stronger. Naturally thin, he wished he could put some weight on. He had his gun and now he wanted to know how to use a knife. Johnny boy was fast. Fast hands, fast runner, and fast talker. He'd have to talk to Al, from across the street about getting a knife and how to use it best. School would be starting soon and there'd be no more humiliation this year. No, Johnny boy wouldn't have any problems with the niggers this year. Every year, the niggers would get him in the bathroom, kick his ass, and stuff his head in the toilet bowl. No more though. Never one to back down, fighting back simply wasn't enough anymore. When they started school again, they'd see a whole new Johnny boy.

As Johnny boy opened the bathroom door, his mother was just about to start banging on the door again.

"What in the world do you do in there?" she asked.

"Just brushing my teeth, Mom."

Johnny boy took the plates from the table and brought them into the kitchen. As he returned to get the last plate and two glasses, Johnny boy saw that his father was lying down, sound asleep on the living room couch. Looking very peaceful, Johnny boy relaxed. There would be no trouble tonight.

"What in the world is that?" yelled a suddenly startled Anatole.

"It's those ass…those people upstairs dad. The new people."

"It sounds as if the ceiling is coming down, Anatole," said Sonia.

"And they're yelling and screaming and using a lot of bad words," added Johnny boy.

"Well, I wait a bit and if they no stop, I go and speak with them," said Johnny boy's dad.

Another loud crash followed by very loud screaming and cursing soon followed.

"Let's go, Dad," said an aggressive Johnny boy.

"Yes, let us go. But John, you stay silent. Let me talk, okay?"

"Okay, Dad."

Johnny boy quickly went into his bedroom and retrieved his gun. Just in case.

"John, now!"

Walking up the stairs, the echoing sounded as eerie as ever. Thump, thump, thump. Anatole gently knocked on the apartment door that was directly above theirs.

"What the fuck do you want?" said a very muscular, Spanish looking man.

"This my son, John and I am Anatole. We are your neighbors from downstairs."

"So? Why do I give a fuckin' shit, old man?"

"We do the nice thing. We introduce and welcome you," said Anatole.

The words barely out of Anatole's mouth, the angry Hispanic man took a vicious swing at Johnny boy's father's face and connected. Staggering backwards, the startled Russian fell to the floor of the filthy hallway.

Johnny boy, reacting with lightening quick reflexes, pulled the gun from the back of his pants waistband and in one motion had it inches from the attacker's face.

"Okay, mother fucker. Back the fuck up! I said back up! Now!"

Slowly, the antagonized man backed into his apartment door. Keeping the gun pointed at his enemy's face, Johnny boy put his hand out to help his father up.

"Dad, you okay?" asked Johnny boy.

"Where you get gun?"

"I found it, Dad."

"Look, I drank too much and I dropped some shit on my foot. I'm sorry old man, okay?" asked the Spanish man. "My name is Carlos. I have little baby's and I just lost my job. I didn't mean anything, okay?"

"Okay, Carlos. But you never raise a hand again, or I will not be as nice as my son."

"Don't fuck with me. Or my family. Ever!" yelled Johnny boy.

The stranger just stared at Johnny boy. Without further incident, the two third floor dwellers bounced back down the stairs and re-entered their own apartment.

"John, give me the gun. Before your mother sees it."

"Dad, I thought you saw it. I threw it down the incinerator. You didn't hear that rusty door? I mean, the thing was empty, Dad. Okay?"

"Okay, son. You are sure?"

"Yes, Dad."

"You no touch guns. Okay? No more."

"Okay, Dad."

Johnny boy's father returned to the couch. He pulled out a writing tablet from under the pillows of the worn and aged couch. Not aware that anyone was looking, Anatole proceeded to write. Johnny boy took a seat on a chair that was close to the couch. Reading a Boy's Life magazine, Johnny boy's curiosities were aroused. What was his father writing and why was it hidden away?

Johnny boy was determined to find out. Someday.

Chapter Sixteen

IT WAS SATURDAY morning and the last weekend before school started. Johnny boy sat down at the kitchen table to eat his steaming oatmeal and his mother poured him a glass of milk. As Johnny boy slowly ate the oatmeal, his eyes scanned the apartment.

The walls, badly stained with grease marks from the previous tenants, still were evident. Johnny boy's mother had scrubbed and scrubbed them, but the greasy residue remained. All the wall switches were stained, the plates that surrounded them, darkened from the constant swiping action of everyone's hands. Johnny boy thought that it was mainly from him as he was quite filthy when he returned from shining shoes. Other than the stains, Johnny boy's mom did quite the job at keeping their home nice and clean.

"Did Dad leave already, to paint?" asked Johnny boy.

"No John. He went to the Salvage store in Canarsie. He wanted to pick up some spare parts for fixing some things as well as making something he has in his mind."

"What does he want to make, Mom?"

"It is funny. When you mentioned about his not painting the walls here, it reminds him of something he always wants to make. To make wall painting easier."

"Are you going somewhere Mom?"

"Maybe to the park to read, I am not sure. Why, John?"

Johnny boy desperately wanted to look underneath those couch pillows.

"Okay Mom, I'm gonna go play some ball or hang out with the boys, okay? And yes, I know—put my dishes in the sink and brush my teeth."

Johnny boy's mother smiled. A softness covered her loving face. Perhaps Johnny boy would leave his father's writing alone. Perhaps he would just wait until he was sure he couldn't get caught.

Hitting the streets, it was about ten in the morning and Johnny boy could just feel the heat of the afternoon coming to visit. It must have already been in the eighties and the air was heating quickly. Deciding to walk down the alley, he slowed down and casually looked into Mrs. Williams' bathroom window. Maybe her tits would come out to play today. Nope, the bathroom was empty. Making a left at the end of the alley, Johnny boy opened the first of two doors that lead to their new hangout. Pushing open the second door and making his way towards the first light, Johnny boy pulled the cord and the dim bulb sputtered on.

"Hey Johnny boy, what's up?" asked Jimmy.

Jimmy was to be the money-man and Johnny boy felt badly. He had been spending so much time trying to toughen up Jackie, that he'd been ignoring his other boys.

"Glad you showed up, Jimmy. I wanted to talk to you."

"What's goin' on, Johnny boy?"

"Listen, you know you're my man, right? I mean, I'm trusting you with all our money, so that tells you right there what I think of you. I've just been trying to toughen Jackie up a little."

"Hey, I know that, no problem. I'm no girl!" said Jimmy with a smile and a chuckle.

Both boys laughed and started to look around their new hangout. Slowly but surely, it was coming together.

"Where's the money box, Johnny boy?" asked Jimmy.

"You know; you guys can just start callin' me Johnny. Johnny boy is when I was a kid."

"Alright. So, Johnny, where's the fuckin' money box?"

"Under the desk, why?"

"I have that thirty-nine bucks. You remember. From the day we got the pocket book?"

"Oh yeah, I remember," said Johnny.

"What, was you testin' me, Jimmy?"

"No way. Listen, we're all family. Anyone fucks with any of us, we all go after them. We all trust each other like brothers," said Johnny.

Jimmy went over to the dimly lit area where the desk was. Pulling out the wooden crate type box, he opened it up.

"I also got this leather pouch, Johnny. We should put all the loot in here always and there's a little compartment on the side here. We'll just drop the pouch right in."

"Listen, you and I will tell the fellas, but if they need money? They have to ask only me or you. Deal?"

Jimmy shook his head yes.

"You know what? When you was little, I gave you that name, Johnny boy. So, it's Johnny boy until I say otherwise."

Jimmy and Johnny locked eyes. A staring contest of sorts was on. It didn't last as Jimmy busted up laughing.

"And I say it's time. Don't fuck with me now!"

Jimmy had a good sense of humor. He had to. His father beat his mother and one time when Jimmy got in the middle, his father almost killed him. Jimmy had a brother, Fred, and a sister named Francis. Being the oldest, he took a lot of shit. Jimmy was smart. Really smart. Ask him any math problem and in a second or two, he'd have your answer. No paper, no pencil, just brain power.

Danny, Jackie, and Mickey pushed open the second basement door and all staggered in, laughing out of control.

"Hey, guy's. Before I ask what the fuck is so funny, I have an announcement to make. From here on in, we call Johnny boy, just Johnny. Okay?" asked Jimmy.

The boys all nodded. Jimmy led them over to the desk and he showed them the money situation and explained the rules.

"Look, Johnny boy…I mean Johnny, I got some light bulbs. Want I puts some in?" asked Jackie.

"Sure. Listen, the rest of you shitheads come over here so I can show you' s too," instructed Jimmy.

Jackie struggled to put in the three new light bulbs but no one offered to help so after about twenty minutes, there was good light in the hangout.

"Hey, I got new lock kits and keys. I got a few screwdrivers also. I'll get to changing both now and then come see me to get your keys, okay?" asked Danny.

"And all of you, when you leave, and you're the last one out, lock both doors. This place will have a lot of money and shit. It will also be our private place to screw girls so we gotta keep it clean. I think girls put out more when it's clean. I think I heard that, you know?" said Johnny.

"Speaking of girls, you fuck Roxanne yet? She wants it bad Johnny," said Jimmy.

"She moved," said Johnny.

"What? What the fuck are you talking about?" asked Jimmy.

"She moved from right above us, to right next door. The apartment opened and cost less, so her parents took it. Me and my old man had to go take care of business last night. Some drunken spic moves in upstairs and he's screaming and yelling all night."

"My old man was gonna whup his ass, but I got between them," explained Johnny.

"Anyway, I was thinking, school starts soon and it'd be great if we could get some jackets, you know and they could say 'Money Boys' across the back. What do you guys all think?" asked Danny.

"Let's see. That's five jackets, right? Danny, you said your dad can get 'em cheap, right?" asked Johnny.

"Yeah, probably three bucks each and with the writing, probably around four bucks each," said Danny.

"Okay, well we have that much in the box right now," said Johnny.

"Let's get some tires. We bring 'em to Al and he'll give us two bucks each. I wanna save some if not all of that money we already have," said Jimmy.

"I'll tell my dad to get 'em. We can pay when they're here," said Danny.

"We still goin' with Money Boys or do you guys wanna change it?" asked Danny.

"I was thinkin' 'The Browns,' for Brownsville," said Mickey.

"Yeah, I like that," said Jackie.

"Me too, let's do it!" said Johnny.

"No way. We decided on Money Boys. We're stickin' with it. Don't be pussies," said Jackie.

Everyone was silent. Eyes darting about, the boys didn't know what to make of this.

"I mean, it is better than Donut Boys, no?" added Jackie.

That was it. The boys all exploded with laughter. Money Boys was it and it wasn't changing.

The boys left the comfort and safety of their hangout to return to the streets above them. Stealing tires was nothing new for them. Danny had learned from his dad how to change them a few years ago and when he showed Johnny and the rest of the boys that it wasn't so hard, they tried a few cars. They learned some lessons along the way. They had to bring something to move the tires to Al, quietly and quickly. No one drove yet. So they couldn't steal 'em and pile 'em in a car and take off. It was best to do it at dusk. A few big screwdrivers and a few large wrenches and that was it.

There was a factory a few blocks away. They had these old and beat up flatbed carts that were just perfect for laying those tires on. A can of oil to lube the wheels a bit and you could push those suckers as fast as you could run and could barely even hear them.

The boys decided to meet in two hours in front of the factory. They had cut back from two shifts to just one as time were tough, so the place would be deserted by the time they needed those carts. Everyone headed home. Soon enough, it would be money time.

Chapter Sixteen

"JOHN, SIT STILL and have some dinner," said Sonia.

"I'm not hungry, Ma. Besides, I have a friend who needs my help. I promised him I would teach him more about reading. Try as hard as he can, he's just not very good. So, I figure I'll help him. That's good, right Ma?"

Johnny's mom just stared at her son. Moms could generally tell when their kids were full of shit and Johnny's eyes had just become a darker shade of brown.

"Okay, Mom, I'll be back a little later."

"John, you stay out of trouble! Okay?"

"Of course, Mom. I love you."

There were three types of tires that John had learned to look for. Firestone, BF Goodrich, and US Rubber. The first two got them the most money. Al would pay two bucks a piece for these and a buck for the United Rubber ones. Now normally, this included the hubcaps but Johnny was thinking and he was gonna ask for fifty cents each for those.

"Hey Johnny, where is everyone, it's getting dark already," asked Danny.

"I don't know, let's give them a few minutes."

"What's that?" asked Danny.

"Hey fellas!" yelled Jackie.

Startled, Johnny and Danny quickly turned and there were Jackie and Jimmy pulling two flatbed carts from around the back of the factory.

"Shhhhhhhh! What the fuck is wrong with you guys? Be quiet. Look, Danny brought the oil can and you're supposed to oil those wheels before you move 'em. Nice and quiet like," said a pissed-off Johnny.

"Okay, I'm sorry Johnny," said an embarrassed Jackie.

"Never mind, it's okay. Listen, pull them off to the side of the driveway, quiet like! Turn them on their sides," instructed Danny.

Turning the flatbeds on their sides, Danny oiled up all four wheels on each of the old carts.

"Let's go. And be quiet!" said Johnny in a hushed tone.

Pushing the carts down the street, the boys followed Johnny.

After walking a few blocks, Johnny veered right, into a movie theater parking lot.

"All the way in the back," said Johnny.

The theater was packed and that was a good thing. More selection, as well as more of a screen provided. No one could see them all the way in the back.

"Work quick, before they start getting out," said Jimmy

Taking the two long screwdrivers that Danny had brought, the boys quickly popped off the hubcaps. All four were quietly placed on one of the carts. Next was the large wrenches and slowly, they pulled each tire off. Using some large rocks that Johnny knew were against the back fence, they propped the car up a bit to make it possible to get all four tires off easily. They were US Rubber. After about thirty minutes, the boys had twelve tires and nine hubcaps. Some of the cars were missing a few.

"All US Rubber. Damn. These people are cheap fucks," said a tough talking Jackie.

"Shut up, fatso," said an angry Danny.

"Hey, what the fuck are you punks doing? What? That's my fucking car!" yelled the middle-aged and very tall man.

It's a good thing that he was with his wife, as by the time he got her situated, the boys had taken off. Those lubed up wheels sure did go fast! The boys tore back towards the alley and quickly took all of the jackpot and brought it down to the hangout.

"Damn, that was close!" said Jackie.

"Too close. Look, we gotta have a better plan next time, okay? You guys understand?" asked Johnny.

Alright, let's take off. We gotta get locks on these doors. Jimmy, you said you could take care of that?" asked Johnny.

"Yeah, be done tomorrow,"

"Hey, Danny, can I talk to you real quick?" asked Johnny.

As the rest of the boys left, Johnny talked to Danny as they stacked the tires and hubcaps neatly in the corner.

"Look, I know that Jackie is a pain in the ass sometimes and yeah, he's fat. But, I'm really tryin' to build him up. You know, in his brain. He ain't got no father so I figure we need to take that over. Who knows. Maybe someday he'll save our lives."

"I got it. I know, I just got pissed. I won't say that shit anymore. Sorry Johnny."

Johnny closed the doors behind him and started walking up the alley. He said goodbye to Danny as Danny took off. Johnny slowly headed up the alley. Looking to his right, his heart started to beat faster. The light was on in Mrs. Williams' bathroom! Johnny walked up and pushing himself against the old and dirty brick wall, stood to the side of the window. Ducking down directly under the window, Johnny slowly raised his head. There she was and the titties were out! Mrs. Williams was about thirty years old, blonde with a huge set of tits. They both stood straight out, even after her bra was off. She was brushing her teeth and when she finished, she slowly slid off her underwear.

What a fucking set of tits. What an ass. Just perfect. Not too big, but just round enough. That's just the way I like my asses, thought Johnny.

Johnny stood there, now almost standing fully upright and continued to watch. He was getting turned on and his dick was swelling up like a hot air balloon. Raising her arms and with the sink water running, Mrs. Williams was shaving her armpits.

Johnny heard footsteps and started to turn around. A large man with a big stick in his hand grabbed him by the neck and started to choke him.

"Get the fuck off me. I'll shoot you," threatened Johnny.

Squeezing even harder now, the man dragged Johnny farther into the alley. Johnny was really scared now. He didn't have his gun and besides, his arms were getting numb and Johnny felt as if passing out was close.

Suddenly, the powerful stranger let go. Johnny fell to the pavement with a thud. His head spinning, he watched as a man grabbed his attacker and pinned him to the wall.

"Dad?"

"Go away, Johnny. Leave, now!" barked his father.

Johnny felt more afraid of his father's tone than he was of dying just a few moments ago. Listening to his father, Johnny walked quickly to the end of the alley but turned around and watched. Johnny knew that when his father drank, and that was often, he had a violent temper but basically, he was a quiet and soft spoken artist.

"You never touch my boy!" yelled Johnny's dad.

"Fuck you. I'll kill him and you. That little fucker and his friends stole my tires!" yelled the stranger.

With speed and quickness that Johnny couldn't believe, he watched as his father, in a flash, reached into his pocket and pulled out a long and shiny knife. He made no threats, and gave no warning but within seconds stabbed the attacker repeatedly until his lifeless body fell to the ground. Grabbing the man by his ankles and shoes, Johnny watched as his father dragged the man to the opposite end of the alley. Johnny ran half way down the alley, just far enough to see his father lift and throw the body into the large communal garbage container.

Johnny knew that his father was indeed a tough and very strong man, but had no idea whatsoever that he could do such things. He also had no idea at all that he owned a knife but was shocked at how incredibly fast and skilled he was at using one. As his father slowly turned, Johnny ran as fast as he could and waited outside of the front door to their apartment.

"Upstairs," said a very soft spoken and calm Anatole.

"Okay, Dad."

As they walked up the stairs, the echoing sounds of the lonely staircase took on a whole new sound of terror. Witnessing a death was always traumatic, but this after all was Johnny's father.

"Do not mention anything to your mother, John. Or to anyone else."

"Yes, Dad, I won't"

In a strange way, Johnny felt a whole new and different type of respect as well as fear for his father. His father after all had just literally saved his life. No doubt about that. Johnny would have been dead by now. Would his father ask him what had happened to start this all or would there just be silence? He had overheard the man say something about tires.

"We will not talk of this until I choose to, John."

"I understand. Thank you. You saved my life, Dad," said a quiet Johnny.

"Last words, John."

Entering their apartment, Johnny said hello to his mother and went straight to his room. The start of school was almost here for Johnny and the boys. He needed to talk to Al tomorrow and get those tires and hubcaps out of the hangout and sold. Once school started, there wouldn't be as much time to make money. Johnny hated school but he'd be much more prepared for the niggers this year. Now having a gun, he'd have it with him all the time. But what he really wanted, was to get a knife. Not only to get a knife, but to be able to use it as his father had.

I will be lightening quick and unafraid, just like my dad, thought Johnny.

Surprisingly, Johnny soon drifted off to sleep. After a few hours, he awoke and had to pee. Getting up, he opened his bedroom door and started to walk to the bathroom.

"John, we should talk."

Startled beyond belief, Johnny gasped in fear. Not only wasn't he expecting his father to be sitting silently in the dark, but he had a strange and different type of fear of the man.

"Use bathroom and we talk," said his father.

"Okay, Dad."

Johnny peed and stood in the bathroom, staring at the mirror. He was a bit afraid of going back out into the dark and quiet living room.

"Sit, John. When I was a young boy, I had wonderful life. My family was very rich. We owned much land in Russia and have many people to work for us. My father was good man. I never knew him to be other than nice and fair. One night, a drunken man, speak bad to my mother and he warned man to stop. This man did not listen and my father grab him. My father had very strong hands and this man could not escape, so he pull knife. I was young and was afraid for my father. But very, very fast, my father grab knife and stick into man's heart. He was dead right away. My mother cried. He tell us to never speak of this. I was frightened and did not bring up until much older. Then I ask him to teach me, and he does. He teach me to never use these skills, unless to protect myself or my loved ones. I listen. I practice much and become very, very fast. I never need to use until I get older and come to this country."

"How did you get here, Dad?"

"When communism take us over, we know that we will be losing everything so my father gives me money and sends me on way. He talks of coming to America and we speak of how this will happen. I started my trip but the soldiers get us."

"Who is 'us,' Dad?"

"My best friend since little boy, his name Christopher. My friend Christopher was shot dead by soldiers. We must dig a large grave. A grave for us to die in."

Johnny sat spellbound. Both shocked as well as fascinated by his father's story, Johnny couldn't get enough.

"When we dig long, long, deep grave, we line up. Maybe more than one hundred men. The soldiers start to shoot all down line. Men, scream and fall into pit. I tell Christopher to jump when I jump, before bullets reach us. We do this and lay in grave for many hours until we feel safe to go. The bodies were bloody and the crying and pain, I never do forget. We climb out of grave and feel safe. Christopher is happy and say to me 'Anatole! Thank you. We did it!' and as I turn, a gunshot bullet blow off entire side of Christopher's face and head. I can never forget this. One thing I never tell anyone is this. When I see that Christopher is dead, I run. I hide. I always regret not getting these soldiers for what they do. To all of us but mainly to my friend. Then after many times, I make it to Europe and then after more time, I come to America."

Johnny boy was wide awake now. He was also in shock but in a somewhat strange way, felt closer to his father. Maybe that is why he drank so much Vodka. To forget these horrific events in his life. Sitting there is an awkward silence, his father simply got up, not another word spoken and went to sleep. After sitting there for a few moments, Johnny got up to return to sleep. Out of the corner of his eye, Johnny saw something next to his father's chair. A bottle of Vodka. An empty bottle of Vodka.

Chapter Seventeen

"WATCH OUT, KID!" yelled the man in the newer looking car.

"Ahh, fuck you!" responded Johnny.

Crossing the street, Johnny opened the door to the candy store and asked if Al was there.

"Yeah, kid, he's in the back. Knock first and go on in," said the man behind the counter.

Johnny had never seen this man before and found it strange that he could just go on back. Knocking on the door, he heard Al yell out, wanting to know who it was.

"It's Johnny, Al"

After a brief pause, Al yelled out "Oh, Johnny boy? Come on in, kid."

"Hey Al, I don't get called that no more, okay? It's just Johnny now. Okay?"

"Sure, kid. Calm down, tough guy."

Johnny spent the next few minutes talking tires and hubcaps.

"Okay Johnny, I'll send the boys over to get them and after we do, I'll pay you ten bucks."

"No fuckin' way, Al. Look, I always give you good prices. I want a buck a tire and fifty cents each for the hubcaps. That's sixteen bucks and fifty cents. I'll tell you what. You guys are picking them up so I'll be nice. Fifteen bucks and we have a deal. Okay?"

Al remained seated and didn't say a word. Nervous, Johnny just waited in silence. Al liked the kid and was gonna give him the fifteen bucks but he wanted to make him wait a bit.

"Okay, kid. Look, here's twenty, but I know you, you slick little fucker, you got five to gimme back?"

"No. But I'm good for it. You know I am. Besides, I don't want you to shoot my fuckin' head off," said Johnny with a big smile.

"Don't talk like that. People have big ears. Got it?"

"Okay, Al. Sorry."

"Now, where is this place?"

"Just down the end of the alley, across the street. In half an hour okay?" asked Johnny.

"Sure, kid. Thirty minutes. Here's the twenty bucks."

"Thanks, Al."

Walking back across the street, Johnny suddenly picked up his pace.

"Hey, Jimmy. Come here. Fast!"

"What's up, Johnny?"

"Just follow me," said Johnny.

As Johnny ran down the alley, he updated Jimmy on the deal for the tires and handed him the twenty-dollar bill. After all, Jimmy was the money man. He also didn't want anyone to know about the hangout, so the boys quickly brought all the tires and hubcaps up the stairs and to the area outside of the clubhouse door. Jimmy picked up some garbage and walked to towards the dumpster and caught Johnny's attention.

"No! Stay away from that!" yelled Johnny.

Johnny hadn't even thought about the dreamlike events of last night. But he was too late. Lifting the top of the container, Jimmy peered in and let out a yell. Johnny ran over as quickly as he could, unsure of what to say to his friend.

"Damn! It fuckin' smells like asshole in there," yelled Jimmy.

Johnny peered inside the dumpster. It was empty.

A few minutes later, a black wagon pulled up and two of Al's goons took all the merchandise. Not saying a single word, they simply drove off.

Johnny and Jimmy went back down to the hangout once more. Jimmy put the twenty dollars into the pouch and slipped it back into the wooden pocket in the side of the wooden box.

"We've been working hard, Johnny. How 'bout we get a ball game goin' today?" asked Jimmy.

"Yeah, that sounds good. Listen, do you think anyone followed us last night, Jimmy? You know, from the movies?"

"No. besides, they wouldn't follow us and not do nuthin', right?" responded Jimmy.

"Good point, Jimmy."

"Listen, Jimmy. You wanna round up the boys and put the game together? I gotta go do some shit. Meet at the park in about an hour?"

"Okay, sounds good, Johnny."

The boys turned off the lights and closed the doors. They still didn't have locks.

We better get them, and soon, thought Johnny.

Walking up the three flights of stairs towards his apartment, Johnny was glad about two things. He now had a key and no one was home. He just needed to think for a while and Johnny did his best thinking alone. Getting to his front door and about to insert his key into the badly tarnished door lock, Johnny had a change of heart. He decided to go up to the roof. Walking to the end of the hallway, Johnny started to go up the stairs.

"Hey! You no piss in my hallway!" yelled that same lady that always seemed to be there.

She must wait on me to show up, thought Johnny.

"And no shit either!" she added.

In quite the somber and serious mood, Johnny couldn't help it and started to crack up.

"I gotta big load of shit in my ass and it's…here it comes. It's coming outta my asshole now!" laughed Johnny as he made his way up the stairs to the rooftop.

"I tell you momma. You piss and shit crazy boy!"

Opening the rooftop door, with lessons learned and never to be forgotten, Johnny took the block of wood that took up permanent residence next to the door, and jammed it into the hinge area. That door would never close on him again.

The dirty city's heat expressed itself as wave after wave of filthy steam rose off the hot roof. It was quiet up there. Seemingly not much traffic below, Johnny, who never minded the heat, found a nice spot and lay down. Stinging a bit from the heat, his white tee shirt soon became wet with sweat. Putting his arms behind his neck, with fingers clasped together, Johnny relaxed and let his mind drift. Oblivious to the heat and humidity, Johnny thought about many things. His father, school starting, the dead man, and what he wanted to be when he was older. Would he ever escape Brownsville, and if he did, where would he go and how could he make money? These things all worried Johnny. Johnny had lots of thoughts but he didn't want to share them with anyone. He knew that the boys surely wouldn't understand. Or would they? Did other boys his age think like this? Johnny wasn't sure. Maybe he could talk to Jackie? It was time to get a move on, so Johnny started his descent back down the stairs. Good, no one was around. As he approached the old lady's front door, he walked as quietly as he could. Getting a few doors down, Johnny boy was in the clear now.

"You dirty boy! I will check the roof! I find piss and shit, I tell you momma and poppa!"

Laughing as hard as he ever has, Johnny turned the key and entered his apartment.

Grabbing something to drink, Johnny had no appetite. Maybe it was the heat. It had to be in the nineties. He was okay with this weather except for when he went to bed. Not having a bedroom window, he sweated like crazy and could never fall asleep. His parents did have a small bronze colored fan. It made a lot of noise and barely moved any air but that was for them only. Actually, it was something that his dad planned on fixing. Johnny's dad could really make or fix anything. Since his father just confided so much personal history in him, Johnny took more of an interest in him. He wanted to ask him what his mother was talking about as far as his 'invention,' the one to make painting walls easier.

Flying down the stairs and now full of energy, Johnny started his trek to the park. About a half mile away, there were always some kids hanging out, smoking, trying to impress the girls, and wanting to play ball. They never wanted to play the niggers, as Johnny knew that there'd always be a fight. Not opposed to fighting, there was a time and a place for that. After all, baseball was baseball! Walking into the park's entrance, Johnny saw Danny, Jackie, Jimmy, and Mickey hanging out behind the badly rusted backstop. The Brooklyn Dodgers were doing well that summer. Over .500, they never gave up. In every game until the last at bat, they were tough. Just like Brooklyn. Each of the boys had their favorite players. Johnny's was the shortstop, Pee Wee Reese, Danny loved outfielder Joe Medwick, whereas Jimmy liked third baseman, Cookie Lavagetto. Mickey was a traitor as he was a Yankee fan and Jackie, well Jackie didn't know too much about baseball yet. But he would. Johnny would make sure of that. And not a damn Yankee fan! He would teach him all about the right things in life. Bleeding Dodger Blue was one of those things.

The park was empty. The boys didn't have any bats or gloves. In fact, Johnny was thinking they should steal some soon. There were usually a lot of kids that wanted to play. Maybe it was the heat.

Yankee fans were fuckin'' pussies, thought Johnny.

When the place was loaded with kids, after playing defense, those with gloves just left them at the position they were playing. Since they needed about thirteen more kids to play, they figured they'd just hang out for a while.

"Hey, Johnny! Look at those girls over there. Nice huh?" asked Mickey.

"Yeah, nice. Big tits and round asses. Just the way I like 'em," answered Johnny.

"The way you like them? You never even touched a big titty, Johnny," said Jackie.

Jackie was slowly changing and Johnny liked it. Instead of getting pissed, he just went along with Jackie trying to feel a part of things.

"Oh yeah? That's what you think, pal. They may not have been huge titties, but a titty is a titty, big or small. Don't forget that," answered Johnny.

The boys all started to walk towards these girls. There was about six of them and five were cute. There was however, one fat girl.

"Hey fellas, I want the chubby one. Fat girls and ugly ones put out. My brother say's that fat girls suck good dick," said Mickey.

"Suck dick?" asked Jackie. "They do that?"

"Oh, hell yeah. They almost all do it. You have to ask 'em though, Jackie," said a half-serious Mickey.

Johnny had struck up a conversation with Jimmy about money as they approached the girls and wasn't really paying much attention.

"So, you mean that if I walk up and ask one of 'em to suck on my dick, they might do it?" a very naive Jackie asked.

"Sure. Now listen, you could pick one out or sometimes they get insulted so you better try askin' them all," said Mickey.

"Jackie. Go for it buddy. Try. Hey, if they say no, it's no big deal. But they're probably gonna all wanna suck on it for you," added Mickey. Mickey tried to hold back a huge laugh.

A now somewhat confident Jackie, separated a bit from his friends, walked directly towards the group of girls. Mickey playfully grabbed Danny to hold him back a bit. They both were trying hard to stifle their laughter. Johnny veered back to the others and noticed what was going on.

"Hey, where's Jackie going?" asked Johnny.

"Shhhhh, watch and get ready to laugh your ass off," said Mickey.

"Mick, what the fuck did you do?"

Just at that moment, Jackie walked right up to the entire group of girls.

"Hi," said Jackie.

"Hello," answered one of the prettier girls.

Jackie just stood there a bit tongue tied. Johnny was gonna step forward but Mickey assured him it was just a little harmless fun.

"So how are you girls all doing?" asked Jackie.

There was no response at all and Jackie was a bit confused.

"I was wondering, would all of you like to suck on my dick right now?" asked a very happy sounding Jackie.

"What did you say?" asked the pretty one.

Clearing his throat, a bit, Jackie thought that they couldn't hear him.

"No! Mickey, what the fuck did you put him up to? Don't do it, Jackie!" yelled Johnny.

As Johnny approached the group of girls, he started to call Jackie off, but it was too late.

"I wanted to know if all of you girls would like to suck on my dick! I don't want to insult any of you, so maybe you could take turns putting it in your mouths?" said Jackie, much more loudly and with more authority as well.

"Oh my God. What did he just say?" asked one of the shorter girls

The girls were all dressed in plaid type of skirts that came down to mid shin. They started to slowly back off and then started to scamper away.

"Man, look at those asses," said a laughing Mickey.

Johnny approached Jackie and told him that it wasn't in fact his fault. That Mickey was playing a silly joke on him and that it was not right to talk like that.

Putting his arm around Jackie's shoulder, Johnny tried to coerce him back to the rest of the boys but with Mickey's laughing, he was too embarrassed. Johnny let Jackie just stand there and went about the business of straightening Mickey out. A few moments later, Jimmy, looking past the group and in the direction of Jackie, yelled out.

"Jackie, turn around. Watch out!" screamed Jimmy.

As the rest of the crew turned, they saw a group of about six boys, all bigger than them, running towards Jackie. Two had baseball bats and were converging on Jackie rapidly.

"Put your hands over your head, Jackie!" yelled Jimmy.

Fearing for Jackie's life, all the boys were running as fast as they could now. It was a race to get to him first. Johnny was shocked at what he then saw. A nimbler and faster Jackie than they suspected, reacted quickly and squatted down as he stuck out his right leg, tripping both boys that carried the baseball bats. The other attacking boys all jumped on Jackie simultaneously and started to punch and kick him. Jackie instinctively covered his face and head. Finally, Johnny and the boys were now upon them.

Mickey and Danny arrived first and with a vicious and aggressive manner, started to pull these thugs off their friend.

"I'm okay," gasped an out of breath Jackie.

Danny had lost his mind and pounced on the biggest of them and was pummeling the kid. He wouldn't stop as the boy's face had opened and he was bleeding profusely. One more vicious right hand to the jaw put the kid to sleep. He was out cold. Someone grabbed Danny from behind and it was on again. Mickey and Jimmy were in the middle of their own vicious fights as Johnny, looking around to survey the situation, picked up the two bats and brought them with him to the fray. Whacking anyone of these punks that he could get a clean shot on, got their attention quickly as they lay on the ground, holding their ribs.

"Here Jackie, hold these two bats. Hold 'em tight now!" screamed Johnny.

Five of the punks were on their knees and now facing Johnny. The other kid, the victim of Danny's beating, was still out cold and bleeding. Quickly, Johnny reached behind him and pulled out his constant friend, his gun. Aiming it squarely at the kid who seemed to be their leader, Johnny quickly walked directly towards the group.

"No! No! Don't fuckin' shoot. The girls are our friends and they said the fat kid was hitting them!" he yelled.

"I was not. I was only asking if they wanted to suck on my dick. All of them, so I didn't hurt their feelings," said Jackie.

"Shut up, Jackie!" yelled Jimmy.

"I'm gonna only say this one time and then I'm gonna start shooting. Get up and run. Don't look back even. Grab your buddy that's lying there and drag his ass with you. Now, or I shoot! Do you hear me?" yelled Johnny.

As fast as they could, keeping an eye on Johnny and his gun, the boys all complied and within a minute or so, dragging the kid that was out cold, were out of sight.

"Johnny? Johnny?" asked Jackie.

"What? What is it, Jackie? Are you hurt?" asked Johnny.

"No. I just wanted to say that they forgot their bats."

Looking at each other, the rest of the boys started to turn and get the hell out of the park.

"Come on, Jackie. You stay with me, and we'll talk. I'll explain everything to you," said Johnny.

Chapter Eighteen

"DOWNSTAIRS, EVERYONE, AND now!" yelled Johnny.

The boys trudged down the stairs, some with a sense of accomplishment, others with a sense of defiance and one feeling like he was gonna get his ass yelled at. He was wrong.

"Look Mickey, are we all family or not?" asked Johnny.

"Yeah, of course, but it was a joke, Johnny!" said a defensive Mickey.

"Yeah, a joke gone fucking bad! Look, let's just be more careful. I gotta say though, Jackie, you did damn good. Two guys running full speed at you with baseball bats? You went down and tripped up both of those bitches but good! Good job, Jackie! I was so pissed, that I really wanted to kill them! No one hurts one of us. The Money Boys stick together! No matter what! But you fought your ass off. You manned up, Jackie. I'm proud of you!"

With that, all the boys started to slap Jackie on the back. Going from fear and feeling like the butt of a joke and a loser, Jackie couldn't help but start to smile widely. Jackie's whole demeanor seemed to change in an instant. Maybe this is what he really needed. Chest now puffed out, his shoulders seemed wider and his voice deeper.

"That's right! And I got two baseball bats too!" Jackie exclaimed.

"Let's get the fuck outta here already." said Johnny.

Making his way home, Johnny tried on his feelings of becoming more and more of a leader. He liked the fit. It was becoming more and more of his role it seemed.

"John! John, please come here," yelled Johnny's mom.

Johnny was lying down in bed and looking at his baseball cards. He would love to trade away all the Yankee ones for all Brooklyn Dodger cards. Log rolling out of bed, Johnny walked to the living room to see what his mother had wanted.

"Listen, John. Please get all your pants together and I will sew up the holes in the knees and it looks as if you get much taller! That is nice for you. I see if I maybe make them longer too. Okay?"

"Oayk, sure, no problem, Mom, and thank you," replied Johnny.

"Your father come soon. He is little late. Friday, he sometime do this. It okay, soon we eat," she informed Johnny.

"I'm starving!" said Johnny.

All that fighting and trouble sure gives a guy an appetite, thought Johnny.

Out of the corner of his eye, Johnny saw the front doorknob start to turn and then watched as his father, shuffling sideways, with his old and dusty shoes, pulled in his folded easel and supplies.

"How are you, John?"

"I'm okay, Dad. We played ball today."

"Okay, this is good. Soon is school again and grades good this year, no?"

"Always, I mean, I will do my best, Dad."

"That is all we can do," said Anatole.

"Anatole, wash please. All this paint all the time. The house smell and everything dirty. Please wash good," asked Sonia.

As Johnny's father walked to the bathroom, he glanced at Johnny and winked a bit. Mouthing the same words as his wife had just told him, Johnny realized that his dad actually did have a sense of humor. Mimicking Mom was funny. But Johnny sure wouldn't try it.

"What Anatole? You have words say to me?" she asked with a smile.

"No Sonia, no," he lied.

Smirking and laughing just a bit, Johnny really liked this side of his father. Perhaps he was drinking vodka, but perhaps it wasn't an entire bottle this time.

"Sit, Anatole, sit, John! We eat now," said Sonia.

There was government cheese, bread, some vegetables, and no tension, no looking and waiting for his father to break a plate, to intimidate him or throw something at Johnny.

"Thanks, Mom. That was really good," said Johnny.

"John…" started Sonia.

"I know, I know. Wash up, John! Yes, Mom, yes," said a bit of a sarcastic Johnny.

After Johnny and his dad had sat down in the living room, Johnny asked his father a few questions.

"Dad? What is the idea you had? You know, to make painting walls easier?"

"Walls, and ceilings too, John."

"Okay, yeah, that one," Johnny clarified.

"A sort of roll-out, round brush. I do not know what it is to call."

"A paint roller?" asked Johnny.

"Yes! That is what I call. Good job, John!"

"Can I make it with you, Dad?"

"Yes. You may watch. Maybe you can make more good thoughts?"

"Sure, Dad."

Looking towards his mother, who was rinsing dishes in the kitchen sink, Johnny asked in a very hushed tone, "Dad, what happened to the body? I mean it was gone…"

Interrupting Johnny, his father, put a finger to pursed lips, as he said "Shhh!"

"Sorry. It's just that I knew she couldn't hear me."

"John. Never do you bring up anymore."

"Okay, I'll never bring it up again."

"I think I'm gonna go to sleep, Dad," said Johnny.

"Goodnight, John. We work on the paint roller tomorrow. Okay?"

"Okay, Dad."

As Johnny headed towards the family's one small bathroom, he saw his mother, still in the kitchen.

"Goodnight, Mom, see you in the morning," said Johnny.

Johnny gave his mother a quick hug. Then kissed her on the cheek. Soon to be twelve years old, Johnny was growing quickly. His mom was about five foot eight and Johnny was almost as tall as her now. He really hoped that he would make at least six foot. His father had told him of uncles and family members that he had in the old days in Russia, who were huge men. One was the strongest man in the entire town. He had hands so strong and so immense that people often commented that he had meat hooks and not fingers. Maybe Johnny would continue to really grow. He had his gun, and he was practicing with a knife and was already very, very fast. He wanted to be the fastest with a knife of anyone in Brownsville. Besides that, Johnny, who had dark hair that was very thick, as well as dark brown eyes, was a very handsome kid. Even at his young age, woman many years older would give him attention. To impress them even more, he realized that he was lean and was starting to get muscular. Not a single ounce of fat was on that frame. When Johnny took off his old and graying tee shirts in the bathroom, he flexed and made muscles. Poses like those big weight lifters like Charles Atlas did. Johnny would see him in the back of magazines at the drug store around the corner and he was determined to get big and strong like him. He was tough already, but he wanted to put some more muscle on that lean frame. He had just started to do pushups and was already up to twenty.

Johnny looked once more at his mother. He really did love her.

"Goodnight again, Mom. I love you."

"And I love you as well. Good night again, John," she said while smiling happily.

It was bedtime. It was pushup time. What else could Johnny find to do?

Chapter Nineteen

AFTER DOING HIS twenty pushups, Johnny collapsed onto his bedroom floor. It was a particularly hot and very humid night.

Twenty more! Come on Johnny, you ain't no girl! Do it!

Johnny, determined now, more by his desire to be desirous, pushed himself to the limit. As he reached fifteen, there was just no way that he could possibly do any more. His arms quivered and he was ready to punk out. And then he thought about Sally.

Sally was one of the prettiest girls in the whole school and Johnny really thought she was hot. There was even a rumor going around that her tits had popped over the summer. One of Johnny's friends, Antonio, had said that Sally's tits had popped so much that they were even bigger now than Mrs. Williams'!

Sixteen, seventeen, eighteen…come on Johnny, you can do this! Do it for Sally's tits!
Nineteen, push it! Push it! Nineteen, almost, almost…twenty!

He did it! Johnny, sweating profusely, lay down on his bed. His sweaty body had made his sheets all wet. None the less, Johnny closed his eyes and tried very hard to go to sleep. Johnny's mind was racing.

He couldn't remove the vision, the vision that his young mind was giving him of Sally, Sally with big, popped out tits, that is.

Deciding to get up to wash his face and get a cool drink of water, Johnny still couldn't stop sweating. Both his mother and father had gone to sleep and all was quiet. As quietly as he could, Johnny opened his apartment door and locked it behind him.

The roof. I think I'm gonna see if there's more air up there. Maybe there is a breeze. Johnny thought.

Almost ten o'clock now, the hallway was quiet. Even his loud neighbors above him must be sleeping. Johnny, as quietly as possible, walked up the stairs and opened the door that led to the roof. Holding the door open, he felt a warm breeze passing by. At least the air was moving a bit. Stepping out a bit farther, Johnny realized that it was indeed cooler up on the roof. Reaching for his block of wood, he securely jammed it in the door to make certain it wouldn't close behind him again. Walking slowly around the roof top and making certain that each step was a quiet one, Johnny found a spot behind a large sheet metal venting duct, and lay down. The breeze was cooler when lying down, and he felt secure, while snuggling up against the ductwork. With his hands now clasped behind his head, Johnny stared intently above. It was a clear night and the oppressive sky was full of stars. It was if the heat had melted tiny specks of shiny metal into the clouds. Johnny stared and stared. He tried to make different shapes and even familiar faces out of all the different configurations of stars above, but his mind kept returning to Sally. And her tits.

Running his right hand down towards his waistband, Johnny, not knowing exactly what he was doing, grabbed his dick. Roxanne had done this, in fact, right up here on the roof, and it felt good. Maybe he would do the same thing, but to himself? Jerking on his dick, Johnny realized that it did indeed feel good, in fact it felt great. He hoped that he didn't have to piss, like he did with Roxanne. That was funny. Jerking and jerking on his dick, Johnny kept thinking of Sally. And her tits. He was squeezing on them and pulling off her shirt. Trying to pop her bra off, he fumbled a bit but then he pulled it off. Those tits were something else! Not sure what he would do next, Johnny never had the chance to find out as he felt this incredible feeling and his dick exploded all over his jeans. Johnny couldn't believe how quickly this huge piece of meat had shrunk to almost nothing now. What had happened? His dick went limp and those good feelings soon went away. Johnny then realized something. Something very important. He could be a father!

Exhausted, he realized that he better get back downstairs before his parents knew he was missing. Maybe he should have just left a note. He kept telling himself that he was getting up. Repeatedly, he tried. He was just so tired.

The car horns blared and as Johnny struggled to open his eyes, he put his hand over his eyes, to block out the rising sun. It was harsh on his sleepy eyes.

Oh shit. Fuck, man. I fuckin' fell asleep. I'm old enough to be a fuckin' father but young enough to get my fuckin' ass beat, Johnny thought.

Running towards the still opened door, Johnny hurriedly pulled away the block of wood and started to run down the stairs. Skipping two and sometimes three stairs, Johnny reached the bottom landing and there she was!

"You foul boy. You piss up on my roof? You smell like shit! You shit again on my roof?" yelled his neighbor from the end of the hallway.

As Johnny ran quickly by the old lady, he turned and imitated jerking his dick.

"But I jerked on my dick! All over the roof! And down to the street!"

"You bad mouth, bad boy! I tell you momma and you poppa!"

Laughing but still terrified of what might be waiting for him, Johnny started to insert his key into his door. The door opened first though and his father was standing right there.

Oh shit! He's gonna kill me. No way that's gonna happen again. I'll do what I hafta...

"Good morning, John. You took to sleep on roof?"

"Umm, yes. I can explain, Dad. It was so hot..."

"Yes, John. I know this. I have done too," said his father.

As his father slid by him, he looked at Johnny's pants.

"John. Clean you pants before your mother sews them."

Johnny looked down at the milky looking stains on his tattered jeans.

Looking up, he was trying hard to think of something to say but his father simply put his hand on his shoulder for a moment and disappeared down the stairs on his way to the streets.

He understands. I wonder if he ever jerked his own dick? Eww, that's nasty. No way. Dad was too serious to do that! thought Johnny.

Johnny said good morning to his mother and quickly walked to his bedroom and closed the door behind himself. Finding his other pair of pants, Johnny quickly changed. He wanted to kiss her but with his pants a mess, he just couldn't. Rolling up his jeans, he walked into the bathroom quickly. He then put them in the sink and ran the water. Taking a towel, he rubbed all around the waistband area. Then Johnny washed his own hands. He wondered if someone could get pregnant from touching those pants.

"John, when you come out, please give me pants to sew for school."

Oh no! What the hell am I gonna do now? Johnny thought.

Opening the bathroom door, Johnny saw his mother. Standing directly in front of him.

"I washed these. I was up on the roof cooling off, Mom, and it was so hot, that some of the tar patches up there, they melted and I got that black stuff all over them. I didn't want you to have to clean them," explained Johnny.

Johnny's mom, with an even expression, just stared at him. She took the wet jeans from him and walked away. Was she mad? She rarely ever got mad at him. A sweeter woman there never was. Did she know what he did?

There was one more week left before school started. Johnny was determined to make it a big one. Wanting to get some money, he would shine as many shoes as possible and when he got together with the fellas, he'd make sure they stole plenty of money, or jewelry, or maybe, if they were lucky, both.

Johnny changed into his one other pair of pants. Going into the tiny bathroom again, he splashed some cold water on his face to help clear his still sleepy mind.

"Gonna go find the boys, Mom. Gonna see if we can get a ballgame going."

"Baseball? Oh John, please wait until your father home. Maybe just one hour. Okay?"

"Sure, Mom. Is everything okay? Did I do something wrong?"

"No, all is okay. We need talk to you and your father has present for you," said Johnny's mother.

He wasn't sure, but this made Johnny very uncomfortable. Sitting and waiting, he could barely sit still. Fidgeting to the point of non-stop movement, Johnny was relieved as he heard and then saw the door handle turn and the door open. His father was home and he had a crumpled brown paper bag in his hands.

"John, come sit on couch please," said his father.

All three of the Rostov's sitting together on the couch didn't exactly happen often.

"John, a few weeks ago, the nurse from school come to door and speak to your mother. There is a bad disease go around, I believe they call Rheumatic fever. I talk to people of this and it is dangerous."

"Wait. Dad, are you saying I have this? I'm sick?"

"No son, but they tell all the parents to speak with children. If you get sick, you must come talk with us. Sometime throat hurts or your skin gets marks all over."

"But I'm fine. Don't worry. I understand, Dad. If I get anything like what you just talked about, I'll come tell you guys right away, okay? Can I go now, Dad? I really wanna get the fellas and play some baseball. When school starts up, you know me, I'm all about studying," explained Johnny.

"Yes son, but wait a minute more for me," said his father.

Johnny's dad looked at his mom. Seeming a bit uncomfortable, His father passed the brown paper bag to his mother. Johnny's mom then spoke in Russian. Johnny hated when his parents did that. Maybe he would learn Russian and not tell them. Yeah, that way he'd know what they were hiding from him.

After Sonia spoke, Anatole held up the bag and told Johnny that this was a present from both of them. Handing it to Johnny, he sat back and a look of anticipation came over his weathered face. Johnny slowly put his hand into the bag and seemed confused for a moment.

Pulling the object from inside upwards, he froze for a moment and then a huge smile came across his face.

"Man, a baseball glove! And this is brand new! Wait. It's a genuine Pee Wee Reese infielder's mitt! Man, thank you, Dad!"

"It is from you mother too, John."

"Your father make deal with a man. He love your father painting and he wants two paintings special for him and then he give us the glove. Your father work very hard to get you this," said Sonia.

"Well, thank you both. So much! Can I go? I'm gonna get a game together right now. It's not even broken in yet but it's so soft, I can use it right away. I've never even seen a new one!"

"Yes, John but…"

It was too late. Johnny had taken off. He knew the fellas were already waiting on him at the park. Hopefully, there weren't any problems like last time.

No, Jimmy was there and Danny also. Even if Jackie said the wrong things again, he'd be ok.

Johnny, now in a full out sprint was running as fast as he could. Baseball mitt, on his left hand, he sprinted into the park. The fellas were all standing behind the rusty old backstop. They were watching the end of a game being played by some older boys.

"Hey, Johnny. Whoa, where the fuck did you steal that from? He musta been some rich asshole, huh, probably a little girly kinda guy," said Danny.

"No way, he stole it from a store fella's, you wanna bet?" asked Jimmy.

"Nahh, he beat someone up and ripped it off their hand, probably right when they were playing a fucking game. Johnny don't back down from nuthin'!" exclaimed Jackie.

"Hey! Shut the fuck up, you assholes. You fuckin'' shitheads don't fuckin'' listen! My father. He bought it for me. He's such a great artist that he made a lotta money. Just so he could buy this for me."

"You still ain't got no food though I bet," said Mickey.

Johnny took a few steps towards Mickey and Mickey didn't back down.

"He didn't mean shit, Johnny. He's just fuckin' with you," said Jimmy.

The two boys glared at each other for a moment and then looked at the game's final out. There was often a tenseness between Johnny and Mickey.

"We play the winners," said Jackie.

"Hey, Johnny, they have six guys but I told 'em we'd whup their fuckin' asses even with just five of us," said Jimmy.

"Winners up first, girls?" said a sarcastic kid from the other team.

Mickey just glared at him. Johnny didn't have his gun but he did have his knife. Brownsville wasn't safe anymore unless you had some sort of protection.

"Ignore him, Mickey. They fuck with us though, and you and I alone will beat their asses and slice 'em up," said Johnny.

Johnny was a smart kid, tough, but also smart. He often knew just what to say to the fellas to make things okay.

"Come on, guys, let's take the field. You girls leavin' your mitts out there for us? What nice girls you are. You can fuckin' see that I don't need shit," bragged Johnny.

As the boys spread out, Mickey, feeling better, but as cocky as ever, positioned the fellas.

"Johnny, you cover third and short, play deep, like you have the outfield too. I'm gonna pitch, Jackie, you stand against the backstop and throw the ball back to me. Be careful though. These fuckin' girls probably throw their bats. Danny, you got first and second, and Jimmy, you're a fast mother fucker, you play center.

As the boys soon found out, these guys were good. After four innings, the game was tied 1-1. Mickey had hit a screaming line drive down towards left and by the time they ran it down, he was flying around first. The other guys had a really big kid, looked about twenty and he lifted one way over Jimmy's head, straight away.

In the bottom of the eighth, Jackie was up. The other team, knowing that he was the worst player on either side, just lobbed the ball over.

"Time out, assholes," said Johnny.

Johnny ran around the backstop and took Jackie aside.

"You wanna be the fat kid forever? Huh? You wanna be the girl, the one that they laugh at? Fuckin' answer me!" yelled Johnny.

"No."

"Well lemme tell you somthin'. These girls are gonna get a fuckin' surprise. I want you to watch the ball. Watch it every second from when it leaves the pitchers hand, all the way till it touches your bat! Loosen your grip and just lift it! Choke up about half an inch. You can do this Jackie! Jackie? I know you can do this!"

Johnny smacked Jackie on the back. He was pumped up but didn't like getting smacked on the back.

"It doesn't fuckin' matter. Hey, fat boy, you can't hit. Go home and suck your momma's tit. In fact, your daddy is probably a fat girl, just like you!"

"Oh shit. What's he gonna do? He ain't got a father no more," said Mickey.

Jackie turned around and looked at his friends. He had tears running down his face and quickly tried to wipe them away. His red face quivered.

"Look! Fatso is cryin'," yelled the pitcher.

Trying to quick pitch Jackie, the pitcher threw a blazing fastball right down the middle.

"No way he catches up with that," said Johnny.

Crack! Jackie had made contact all right and the ball was smoked over the third baseman's head and rifled down the left side of the outfield. Jackie just stood there, almost frozen.

"Run, Jackie! Run!" screamed all of the boys.

Jackie, looking back at them, suddenly snapped out of it. Taking off for first, Jackie's large and lumbering body chugged along. As he rounded first, the first baseman stuck his foot out and tried to trip up the bloated baserunner. But Jackie had quick reflexes and jumped over the foot. Spitting right in the kids face, he tore towards second. The boys were going crazy.

"Go, Jackie, go!" they all screamed.

Please. Please God, let him score. I'll be a good kid. Most of the time, I mean, thought Johnny.

The outfielder raced to the ball and scooped it up, right as it was rolling to a stop in the high, un-mowed grass. Jackie, rounding second was totally out of breath. He was shot.

I'm gonna score. No matter what! I'm gonna score! thought Jackie.

You could almost hear the thud from Jackie's heavy steps. As the outfielder picked up the ball, he slipped a bit. Regaining his balance, he let go a blazing line drive of a throw. Johnny went around the backstop and stood to the side of the plate. The catcher was a big muscular kid.

"Go, Jackie, go!" yelled Johnny.

Jackie, tears running down his face, chugged towards home. Totally exhausted and almost falling, he watched as the ball beat him home by about ten feet.

"Slide, Jackie, slide!" screamed Johnny.

Preparing to slide and certain he'd be out, certain he'd be the fat kid, forever, Jackie saw the catchers face. He was smiling. No, he was laughing and laughing out loud.

Jackie saw red. That was it! There's just no way he would be denied.

"Slide, Jackie! Slide! Slide!" yelled Johnny as he waved both arms in a downwards motion.

Jackie dug deep and with every last bit of strength, every last bit of resolve, stood up and blasted his body right into the catcher. At the point of contact, he raised his elbow, straight into his opponent's jaw. That was it! Jackie literally ran the kid over. Sprawling backwards as Jackie stomped on the plate, everything slowed down. Johnny and the boys watched as the catcher fell over. The ball popped loose.

"Safe! He's safe!" yelled Johnny.

Sweating profusely and feeling unlike he'd ever felt in his life, Jackie walked and stood over the fallen giant.

"Now you can tell your daddy to suck my dick! Bitch!"

As he turned around to head towards the fellas, he was mobbed. All his friends were slapping him on the back and jumped on top of him.

As the game resumed, Johnny struck out for the last out in the eighth.

Three more outs, just three more outs, thought Johnny.

As the boys jogged out to their defensive positions, Johnny put his arm around Jackie.

"The old Jackie is gone. Remember this. This is you now!"

Shaking his head in agreement, Jackie went to the backstop. Something told Johnny that the game would end with another play at the plate. But this time, it would be Jackie doing the catching.

After retiring the first two batters routinely, the next batter laid down a perfect bunt. Johnny raced towards his right, came up, but held on to the ball, knowing he had no shot. The next batter followed with a single, putting runners on first and second. The following batter hit a line shot, right towards the mound. Barely getting his old glove up in time to keep the ball from taking his head off, Mickey picked up the ball, looked all around and held on to it. Bases loaded and two outs.

Fittingly, up next was the catcher. Wanting revenge, he looked at Jackie and said, "You better hope I get a hit, fatso, or it's you and me."

"Your momma has a cock," said a totally confident Jackie.

Strike one. Mickey took a deep breath. Strike two. Jackie started to laugh. He had learned enough from Johnny to know how to get into someone's head. He knew this would infuriate his enemy and he'd over swing, hopefully striking out to end the battle. As Mickey reared back, exhausted, he gave it all he had. A blazing fastball, but the kid was right on it. Swinging with all his might and just barely missing a crush shot, he lifted an amazingly high pop up towards left field. Jimmy, with all his speed was the only one who could possibly get there in time. Running all out, he ran in and to his right. He wasn't gonna get there in time. All three runners crossed home plate. They were gonna lose this hard-fought battle.

Johnny, however, had other ideas. Pounding his new Pee Wee Reese mitt, he made believe he was at Ebbetts Field. Racing as fast as he could, Johnny jumped, stretching completely out. As he hit the ground, the huge catcher scored. It was gonna be a game winning grand slam. Jackie readied himself for a fight, dropping his mitt and clenching his pudgy fists. As Johnny lay on the ground, Jimmy let out a scream.

"He got it! Oh, my God, what a fuckin' catch! He got it!"

Squeezing his brand-new mitt as hard as he could, Johnny held the magical glove up for all to see. The ball, three quarters out of the mitt, was stuck in the very end of the webbing. They had done it. Jackie had done it. Johnny had done it. As the entire team raced out towards Johnny, Johnny thought of his dad. Perhaps being an artist was a real job after all.

Chapter Twenty

"JOHN! WAKE UP, John! Come on now, John. Wake up, my sweet son. You have new start to school!" pleaded Sonia, with a laugh.

"Ahh fuck. I hate this shit," yawned an extremely tired Johnny.

"John. What you say? You use bad words with your mother?"

"What? No! No way, Mom!"

Damn, I'm so used to cursing with the boys. I gotta be more careful in front of Mom!

"Okay, John. Fast. Get dressed and wash face, brush teeth. Eat and then go, please," instructed Sonia.

Johnny put on his newly sewn jeans and found the one and only button-down shirt that he's ever owned. He wasn't sure what his mom had done to those jeans but they were actually blue again. Not a dark blue, like Johnny had seen on the rich kids that occasionally walked through the hallways at school, but they looked really clean. The boys were gonna get on him about that! For Johnny, the start of seventh grade was a big deal. First of all, it was in a different school. Johnny had gone to Brownsville Elementary school from kindergarten through sixth grade. They went to one class in the morning and that was it. They sat there all day long until the bell rang, telling them it was time to go home. Today though, Johnny and his friends were about to start the first of two years at Brownsville Junior High. They had home room and then six more classes, and each on was in a different part of the school. Johnny thought that they had about five minutes in between classes, but he knew he would probably take more time than that. After all, Johnny was an experienced man now. Plus, he could be a father! That was a big deal and the girls would probably want to screw him in between every class, he was certain of this!

"Hey! Wait up!"

Johnny saw some of the fellas up ahead. They might as well walk together. When were they gonna get those jackets anyway? Then they'd really be intimidating. The niggers and micks wouldn't dare fuck with them then!

"Hey, Johnny! New jeans? Ha, your mom got to you huh?" asked Mickey.

"They look new to me too," said Danny.

"Nobody can be the boss of their own mom. Shut up guys. If Johnny wants to look like a rich fuckin' fruit, leave him alone," teased Jimmy.

"Hahaha, he called you a rich, fruit!" added Jackie.

"Okay, you bunch of dick bags! I'm sick of you guys already!" yelled an agitated Johnny.

The boys were all together now and they were gonna try and keep it that way all year long. Everyone was gonna know the Money

Boys. They'd killed and robbed. They'd hid from the police, beat the shit outta everyone on the ballfield. And, Johnny could be a father. Johnny just knew that this was a very important point.

As the boys walked up the twenty-five or so steps that led to two faded double doors, they each pulled out a small slip of paper from their pants.

"I got room one eleven," said Johnny.

"Yes! Me too!" said a relieved Jackie.

Danny, Jimmy, and Mickey all had room ten ten. It didn't really matter. Home room was pretty much for attendance. And looking up girl's skirts. You had to have really good eye sight, but the boys would sit there and wait for the girls to stretch or move and try and look right up their skirts. It was cool looking at the different colored panties they had on. And then on a really good day, they could see some hairs coming out of the sides of the panties. Johnny could never understand why, but even the blondes had dark pussy hair.

Maybe these blondes that had dark colored pussy hair, just had dirty pussies, thought Johnny.

Mickey was really smart though, and taught Johnny and the rest of the fella's a few extra tricks. You would try and sit a few rows in from the windows. On a really bright day, with the sunshine streaming in, you could see right through their shirts, especially if those shirts were white. Now, if the girl's tits were already popped, you could see the big bra, and that was cool because you would know a few important things. The true size of the tit, the actual shape of that

- 175 -

titty, and which girl's tits hadn't popped yet. Well, most of the time, they just had those little baby tits and no bra. But even tiny titties had nipples. And that was the real prize. You saw some nipples? You had a weeks' worth of jerk-off material. So, you had to be slick. You know, you glance out the window, just faking like something important was going on, or caught your eye. The other trick took a lot of concentration but was worth it when it worked. If you were good, you could even help it happen. When the girls shifted, and moved, you needed to stare hard and wait for the fabric in-between the buttons to puff out a little. Bingo! Clear as day, direct sighting tittie-time!

There were times, when a guy could actually go home and have seen, tits, legs, bras, panties, and even some pussy. But it was exhausting work. Just shot your energy to hell some days. When things were really clicking, you could spend most of a class, looking for tits and then when class was over and you had to change classes, you would hope to have to go up or down the stairs. When you got good at it, no one could even tell you were doing it. You would casually glance as if you knew someone up above, on the next staircase and the eyes would just zero-in on those panties. Sometimes you could even see a little ass. The bad part was all the fat and nasty bitches. Nothing was worse than a fat and chubby butt. Johnny was sure of this.

"Let's go, Jackie. We don't wanna get in trouble our first day now."

"Yeah, we should wait until the second day," said a newly confident Jackie.

"Jackson Matthews?" called the teacher.

Who the fuck would name their own kid, Jackson? thought Johnny.

"Here," said Jackie, as he raised his hand.

Woah, I had no idea that Jackie's name wasn't Jackie, thought Johnny.

"Jonathon Rostov?" asked the teacher.

"Right ova' here," said Johnny as he also raised his hand.

Did they just call Johnny, Jonathon? What a weird name! thought Jackie.

The day went pretty quickly and before they all knew it, the final bell had rung. No homework on the first day, but all the teachers had warned them. There would be a lot more homework in middle-school than they had in elementary school.

Johnny and Jackie waited out on the steps for the rest of the boys. Some big kids, probably having been left back a few years, approached the two.

"Hey, gimme a light," said one thuggish looking kid.

"What do I look like, a candy store to you?" asked Johnny.

"Okay, so we hava wise ass here. First day of school and I'm gonna have to bust his ass up a little!" said the big kid.

"Fuck you! You don't mess with us; you understand?" countered Jackie.

"So, whatta we have here? The poster boy for a fat farm?" laughed the thug's partner in crime.

"No way. That might have been, but that's not me anymore, right Johnny? I'm a new kid now!" said Jackie.

"Hey boy's. What's up?" asked Mickey.

Mickey, Jimmy, and Danny all ran down the stairs and the five boys now surrounded to two really big kids.

"Okay, I see the way it works around here. You punks can't fight by yourselves. You hafta get all momma's little helpers," said the thug.

"Hey, no momma's! In fact, I just got off your momma! And man oh man can that bitch suck a dick!" said a pissed off Mickey.

All seven of the boys converged and started pushing and shoving. Johnny was double prepared. He had both his gun and his knife with him.

"Okay, boys! Separate! Do I need to suspend someone on the first day?" barked Mr. Welch.

Tall and lean, Mr. Welch had a reputation for always making good on his threats. He was the Vice Principle, as well as the Disciplinary Officer. The two thugs walked off slowly, glaring at all five of the boys.

"Let's go," said Johnny.

"This school is for losers," said Mickey.

"Yeah, losers," echoed Danny.

The whole of Brownsville is for losers, thought Johnny.

"Someday I'm gonna write a book about this place," said Johnny.

Not saying a word, the boys just looked strangely at their leader. As much as they respected, and even depended on Johnny, they knew he was a little bit *different*. For as tough and fiery as he was, he was also sensitive and intellectual. But he did his best to hide it.

The boys walked home, and walked home with an attitude. Walking five across the sidewalk, no one could get by. This made them feel good.

"Okay, so we got this stupid school shit started. You know what I was thinking?" said Jackie.

"That you want another shot at that catcher?" answered Jimmy.

"No, I mean yes, but somethin' else too."

"What's that, Jackie?" asked Jimmy.

"We need our Jackets!"

"Yeah! I forget, who was supposed to take care of that?" asked Johnny.

"Me, I asked my dad about it. He said he could get six of 'em and get 'em for free too. Somebody owes him a favor I guess. Only one thing. They all gotta be the same size, medium," said Danny.

"That's no problem. Jackie used to be the fat kid, but no more. I'm the new Jackie. I'm losing weight," said Jackie.

"Yeah, we can see that," said Johnny.

Johnny sure was glad that Jackie was getting more and more confident. He just wanted to make sure Jackie didn't over-do things. You know, take on anyone, or more than one guy at a time.

"Okay, so we started out with The Money Boy's and then we changed it to The Browns, but I don't like it fella's. Sounds like we're niggers or somethin'," said Mickey.

"I kinda always liked The Money Boys, but you guys wanna vote on it?" asked Jimmy.

"I mean, we're gonna be all about the money, right?" asked Johnny.

"That and popped out tits. I guess we could be called The Tit Grabbers," Jackie said.

The boys shot Jackie a look.

"What? What did I say?" said Jackie.

"The Money Boys it is. We went over all of this already!" said Johnny.

"Look, let's all check in at home and meet at the hangout in about two hours, okay?" asked Johnny.

"We need those fucking keys," yelled Johnny as he walked away.

Johnny opened the large door that led to his apartment. It's funny. At one point in time, Johnny struggled and struggled with that door, but now, after doing all those pushups, there was nothing hard about it at all.

The shuffling sounds, combined with the echoes of Johnny's fast walking, always reminded Johnny that he was home. Unlocking his front door, Johnny was surprised to see his father home. Smoking a cigarette, he was working on some project.

"John, sit. I have idea that will make us all money," said Anatole.

Johnny had heard all of this before. Nothing really ever happened, but his father was amazing with what he could make with his hands. A large piece of paper, several charcoal pencils, pieces of canvas, wood, and some carving knives were strewn all about the kitchen table. Johnny noticed a glass jar. It had some sort of thick looking liquid in it.

"I make paint roller machine."

"A what?" asked Johnny.

"Here. Look at paper," said Johnny's dad.

Johnny looked at the wrinkled piece of paper. It had drawing after drawing of designs for something that his father had in his mind. He also seemed to be struggling to take that vision and translate it to a picture set to paper.

"You like, John?" asked Anatole.

"Well, yes. It's kinda hard for me to see it in my mind though," answered Johnny.

"Look, John. I take round piece of wood and carve. I have friend that has store, make chairs. I ask him and tell of idea…"

"Dad, maybe you shouldn't tell anyone?" said a thoughtful Johnny.

Anatole's expression went from genuine happiness to a look of frustration, instantly.

"I didn't mean nuthin' by that. I just wanna see you get credit. And the money, Dad."

Sitting in an all-consuming tenseness for what seemed like forever, finally, Anatole's face changed. The tightened muscles all throughout his face relaxed. Teeth, now unclenched, opened a bit as he took another drag on his cigarette.

"Friend make chairs. So he said something he call 'mohair velour' would be perfect to use. Hold wood, John. Yes. I wrap fabric around the wood now."

"Maybe two times, Dad. So the roller absorbs more paint?"

Johnny's dad's head spun around in the direction of Johnny. His eyes, darting all about, mellowed.

"Good idea, John."

Whew. Johnny was still afraid of his father. But his mind was full. Full of conflicting emotions. Fear, adulation, anger, rage, and yes, love. It was too much for any eleven-year-old to figure out.

"Bring me wooden tray. Over there, John."

Johnny's dad had taken a small children's dresser drawer and cut it in half. He meticulously reattached the side panel and sanded it. The wood was now so smooth that it felt like glass.

Taking the smallest little nails that Johnny had ever seen and tapping them completely around the fabric, his father asked Johnny to open the glass jar. It had a funny odor.

"No, John. Add a few drop water. Put back on top and shake bottle very much hard," instructed Anatole.

Following his father's advice very carefully, Johnny was next told to pour the greenish contents into the silky smooth sanded box. The box must have been about twelve inches wide and the fabric covered roller was about half that size in width. His dad had fashioned a wooden handle, also sanded smooth to the touch.

"Follow after me and bring with you tray."

"Be careful, no spill."

Placing the tray next to the wall in the living room, Johnny watched as his father slowly rolled his invention forward and back, forward and back. The green fabric was picking up the liquid, some sort of a homemade paint. Picking the roller up, slowly, he started to roll the invention back and forth, over and over. While the choice of green was a little strange to say the least, the paint did in fact, roll out smoothly, and also covered those stains that Johnny's mom had tried so many times to scrub clean.

"Wow! Just like that! The wall just changed, just like that! So, what do you think, Dad, is Mom gonna like it?"

"She woman. One never know. I stopped to guess long time before."

It wasn't often, but Johnny absolutely loved when his father was in a good mood, he was actually funny. Not only did it remove that tense feeling that he had in the bottom of his belly, but he was learning that his father really had a sense of humor.

"I want to soak in solvent. See if we clean, can be use more over and again," said Johnny's dad.

Oh shit! Fuck! What the fuck am I gonna do now. I used that solvent to start that fire for the guy who bitch slapped Jackie, Johnny thought.

"John. Look closet to get solvent. In small metal can."

"Okay, Dad. I was looking through this closet the other day for Vaseline to break in my mitt, but I didn't see anything."

"Let me. I look for."

Johnny stood aside as his father went through the contents of the closet.

"Here is! I knew we have. But…I think before maybe two cans."

Johnny breathed in deeply and exhaled all of his worry.

"Ahhhh, that's okay, Dad. You have what you need now. Want me to clean the roller, Dad?" asked Johnny.

"No, I do. John, you mother be home fast now. Go to bathroom. Clean you self-please. Otherwise she will hit me with her shoe once more again." said Johnny's dad.

Johnny headed for the bathroom but did a double take and started to laugh when his father said this. Bending over, with his two hands on his knees, Johnny couldn't stop laughing.

"John. Go. Soap and wash good," he told Johnny.

Johnny nodded yes but couldn't hold in the laughter.

Looking very sternly at Johnny, his father looked as if he was going to start to scold him. He didn't. In fact, Anatole Rostov not only joined in the laughter but was laughing harder and louder than Johnny.

While Johnny and his father continued their out of control laughter, the door handle turned and the door slowly started to open.

"Anatole! What is this metal smell?"

"It's solvent, Sonia, it's just to clean my paint roller. John and me make together. You like?"

"I like when this mess be cleaned all up. Then you two!" answered Sonia.

As hard as she may try to sound stern, Sonia just couldn't pull it off. She was a wonderful woman, sweet, caring and loved her two Rostov men.

The chicken soup went down easily. It was the first of the month and the Rostov's had just gotten their relief check from the government. The family usually had enough money to get them through three weeks. It was that last week that became so difficult. The end of the month is when Johnny usually had to resort to "borrowing" things from people.

"May I please be excused?" asked Johnny.

"Why such you rush?" asked Sonia.

"Nothing. But I told the fellas I'd meet them, Ma."

"Yes. But first…."

"Yes, Mom, I know, wash my hands and face and brush my teeth," said Johnny.

"How this you know?"

"Lucky guess, Mom," said Johnny with a happy and heartfelt laugh.

Johnny washed up, brushed his teeth and stared at himself in the mirror. He did that pretty much every time he was in there. Flexing, he could see that his muscles were growing, getting bigger and harder. That's not the only thing that had been getting bigger. Johnny had noticed that his manhood had been growing as well. Sometimes it felt as though he was carrying a lead-pipe in his tattered pants.

Coming out from the bathroom, Johnny started to say goodbye to his mom but his father interrupted.

"John. You go?"

"Yes, Dad. I told the fellas that I'd meet them down by the...umm, outside. Why, Dad?"

"No important. I want know you work with me on roller painting."

I can't figure this guy out. He got me so mad that I wanted to hate him forever. I'm not taking any shit anymore! From nobody, thought Johnny.

"Okay, Dad. I'll stay."

Anatole had seen a lot in his life. He had also been through a lot. Part of him felt abandoned, but as he grew older, he understood just how much his parents loved him. Enough to let him leave. As Johnny had paused, thought a bit, and decided to stay and hang out with his dad, Anatole had been certain that his son would leave. He didn't really understand how to express himself to Johnny. To his wife, he would just say the words, but he felt awkward with his son. Like he was always doing, or saying, the wrong things.

Sonia has told me that all I need to do is speak naturally to John. Even try calling him Johnny. Why do I feel so uncomfortable? Why can't I tell him how I feel? In my heart ,that I love him?

"Yes?" said Johnny's dad. He smiled widely and looked like the happiest man in the world.

Then that uncomfortable feeling overwhelmed him again.

Chapter Twenty-One

JOHNNY JUST SAT and watched. How did his father know all of these things? He took some of the paste like substance and added just a bit of solvent to it. Rolling it thoroughly with their homemade paint roller, it was a nice, creamy consistency. A nice creamy green consistency.

"Dad, you weren't thinking of painting all of our walls green, were you?"

"No, of course not John. We do kitchen white!"

Johnny couldn't believe that his whole house, except for the kitchen, was going to be green. He would have girls over and he'd have to bring them straight to the kitchen.

I can just see it now. I'll bring home this hot blonde. Maybe that hot one who smoked the cigarettes in front of the candy store. And who cares if she's Al's lady? I'll fuck up Al too. Yeah, I bring home some hot dame home and I romance her. I'm definitely gonna fuck her. Oh yeah, she wants it. But I'll have to take her and fuck her in the kitchen! Oh yeah, that'll be real romantic like," Johnny thought.

"John, go to closet. I have one more tray I make other day."

You hafta be kidding me! Oh shit! Not only is my fucking home gonna be green, but I'm the one who's gonna paint it?

"Okay, Dad."

By the time Johnny had gotten the homemade tray, his father had the greenish mixture all ready. Smoothed out and filtered through a small piece of screening, it was all ready to hit the walls.

"You must be excited, John?"

"Yeah, Dad, I'm real excited."

"I have surprise for you, John."

Oh no, not another surprise. I can't take anymore, thought Johnny.

"Really? What is it, Dad?"

"I make second roller. I just need put on fabric."

Attaching the fabric to Johnny's own personal home-wrecker, Johnny's thoughts drifted to the hang-out. All the more reason to get it all finished. He sure would never bring girls home to this green-walled embarrassment. Pouring some of the glistening liquid into each tray, Anatole slowly showed him the proper way to roll the paint out. He had him apply a thin coat & roll out the letter "W" over a few feet at a time. Then he would retrace his steps and fill everything in. Johnny did have to admit that green or not, it sure was a huge improvement.

"How am I doin'?" asked Johnny.

"Good. You do good."

After pulling the furniture away from the walls, Johnny laid down paper on the floor, in the areas that they were painting. Johnny was actually enjoying the painting. He also was enjoying the time spent with his father.

Before he knew it, the small living room area was finished, as well as the two bedrooms. Washing off both trays as well as both rollers, they were ready to switch over to the white paint now.

"Dad, should we use the solvent to clean off the rollers?"

"Yes, good think. We take rag and wipe off with solvent. Good think, John."

Johnny's dad did all of the cutting in and edging. He had a variety of brushes and Johnny was impressed at how precise he was. He could actually turn his head and talk to Johnny and paint lines that were straight as an arrow each and every time.

"I can't believe how much bigger the kitchen and bathroom looks and how much cleaner everything looks," said Johnny.

It had gotten pretty late. Johnny wondered what the boys had done in his absence.

"It warm in here. Paint no dry too good. Sonia, get fan."

Setting up the old, noisy metal fan in the middle of the living room, they would wait and do the bathroom next. Johnny's room would follow as the fan would make its home, like most nights, in Johnny's parents room.

Soon, what started as a labor and ended as a labor of love, was all finished.

After cleaning up in the bright and clean looking bathroom, Johnny said goodnight and started towards his bedroom.

"John, make sure you wash face and brush teeth."

Johnny, exasperated, knew this already. How many times would his mother tell him? Over and over and over.

"Yes, Mom, I did."

Entering his bedroom and closing the door behind him, Johnny wished that his door had a lock. He had found a new hiding spot for both his gun and knife and he wanted to check on them. He also would like to know that he had some real privacy in case he wanted to play with his dick again. In fact, Johnny pretty much wanted to do that every day.

Even though they had set up the fan earlier, the room was muggy. The still air seemed to reach out and grab the paint's smell and wasn't letting it go anytime soon. This would be the perfect night to sleep on the roof. As he was considering it, Johnny drifted slowly off to sleep. He never realized that painting such a small apartment could be so tiring.

In the living room, Anatole and Sonia finished cleaning up and were about to go to bed.

"Sonia, he sleep now?"

"I don't know, Anatole. Why ask?"

"I wish I can say to him how I think inside."

"Well, it is not so hard, Anatole. You say the words that are in heart. Don't worry about thinking from your mind. Your true feelings always keep a home within heart. Sometimes, if important to you, they lock in your mind. But if you let go from heart, it is always much easy."

"How do I get so lucky? I marry smart woman. Wonderful woman. Perfect mother and wife too."

"I marry artist. Someone need to have brain."

When the whole house was quiet, Johnny stirred. As tired as he was, he slowly opened his eyes. In the next room, he could hear the sound of the fan. Johnny felt thirsty and quietly got up to get a drink of water from the kitchen sink. As he shut the water off, it sounded as though there was someone behind him. Turning quickly, and to his relief, there was no one there. Standing perfectly still, Johnny realized that the sounds that had frozen him were coming from the front door handle. Scooting across the floor and into his bedroom, Johnny quickly put his pants and sneakers back on. Grabbing his knife and putting it in his pocket, Johnny also grabbed his gun. The gun that he had lied about to his father, the one that he had said he had thrown down the incinerator. Holding the gun at his side, facing downwards, Johnny slowly made his way to the front door. The door handle was still moving slightly as Johnny suddenly opened it. Standing directly in front of him was a large stranger. The man looked to be about thirty years old. Pointing the gun directly at the stranger, Johnny's finger twitched. The man had a bit of a smile that slowly spread across his weathered and tired looking face.

"Look, kid…"

As the potential intruder was finishing his thought, Johnny pointed the gun directly at the stranger's face. Suddenly, he turned and took off running from Johnny. Johnny took chase and as they approached the end of the hallway, the man, looking in all directions, tried to determine which way to go. As he was all set to take to the stairs, the last apartment door opened.

"You bad men, get away from my building. Go!" said Johnny's friend, the old lady.

As Johnny was explaining that this man was indeed an intruder, the man bolted past Johnny and proceeded to run down the stairs and into the night.

"You're a bad boy! I tella you father!"

"I'll never win with you. Maybe I should just take a shit on you, because the roof is close to full by now!"

"You poor parents. They know how bad a boy you are?"

"Look, you should be thanking me! I chased the bad guy away. Away from all of us!"

Shaking his head and putting the gun in the back of his pants, Johnny turned and headed back towards his apartment. It then occurred to him that he didn't have his key and the door was in fact locked. Now unsure of what to do, Johnny just stood outside of his door. If he knocked and startled his parents, who knew what would happen? Maybe he should just head to the roof and tell them in the morning that the paint fumes were just too much, and that he needed to get some fresh air. The only thing was, it was a school night. No

- 194 -

matter what, Johnny was gonna be in for it. The apartment door suddenly opened.

"John. What you do?"

It wasn't Johnny's dad, but in fact his mother.

"Mom. I…I heard a sound and…And I wanted to make sure everything was okay. I didn't wanna wake you and Dad, but the door locked behind me."

"John, you have a father, and it he job to do this! Not you. You have school tomorrow! Go to sleep! I no want to you be hurt. I love you so much."

"Okay, Mom. I'm sorry."

"Whew! I can't believe I got away with that one. Thank you, God. I'll never do anything wrong again. Well, at least until tomorrow." thought Johnny.

Johnny tip toed across the apartment, reached the safety of his bedroom, and quietly closed the door behind him. Laying back down on his bed, the paint didn't even bother him. Nothing bothered him. Except getting that bastard.

Chapter Twenty-Two

THE REST OF middle school had gone pretty well. Johnny actually got pretty good grades and so did most of the boys. Johnny, thinking he was gonna fuck every girl that he laid eyes on, was disappointed. Oh, he made out with a few, but just squeezing tits was getting old. He did like the titty variety. There were big tits, small tits, and medium tits. And then there were the nipples. Big ones, small, and medium as well. But he wanted some real action.

The boys all got the hangout just the way they wanted. Every week they added something new. Another couch, some throw-rugs and more lighting. Johnny continued to take Jackie under his wing and Jackie grew in confidence, more and more. He was even losing weight and though there was some doubt, even claimed to have grabbed some tits. No one really believed him though. Two years of middle school was quite enough though. Johnny just couldn't wait to get to high school. That's where the grown girls were. The ones who really put out.

With middle school in the rear-view mirror, Johnny, now fourteen years old, had just started high school. Things were going pretty well. Johnny had stuck to his plan to add muscle to his rather lean frame, and the results had started to really pay off. Johnny, now about five foot nine and weighing about one hundred twenty-five pounds, held his own against pretty much anyone that messed with him. The boys all wore their Money Boys jackets every day, and people feared them as they walked down the streets. All was good.

"John? John? Where are you?" called Sonia. "Your father and me need to talk to you."

"What, Mom?"

"Sit, John," said Anatole.

Oh shit. What the fuck did I do now? What did they fuckin' find out about?ed thought Johnny.

"John, we have visit from few people, the last week or two. We have police come. They say you have been in lot trouble. You with wrong boys and you steal. They say because you young, that they no want jail yet. Fresh Air Fund say that they have nice, nice place for you. Just one year. You will finish school freshman year there," Anatole said in a very even and emotionless tone.

Johnny just sat there. A bit stunned, hurt, as well as scared, he knew that when his parents were speaking to him in a serious manner, that he was best off just listening. To interrupt would be a huge mistake.

"John, would you like to say things?" asked Sonia.

"Well, that stuff about stealing is just not true."

As Johnny spoke, his eyes darted around the apartment. He wanted to avoid his father's eyes but he couldn't.

"I don't wanna go. I have my friends here. Do I have to? Why?"

"It will be good. You stay nice place in country. Fresh is the air and you have no danger streets. You have many nice boys and new friends to you," said Anatole.

Johnny knew that the decision had already been made. Arguing would do no good. But his quick thinking mind was already putting a plan together to get out fast. He'd go. He had to. But, it wouldn't last long. He would figure this out. What he really needed to do is speak with the fellas.

Johnny's eyes darted back and forth between both of his parents.

"Where is this place and how do I get there," asked Johnny.

"It is Catholic Charities Home for Boys," said Johnny's mom.

"All boys? No girls?" asked Johnny.

"Yes, all the boys only. You will leave this Saturday. Time will go fast. You learn to not make trouble. Your father will agree that he get different job and when you come back, we want move to much nicer place," said Sonia.

Sonia was putting on a brave face. Inside, she was very troubled, and very sad. Johnny was her little boy. He always would be. Who would make sure that he ate well, and that his jacket was buttoned up when it got cold? And who would kiss him goodnight. Who would remind him to wash his face and brush his teeth?

Johnny was in a daze. All he could think of was his boys, the hangout and not getting laid for even longer now. This wasn't fair, but he would get out. But even more importantly, Johnny didn't want to leave his mom. He was a tough kid, but Johnny would miss his mom terribly.

Johnny tossed and turned all of that night. His mind, racing and plotting, would never stop. In the morning, while tired, he knew he needed to get organized.

Johnny called a meeting with all the boys. They met in the hangout and he gave his gun to Jimmy for safe keeping. Never his knife though. He would never again go anywhere without his knife. Johnny motioned towards Jimmy.

"Hey, listen. You know you're in charge, but watch out a little extra for Jackie. He's getting' there but he's still a little soft still."

"Okay, Johnny. Don't worry. I will."

Saying his goodbyes, Johnny returned home.

Saturday morning came too fast. Johnny's mom packed a small bag for him and they waited at the school that morning for the bus to pull up. Johnny kissed his mother goodbye and his father gave him a hug. A hug without much feeling but a hug none the less. As the bus pulled up, his parents started their walk home. Johnny looked out the window. His lips trembling a bit, he fought the urge to cry.

"Anatole. We need to move to nicer place for John. So they let us take him back. We should have tell him to the truth, Anatole!"

"What do you mean, Sonia? We tell him truth."

"No. We tell him so sounds like his fault but it our problem. We need you to get different job, Anatole. You are great husband and I love you. But we need nice place to keep John from bad people."

The old bus was loud. The passengers barely made a sound but the engine sounded as if it would explode.

Scanning the mostly empty bus, Johnny decided to sit towards the back. Tapping his pants pocket, Johnny felt reassured when he felt his knife, safe and sound. No one would fuck with him. Ever.

"What's your name, kid?"

"It's not kid. It's Johnny."

"Hey Johnny, I'm Paddy. You ever been where we're going?"

"No. You mean you've been there before?" asked Johnny.

"Yea,, this is my third time. It's okay. My parents can't afford to keep me. My father drinks too much and when he's lucky enough to work, he gets drunk and he gets fired," said Paddy.

"My dad has a job. A real one too," said Johnny.

The two boys talked awhile and Paddy soon fell asleep. Johnny wouldn't let himself though. He wanted to stay awake and see every single boy that got on that bus. After stopping at four more schools, the bus hit the highway. Johnny just stared out the window. Mostly everyone was sleeping but Johnny's mind never stopped.

I guess I should wait. Size the place up and then I'll figure a way out. They think I'm gonna like this place? Fuck that! I can't wait to get back to my school and my friends and all those girls that wanna fuck me, thought Johnny.

Slowly, the scenery started to change. Johnny had never really seen places that didn't have buildings. Becoming farther and farther apart, the buildings soon disappeared from his sight altogether. As if leaving one world and slowly landing on another, Johnny saw things he had never really seen before. Large trees, soon standing shoulder to shoulder and covered with brilliant colors, lit up the view. Interspersed between these wondrous newcomers were long stretches of fields. Golden amber in color, Johnny was truly taken aback. Realizing that his guard had become less strong, Johnny snapped out of this nature induced coma, and focused on what he really needed to be thinking of-staying safe.

The dirt, loud noises, and troubles of Brownsville were almost a distant memory. Johnny felt himself being pulled in, pulled into a very strange, but beautiful and peaceful new world.

"Hey, Johnny. Wake up," said Paddy.

"What the fuck are you talking about? I've been awake every single second," said Johnny.

The bus seemed to be slowing down. Veering off to the right, it followed a narrow road, more of a path actually, and soon enough, Johnny could see an archway type of sign. "Catholic Charities Home for Boys."

Johnny was there. His new home. But for how long?

"Okay now. Everybody out."

The bus driver barked out the orders, and the thirty or so boys started to stand up and make their way towards the front of the bus.

"Any weapons? Knives? Guns?" asked a security type of guy as the bus full of boys emptied.

"No," answered Johnny.

"Turn around now. Arms up. Come on, let's go now."

"I ain't got nothin' I said!" said a defiant Johnny.

"Just do it," said Paddy.

Johnny was angry but figured that if they found his knife, maybe they'd send him home.

Standing just outside of the bus, he patted Johnny down. Johnny's natural inclination was to clench his fists. Someone put their hands on you in Brownsville and you had to be ready to fight.

"Look what we have here," said a smirking guard.

Removing the knife from Johnny's pocket, he threw it into a box. It clanged around as it bounced, and then settled upon all of the other weapons.

After being brought to a classroom where instructions were given by a teacher who happened to be a nun, she also led a large group of newcomers around the premises. Johnny was in another world. He wouldn't like it though. He wouldn't let himself. The property was divided into many different sections. The two large, red buildings were the school houses. A group of much more narrow buildings, a drab gray in color, lined a hilltop. These were the buildings where Johnny would sleep.

Entering one of them, the nun showed the boys where the beds were, and at the far end of the building, the showers. Standing in the center aisle that separated the two long rows of beds, the nun called out names and each boy was to respond with a "here."

"John Rostov?"

"Rostov? What the hell is a Rostov?" laughed one of Johnny's new roommates.

As she turned in the direction of the laughter, the nun walked purposefully towards the comedian.

"Put out your hand!" she yelled.

"Who, me?" answered the boy standing directly in front of her.

"Okay, sure, but……"

Smack! Smack! Faster than Johnny could believe, the nun had grabbed a long and thick wooden ruler from beneath the cluster of papers she held. The hits were direct and they were hard.

"What…what the fuck?"

Smack! The ruler came down even harder this time. Its intended target had nothing more to say. There would be no more jokes. No more sarcasm. Too frightened to directly look, Johnny peeked sideways and could see that the boy's right hand was swelling up. Red in color, his hands quivered just like he did. Trying hard to hold it in, the wounded roommate sniffled as a few tears rolled down his unshaven, smooth cheeks.

Sister Mancini was a short, but wide and stocky woman. Growing up in Italy, she worked the farm that her family had owned for generations. The family had resided in Calabria for generations. Those from Calabria were known to be exceptionally smart, but equally as stubborn. Very strict disciplinarians, both her mother and father were big believers in corporal punishment. Sister Mancini held the same beliefs. She may have even enjoyed implementing this physical sort of punishment.

Continuing her tour, Sister Mancini led the boys beyond the hill where their new housing was located, to an area that had long and wide areas of overturned and very rich looking soil.

"Pay attention now. You're here to learn. To learn to behave and to learn whatever it is that I care to try and teach you morons."

No one dared to say a word, for despite her limited stature, the group of boys were intimidated by their new leader.

"It may already be September, but these large areas of dirt still need working on. And who better to work the soil, than a bunch of wannabe hooligans? A bunch of little boys who think they're men? We'll see exactly how tough you little girls will turn out to be. Okay, get back to your rooms and pick your beds out. There are toothbrushes and soap on each bed. Don't you even think of fighting or even arguing over your spots. If I hear one word of disagreement amongst you, I'll break out my big ruler. Do you understand me?"

As she looked at all of her new prisoners, Sister Mancini glared into their eyes.

"Move!"

Turning around, the boys quickly made their way back to their cottage. Filing in quietly, they realized that their housing unit was just one the first of maybe ten or so units. This place sure was big. Walking single file, they stopped at their beds, picked up their toothbrushes and soap, and scrubbed up.

"What the fuck are we supposed to do now?" asked a taller and very lean boy.

"Hey. Shut up!" said Johnny in a loud but hushed tone.

"Why? You really afraid of that short little piece of shit? You see that cross around her neck? She fucks with me and I'll choke the shit outta her! I'm from the Bronx. We don't go like that!"

"Listen, tough guy. What's your name?" asked Johnny.

"My name is Herbie but you just call me Slim. Got it?"

"Yeah, okay Slim. Maybe we should just keep things kinda quiet for a few days. I don't plan on stayin' here too long, but let's make the time here as okay as we can. Okay?" asked Johnny.

The boy's eyes connected, and they just stared each other down. Each one wasn't gonna look away first.

"Okay, that sounds okay, I guess, Johnny," said Slim.

"Shake on it," said Johnny.

The two boys were both natural leaders. They were either gonna get along really well or it would lead to an explosion. Neither one really wanted that.

"I think she wants us to get down to the mess hall. It's down the hill…" started Paddy.

"Yeah, we know where the fuck it is," said Slim.

"He's okay," said Johnny. He gave Slim a little nod in Paddy's direction.

The boys all walked down the hill to the mess hall. Most of the group was about ten to fifteen years old. They all seemed to assume that they'd all be about the same age.

"Shit. Are there any fuckin' seats?" asked Slim as he looked towards Johnny.

As Johnny looked around the large cafeteria type building, he saw mostly boys that looked much older. Some were already shaving. These guys looked like men. Dangerous men.

"Hey lookit. A bunch of little pussies just walked in! Fresh meat!"

"Yeah, Stevie. You ever seen such a sorry assed bunch?"

"Naahh, look. I think the fat kid is gonna cry, Joey!" laughed Stevie.

Most of the younger boys would normally confront people that talked about them that way. Johnny surveyed the room and looking at his new friends, realized that they were afraid alright. But not of the older boys. They could hit those guys. Win or lose, they had little fear. But it was Sister Mancini. They were all strangely shaking in their boots at the thought of that ruler. No one wanted to be humiliated. No one could imagine a nun making them cry. And in front of everyone.

Truth be told, they were stuck. They couldn't hit her back, for even they knew not to strike a nun. And they sure couldn't run. Imagine running from a woman?

"Okay, boys. Find seats at the other end. Stay away from the older boys. You don't worry about them. We have an understanding, so you just watch out for yourselves," explained Sister Mancini.

Standing in line with a tray in hand, the boys waited for their ration of some sort of grayish meat, a pile of vegetables that didn't smell too fresh, and a red liquid that seemed to have something moving around in it. While the place wasn't filthy, it surely wasn't clean either. As the boys finished their less than appetizing rations, they got up and started to walk out.

"Oh hell no! Pick up your own trays, and all of ours as well. Now! Then go back to where the trays are and pick up some rags and wipe all these tables down. And who the fuck you lookin at?" one of the older boys, Joey, asked.

Joey was looking at Paddy. Paddy seemed so scared, that he might have peed his pants.

"He ain't lookin at no one," said Johnny.

Joey walked up to Johnny and poked the smaller boy several times in the chest.

"Shut up. You talk to me when I tell you to! You understand, kid?"

Johnny nodded but there was no way he was gonna answer.

As Joey stepped farther into Johnny's space, Sister Mancini approached.

"A problem, Joseph?"

"No ma'am, Sister Mancini. None at all."

"That's a good boy, Joseph."

"You'd be wise to behave like Joseph, mister," said Sister Mancini, while staring right at Johnny.

The boys finished their cleanup and headed back to their sleeping quarters for the night. As they got closer and closer, Johnny could hear the laughter coming from a few cottages down. They were mocking the younger boys.

"We might as well do our best to ignore these guys," said Johnny.

"I'm goin' over there. I'm not gonna take any shit!" yelled Slim.

"Hey! Are you crazy? Yeah, okay. I'll go with you and we'll probably knock out a few of these bitches, but then what? You gonna beat Sister Mancini's ass too?" asked Johnny.

"She's got a big fat, old ass!" laughed one of the boys.

After a brief and frightened pause, the boys all exploded into laughter. The laughter was huge. Pent up for what most likely was a few days, collectively, they all needed a good laugh.

Eddie McGuire was a short and wiry boy. Hailing from Coney Island, Brooklyn, he was as tough as they come. But Eddie had no need to show it. He had learned a long time ago, that when he wanted to stay out of trouble, there was an easy way for Eddie, and it was to make people laugh. And laugh, they did! All night, almost all the boys, as tired as they were, just couldn't stop laughing. Eddie also did imitations, and in the few short hours that they were at their new home, he did an outstanding Sister Mancini. He even had her walk, plodding and deliberate, down perfectly. Stevie and Joey were next and by the time the night was over, Eddie was doing all three at once. He even had the boys crying in laughter at one point as he bent over to simulate Joey and Stevie putting their dicks in each other's asses as Sister Mancini got all hot and bothered. By the time most of them were falling asleep, Johnny, fighting off the inevitable yawns of what was coming, had one final, sleepy thought.

Maybe this place wasn't gonna be all that bad after all.

Chapter Twenty-Three

"COME ON! LET'S go, young ladies! Up. Get in the showers, wash and brush those teeth!"

Sister Mancini must never sleep. Johnny strained his tired eyes and tried to make out where the hands were on the old clock hanging a few feet down from his bed.

Five a.m.? What the fuck was wrong with this fuckin' lady? She needed some dick. I wonder if she ever got any? These nuns had to be horny. Ugly as hell though. She must have a nasty old, grey winter bush, thought Johnny.

"Make your beds! Tuck in those sheets. Let's go now!"

Beds? These aren't fuckin' beds. They could barely pass for broken down cots! thought Johnny.

It was nearly mid-September and while the days were a special kind of beautiful, the mornings brought with them the first signs of what was to come. Winter. Only wearing tee shirts, most of the boys shivered as they made their way to the mess hall.

"I wonder what kind of fuckin' slop we get for breakfast," said a sleepy-eyed Slim.

Looking around before answering, Johnny was gonna make sure to avoid any problems with the old hag Mancini.

"I don't know, but it sure as shit couldn't be any worse than what they tried to pass off for food last night," Johnny answered.

"What do you wanna do about those fags?" asked Slim.

"I don't know. Maybe that was a first day kinda thing. You know. Like an initiation," suggested Johnny.

The boys all walked in and headed for the same seats as last time. Strangely, their tormentors barely took notice. As the boys settled in, they chatted amongst themselves.

"Maybe we should just get up and get our food? I'm hungry," asked Paddy.

The boys decided to do just that. Noticing that the older guys were still sitting and barely saying a word, Johnny just felt like something was up.

"I don't trust those fuckers, Slim."

"Me neither," answered Johnny.

Loading their trays with the cold and gray looking mounds of slop, Johnny guessed that they were supposed to be eggs. Some sort of a meat patty and a half glass of orange juice rounded out the meal for the morning. Sitting back down to eat, Johnny turned to check on the older guys just once more.

"Good morning, sunshine! Now get the fuck outta my seat," yelled a now furious sounding Stevie.

Stevie grabbed a still sleepy Johnny by his tee shirt and pulled him backwards. Falling feet over head, Johnny landed hard and came up swinging.

"Johnny! Wait! Sister Mancini is coming," warned Slim.

As Stevie turned to see who was approaching, Johnny, in a rage, reared back and kicked Stevie in the balls with all his might.

"Shit! You little fucker. I'll get you. No matter what, I'll get you," he yelled while staring directly into Johnny's eyes.

"Steven! You young men, please don't stoop to the level of these bad little boys. I will take care of them," warned sister Mancini.

As she spoke those words, her eyes darted around the mess hall. Settling in with a scary and hateful glare, she stared at Johnny. Yes, not only would Stevie have it in for Johnny, Sister Mancini would as well.

Sister Mancini spoke to Joey and Stevie, and the older boys quietly served themselves and went back to the first set of tables. Breakfast went by quietly and quickly. Things were too calm. When the boys finished up, they brought their trays back to the front of the cafeteria and grabbed some cloths. Dampening them, they proceeded to wipe down their tables.

"Hey, Slim! What are you doin'?" asked Johnny.

Slim took a few of the already wet rags and walked towards the older boy's tables. While they were just about finished, Stevie still was munching away on his eggs and some toast. Slim started to wipe the table, carefully wiping around the plates and making sure not to bump into any of the plates that still had food on them.

"Thank you for letting me wipe your table," said Slim.

"Well we finally have a bright one," said Stevie.

"It's about time. I thought they were all losers," agreed Joey.

"Are you done with that yet?" asked Slim.

As Joey started to answer, Slim cleared his throat. Mustering as much spit as he could, he spat it all into Joey's plate.

"Eat that! You wanna fuck with us? Come on, bring it!" he screamed.

Johnny, Paddy, and the other boys just sat there for a few moments in stunned silence. Then, as reality hit him, Johnny just shook his head, and in unison, all of the boys got up and raced to their friend's side. It was on. Food went in every direction. For all the wrestling and cursing that was going on, no real damaging shots were landed. Sister Mancini raced her wide body out of the cafeteria and returned moments later with two of the priests.

Johnny and Stevie were locked up, wrestling and rolling all about the food filled floor. Slipping and sliding, neither one could get in a clean shot. Stevie was much bigger than Johnny, but all of those pushups, as well as growing up on the mean and dangerous streets of Brownsville had prepared Johnny for the likes of Stevie. The priests, large and strong, threw the boys in two separate directions and marched the older boys out and back to their bunks.

"Okay, you little trouble makers, all of you! Listen up. Clean all of this up, and when I get back, it all better be done and looking brand new!"

They worked in a slow and deliberate manner. Johnny, Slim, and company cleaned up all of the mess, and Sister Mancini, accompanied by one of the priests, led them back to their bunks. The sun had now come out, and was showering the once brisk morning with a bright and wonderful feeling warmth. As they approached the white and peeling, washed out looking front door, Johnny noticed a few large wheelbarrows sitting in front of the entrance. Loaded with shovels, rakes, and some bags filled with white looking powder, Sister Mancini instructed the boys to bring the tools and supplies to the large dirt patches. Doing as they were told, the boys pushed and carried their work utensils to the barren garden area.

"Okay, so I see we've had a lot of energy today," said a sarcastic Sister.

"Take these four bags and divide them up evenly over all of the gardens. The take the shovels and turn over the soil. And then again. And again. This should take hours if done properly. Then the rakes and smooth things out. The more work you put in now, the greater chance you have of winning, come spring."

"Winning what? I mean, what do we win in the spring, Sister Mancini?" asked Paddy.

"Come spring, we have a competition. You boys against the older group. You'll be planting and growing tomatoes, corn, peppers, and melon. The winner gets to take two weeks off from all work and we also drive you into town. The girl's division winners are there as well."

"Girls? Where are they?" asked Slim.

"Far enough away that you shouldn't even think about it. Okay! Get to work! Water break when I come back. Not before."

The chill now out of the air, the boys worked until the sweat literally poured off of them. Several hours passed and they were thirsty. Slim, Paddy, and two other boys, Fred and Andy, took a slow walk over the peak of the rolling green hill and silently observed the older boys. They were digging also.

"What the fuck are you guys doin'?" asked Johnny.

Johnny had quickly followed his friends and tried to convince them to get back and get back fast. Sister Mancini was on her way and the last thing the boys now needed was that ruler. Or worse.

"What are they diggin'?" asked Johnny.

The boys, turning in unison, made their way back to their own jobsite. "Looks like they're diggin' a fuckin' grave," said Fred.

"Yeah, probably a grave for all of us," added Andy.

Suddenly Johnny thought of his father. His father had explained to him just how he made his way to America, self-dug graves and all.

"Well, it's about time that you boys listened to me. Maybe there's hope for you all yet," said a much calmer and less intimidating Sister Mancini.

"Thanks, Sister," said Paddy.

"That's Sister Mancini!" she barked as she felt for her trusty ruler.

"Oh, I'm sorry Sister. Umm, Mancini. I mean Sister Mancini," Paddy added.

"Good job, boys."

It was amazing that even in a few days, the boys had developed a deep-seated hatred for the Sister, but just like that, she humanized herself. These weren't bad boys. Not a bad one amongst them. Most were there as their parents couldn't afford to keep them.

"Please load everything back into the wheelbarrows and bring them back to your cottage. I'll make sure that they make their way back to the shed. When you get there, please sweep up all the dust from the floors and then wash up and brush your teeth. There's some time left before lunch so just rest. Now listen. When we have lunch, I want no repeat of the activities of this morning. Have I made myself clear?"

The boys all nodded yes and started their walk back. Johnny wondered where the shed was. Must be close to the older boys, he thought. Lunch was calm, the food terrible and the two groups continued to exchange dirty looks as well as middle fingers when no one was looking. Johnny mouthed "Fuck you!" towards the older boys and the middle fingers were popping.

Sister Mancini had also said that after lunch, the younger group was to meet at the smaller of the two red school-houses, for an orientation of sorts. Although the majority of the boys were close to Johnny's fourteen years of age, not everyone was equally educated.

The orientation lasted about two hours. Some books, a schedule, and more rules were given out. Every morning, the boys were to arise at five in the morning. After making their beds and washing up, they would make their way for breakfast. Chores would be next, followed by five hours of classroom work. They would have a thirty-minute lunch break and then, when the school day was done, they could rest, play, and relax. Dinner was at six and would be followed by studying, doing homework, and showering. Lights out and silence commenced at nine. Weekends were dedicated to chores. They would work outside, as long as the weather permitted, but when the bitter cold and snowy season was upon them, they would do all of the shoveling.

Didn't the older assholes ever do any work? What, did they just eat, jerk-off and sleep? thought Johnny.

The days of fall, slowly but surely, morphed into winter, and a bitter cold one it was. While Johnny found his new, temporary home tolerable, he still planned. He would be out soon enough. It had been almost five months now, and January brought with it the most bitter of cold winds that Johnny could ever remember. Maybe the large brick building that was his home in Brownsville shielded them somewhat from nature's arctic blasts but this was brutal. Johnny had never shoveled snow before and while he didn't exactly love it, he looked at it as muscle building. Johnny hadn't abandoned his push-ups either. Hitting the dirty and dusty wooden planks of their cottage whenever he could, Johnny was closing in on a hundred straight, each night. When no one was looking, he had also lifted a few knives and forks from the cafeteria and practiced his moves. Storing them in the metal frame under his cot, Johnny needed to stay sharp. For the older boys. For his return. To Brownsville.

It was a Saturday morning and it was nice to not be rudely awakened. Johnny still woke up at five. His parents would be impressed. Especially his mother. Johnny could hear her voice.

John! Wake you self now! Brush teeth and you wash face please…

Johnny missed his mother. He loved her so much. His relationship with his father was complicated, but with his mother, it was just pure love and adoration. When he got back, he'd tell her so. He also had spent a lot of time thinking about her. His father had such a dominant personality that his mother sometimes got lost in his thoughts. While aware of his immense love for her, he wanted to know more. He was really interested in his mother's passion, her writing. Johnny wondered if he could ever write. What would he write about anyway? His thoughts would often turn to his boys. He especially worried about Jackie. Growing bigger and stronger over the last few years, Jackie would turn out to be an imposing sort. Johnny just knew this. But he worried none the less. His soft heart wouldn't match his slowly developing toughness. Jackie was pure. A sponge that absorbed all that surrounded him. Johnny needed to get back to helping his buddy.

Jimmy, Danny, and Mickey. He missed his other friends as well. Soon. Soon he would leave. This place would be a distant memory for him. Johnny wanted to go home.

"What the fuck are you doing, jerk-off?" asked Slim.

"What?"

"It's fuckin' Saturday morning. If you had some normal in you, you'd be sleeping!" joked a bleary eyed Slim.

"Ah, fuck you," said Johnny as he good naturedly pushed his friend.

Breakfast was lousy and the boys made their way back to their cottage. Some of the older boys walked close by.

"Hey, Johnny. Hey, what's up? Listen, I know we started off rough, but we fuck with all the rookies that way. You'll see. You'll do it also, later this year when the new meat comes in," explained a very convincing Stevie.

Johnny's fists clenched. He didn't trust this guy.

"Look, soon enough, we're gonna start the plantings. I don't know if Sister Mancini explained it all to you, but all of us compete against the other boy's home down the road. I want that win. We need to work together. Okay?" added Stevie.

There's another boys- home? I thought it was against these older jerk-offs, thought, a confused Johnny.

"Did Sister tell you about the special fertilizer that we use? I know you guys already put the lime in, right?" asked Stevie.

"Nope," answered Johnny.

"Ya gotta do it right though. Ya mix the lime and the fertilizer together. Then ya…wait. Come on, lemme just show ya. I want to win this. Bad," said Stevie.

Johnny looked around. Most of his friends were still asleep. He didn't wanna wake them. Stevie and the jerk-offs hadn't bothered them in months. Maybe it was just a thing that happened to all the newer kids.

"Okay, let's go," said Johnny.

The two walked together and quietly chatted. Mostly about the garden and the competition. Walking towards the shed, Johnny felt a sense of relief that there was no one else around.

"Here, gimme a hand, we'll take a bag of each and a screen and dump it in our plot. Over there."

Stevie pointed to a very large expanse of soil. Beyond that was a large piece of burlap.

Opening the shed's door, Johnny sensed that something was wrong. They were on him in seconds. Four. Five, maybe six of them. The older boys pounced out of the shed and pinned Johnny to the still cold ground. Taking turns, they kicked him and kicked him hard. Johnny did the only thing he could think of and rolled into a tight human ball. It took all of them, as he was strong, but they pulled off his sneakers and socks as well.

"Get the fuck off me. I'll fight each one of you rat fucks. Come on!" Johnny screamed.

"Get him over to the hole! Move it," yelled Joey.

Half dragging and half carrying Johnny over to the burlap on the ground, they stopped short a few feet. Letting him fall to the ground, Stevie grabbed him by his plaid shirt and pulled him close.

"You think you're gonna kick me in my balls and get away with it? Huh, punk? See that burlap, asshole? You know what's underneath that? A pit. Four feet deep. And full of rats. Huge rats. Those rats are hungry and we'll tie you up and throw you face first in the pit. They'll eat you alive, you little fucker!" yelled Stevie.

Stevie had pulled Johnny close. He could smell his breath.

"Your breath smells like shit. You've been licking Sister Mancini's shitty asshole, you jerk-off?" countered Johnny.

"Hey, Stevie. Not face first. It'll kill him. Seriously, man. Those rats are huge."

"Okay, drag him over. Feet first. Hold him and lower those feet, nice and slow. When they start chewing off his fucking toes, he might just die from the pain. Or the bleeding! Take the burlap and tie it around his head" yelled Stevie.

Johnny was scared. You never get used to rats. But the fact that he wouldn't see his enemies, that he didn't know when the pain would start, really scared him. Sweating profusely, Johnny used every bit of strength he could muster. He stomped on one of the boy's feet, spun and broke loose. Starting to run, he reached low for his sneakers but they got him again. Then the silence. Struggling every second of the way, Johnny wasn't gonna go down this way.

"Okay. Lower his feet in," ordered Stevie.

"I'd just let them eat him. Kill the little fucker. We'll burn him to death with the kerosene in the shed. They'll think he ran away, it's the perfect plan. I wanna smell this punk's flesh as it burns!" said Joey.

Lowering his feet into the pit, Johnny started to scream.

"No! No! Shit, they're chewing my fuckin' feet! I can't take it! I'm bleeding! You mother fuckers! I can't take the pain. I'll kill you fuckers. I'll get you back!" screamed Johnny.

With the burlap bag over his head, his senses were hard to identify. And then he heard it. Laughter. Pulling him out of the pit, Johnny was shaking. Johnny reached for his bleeding and chewed off toes. Laying him down, they pulled off the bag and a red faced and petrified Johnny, was confused. There was no blood and all his toes were still there.

"Look at that little bitch cry. You want your mamma? You can't have mamma. Mamma is with my daddy right now. Cry, you little bitch!" yelled an angry Stevie.

As he slowly calmed down, Johnny started to realize what had just happened. Even worse than being eaten up by the rats, worse than having his toes chewed off, worse than focusing his bleary eyes on his bloody stumps, these guys had humiliated him. There were no rats. No blood. In fact, except for a sore leg from a few kicks, Johnny was okay. Physically, that is. This was worse than the beating that Johnny had gotten from his father.

"Ahh, look at him. I told you guys that he was a little bitch,ay" yelled a laughing Stevie.

Johnny composed himself and wiped the tears from his face. His heart was racing and he still was gasping for the warming spring air. Putting on his socks and sneakers, Johnny ran. Slipping on the wet grass, he fell. Adding even more of a laughter soundtrack to his ears and mind, Johnny got up and kept going. He glanced at the shed as he ran by. Four large metal cans were stacked upon each other. Taking deep breath after deep breath, Johnny finally composed himself. He felt an overwhelming sense of calm.

"Hey. Where have you been? You okay, Johnny?" asked Slim.

"All is fine. Just went for a walk. Nice out," answered Johnny.

"Just be careful. I still don't trust those assholes," warned Slim.

Johnny just nodded. He was calm on the outside but his mind slowly started to race. He would never again let someone, anyone, hurt him. The humiliation he felt was worse than any pain he had ever felt. Johnny sure wished he had his gun. He'd have to come up with another way. Payback would surely be a bitch.

Chapter Twenty-Four

HE WOULDN'T SAY a word about what happened. To anyone. Ever. Thinking about it, Johnny was sure that they older boys surely would though. If he could just not react. Just ignore them. Yeah, that was it. Just ignore them he thought.

Johnny felt as though all eyes were on him as he and his friends entered the cafeteria. Quickly finishing their breakfast, the boys waited and waited for the older group to finish. As had become the way, they grabbed some rags, dampened them and started about the business of wiping down the older boy's breakfast tables. Johnny had grabbed a few extra rags and stuffed them into his pockets.

"How was breakfast? Mine was great We had baked rat!" laughed Joey.

The whole group burst out in laughter. Johnny's friends looked at him, and he just shrugged.

As the boys walked back to the cottages, Johnny veered off slightly from the normal path. The grass had been beaten down from the thrice a day beating it had taken over the years. Getting closer and closer to what looked to be a rusty old pickup truck, Johnny could see that the keys were in the ignition. Reaching inside, pulled out the key and stuffed it in his pants pocket.

The day dragged on and on for what seemed like forever. Lunch and then dinner, were uneventful. The boys all seemed to smell spring in the air and thus had a burst of energy that evening. Johnny made sure that the rags were stuffed into his pockets as well as several dull looking metal knives. And the key was still there.

As darkness overwhelmed the drab and musty cottage, all were asleep. Except for Johnny. Waiting at least an hour, Johnny grabbed his sparse belongings, and as quietly as he could, headed out of the cottage. It was a short walk to the pickup truck and after making certain once again that they keys were in fact in his pocket, Johnny tossed a bag with his belongings into the front seat.

Moving quietly but quickly, Johnny removed the knives and forks from his pockets. Approaching the tired looking shed, he used his tools to pry open the doors.

Shit! Matches. I forgot about matches! thought Johnny.

The moonlight served as his only vision and Johnny felt relief, as he saw a box of cigarette lighters. Bronze in color, there were several that still looked brand new. Grabbing two of them and then one of the large metal cans of kerosene, Johnny quietly closed the doors to the shed behind him. Still walking as quietly as possible, Johnny got to the front door of the older boy's cottage and peered into the single glass pane. Two long rows of bunks contained about twenty sleeping boys. As Johnny opened the door, he walked as quietly as possible towards the back of the cottage. Opening the top of the kerosene can, he tilted it downwards as the pungent smelling liquid spilled out onto the dusty floor. With his eyes scanning the room, Johnny was looking for something. For somebody. And then Johnny froze.

Harmless as a baby, Stevie was curled up in the fetal position. Luckily for Johnny, his bed was right at the front of the cottage. Lowering the now empty, large can by Stevie's bedside, Johnny knelt down and lit the lighter. Johnny surely was lucky. At the back of the cottage he had found the burlap bag. The same one that he had worn over his frightened face. Leaving it right in the center of the last two bunks, Johnny watched as the low-lying flame traveled farther and farther towards the burlap. Now moving as fast as he could Johnny poured the remaining kerosene onto the rags that were stuffed in his pocket.

Johnny was out the front door in seconds. However, he couldn't resist pushing his face against the single glass pane, if only for a moment or two. Peering inside, Johnny saw the flames start to engulf the entire room.

No! Shit! I can't do this, I'm better than them!

Johnny opened the door and started screaming, "Fire! Fire! Get the fuck outta here! Now!"

Johnny ran outside. Waiting long enough to make certain that every last miserable prick was safely out, he then took off. The cottage burned.

The pickup started on the first try. Johnny had only driven a few times when Al would let him move the long, black limousines, but figuring out the clutch and shifting was going to take some time. Passing through the archway that said "Sorry to see you go. Come again", Johnny knew that he'd never be back. He'd never let anyone else hurt him. Ever.

As Johnny and the old pickup passed through the archway, he started to get the coordination of shifting down a bit. And then the old pickup lurched and stalled. Getting out, he wasn't sure what to do, but he did realize that he had been driving without his headlights on. Looking backwards, Johnny could see the amber light that rose into the darkness from the inferno that he had just created. He could also hear a commotion, a panicked combination of fear as well as desperation. Screams of fear and agony were very distinct.

Getting back into his escape vehicle, Johnny started the old clunker and then took off. Fumbling for the light, he realized that it was indeed easier to drive once he could see where he was going. Nearing the end of the long and winding road, Johnny came to a stop.

New York- Keep Left, said the sign.

I thought I still was in New York? Okay, I'll just go left and see where it leads me. Maybe that meant the city? I think it took us about three hours to get here. Where's the fuckin' gas gauge? Okay, three quarters of a tank. I wonder how far I'll get with that? What if the cops come after me? Calm down. There's no way they can prove anything. Worse comes to worst and I'll just say that I ran away 'cause Sister

Mancini grabbed my junk or somethin', yeah, that's what I'll do, thought Johnny.

Finding his way through the old, noisy, and grinding gears, Johnny was now doing about forty miles per hour. The sun had come up and as if learning how to drive in an old, beat up truck wasn't hard enough, now he had the bright glare of a new day's sunshine practically blinding him. Figuring that he had driven about an hour or so now, Johnny had to take a piss. Pulling over, he misjudged the embankment and for a second thought he'd flip the old farm truck. Straightening the wheel out, he was lucky as the truck rolled to a stop. Getting out, Johnny started to walk around the front and then thought better of it. He poked his head back into the driver's side door and turned off the truck and shut the lights. Brownsville still coursed through his veins and he didn't trust anyone. No way he'd have his truck stolen! Standing next to the passenger side door, Johnny relieved himself. He pissed his name on the side of the old rusted door and made himself laugh. It was a hollow laugh, as Johnny was confused. He never started with anyone, and when they messed with him, he fought back. But they had really gone too far this time. They humiliated him. He could still see Stevie's face, as the pain, too severe to allow him to even cry out, froze as the skin just melted off his facial bones. Johnny had seen his share of horrors before, and fires and death were nothing new to him, but this was different. Even though the cottage door was closed, he could smell it. The smell of death. It was still with him.

Starting the engine and pulling out onto the main road, Johnny looked for signs towards his destination. Looking far ahead, through some of the rolling fog that seemed to come out of nowhere, Johnny strained his vision to make out what he saw in the distance. It was a hitchhiker. An older boy, maybe eighteen, he was a big kid, standing well over six feet tall.

"Need a ride?"

"Yeah, where you goin?"

"Tryin' to find my way to New York," said Johnny.

"New York? You are in New York," said the stranger.

"Brownsville," said Johnny.

"Where? Did you say Brownsville? I know Brownsville. When I was little, I used to go visit my Uncle Al there. He was in his own business. Think he owned a garbage hauling company or whatever. My name's Vinny."

"Johnny. Johnny Rostov."

"You know Johnny, it's about four hours away still. You have money for gas?" asked Vinny.

"No. I don't have shit."

"What's in the bag?"

"Don't fuckin' worry about it," said Johnny as he glared at his new traveling partner.

"Hey. How old are you Vinny? Do you drive?" asked Johnny.

"Yeah. Shit. I'm seventeen. Been driving for years."

"Okay, wanna drive?" asked Johnny.

"Sure. And Johnny. Next gas station we see, we'll pull in and you just follow my lead. Okay?"

Johnny drove a few more miles and pulled over. Passing each other as they ran around the front of the old farm truck, Johnny sized up his companion.

I could kick his ass if I had to.

"Okay, let's see. Four- speed huh? Damn, the clutch is worn. Right to the ground. No worries though. We'll get there. I sure hope that gas station isn't too far," explained Vinny.

"So, Vinny, what were you doin' walkin' out here in the middle of nowhere? I mean, it's nice out here and all but, well, where do you live?"

"Bronx. Been moved around a lot. My mom couldn't put up with all the fights I got into I guess, so her sister and boyfriend took me in about six months ago. She's okay, but her boyfriend was a dick. A real tough guy, you know? Then when he started suckin' the whiskey back, well... he would get nasty. To my aunt and then to me. I just put up with it until I couldn't take it no more."

"When was that?"

"Last night. We got into it. I whupped his fool ass and broke that damn whiskey bottle right over his fuckin' head. Blood was awful. Still have some on me but, that was that and I just walked out."

"Last night? Are the cops lookin' for you too?"

"Me too? Why? What'd you do, Brownsville?" asked Vinny.

"Ah, nuthin' really. Folks just wanted me to get outta Brownsville for a while. Homesick. Found this old pickup and, well, makin' my way home."

"Yeah, okay. If you say so," smiled Vinny.

Up most of the previous night, Johnny's eyes were closing. But he fought it. He didn't really know this Vinny guy and wanted to keep an eye on him.

"Go to sleep, Johnny. I can see the eyes closing. Brownsville, huh? Yeah, you don't trust nobody. I get it. I'm cut the same way," explained Vinny.

Before he knew it, Johnny was out like a light. His mind was racing however. Thoughts of his mom and dad, the cottage, Stevie, and more, raced through his memory bank. Vinny, occasionally glancing at Johnny, knew that Johnny was as full of shit as he was, as far as what had been going on in their lives.

"Wake up, Johnny!"

"We're home?"

"No, pulling into a Shell station. Here's what we do. Looks like an old man in there. He looks fat too. Good. He's gotta be slow, the fat fuck. Look, he fills up the truck. I ask to use the shitter and you talk to him. Talk real nice, okay?"

"About what? What the fuck you want me to say?" asked Johnny.

"Don't matter. Make him like you. You know '*you miss your mom,*' shit like that. Then when I come out, I get in and tear off. Now look, he's a big 'ol boy so stay clear of those big assed meat hooks, but as soon as pappy sees what's goin' on, run! As fast as you can. I'll stop about a hundred feet or so down the road and you hop in. Home free!" smiled Vinny.

Johnny wasn't so sure about this. He'd feel a hell of a lot better if he had his gun.

"What can I gethcha fellers?" asked the attendant as they pulled up.

"A fill. Umm, please sir. And, can I use the shitter. I mean the facilities, sir? Sorry about my language sir. I've been driving with my little brother Johnny and well, he's got a toilet mouth. Rubbed off a bit on me."

"Sure, sonny. Right 'round the corner," as he pointed to the right side of the cleanly painted white building.

"So, where you young men goin' to?"

"Umm, Brownsville. I mean the Bronx," stammered Johnny.

"Well, which one is it?"

"Umm, both. We're gonna go to both, mister."

As the old man put the gas hose back into its receptacle, Johnny could see that Vinny was quickly making his way back to the driver's side door.

"Okay son, that comes to…"

Before the old man could get the words out of his mouth, Vinny started the old truck and peeled out on the mostly dirt and gravel lot.

"Hey, where the …," started the old man.

Johnny took off running. Giving with every bit of energy he had, he raced to meet Vinny.

"Ima get my shotgun!" warned the old guy.

"Go! Go! He's gonna shoot my nuts off!" Johnny yelled to Vinny..

Both boys looked at each other and started to laugh. If the guy did fire off a few shots, they didn't know it.

Vinny figured they had about an hour to go. Traffic was smooth sailing on Interstate 90.

"Need to look for signs, Johnny. I-81. I think."

"Wait! Right there," said Johnny as he pointed to the exit.

The old truck veered side to side. If Vinnie had been driving "for years" he sure needed to work on his turns. Johnny slid towards the driver and almost knocked Vinny's arms from the steering wheel.

"I guess we're getting' pretty close. I'm starvin'," said Vinny.

"No! Shit, let's just wait, okay?"

"What? I have plenty of money," said Vinny.

"What? Why did we almost get shot then stealin' gas?" asked Johnny.

"Can't eat gasoline. Need to save that money for the important stuff."

Johnny just shook his head. He liked Vinny, but outside of Jackie, Danny, Mickey, and Jimmy, he didn't trust many people. He wondered how his boys were doing. It had been about half a year now.

He left so suddenly. What was he going to tell his parents when he just showed up?

"Here we go. This place has burgers, sandwiches, and pop," said Vinny as he slowed and pulled into the parking lot.

Entering the clean looking eatery, the two took seats up at the counter. After a few minutes, a pretty waitress approached and took their orders.

"Anything you want, little brother," laughed Vinny.

Johnny wasn't laughing though. He'd gone through too much to think too much was all that funny right now.

"Cheeseburger, a pop, and some fries. Please," said Vinny.

"Umm, I guess I'll have the same," said an uncomfortable Johnny.

"What's wrong, Johnny? You look a million miles away. Like you're here, but you left your brain on a back road somewhere."

"I'm just tired," answered Johnny.

"Look. Look at that other waitress over there. See her? The Blonde. Johnny. She wants to fuck me. I know it. See the way she's lookin' at me?"

"What? No way. She ain't lookin' at you special. She got gas in her ass, Vinny. She probably farted. She aint' smilin'."

As the boys munched on their food, they finally started to feel a bit more at ease with each other.

"Oh shit," whispered Johnny.

"What?"

"Sherriff. Those bastards are mean out here. They don't have much trouble out this way, so when they do, they have as much fun with it as they can," explained Vinny.

"Hey there, darlin'. Get me a coffee, sweetheart," said the large and balding man of the law.

As the sheriff sat there sipping on his hot black coffee, a middle-aged man, wearing a tee shirt with yellowish stains under each arm, and pushing a mop, worked his way to the counter.

"Hey, Sheriff. How are you today?"

"Frank. How's business? Why don't you have one of your girls do the mopping?" asked the Sheriff.

"We're busy, they're busy. Those are good things. Besides, it keeps me in good shape. Some little shits come in here and don't pay? I have my legs to catch 'em and my gun here to drop 'em," said Frank.

Johnny and Vinny knew at that moment that they'd surely be paying for lunch. No shenanigan's today. That sheriff looked like he wanted a reason to clean out the barrel of his gun.

"Okay, young men. Will you guys be having some desert? Hot fudge sundaes are the best, so is the chocolate cake."

Johnny wasn't really used to desert. That would be a real prize to him. He did remember his father selling a painting to a local baker once and they had fresh rye bread, as well as chocolate cake. Boy, that was good. One time, after shining shoes and giving his parents the money, he kept a little and bought cookies and an ice cream cone. He hid in a closet and ate all of it.

"I'll have the chocolate cake. Umm, please," answered Johnny.

Vinny just shot Johnny a look. After all, he was the one paying.

"Sure, I'll have the sundae please," answered Vinny.

"Okay boys, that'll be about five minutes. Either one of you want some pop?"

The boys shook their heads no, and hunched over a bit so as not to draw too much attention to themselves. There was really nothing to worry about, they figured. That gas station was pretty far away.

"You hear about the fire upstate?" asked the sheriff.

"Why, yes, I sure did," answered Frank.

"Terrible. Burned down a cottage with about twenty young boys in it. Who knows? At that age, they coulda been smoking and fell asleep."

Vinny and Johnny's heads slowly and deliberately turned towards one another.

"Fellas. Here you go," announced the waitress as she put the desserts on the counter.

Johnny had jumped a bit, startled at her sudden announcement.

"You okay there, son? Little jumpy now, aren't we?"

"Just sleepy. We've been…"

"We've been driving all day. Me and my little brother had been tending to our grandparents over the weekend. On our way back home now," finished Vinny.

"Well isn't that sweet. Hey fellas, these boys are nice enough to give up their weekends to care for their grandparents," said the waitress as she glanced towards the sheriff and Frank.

As the boys started to devour their desserts, Vinny kept an eye on the sheriff's hand. Absent mindedly, he buttoned and unbuttoned the worn leather holster. The two men just took Johnny and Frank in, almost as if they were memorizing their faces.

"Man, this is good. No, this is great! Can we have two more pieces of the cake wrapped up to go?" asked Vinny.

By the time she returned, round one was done and Vinny asked how much the total came to. Paying their bill, Johnny got up to use the bathroom and the two boys made their way out to the parking lot. Getting in, they noticed that both doors creaked of age, so much that it almost had a melodic tone to their closure.

Whew! Damn, I was scared as shit! But I don't feel bad. Those fuckers deserved it! Especially Stevie. And Joey. The others knew what was happening and they didn't have the balls to stop it. Nobody was ever gonna hurt me again. Nobody, thought Johnny.

The old pickup truck strained its mighty muscles to make it up the hill. Johnny noticed that there were less and less trees now. As they came down the steep slope, after passing the top of the hill, they could see an entirely different landscape in the distance. Little by little, the trees would disappear, and their replacements were more of the brick and mortar variety. Yes, Brownsville was coming. But was Johnny ready for Brownsville?

Chapter Twenty-Five

"WE'RE GETTTING PRETTY close, Vinny. Look, I guess you kinda figured that my folks didn't wanna just get me outta Brownsville, huh?"

"No, I never woulda guessed. Hey, none of my business. Listen, I figure, that as we get closer and closer, I should probably drop you off within walking distance of your place? Again, none of my business, but you're only fourteen. Do you want me to just take this piece of junk and keep driving?" asked Vinny.

Johnny thought for a moment. No way he'd wanna keep that truck. First of all, where would he keep it? Secondly, he didn't want any connection with that home for boys. But he wasn't giving anything away!

"Listen. I like you, Vinny. I was gonna keep this, my dad can fix anything and he was gonna drive it. You gimme a hundred bucks and it's yours."

"A hundred bucks? No way! Look, I'll give you twenty and you can keep the damn piece of cake," said a smiling Vinny.

"Forty bucks and the cake. That's it. No less!"

"You drive a hard bargain, but yeah, okay."

"Pay me now," said Johnny.

"You don't trust your buddy?"

"I don't trust anybody. Except my mother. Pay me now or the deal is off," said Johnny.

Vinny had the money and Johnny knew it. Reaching into his pants pocket, and with Johnny watching every move, Vinny counted out forty dollars. Handing it over to Johnny, Vinny watched as Johnny counted every single bill.

"Nice doin' business with you. Drop me off up here. It's only a few miles. I got it."

"You sure?" asked Vinny.

Vinny pulled over and Johnny quickly jumped out. Turning away from the pickup and with the small bag containing his possessions, Johnny started on his walk home. Vinny honked the old horn and gave Johnny a wave.

"Take care of my pickup!" yelled Johnny.

"Maybe I'll come see you sometime!" said Vinny, as he took off.

As Vinny took off, Johnny turned to look at the pickup, one last time. What a strange seven or so months it had been. Johnny never forgot when somebody hurt him, but he was determined to draw a line in the sand and put his time spent at the home for boys, deep within his memory banks.

Johnny had walked about three miles or so and things were now becoming familiar. He was almost home and he still hadn't thought of what to say to his parents. While he sure couldn't be honest, he could say that he became homesick, that they hit him, and that he ran away. He didn't like that idea, as if his parents ever spoke to anyone from the home, they'd possibly piece everything together.

Continuing to walk, it wasn't just the sights that became more and more familiar. It was the smell, the horns honking, the yelling, and the danger. Danger had a feeling. A presence. This was a strange feeling.

"Hey! Look who it is! Johnny! When did you get back? You look different. Skinny. They don't feed you, those fuckers?" asked Jimmy.

"I'm just getting home. Just rollin' up. Haven't even gone upstairs yet," answered Johnny.

"Come on, come to the clubhouse. We've been working on things the last six months. We even saved up some money," said Jimmy.

"Okay. I gotta figure out what I'm gonna tell my parents, Jimmy," said Johnny.

"Whatta you mean? I thought you did your time in 'farm-jail' and now you're out. Wait, did you bust outta there? What the fuck did you do, Johnny? Are they lookin' for you? How did you even get back?" asked Jimmy in a rapid-fire staccato.

"Slow down, Jimmy. Let's take a walk."

"No one's down in the hang-out, let's just go down there. But Johnny, you gotta tell me all the truth, okay? Everything," said Jimmy.

It must have been about four o'clock in the afternoon. Johnny figured that it would be good to get some of this stuff off his chest, and maybe Jimmy could even help him figure out how to handle the situation with his parents. The boys sat downstairs for about an hour. Johnny really was impressed with the way the place looked. No more dimly lit, old light bulbs, there were now lamps and the doors were furnished with new locks. There were also some new throw rugs and a few pictures of naked girls on the walls. The 'safe' was now camouflaged by a large dresser that fit caddy corner in an area farthest away from the door.

Johnny took Jimmy on a six-month journey of his experiences at the boy's home. Listening intently, Jimmy's eye became focused and his fists became tightly clenched when Johnny filled him in about Stevie and Joey. The look of anger soon gave way to a look of astonishment as soon as Jimmy heard about the fire and the stolen pickup truck.

"Holy shit, Johnny! What about your parents?"

"I know. I've been thinking that over. I don't see how I can go wrong if I just tell them that I got serious about coming home, got good grades and worked hard. I'll tell them that the nuns drove a small group of kids back and dropped me right by the front door. I'll even tell 'em that nuns are the worst drivers. That they think God is just gonna protect 'em"

The school year wasn't over, so Johnny figured that he could just pick up where he left off. He was sure that he'd be fucking girls in a few days. They must have missed him, how couldn't they have? Johnny and Jimmy figured that they'd meet up later on in the early evening, and Johnny headed towards his parents. He didn't have a key so he hoped someone was home.

Man, this is a weird feeling. I've lived here my whole life but being away, for even seven months, it all looks so different, Johnny thought to himself.

One thing sure wasn't different and that was that hollow sound as he headed up the wooden steps. Johnny knocked on his apartment door and waited. Nothing. Okay, he'd just wait around a bit. Shuffling down the hall a way's, Johnny figured that he'd go up to his favorite place in Brownsville. Heading up the stairs, he was startled and tripped a little.

"You no go shit on my roof! You bad boy! I think they final get rid of you. You come back. Jesus, Mary, Joseph. Whatta I do with you?"

"I don't have to shit, but when I do…"

Before Johnny finished his thought, he had to side step his friend, "the old lady" as she took a swipe at him with her old and well-worn broom. That broom must have been older than her.

"I get you. Someday, I get you, you bad boy. I tell you momma that you come back to go shit on my roof again!"

Johnny skipped a few feet down the hall towards her apartment. He would never really be disrespectful, well not too much at least, but he didn't even know the old-lady's name.

"Ma'am. I am not going to shit on your roof. I promise. I'm also sorry. I'm sorry if I've ever said anything in a disrespectful way. What is your name?" asked Johnny.

The old lady just stood there. Almost with a frozen look of surprise, stunned that Johnny *actually did* have manners.

"Mrs. Mangione," she answered.

As Johnny looked at her, he saw a completely different woman. Gone was the disapproval, the suspicion and the anger.

"Nice to actually meet you, Mrs. Mangione. My name is Johnny. Johnny Rostov. Is there a Mr. Mangione? I've only seen you when you were sweeping up and keeping the hallway so neat. You do a great job," Johnny added.

Mrs. Mangione's eyes glistened and had a sparkle to them. An immigrant from Catania, Italy, she had lived in that apartment for years and years.

"No more. No more Mr. Mangione. Alfredo. My Alfredo leave me. Ten years now he gone."

Pausing for a moment, she leaned slightly on the outside door frame of her apartment.

"You can call me Mamma. Yes, Johnny. You call me Mamma," she said while breaking into a huge grin.

"John! Is that you?"

"Mom! I'll be right there! I have to go, Mrs. Mangione, I mean Mamma," said Johnny as he backpedaled away.

"I'll talk to you tomorrow, okay? Maybe I can help you sweep?"

"Okay, Johnny. You be good boy. You are good boy."

As Johnny turned to head back to his apartment, he was surprised, as his mother was still standing in front of the door. Johnny assumed that she'd unlock the door and they'd talk once he met her inside. With her lower lip quivering a bit, Johnny's mother began to cry a little.

"Mom, what's wrong?"

Before should even tried to answer, she took the remaining few steps towards Johnny and embraced him. Hugging Johnny and then kissing him on his cheek left Johnny confused. While fully knowing that his mother loved him, he had never seen her cry.

"I miss you so much. How are you? You look skinny. I love you, John."

Johnny adored his mother but secretly held some anger towards her for not taking his side after his father gave him that terrible beating.

"John, I am glad you home. How did you arrive? It is not time yet."

"Well, they liked me a lot there, Mom. I'll tell you everything later but, it was crowded and they let the best kids decide if they wanted to leave early. I decided to come home because I missed you and Dad so much," said Johnny. "Mom? Can we talk later? I hafta pee really bad!"

As Johnny closed the bathroom door behind him, he glanced at the mirror. He liked what he saw. There weren't too many mirrors at the home, and Johnny was too busy keeping his guard up to admire himself all that much. After taking his piss, Johnny pulled off his dingy tee shirt and flexed his muscles. Yeah, he was getting there. His biceps now had some definition and his chest and shoulders were really starting to develop. Pretty soon he might even be shaving. Johnny had hair on his balls so he wondered when the facial hair was coming in.

"John! You drown? Come on, wash you hands, brush you teeth and wash you face. I miss so much to tell you that."

"Okay, Mom."

"You hungry, John? I can make you soup. We have bread and the cheese came today too," she said about the government cheese that was delivered once a month.

"Yeah, Mom, that sounds good. I'm hungry!"

"You always be hungry," said his mother with a slight trace of a smile. "So, tell you mother about this place. We want to see you, but too far."

"I understood, Mom. It was okay. The nuns were really nice and all of the kids got along really good," Johnny lied.

"You have school class? I mean, you just go back to school or you need me to go with you?"

"Yes, oh that's right. Do I just show up? I mean, I'm a high school freshman now."

"I go to the school with you tomorrow and we will find out," explained his mom.

Believe it or not, Johnny was anxious to start school. He knew a few things for certain. He had to get another knife. That was most important and at some point, a gun. He would have to remember to wash his balls. At least two or three times. He was going to be seeing a lot of girls and he wanted to stay as fresh as he could.

Johnny made quick work of his food. Even though his mother had put it together quickly, it was sure better than anything he'd eaten in a long while.

"Okay, Mom. I'm gonna head out and find the fellas. It's kinda cold out, do you know where my jacket is?"

"What jacket you mean, John?"

"Money Boys. You know, the one we all have."

"Yes, it is in bottom drawer your room. I fold it," said Sonia.

"Where's Dad?"

"He is painting, John. Maybe one more week and he has new job,"

"What? What job? He's not gonna paint anymore? He loves to paint," asked Johnny.

"John. He lose all money for his paint roller. He shows to friend and now friend sell to big business. He very mad. Not first time he has this happen. Long time before, same thing. He done with paint to take care of us."

"Well, where's he gonna work?"

"At Brooklyn Museum. He will do security."

"Wait, how far is that?"

"Maybe twenty minutes. He can take subway. Right to Eastern Parkway. Not far. Nice hours. It is art museum too. He will love that too."

"Okay, so long as we don't have to move. I gotta go mom."

"Okay, but John. We move maybe. Maybe soon. We look to nice place. Apartment, maybe in the Ralph Avenue. It still will be to Brooklyn."

"I'm still gonna go to Brooklyn High School, right?"

"I think yes. Do not worry. We will find this out," she explained.

Johnny's head was spinning. During the last few days, he was frightened half to death, gotten all of those deserving bastards back, escaped in a stolen pickup truck, made friends with a guy named Vinny, and now his dad was starting a new job and they may have to move!

"Okay, Mom. I won't worry. Listen, I think I'm okay just going to school tomorrow by myself. I'll just go to the office and explain that I'm back, okay?"

"Okay, John, please not too late to stay out tonight, please," she asked.

Johnny looked at his mom. Something seemed different. He wondered if everything was alright between his mother and father. He sure did miss her though.

"Okay, Mom. Gotta go!"

As Johnny exited the apartment and entered the hallway, he pulled the door closed and waited for his mother to put the lock on. As he headed towards the staircase to make his way to the streets Johnny heard someone calling his name.

"Johnny! Hello. You are a good boy! You stay off the roof when you need to shit and I kiss you everyday!"

"Okay, Mamma! I will see you later. I gotta go," said Johnny in the nicest way possible.

"You be good boy!"

"I will, Mamma!"

Johnny flew down the stairs and onto the street. The early evening air was March brisk, and he had forgotten to get his jacket. He was just gonna go to the hangout. Not only did he need a key for his apartment but also one for the hangout.

"Johnny! Hey Johnny!"

"Jackie, hey, how are you? What the fuck? Did you eat Danny and Mickey? I thought you were gonna lose weight and get stronger?" asked a disappointed Johnny.

"I'm trying Johnny. I went backwards a little. I'll start over. You'll see!"

"Johnny! You're back!" said Mickey, as he approached with Danny right behind him.

"Jimmy said he'll be here in about ten minutes," said Danny.

The boys all walked slowly down the alley. They figured they'd hang out there tonight, and catch up with Johnny.

"Anyone see Mrs. Williams' big assed tits?" asked a curious Johnny.

No one answered, so Johnny guessed that there was no action that he had missed.

"Hey Johnny, Jimmy has a key for you when he gets here," said Mickey.

"You know what we need? We need some whores to bring down here. You know, the grown-up ones like, that hangout with Al the gangster," said Danny.

"Yeah, good luck with that. They gotta be about twenty bucks to fuck us all, no?" asked Jimmy as he made his way over to the rest of the boys.

"Here, Johnny. Here's your key. Hey, all okay?" asked Jimmy in a hushed tone.

Johnny nodded yes and wanted to talk more about getting some whores down there.

"Lemme ask Al. You guys stay away from there. I've known them since I was a little kid," said Johnny.

"We have the money. We should get two whores. Let 'em get naked and dance and then we'll fuck their brains out. We gotta get bags though. I ain't stickin' my dick in no whore without a bag. No fuckin' way," said Mickey.

"No Jap whores though. I hear they put razor blades in their pussies," noted Jackie.

"What?" asked Johnny as the whole group exploded into laughter.

"So, any tits popped while I was away?" asked Johnny.

"Oh, hell yes! Johnny, you wouldn't believe it. You know that pretty little girl? You know, the one that's real skinny and you pissed on her on the roof, when you was feelin' her tits?"

"Who, Roxanne?" asked Johnny.

"Yeah, that's her. She popped! And I gotta good look at 'em also. I had to change my fuckin' seat, three times! I finally got a good seat, where the sun was comin' in and I could see right through that white shirt. Nice!"

No was no reason to, but Johnny found himself feeling a little jealous. He and Roxanne had drifted apart a bit and he had rarely even thought about her. However, as pretty a girl as she was and now with the announcement of the arrival of tits, Johnny was intrigued. Johnny made a mental note to meet with Roxanne and her tits. Tomorrow in fact.

The boys rounded the corner and headed downstairs. Popping all the lights on, Johnny just took it all in. It was different. Filled with all his childhood pals, they made this place. And it was going to get better. They were going to get some whores down there and they would grow up together and probably grow old together.

"Johnny! Hey, Johnny! You here with us? You look like your brain took a fuckin' vacation," said Jimmy.

"Yeah, I'm here. I was just thinkin'. My mom just told me that my dad is getting a job. A really good job and it's at an art museum."

"So what?" asked Mickey.

"So, that's really important to him, asshole!"

"Calm down. I was just sayin'"

"Anyway, I might have to move. I mean, I'm probably gonna have to move."

The hangout became silent. Johnny could hear the rats humping each other but no one dared say a word. Looking around, Johnny could feel the sadness.

"Even if I do, it ain't gonna be far. Ralph Avenue, and my Mom said I'll still go to the same school and all," explained Johnny.

The downcast mood still remained, but the boys really didn't know how to express themselves. When they were happy, they all laughed. Mad? That was easy. Just break something, curse or hit someone. Horny? Grab some tits or jerk-off. But sadness? No, they had no clue how to express that.

"So, Mickey, how much money do we have in the box?" asked Johnny.

"A little more than sixty bucks. Why?"

"Well, we all have the jackets and we're fixin' this place all up. We can get some whores. I'll talk to Al as soon as I see him. Who's gonna get some bags?" asked Johnny.

"I will, I get 'em all the time," lied Jackie.

"What? When did you ever buy some bags. You don't need bags when your jerkin' off! You need a bag for spankin' the monkey? Hahaha, Jackie, I love you, you're somethin' else" laughed Jimmy.

"No. I stole some. I had no idea when I might need them but…"

"It's okay, if you can get 'em and not get caught? Go for it," said a reassuring Johnny.

"I still say we need more money. Girls like money. We can buy 'em shit and then bring 'em down here and fuck 'em. Or at least they will suck our dicks," said Johnny.

"Oh, without a doubt, they'll suck our dicks," said Jackie as the whole place erupted in laughter once again.

"Look, I better be getting' back home. I ain't seen my father yet and I gotta make sure I have some clean clothes for school tomorrow," said Johnny.

"Okay, we're gonna hang here a little bit. We'll lock up. See you tomorrow, Johnny. I'm glad your back," said Jimmy.

Johnny jogged back down the alley. It was starting to get dark so he slowed down as he got to Mrs. Williams' tits window. Looking inside, there was nothing but darkness. Another time.

Taking the stairs two at a time, Johnny couldn't wait to see his mom. He wished that he could have her all to himself sometimes.

"Mom? Open up, it's me!"

The door slowly opened and as Johnny was about to say hi to his mother, he took a step back.

"John. You get back today, son? How does this happen, John? They say that you stay until summer is finished, no?" said a stern looking Anatole.

"Dad. Hi. Umm, I did good, Dad. They are so crowded there, that the top kids got to choose on whether they wanted to stay or go home. I missed you guys, I missed my friends and, well, they drove a few of us home."

As Johnny was finishing his sentence, his father's suspicious glare softened a bit. As his father moved to the side a bit, Johnny squeezed through the narrow opening and into the living room.

"Mom said you're getting a new job?"

"Yes."

She said it's at a museum, right?"

"Yes. A museum."

"Do we have to move, Dad?"

"Yes. I want better place for you. Nicer for all of us. It is good."

"Will our new apartment be close enough so I can still hang out with my friends here?" asked Johnny.

"Yes, I think you can walk, maybe fifteen minutes. Maybe twenty. But John. When I was little boy in Russia, we move. We lived in big, big house and we have anything we want. My father and his father own much land. Fields that grow wheat. We own the mills that cut up and make fine. My father want a different place. Better for me. More friends. But I was mad. I was very angry, and we move to new home, I stay inside. My father promise to me, that I make new friends. Good friends. I no listen though. After time, I see my father was good man. I make very good friend. Christopher his name. When I explain of how I come to here, he, Christopher was shot and they kill him. The soldiers."

Johnny just stood there. Spellbound by his father's words, while his father had spoken of this once before, Johnny couldn't get enough. All was going to be okay. Johnny just felt it. Now, if the girls at Brooklyn High would just understand how much Johnny and his friends wanted to fuck them.

Chapter Twenty-Six

THE NOISE SEEMED almost deafening. Johnny hadn't seen this many people in a long time. Making his way to the main office, he would occasionally turn as someone yelled his name or slapped him on the back. He was a little tense, not used to the friendlier atmosphere.

"Yes, may I help you, son?" came the voice of what, to Johnny, looked like the oldest lady in the world.

"Yes, ma'am. I am starting my first day today. My name is John Rostov."

As Johnny uttered his last name, he heard a voice from behind him.

"Rostov? What the fuck a Rostov?" asked the tall black teenager.

"What the fuck you lookin' at, white boy?"

Johnny stiffened. He had dealt with guys tougher than this kid. Clenching his fists, Johnny redirected his attention to the older lady behind the counter.

"Yeah, I'll see you later, white boy. Just don't step into a bathroom to grab a smoke! You hear? I'll flush that head right down the toilet like I do your fat friend," the kid warned.

Johnny started to feel that rage. It started in his legs and boiled its way all the way up to his face. Who was he talking about? What fat friend? He better not be talking about Jackie! That was it. While there was no way he could get in trouble, at least not for a long while, Johnny knew one thing and knew it for sure. A knife. He needed another knife. You just didn't walk around Brownsville, whether it was Christopher street or Ralph Avenue in Brooklyn without a knife. Johnny never started any trouble, but if trouble came looking for him, they'd be sorry. Johnny had learned his lessons well.

"*John, you only fight to protect yourself or your family.*"

These wise words came from Johnny's father and Johnny agreed with them. Except for one small thing. Johnny added "and your friends."

"Son? Son?"

"Oh, I'm sorry," said Johnny.

"Here is your schedule, Mr. Rostov. Now do you know where you're going?"

"Yes, ma'am, and thank you, ma'am," answered Johnny.

Being on his best behavior sure wasn't going to be easy. But Johnny knew that any trouble may lead to discussion about the boy's home, and for Johnny, he'd much prefer to just leave that far, far away, as if it never happened.

Johnny was early, so he could find homeroom quickly. Entering the classroom, Johnny took a seat all the way in the back.

"May I help you?"

Man, why couldn't he get a pretty teacher. This one had a face that made Sister Mancini look like a starlet.

"Yes, ma'am. Here is my schedule and my papers. I just need you to sign them?" asked Johnny.

"Okay, Mr. Rostov. Now listen, there's to be no talking when..."

"Johnny! Hey! Shit...Oh shit, I mean. Sorry..."

Jackie was so excited to see Johnny that he forgot where he was. Johnny couldn't tell by the teacher's expression whether she was mad, as her face was most likely not capable of smiling.

"To the office! Now! Not a word!"

Jackie, head down and shoulders slumped, exited the classroom and made his way to the office.

"I hope this isn't representative of what you think is proper classroom behavior, Mr. Rostov!"

"Well, umm...could you say that once more?" asked Johnny.

The teacher just shook her head in disgust and assigned Johnny a seat. At least that worked out well, as it was on the opposite side of the classroom's windows. Always having girls on the mind, this would provide Johnny with the perfect viewing angle.

Homeroom went quickly and Johnny had little problem finding his classrooms. Feeling a bit tired, and hungry as well, Johnny headed for his last class. English literature. Upon looking at his schedule, Johnny thought this might be a mistake. English literature sounded like a college course. Johnny went through the same routine with his teacher and sighed a bit when assigned a seat. Right smack up front. Front row, exactly in front of the teacher. There wouldn't be much of an opportunity to look through girl's shirts there. Mrs. Stevens handed Johnny his textbook, and he tried to follow along as best as he could. Something very strange was happening, as Johnny was interested in this class, in this textbook especially. Gone, for the moment at least, were thoughts of pretty, young girls and what he wanted to do to them. His thought systems were now being aroused by the likes of the epic poem *Beowulf* and *The Canterbury Tales*.

Before Johnny knew it, the bell had rung and as all his classmates jumped up and rushed for the schools exit doors, Johnny just sat there.

"Mr. Rostov? Are you okay?"

"Yes, Mrs. Stevens. I'm just, I don't know, I'm really interested in this class," said Johnny.

"Why, that's great. Does this surprise you?"

"Yeah, I mean, the school is nice and all, but I just go because my parents make me. And the girls. I mean…"

"Yes, Mr. Rostov, I know," said a smiling Mrs. Stevens.

So, she could smile after all.

"Okay, well read as much as you can. You have a way to go, before you catch up."

"Okay," said Johnny.

"See you tomorrow, Mr. Rostov."

"Okay," answered Johnny.

A bit dazed, Johnny entered the hustle and bustle of the real world. The hallway had emptied out some, but it was still crowded.

"Fuck you, nigger! Let me go!"

"Come on, fatso, your hair needs some washin' now."

Johnny looked up, just in time to see his friend Jackie being dragged into the boy's bathroom. As he took off, Johnny spotted Jimmy.

"Jimmy! He's got Jackie! Come on!"

"Who does?" asked Jimmy.

"Some tall nigger," answered Johnny.

The two boys rushed to the bathroom and witnessed their friend Jackie getting his head dunked into the toilet bowl. Letting him up for a moment, he told Jackie that he was now going to piss in the bowl and dunk him again.

Johnny couldn't believe this. After all, they had all called him "the knife guy" and now he was a guy with no knife.

"I'll slit your black throat, mother fucker! Back up. Now!" screamed Jimmy.

"Okay, white boy, we just havin' a little fun here. Betta put that knife down fors I shove it up yo' ass!"

Jimmy was on him in a flash. As Johnny quickly helped Jackie to his feet, and grabbing some paper towels to dry him off, Jimmy had the much taller boy trapped in the corner. Putting the sharp knife to his opponent's throat, Jimmy warned him.

"One time, mother fucker! Just one time, I'm gonna warn you! Stay away from him. You want some of me?" Jimmy screamed.

As Jimmy put just a little more pressure on the knife, blood droplets started to trickle down the tall youngster's neck.

"Alright. Calm. Calm. All good now," said the now shaking and frightened youth.

Before exiting the bathroom, he turned and offered a warning to the three friends.

"I isn't the only one. We gonna get you," came the warning.

As Jimmy and Johnny dried off and calmed down their friend, Johnny burned inside. A knife and a gun. Yes, he would carry both from now on. The three boys left school together. But Johnny wasn't going home. Not right away anyhow.

As the boys got close to their homes, they agreed to meet up at the hangout in about two hours. Johnny was distracted, as they separated and instead of entering his apartment's large heavy door, he took off and quickly ran across the street.

"Hey kid, long time no see. Your candy stealing days are over I hope," said the guy behind the counter.

"Is Al here?"

"Yeah, I'll get him. Watch the counter, okay kid?"

Johnny looked all around the small candy store. He hadn't been there in a while but it all looked the same.

"Johnny boy! What is this? You finally come to visit your good friend Al?"

"Al, can I talk to you? Private like?"

"Yeah, sure, kid. Come on back to the office," said a very friendly Al.

Johnny had no illusions about Al. A cold-blooded killer, you would never have a problem with the head neighborhood gangster. If you never crossed him, that is. There were many stories of bodies, bodies stuffed in wall cavities, in crawl spaces, and thrown from roof tops.

"It's Johnny, okay?"

"What? What the fuck are you talkin' about?" asked Al.

"No more Johnny boy. I changed that years ago. Remember?"

"Well yeah, Johnny. I have nuthin' better to do than remember your fuckin' correct name! You crack me up!" said Al as he burst into laughter.

Johnny spent the next thirty minutes or so, catching up with Al. When he left, he had a brand-new switch-blade and the order placed for a gun. Johnny would pay Al and do some work for him as well. Feeling a lot better, Johnny started for the front door.

"Hey, Johnny. Look, you want me to have the boys take a visit to these damn niggers? Mother fuckers stink. Their skin don't breathe right. You know that, don't you? It's a proven scientific fact. They should teach this shit in school" said Al.

"Thanks, Al. I'll let you know. But thanks for everything."

Johnny opened the front door to the ever-familiar chimes that he'd heard since he was a little kid. Stepping out onto the sidewalk, Johnny exhaled forcefully. Although he didn't quite understand it, Johnny couldn't wait to get home. English literature. Book in hand, knife in pocket, Johnny crossed the street.

Johnny knocked on the door. When was he going to get a key? By the time, he finally got that key, the family would be moving to Ralph Avenue. Johnny had to piss and he couldn't hold it much longer. Squeezing his thighs together, the fountain was going to start soon. Johnny contracted his stomach muscles and attempted to make it to the stairs and then hopefully, the roof.

"Johnny! How school today? You come talk to Mamma now," said the suddenly caring older lady.

"Umm, umm…"

"You hafta to take leak, Johnny?"

"Yes!"

"Come fast. Go ahead I open door. Go down hall, and on right. No piss on seat! I check!"

Johnny hurried down the hallway and barely closing the door behind him, he took aim and peed. His aim was spot on, not a drop on the seat. Johnny ran the bathroom sink for a few seconds so it'd sound like he washed his hands and opened the door.

Wow. How can an apartment just a few doors down from mine, look so much different? I mean, Mom keeps ours clean and Dad and I did some painting, but this is beautiful, thought Johnny.

As Johnny walked back up the narrow hallway, he noticed all the pictures on the wall. The walls had a beautiful printed wallpaper, and each picture was perfectly level and square. From very old pictures that looked to be from a faraway land, to one that looked like it was taken yesterday.

"That is my Alfredo. He has been in heaven ten years now. I miss him. We come together from Italy. Alfredo comes first and I come one year more with my three babies," explained Mrs. Mangione.

"You have babies?" asked Johnny.

"No, Johnny. They all big now. They move. No come love Mamma no more," she explained with moistened eyes.

Johnny could hear the slight tremble in her voice as well as see a single droplet, slowly falling down her wrinkled but beautiful face.

Johnny continued to look with amazement at all the pictures. He found it amazing, that just outside of this very building, there were murders and fights, thieves and drive by shootings. Gangsters instilled fear in everyone and no one had money. But inside Mrs. Mangione's apartment provided an insulated private viewing of a land afar. Her apartment even smelled different. It smelled great in fact.

"What smells so good, Mamma?"

"I simmer some sauce. Some people say gravy. In Catania, my mamma teaches me sauce, no gravy! I have an Aunt Mary, she and Mamma argue always. She comes from different part Italy, her family, the Balderose's, say gravy. Not me!"

Wow, she really fuckin' cares about her sauce," thought Johnny.

"Johnny, you want stay with Mamma? I cook you a good supper?"

"Umm, well, sure. I hafta go ask my parents first. Would it be okay if I brought a school book over so I could study a little bit? I like it here," asked Johnny.

"Of course. You go! Ask you mamma. Come back not too much, food ready in half hour, okay?"

"Okay, Mamma. Thank you,"

"And please be hungry, Johnny. Mamma need someone to cook for. My food is my love."

Letting himself out, Johnny waited in front of the door for a few seconds. He wanted to make sure that Mrs. Mangione locked the door, and she did.

Johnny knew that he had so much to deal with still. He was only home a short while, he had a sudden love for literature and he really wanted to spend time with his mom. But tonight, would be Mrs. Mangione.

Johnny knocked on his front door. Sonia answered and let him in.

"How school today, John?" asked Sonia.

"Actually, it was great."

"Really? That so good, John."

"Yeah, I was doing okay and my last class, English Literature, well, I was tired, bored, and dreading it. I just wanted to get home and hang with the fellas. But Mom, I started to really get interested. I think I really like it. Maybe I could be a writer someday."

"John, you can do whatever you please to. I am writer and I have no school for it. I am proud for you."

"Mom, would you mind if I had dinner with Mrs. Mangione? She's lonely and I want to bring my literature book over and study after dinner."

"Well, okay. Why not? You be nice her, John, okay?"

"Of course, Mom. I really like her. I can learn so much from listening to her. She's from Italy. It's interesting, how things are so different around the world, you know? Who knows, maybe I'll marry an Italian woman someday!"

"You please say thank you for Mrs. Mangione, okay, John?"

Johnny washed up, grabbed his book and took off down the hallway.

"Mamma, it's me. Johnny. And I'm hungry!"

Letting Johnny in, Mrs. Mangione looked so happy.

"You must be hungry, I hope? I make special for you, also Italian bread!"

Mrs. Mangione had a sparkle in her eyes and a reborn smiling soul and spirit. Her happiness had been in hibernation and it seemed to have just awoken. Spring had released her sadness and replaced it with a new season, one of hope.

"Can I help?" asked Johnny

"No, you be good boy, here you go. You like the Italian food?"

"Umm, I never had any. It sure smells great!"

Johnny sat down at the small kitchen table. I simple, delicate tablecloth covered the wooden set. Johnny dug in. He couldn't believe how good this food was. The sauce was incredible!

"Mrs. Mangione..."

"Mamma! You only call me Mamma!"

"Mamma, this is amazing! This is the best food I've ever had in my life! The bread is so good. The cheese is amazing! I'm used to stale bread and government cheese," explained Johnny.

"When I live in Italy, my momma, she teach to me the secret recipe for her sauce. I no tell anyone her secret. You like? Mangia! I am happy to eat with someone. You nice boy. I always know you nice boy. You just make mistake, shit and piss all over my roof! I know that someday I straighten you out. Like my own little boy."

Johnny took a moment from devouring his dinner, to sneak a look at Mrs. Mangione. His eyes darted around her entire apartment in a matter of seconds, and he became startled as she literally exploded in laughter. Just looking at Johnny's happy face made her smile. And the smile turned to laughter. Real laughter, belly laughs that hurt, they were so strong. Johnny just shook his head. Partly embarrassed, he started to relax and found the humor that had been hidden in Mrs. Mangione's stern exterior.

"It's okay, I joke and funny with you. I no laugh like this in so long. My Alfredo and I laugh so much. If you find someone who you laugh with, you take them and never let away from them. Okay, Johnny?"

"Okay, Mamma. That was amazing," said Johnny.

"You ready I hope for desert? I make a nice cake for you."

"Yes! I'm still starvin'. Shit, I mean…I'm sorry. I have to watch my language, Mamma. I'm used to cursing with my friends."

"Johnny. You listen me. I say 'shit' many times. I tell you 'no shit on roof,' remember? It is okay. Besides, you shit anyway!" she reassured Johnny.

Another explosion of laughter soon followed. After desert, Johnny helped to clear the table and do the dishes. He had eaten so much, that he was starting to become very sleepy. But Johnny didn't want to sleep. He had his English Literature book and besides, Mrs. Mangione had plenty of stories. Johnny couldn't help but think just how much his life had changed in a matter of just a few days.

Sitting down on the plush and immaculate couch in the living room, Johnny opened his school book and started to jump all around, looking for something that really interested him. To his surprise though, everything was of interest. Johnny read and read as Mrs. Mangione worked on knitting a sweater. Johnny's mind was like a vacuum and all the knowledge that was put in front of him was being sucked from the world around him and stored in his own private hideaway, his mind. Johnny spent a relaxing evening with both Mamma and English literature.

Chapter Twenty-Seven

"WHERE WERE YOU last night?"

Johnny looked up and couldn't attach the face to the voice. After all, Brooklyn High School was a crowded place.

"Hey Jimmy. I umm, my mom had me doing chores so I didn't come out," answered Johnny.

"Listen, I found out where we can get some whores. Twenty-Five bucks and she'll fuck all of us. Even Jackie," laughed Jimmy.

"Okay, that's good."

"What's wrong, Johnny? I thought you'd be really happy."

"No, I am. I'm just tired and thinking about my last class of the day, English literature."

"What? What the fuck are you talkin' about? Some girl in that class?" asked Jimmy.

"Yeah, that's it. Tits popped and I'm workin' the angles, you know how we do it."

"Listen Johnny. I was thinkin'. We have some money but we need more. How 'bout we get somethin' goin'? If we steal a car or two, can we sell them."

Still distracted, Johnny really was having to push himself to get back into the life of theft and law breaking.

"Yeah. Definitely. Okay, after school, we meet right away. Plan it out and let's do it! Fuck these people with money. Or, better yet, maybe that warehouse with all the tires. Cars are high risk. With tires, we know we can always sell 'em to Al.'"" said Johnny.

School went by quickly. Johnny found out that his tall black friends name was Douglas. No sign of him all day. Maybe he was scared to show. Somehow Johnny doubted that was the case. He had his knife though.

The fellas all met up at the hangout and they decided that tonight would be the night. Johnny really wanted to hit the warehouse. Tires were less risky, but the fellas all wanted cars. A few blocks away, the Jews always had some nice cars. Mickey could hotwire a car, and they'd make it quick. In and out.

"Listen, we can't get greedy. We get greedy and we get caught," said Johnny.

"We gonna wait until it gets dark?" asked Jackie.

"No, let's do this, fellas. No sense in waiting. People are home. Mickey, you good?" asked Danny.

"Good," said Mickey.

The boys made their way up the dirty stairs and back onto Christopher Street. They walked about six blocks and it was sitting right there. A black Chrysler. The boys guessed it was about a 1940.

"Shit, we should get about four-hundred bucks for this," said an excited Jimmy.

"Listen, we sell this to Al and we'll be lucky to get a hundred bucks, if that. He might give us fifty." said a more reasonable Johnny.

Danny, Jackie, and Jimmy spread out a bit, walking about fifteen feet ahead of, as well as behind the black beauty. Johnny took a small screwdriver and tried to jiggle the door lock open.

"Shit, it's open," said Johnny in a hushed, soft voice.

Johnny and Mickey both knew that they should wait until dark, but they were in the middle of it now and there was no turning back. Johnny looked around and opened the large and heavy black door, just enough for Mickey to get in and crawl under the dashboard. Yanking on two wires, Mickey brought them together.

"Shit! It's not working, Lemme try again."

Becoming nervous, Mickey tried desperately to get the car to start.

"Hey! What the fuck are you kids doing? That's my car!" yelled a middle-aged man walking briskly towards them.

"Let's get the fuck outta here!" yelled Johnny.

Mickey was stubborn. Determined not to fail, he continued to touch wires together. Suddenly, Johnny felt a strong hand grab ahold of his shoulder, and spun him around. Instinctively reaching for his knife, Johnny pulled it out and the man's grip lessened and Johnny pulled away.

"Let's get the fuck outta here, Mickey! Mickey, now!" screamed Johnny.

Reluctantly, Mickey pulled away from his failure and in a pack, the boys took off running.

"We should separate," yelled Danny.

"I'm going to call the police! You little rat bastard, mother fucking thieves!"

Running as fast as they could, it sure seemed that they were home free. Slowing to a walk now, Johnny looked around and the coast was clear.

"Never again. Nighttime only fellas. Everyone okay?" asked Johnny.

"Oh shit. Listen!" yelled Jackie.

"It's the cops! You guys hear the siren? They're close! Look, let's run into this General store and mix in with the customers. Be quiet and just act normal," said Jimmy.

"We really should split up. Shit it's too late now, they're getting closer," said a scared Jimmy.

The boys tried to act as casual as possible. Anytime five boys walked into a storefront, all eyes would be upon them. Maybe they should just run.

Jackie stood close to the window. Jimmy was trying to wave him farther into the establishment and away from that front window but Jackie didn't understand. As Jackie glanced outside of the grocer's window, he saw a patrol car slowing down. Two cops were looking all overt for the boys, and they spotted Jackie.

"Shit, they found us!" yelled Jackie.

"Backdoor! Where's a back door?" yelled Danny.

They boys pushed and shoved each other as well as the stores few customers, until they reached a back door. The door was locked. The man behind the front counter, wearing a white apron with blood stains on it from butchering meats, saw the boys and started to yell.

"Hey! Get outta my store you punks!"

Danny became overwhelmed with fear and with his shoulder, rammed the door as hard as he could. With a final kick, the door burst open and the boys nearly trampled each other to get out, and get away! Except for the fact that this was no backdoor, and staring them right in the face was a very narrow and winding staircase. These stairs didn't lead outside. They led to the roof.

"Shit, we ain't got no choice now! No going backwards, only up. Let's go!" yelled Johnny.

The boys made their way up the stairs and were breathing hard. Not realizing that they were in a one-way stairway, with no exit until they reached the fourth floor. The roof!

Johnny, Jimmy, Danny, and Mickey ran up the final few stairs and opened the door to the roof.

"Let's go!" yelled a frantic Jimmy.

"Wait! Where's Jackie?" yelled Johnny.

"I told you that fat bastard was gonna get us killed," said Mickey.

"Shut the fuck up! We stick together," ordered Johnny.

Looking back towards the stairwell, Johnny saw a red faced and exhausted Jackie emerge. His face beaded with sweat, he had barely made it up the stairs.

"Let's go. They're right behind us," said an out-of-breath Jackie.

Taking off running, the boys were soon out of real estate. Ducking behind a large sheet metal exhaust housing, they squatted down, and rested.

"Look, they're coming. What the fuck are we gonna do? Shit! We're gonna get shot," exclaimed Mickey.

"Look! We gotta jump. It's a really, narrow alley. We make it and there's a fire ladder right over there! We're down and they'll never find or catch us!" yelled Danny.

"Okay, let's do it!" said Johnny.

Danger wasn't going to afford them any time to discuss an alternative.

Taking a running start, Danny, then Mickey, and Jimmy all leapt across the alley, falling onto the adjacent rooftop, rolling to a stop.

"I can't do it," said a quivering Jackie.

"Jackie, you have to and we need you to, now!" ordered Johnny.

"Look, you go and I'll watch you," said a frightened and red faced Jackie.

"Okay. Look, it looks like that roof is a little higher than this one. But you can do this Jackie! Jackie! Look at me. Look at me! I wouldn't lie to you! You can do it. Okay?"

Jackie slowly nodded his head up and down.

"When you push off, get some lift so you make up for that roof being a little bit higher," said Johnny.

Johnny backed up and could see the police coming. It was now or never. The athletic Johnny made the jump easily, dropped and rolled to a stop and looked back towards his hesitant friend.

"Come on Jackie! Come on!" pleaded Johnny.

Jackie looked back towards the approaching police. Guns drawn now, he'd have to jump and jump now.

Running as fast as he could, the large and sweet souled friend leapt. As he crossed over the narrow alley, his eyes locked with his trusted friend Johnny. Johnny could see the fear in his friend's eyes. He could also see that it was gonna be close. Holding his breath and instinctively squinting his eyes closed, Johnny waited for his friend to land. But he didn't

"Help me. I can't hold on! Johnny. Please! I'm scared. Please, Johnny. I'm scared to fall. I don't wanna die!" pleaded Jackie.

Jackie had come up just a little bit short. Walking to the roof's edge, the boys could see Jackie's fingers desperately holding on for dear life.

"Shit! Shit! Don't let go!" pleaded Johnny.

"They're comin', Johnny. We gotta go or we'll all be dead!" yelled a backpedaling Mickey.

Johnny reached down and put his hand over Jackie's sweaty and soft wrist. Grabbing on as hard as he could, he begged Jackie to pull himself up.

"Here, lemme put my arms around you and pull, Johnny. I ain't leavin. We're all family!" added Jimmy.

"Pull Jackie, pull!" yelled Jimmy.

"I can't do this. I'm slipping. Johnny. I'm gonna die."

With those last words, his friend Jackie fell. As he watched his large body twist and turn, he could hear his screams. And then they stopped. Jackie lay motionless. He was crumpled and laying in a pool of blood. His own blood.

Johnny and Jimmy stared in disbelief and shock. They both were shaking and had no way of stopping it.

"Maybe he's alive!" said Johnny.

"Look, his legs are all twisted and…Johnny, he's gone. Jackie's dead."

Pulling Johnny as hard as he could, Jimmy implored Johnny to go. To run. The cops had their guns drawn.

"Stop! You fuckers!"

"Just shoot 'em!" said the largest cop.

Shots rang out, but Johnny had listened to his friend, and took off running. They'd escape. But the gang was now one member short.

Johnny had heard that Jackie's mom tried to kill herself. That with both her husband walking out on them and now to lose Jackie as well, it was just too much for her. After a long stay in a mental hospital, she vanished.

The boys were a changed bunch. Oh, they still got in their fair share of fights, and trouble as well, but things were never quite the same. To Johnny, the next few years were a blur. Girls had come and gone. Johnny had fallen in and out of love, time after time.

Now seventeen, Johnny was still a leader. But he had also immersed himself in his new passion. Literature. He hoped to someday go to college. No way he could ever tell the fellas though. No way they'd understand.

Anatole and Sonia found a nicer apartment in Brooklyn, on Ralph Avenue. It was still a small place but all in all, much nicer. Johnny was okay with it. He still went to Brooklyn High School, and still had the fellas.

"One more year, Jimmy, one more year and we're out," said Johnny.

"You know, Johnny; I was just thinking the other day about Jackie. He woulda been seventeen now. These last two years, I've been scared always; kinda inside, you know? Always lookin' around; hearing his voice. I think I feel guilty. I don't know," explained Jimmy.

"I know what you mean Jimmy. When it first happened, I used to go to sleep at night and think I was hearing his voice. I could see his eyes. I talked him into it, Jimmy. It was my fault, and I've been carrying it around for over two years now. Sometimes I can't even sleep. I get scared. Scared that I'm gonna see him, or I'm gonna hear him, and he's gonna be pissed."

"Tomorrow is our last day of our junior year, man. What are you gonna do this summer? My parents really need me to work," said Jimmy.

"Well, it's better over on Ralph Avenue. More guys have more money. I shine a lot of shoes and I have a job lined up at the cafeteria at the museum where my dad works. He's doing good there. He's a security guard but they have him doing more stuff. He knows so much about art that they've had him give some tours. I mean, his English still ain't too good but, you know, he tries. It makes him feel good not to hafta just stand there guardin' the air, you know?"

"Listen, I told my parents that I'd be a little late today. I wanna go up and visit Mamma Mangione for a while and then you wanna get together with the fellas?" asked Johnny.

"Yeah, okay. Meet at the hangout in about an hour?" asked Jimmy.

"Okay, sounds good. Hey, Jimmy…"

"Yeah…what's up, Johnny?"

"Do you think he blames us?"

"He's Jackie. He's family. I'll never forget him. I don't know what I believe in but, I know he's smilin' that big goofy grin. And probably eatin' the biggest donuts, we've ever seen. And you know something?"

"What, Jimmy?"

"You remember when we was kids and he runs over that big assed catcher?"

"Yeah. I remember. He told me that was the best day of his life," answered Johnny.

"Well, that's what he's doin' now Johnny. Every day is the best. The best day of his life. Over and over."

Johnny took off running the two more blocks he had to go, before he got to his old apartment. It still felt weird, the place was the same dirty, old looking building, but it felt different. After climbing those same old stairs, and hearing that familiar thumping, Johnny knocked on the door.

"Who be to my home?" came the Italian scented voice of Johnny's second mamma.

"It's me, Mamma. Johnny."

"Who?"

"Johnny. You know, Johnny Rostov!" said Johnny with a bit more assertiveness.

As the door opened, Mrs. Mangione was holding her right hip and looked to be in some pain.

"Mamma. What's wrong?"

"Oh, Johnny, Mamma is old. I fall the days before and no one was here for me. I forget and call for my Alfredo. I lie down kitchen floor for long time. I have some trouble with walking so my friend buy me this," Mamma said, as she pointed to the dark brown wooden cane that was leaning against a chair.

Johnny entered the neat little apartment and could see that things were a little off. The pictures in the hallway hung a bit crooked, the dust piled a bit higher and the place just wasn't the same. What the hell was going on anyway? Everything seemed different in Johnny's life now. Everything kept changing.

Johnny sat on the plush couch and talked to his mamma. Mamma sure could spin a yarn; but Johnny found out that she was also an amazing listener.

"Johnny. Let me tell to you something that take us many times to understand. Everything changes Johnny. People, they change, the world does it change too. Mamma knows things. You change you girlfriend too. Mamma knows," she said with a smile.

"How did you know that? I was goin' out with Roxanne for a while and especially since I moved, even though we saw each other in school? Wasn't the same. See what I mean?"

"But, who is this new girl now, Johnny? Tell Mamma."

"She's nice, Mamma. She wants to be an actress. She acts in the school plays. She's even trying to talk me into doing some acting. I might try it. Mamma, do you remember when I ate over here for the first time?" asked Johnny.

"Oh yes. I do. Mamma was very lonely and then Johnny come to visit. I used to think you very bad boy. Johnny, you shit all on top of Mamma's roof! And piss! Piss and shit like a dog! A dog on no leash!"

Mrs. Mangione was really laughing hard now. She could barely get the words out, she was laughing so hard.

"I know, I know. But, after dinner, I brought over a book."

"Yes, I remember. English Literature. I was proud for you, Johnny."

Mrs. Mangione was probably close to eighty years old now. With an achy hip and her share of other aches and pains, she sure looked it and felt it. But she was still sharp. Sharp as a tack.

"Well, that was a strange day, Mamma. I always went to school to, well…"

"Yes, Mamma know. You go school to look at the girls. The tits. The bigga tits and the asses. If you like my Alfredo, you like the bigga asses."

"Mamma! I didn't know you talked like that!" said a surprised, but entertained Johnny.

"Mamma knows."

"So, yeah, that was it, until that day. I fell in love, Mamma. But not with a girl, but with a book. Something inside changed. And it's gotten bigger and bigger. My grades are okay, but they're really good in literature. I love it, Mamma, but I don't tell the fellas," explained Johnny.

"Why? You think they laugh? So what? You teach them. You always a leader, Johnny."

"You know, Mamma, I think I wanna go to college. My parents don't have money but I'm a very hard worker. I'm getting a job this summer and I'll hustle…I mean I'll also shine shoes and…well, I'll do whatever I have to do to make money, and start saving for college. Brooklyn College is a good school you know."

"Listen, Johnny. I want you do favor for Mamma. Remember, you are different from the other ones. You are special. You smart. You can do something you life. Okay? Promise Mamma. Promise you do something special"

"Okay, Mamma. I will. I promise. I better get going. I promised the fellas I'd meet them."

"Okay, Johnny. You come back soon, see Mamma. No forget. Mamma gets lonely. Mamma old, but I have one more special dinner to make. For you Johnny."

"Bye, Mamma. Oh, Mamma…one more thing. I like the girls with bigga tits and the bigga asses too!"

Johnny was really laughing now. And so was Mamma. It was just a few minutes ago that he felt like crying. Jackie was on his mind. But Mamma had lifted his spirits.

One more year, thought Johnny. So far he had been lucky. He had done a lot of things the wrong way, but he was still standing. Maybe he was going to turn out okay. Maybe he would finally get completely away from Brownsville. He was away, but he wanted to get much farther away.

Chapter Twenty-Eight

BY THE TIME Johnny got home to Ralph Avenue, it was starting to get dark. It was a Friday, and Johnny knew that his father sometimes worked Saturday's when he could, to make some extra money. If he was working tomorrow, maybe Johnny could take the train with him.

The Brooklyn Art Museum was a large and imposing looking structure. From the outside, it was difficult to imagine the wonderful treasures that were at home within. Set up high on what was almost a completely cement hill, the six pillars that spanned the front entrance served as an invitation to the tremendous beauty they stood guard over. Johnny would be working as a dishwasher at the cafeteria. His father told him just who to talk to, and to Johnny's amazement, he got the job.

Walking in the doors, you would see signs for upstairs and downstairs as well. The cafeteria was on the third floor and the way Johnny figured, he'd be able to clear about forty bucks a week. Cash! This was a fortune, and while there were many things to use that money on, Johnny wanted to give both his mother and father some, each week. Twenty bucks a week sure could help them out a lot. Then there would be savings for college, maybe a car, and whores. Johnny and the boys still needed to get some whores down at the hangout.

"John, how was school today?" asked Sonia

"Okay, Mom. It easy and fun but hard and boring also."

"Why you say this?"

"The last day. You know, we all just wanna get out!"

"Yes, I see this."

"Mom, what time does Dad leave for the museum in the morning?"

"Your father leave at eight in morning. Good hours. He stays nine to four."

"Okay, well I start my job tomorrow at nine, so that's perfect. I'm gonna be washing dishes in the cafeteria. Good money. I wanna give some, every week to you," said Johnny.

"That will be wonderful, John. Listen to me, John. Please sit with me."

"What is it, Mom?"

"The museum. The cafeteria, it is very important. To work hard is good. For you, the money, but to work hard and your best, always good things."

"I always work hard, Mom. Don't worry. I'll have money every week to help pay the bills," said Johnny.

"No, not what mean. They also have library. For you John, you can study. Read the classics. I know you have love for books. Like me, same love."

"They have a library?"

"Yes, John. It is very good for you to read."

This was great news. Even though the fellas would never understand, if he was able to, Johnny would be off every summer morning, straight to the library, to read. His dream would be to read until they turned the lights out. His recently found passion for learning, specifically reading, was immense. It's as if he had an unquenchable thirst for knowledge.

Johnny's dad walked in the door. He looked very tired and smelled of vodka. He looked harmless but Johnny still became tense around his father. He understood him much more as he had become older, but the anger was still there.

Johnny had brought his knife skills all the way back, and within a week or so of his visit to Al, he had his gun back as well. After dinner, Johnny read for a while and figured he'd get some sleep. It was a warm night. Johnny hadn't yet gone up to sleep on his new roof on Ralph Avenue, but he was so tired that he figured he'd just drift off. His overnight stay on the roof would have to wait until another night. Johnny's eyes slowly closed. His rapid but subtle thoughts raced across his mind with amazing acceleration. His eyes would startle open briefly but after a few more minutes, he fully relaxed and his mind gave in.

"Hey, Johnny. What's up?"

Johnny looked around. He didn't see anyone though.

"Over here! Come on, Johnny. You can see me."

Looking down and up once again, Johnny became paralyzed with an all-consuming fear. It was Jackie.

"Jackie? Jackie? Wait, you're dead! What the fuck is going on here?"

"It's not your fault, Johnny. I heard you and Jimmy talkin' today and I need to make sure you know. Don't feel guilty, Johnny. Don't feel badly either. It's great here."

"Where? Look, I'm getting the shit scared outta me, Jackie! What the fuck is goin' on?"

"I'm at a place where every day is better than the one before. That I can be anything and everything I wanna be."

"Where? Come on, Jackie! You hafta tell me."

"Look, I'm okay. That's all you need to know. Well that and..."

"What? Don't leave me hangin', Jackie!"

"Well, I'm not supposed to be doin' this. I'm gonna get in trouble...but watch your back. Remember that cart guy who caught on fire? He's been tryin' to get you back. It can work like that. He's tryin' to set something up. He's using someone, kinda goin' through him. It's a guy that you know Johnny. You drove with him...I gotta go. I'm really gonna be in trouble now. Listen. Don't forget. Nothing was your fault! I love you, Johnny."

"Wait! Jackie!"

It was too late. Whatever had just happened, it was over. Johnny was wide awake. Getting up to get a drink of water from the kitchen, he glanced at the clock. This couldn't be right. It was already six in the morning. But he just had closed his eyes for a minute. Two, at the most. Drenched with sweat, Johnny forced himself to slow his breathing.

Calm down. Take it easy, it was just a dream, thought Johnny.

"John, you awake already? That's good son. We should always be early for work. So important. Good job. You need change clothes. We eat and then we go," said Anatole.

After changing, Johnny and his father ate a small breakfast and took off. Walking down the wooden steps, Johnny noticed how quiet those steps were in comparison to his old place.

"Dad, is it just me or are these steps different than our old place?"

"You very smart young man, John. Yes, they have better quality in all this building. Much better. Building is newer also. Your mother and me, we like much better. More money, it costs, but we like. Do you feel happy here, John?"

"Yeah, Dad, I'm good."

Johnny wasn't used to talking to his father like this. As much as his father was a talented artist, he wasn't a talented talker. Especially when that talk involved feelings of the mind. He expressed himself through his paint laden brushes. Perhaps Johnny was learning about a whole new side to his dad. As much as he tuned his dad out, felt angry with him and if he looked deeply enough within himself, feared him, Johnny loved his father.

The summer's morning held the heated moisture of what was to come. It was going to be a hot one.

"Yes, it will be hot today, son. Museum is with the air condition. It is nice. Not so sure about cafeteria. I never go, your mother makes me lunch to bring. I forget today."

"That's okay, Dad, I'll cook you up something special. On the house, of course!"

Johnny's dad's expression changed a bit and that nervous feeling came back over Johnny.

The subway ride was relatively quick. Within fifteen minutes, they were there.

"I will see you at four-o'clock, John? Have good day. Work hard. Rostov's always work very hard."

Johnny nodded. They climbed the many cement steps that led to the museum's front door. As Johnny looked to say goodbye to his dad, he just saw his back. Anatole Rostov had done enough talking. Now was time for work.

Johnny found the cafeteria with no problem. He was to find a man called Leroy. Leroy was an older black man and ran things in the kitchen. Johnny had never really had any black friends, but he kept an open mind.

"Excuse me, can you tell me where Leroy is?"

"My man. You be lookin' right at him, youngster."

"I'm Johnny. I'm supposed to start workin' today?"

"That a question, young man? Come on now. Be sure of yourself. A man ain't nothin' unless he's sure of himself," said Leroy.

"Well, I'm sure that I'm Johnny, and I'm sure that I wanna start makin' some money!"

"Alright! My man has a funny side. Step into my office, Mr. Johnny."

Leroy waved to Johnny to follow him. Johnny wondered where Leroy's office was.

"Okay, my man, here we be," said Leroy.

"I thought we were goin' to your office?"

"Oh man. This is my office, Johnny. And there's yours. Come on now. Put on these rubber gloves. You washed many dishes, Mr. Johnny?"

"Oh yeah, sure. Millions," said Johnny as he shook his head side to side, admitting that he never had.

"White boys probably got them some fine lookin' maids that do them for ya, right?"

"Maids? No, Leroy. We're broke. I never met a maid in my life."

"Okay, then! Johnny, see those three big sinks over there? The first one, that's for the soakin', the big pots and pans. The second one is for washing. Scrub them suckers up with soap and get 'em squeaky clean. Then there's the rinsing in that last one. There's that hose you pull down and squeeze the end. Rinse 'em real good. That water all needs to be hot. Okay now? Go get 'em boy."

Johnny got right to work. Rubber gloves on and scrubber in hand, he started on the pots that had been soaking. Leroy reminded him to be careful when cleaning the large knives and forks. There may have been air conditioning in the museum and the cafeteria felt okay, but Leroy's "office" was hot as hell. All that steaming hot water didn't help either. Johnny's back started to ache but he wasn't going to complain. Forty bucks a week was too good to be true. He wasn't going to mess this up.

Continuing to scrub, clean and rinse, Johnny was getting tired. His arms felt achy, but there was no way he was going to say a word. It must have been about two hours of nonstop work, and Johnny exhaled forcefully.

"Alright there, boy. Ready for a break? Come on over to my other office," said Leroy.

"What, am I gonna clean the shitters next, boss?"

Leroy laughed a big, from his belly, laugh. He seemed to like Johnny.

Leroy led Johnny to a small little office in the back of the kitchen. Sitting down at the table, Leroy put down a plate with a hamburger and some Pepsi Cola.

"Eat up, boy. Gotta long way to go. Go on!"

"Thanks Leroy, I'm starvin'"

"That's okay. We take about ten minutes, Mr. Johnny, and then we back at it. Later, when dishes be all caught up and what not, I teach you how to bus them tables and make you some real money."

"Bus?" asked Johnny.

"Boy, what in the ham sandwich you been doin' all you life? Bussin' mean getting' all the dishes and glasses and shit and bringin' 'em on back. You be splittin' them tips with the waitresses too," Leroy explained.

Leroy went on to explain that he used to be a car mechanic and a good one.

"What made you stop that?" asked Johnny.

"Well, the new boss man, he didn't take too kindly to what he called 'niggers.' Johnny, lemme tell ya somethin' son. Try to never use that word 'round a black man. It's a very ugly, hurtful word."

Johnny nodded his head in agreement. After eating, Johnny went back to his rubber gloves, and steamy hot water. True to his word, Leroy took Johnny out to the cafeteria and showed him how to clean off the tables and then wipe them down. Whatever tips were left were split up with the servers.

"When do I get to be a server?" asked Johnny.

"Mr. Johnny! You no like worken with your favorite black man in all history, now?"

Leroy said this with a huge smile and that big belly laugh of his. Johnny liked to work with Leroy. He was funny, smart and the time went fast. Before he knew it, it was time to go.

"Oh man!" said Johnny.

"What is it, son?"

"I promised my dad I would make him some lunch."

"What your daddy like to eat? Old Leroy will make him up somethin' and you can give it to him, okay?"

"Well, thanks Leroy, but he's kinda stubborn. He always wants to pay his own way."

"Well, no worries, we be takin' it off your pay!"

Johnny had a surprised look on his face. But Leroy was just messing with him. Johnny had a strange feeling that he had seen Leroy before. Perhaps when he was young, maybe even very young. Thinking back to when he was about five, Johnny could remember walking down the dusty apartment steps on Christopher Avenue. That distinctive hollow thud, followed by the rusty sounding creaking of that heavy metal door. Johnny could barely open that big door, but one evening when he did, he saw something that he would never forget.

Across the street, a group of about ten men, all of them white, were giving a terrible beating to a black man. They beat him so badly that Johnny started to shake with fear. But he couldn't look away.

"Lay him down in the street!" yelled one of the men.

"What did I do? I didn't do nothin'. Please lemme go. I have kids and a wife," pleaded the bloodied and battered man.

"Fuck you, nigger! Don't you be walkin' down our street. We don't want your kind around here!" yelled another of the men.

"Please just lemme go. You won't see me ever again. Please! I needs to take care of my family. Please…"

"Stop your beggin', coon. Open his mouth and put it on the curb. I'm gonna stomp on his head 'till his brains explode!" screamed an angry man.

"Nah, let's string his black ass up. You know, like the good 'ol days. Lynch a damn nigger. We were born too late. Missed out on all that lynching fun!"

As the men pulled the poor soul back up, they dragged him into a building across the street. Johnny boy just stood there. Almost frozen, he watched as the men pulled the man out of a first story window and out onto the fire escape. With an uncaring brutality, the men aggressively tied a heavy and coarse looking rope around the crying man's neck.

"Look at him shake! We ain't gonna let these damn niggers take over!"

As they tied the rope, tighter and tighter, the man's screams were stifled and he gasped for air. With no warning at all, they shoved him off of the fire escape and the short rope came to an abrupt stop. An agonizing sound of air coming from the tortured man's mouth, brought Johnny boy to attention. He watched as the man swayed back and forth, white foam starting to escape from the corners of his mouth. His dark facial skin started to take on a purplish hue. Eyes bulging, he was losing his fight…his will. Soon, his head hung. He was dead.

"John! Come back to apartment!" screamed his father, as he dragged him from behind, back through that metal door and up the old wooden steps.

"Where you be at boy? Where you done gone?" asked Leroy.

Johnny snapped back into reality and focused his eyes back to his new friend.

"I'm sorry. I was just thinking back to something horrible that I saw when I was a little kid."

"Care to talk about it?"

"I didn't grow up with many black people, Leroy. I remember though, a terrible scene…"

Johnny went on to describe what had happened. Expecting Leroy to recoil in horror, that's not what happened at all.

"Shit, that ain't nothing. When I was oh, 'bout in my mid-twenties, I was livin' in Georgia. I found work in a shoe factory in Atlanta, when the race riots broke out. He musta been 'bout fifty or so but they got my daddy. Said he raped a white woman. They hung a damn rope under his armpits and lowered his feets into the fire. He screamed and screamed. They just laughed. You could smell the skin on his feet's cooking. But they cared none. Thought it was all fun. We cared for him best we could but infection set in and he passed about a month later."

"John? We go now."

Johnny's father had come into the cafeteria and it was now time to go.

"Okay now, Mr. Johnny, see you tomorrow, now."

"Okay, Leroy. Oh, Leroy…"

"Yeah, Leroy know. Bus them tables. I know. I know!" said Leroy as he laughed and laughed.

Asa they walked away, Anatole glanced back towards Leroy.

"Good man?" asked Johnny's father.

"Yes, Leroy is good. I like him."

"You know, John, manners say you introduce your father. You ashame I no speak good English?"

"No, Dad. No way. I just forgot. I'm sorry."

Johnny and his father made their way home. Both were tired and in fact, Johnny couldn't keep from having his head drop down in exhaustion. Johnny sure did have fun and Leroy was a great guy, but he was exhausted. Johnny said a little prayer that he'd never have to wash another dish in his entire life. As Johnny and his dad approached their Ralph Avenue apartment, they spotted a gorgeous red Cadillac sitting out front. This wasn't the type of car that you'd normally see in this neighborhood. In fact, Johnny had never seen a car like this. The setting sun cast its amber hues on the deep red paint, and the beautiful car looked as if it was glowing. Luminescence, and not the usual dirt, seemed to rise from this amazing looking vehicle, forming a halo of beauty.

"Mr. Rostov? Anatole Rostov?"

"Yes, who are you?" asked Anatole.

"I'm a fan. Of your painting. I'm on the east coast on business with my wife Helen. I'm sorry, where are my manners? My name is Harry. Harry Donegan. I have friends that know Herbert Hoover. Our former President."

Johnny noticed the expression on his father's face suddenly change. His eyes filled with passion, his energy returned.

"I sell paintings to President Hoover, many years back."

"Yes, I know. My wife Helen is a big fan of yours. She'd like to commission you to paint some pictures. Top dollar we're talking about now."

"Would you like come in?"

"Why, thank you but I'm late for dinner plans. Helen doesn't like it when I'm late. Woman, you know."

"Yes, woman. I know," smiled Anatole.

"Here, if I leave you with these pictures, could you paint them? Standard sizes I suppose. Color. Even the black and white ones, she'd like painted in color. Can you do that, Anatole? I guess there's what, six of them? How much will that be?"

"Well, six? I can do for…"

"One hundred each. He's not cheap but he's good," interjected Johnny.

"John!" said an irritated Anatole.

"No, that's quite alright, Anatole. I like it. The kid has, well you know. He's not scared. We're in town for about ten days. Is that enough time? Here's three hundred dollars. A down payment. Is that enough?"

"Yes, this is good. Very good. I will do for you good job. Ten days. All done for you."

Harry Donegan got into his shiny car and took off. Just like that. Within five minutes, Johnny's dad had more money in his pocket than at any time since he was a very young man. When his own wealthy father had given him cash. Cash for his journey. To America.

"We're rich, dad!"

"No, but we eat good and pay electric. I take you to opera. You will like," said Johnny's dad.

The opera? Just what I fuckin' need. I need some pussy. I mean, can I get pussy at the fuckin' opera? I can't take this anymore. Maybe Mrs. Williams and her big tits were out?" thought Johnny.

Anatole and Johnny made their way up the stairs. Their tired legs felt heavy. Once inside the apartment, Anatole kissed Sonia. It was rare that they were affectionate in front of Johnny. As Johnny hugged his mom, Anatole sat on the couch and looked at the pictures that Harry Donegan had given him.

Anatole was excited by what he saw. Always a fan of painting pictures of nature; trees and leaves were plentiful in these pictures. There was a charming looking hotel set back off a dirt road. Beautiful and majestic trees filled the landscape, surrounding the structure. Every painting must have a focal point and the hotel would be it. Golden leaves interspersed with dark reds and browns covered the rustic flooring, much like an outdoor carpet laid by nature's finest craftsman. Yes, Anatole had a sparkle in his eye. Perhaps things were getting better.

Chapter Twenty-Nine

JOHNNY CONTINUED TO work hard. He worked Monday through Friday and on occasion would get some weekend hours. Finally, Johnny had a day off. As he thought it over, there were two choices: Girls, or the library. Maybe he'd meet up with the fellas and they'd finally get some whores down in the hangout. The library would still be there.

"What are you to do today, John? Today is Sunday. Maybe you go to library. Read. In fact, let us do this together. I very much want to go. Come with me, okay, John?" said Sonia.

Johnny had already made up his mind that it would be the perfect day to take a walk over to Christopher Street. He hadn't hung out with Jimmy, Danny, and Mickey in quite a while. It still seemed strange to think of the boys without including Jackie.

You know…I can have a million friends, but I'll only have one mom.

"Sure, Mom. I'd love to go to the library with you. That's exactly what I'd love to do."

Johnny's mom's face lit up. A bit shy by nature, she loved her only child and always wanted their relationship to stay close. After all, while Johnny resembled his father as far as looks, it was becoming clearer daily, that they shared a love for literature, for books of all kinds. Johnny also got his sensitive side from his mother. Perhaps Johnny would even become a writer someday.

The Brooklyn Public Library was about a fifteen-minute walk. As Johnny and his mom approached the rather small brick building, Johnny abruptly grabbed his mother's arm.

"What is it John?"

"Mom, lemme walk you inside. Then I just must come out for a few minutes and then I'll come right back in to sit with you. Okay?"

"What is wrong?" she asked.

"Umm, nothing. I just see someone down the road that I think I recognize. Just wanna go and say hello. You know, real friendly like. Like you always want me to be."

Johnny, holding his mother's arm, escorted her up the ten cement steps and brought her to a nice quiet corner.

"Be right back, Mom," said Johnny in a very hushed tone.

Johnny gave his mom a kiss on the cheek and quickly exited the library and ran down the steps. Making a left, he walked in a very determined fashion up the block. About a hundred feet, on the right-hand side of the street, Johnny saw a pickup truck. An old and rusted one.

"Hey, if it's not my little friend from the boy's home."

"I thought that was you. What are you doin' around here Vinny?"

"Who me? You're not happy to see me, fire boy? What? You didn't think I'd hear about that? I know everything. But, I'm just here to visit my Uncle. My Uncle Fred," said Vinny.

"I thought you said he was your Uncle Al?"

"What? A guy can't have more than one uncle? So, how's high school treating you? You burn down anymore school houses, pal?"

Johnny could feel his body stiffen. He was getting that feeling. When Johnny got mad, his entire body felt like a searing heat was coursing throughout it. Hands clenched, Johnny felt for his knife. He had it.

"I have no idea what the fuck you're talkin' about, Vinny. I don't want you talkin' shit about me. Why don't you just get the fuck outta here, okay?"

"What, are we a tough guy now? Listen, asshole, I'm not some sleeping little boy that you're gonna set on fire. When you deal with me, I won't wind up lookin' like a burnt fuckin' match. I'm the real deal. A badass, that you want no part of. So, jerkoff, I want a hundred bucks. That buys you my silence. Otherwise, I go see that pretty lady you walked in with. How do you guys like living on Ralph Avenue? Nice over there, huh?"

Johnny saw red. Reaching for his knife, he stopped in his tracks as Vinny had a gun pointed right between his eyes.

"Whatever plan you got? Get another. I'll be back in a week or so. Don't worry. I know where you live. And that pretty lady!"

With that, Vinny hit the accelerator. A blast of foul smelling exhaust was all that was left in front of Johnny. Standing still for the moment, Johnny had a million thoughts run through his mind. Memories of that night returned. The sounds of the fire. The look on Stevie's pained face as his skin melted. The plan that he would have to come up with to deal with his new nemesis. For there was only one solution to this problem. He would kill Vinny. He simply had to.

Standing still for a few minutes, Johnny wanted to make sure that Vinny wasn't on his way back. His mind full of rage, Johnny felt confused. He wasn't gonna take shit off anyone. No one would ever hurt him again. But this time, there were other people involved. People that he loved. In fact, the person that he loved more than any other. His mom. Slowly turning back towards the library, Johnny made his way inside and found her sitting at a small table.

"John. What is it that is wrong?"

"Nothing, Mom. Really. I didn't know that guy. Was someone else."

Johnny and his mom both enjoyed their time together. This was nice. As Johnny sat there reading, he realized that he never really spent much time alone with his mom. His dad was always around. Johnny realized just how much he adored his mom. A tall woman, Sonia had a tough life growing up in Russia. Unlike Johnny's dad, Sonia's family was poor. Her father, a quiet and gentle soul, was a school teacher. During the summers when school was out, he would find work doing what was his true love, his passion…singing. Sonia's father would sing anything and everything. From jazz to opera. Sonia loved her father's singing, especially when he sang songs from the opera. Her mother worked in a factory that upholstered chairs. It was difficult work and was painful for her, as she developed arthritis in her hands. The cold temperatures of Russia made this even worse.

Growing up in the industrial region of Kiev, Sonia would often hear her parents talk of a simpler time, a better time. Both of her parent's families were involved in agriculture. It wasn't an affluent life, and the winters were harsh and long but there was always food.

As Johnny and his mom made their way home, Johnny stayed tense. As they walked, he kept one eye on the road ahead of him, and the other, constantly scanning in all directions, looking for Vinny. Things were going good for Johnny and the Rostov family. Johnny wasn't going to let anything change this. Certainly, not a guy like Vinny. Vinny was what Al would refer to as a "wannabe," a fake mobster.

Once safely home, Johnny started to plan. His number one goal was to make sure that his mother was safe. Johnny had a strong feeling that Vinny would be back, and when he least expected it. But, he would die for his mother. He loved her that much.

In deep thought, Johnny startled when his father, turning the apartment's doorknob, entered and dragged in his easel and supplies.

"Hello, John. Remember, we go work tomorrow. You be ready, okay?"

"Of course, Dad."

"Dinner almost ready, Anatole. John, go wash up please."

The family sat together and ate. It was quieter than usual and Johnny felt strangely uneasy.

"What is it that is wrong, John?" Anatole.

"Nothing, Dad. I'm just thinking."

"What is it you think so much concerning?"

"Nothing. You know. Girls, money, getting a car someday."

"A car?" asked Sonia.

"Good to dream, Sonia. Let him have goals. Want him to have better than we do."

"I want to go to college someday also, Dad. I really love to read and I think I'm interested in writing as well."

"This is good. I am artist. Your mother is writer. We no have lots of money but we are talented family."

All that Johnny really had on his mind was Vinny. Vinny, knives, and guns. Maybe he should talk to Al. Actually, maybe not. The less people that knew about this, the better.

"I'm all done. May I please be excused, Dad?"

Johnny's dad simply nodded.

"Wash up, brush teeth," added Sonia, with a gentle smile.

"Always, Mom."

As Johnny lay in bed that night, he couldn't get Vinny out of his mind. He knew what he had to do. He just had to pick the right time. Johnny was never going to let anyone hurt him again. And that included no one hurting his family. Johnny's father had always taught him to walk on the other side of the street to avoid a fight. But to fight when he had to, to protect himself or his family. Well, Johnny hadn't always crossed that street, but this time, Vinny would feel his wrath.

Chapter Thirty

"HEY, JOHNNY! YA prick. Nice of you to visit," yelled Jimmy.

"Hey ,Jimmy. Day off today and wanted to come hang with the fellas."

"Yeah, it's been awhile. You know, we need to get some whores. My dick aches. I need pussy almost every day you know," said Jimmy.

"You crack me up. The next time you get some pussy will be your first," added a laughing Johnny. "I think I wanna go and visit my old neighbor, Mrs. Mangione.".

"She gonna give you some pussy?" laughed Jimmy.

"Hey! Fuck you. That's Mamma! She a sweet…"

"I know, I know. I was just kidding! Calm the fuck down."

"Come on Johnny, let's you and me get some whores. I need some pussy," added Jimmy.

"Okay, I'll go see Mamma afterwards. And shut the fuck up with the wise cracks, asshole."

"I didn't say shit, Johnny!"

Johnny's next pussy would be his first also. He wouldn't tell Jimmy that though. Hell, he wouldn't tell anyone that.

"I usually go see Al and he sets me up with some whores. I'll go over and see him now. Meet you in the hang-out in a little while?" asked Johnny.

Walking to the run- down candy store, Johnny hoped that this would go well. After all, he needed to get some pussy experience. His senior year was approaching, and with his big dick and great looks, he was gonna have the time of his life.

"Johnny boy! How are ya, kid? You need more guns? Knives?" laughed the large Italian mobster.

Al was a large man. No matter how hot it was out, or how cold it may be, Al always wore that overcoat. Made him look classy. A sharp dresser no matter what the occasion, Al demanded respect. He was distinguished. But the murderous hitman always resided below the coat.

"Come on Al. My name is Johnny! No more Johnny boy!"

"Okay, okay. Calm down, kid!"

"Listen Al. I have an achy dick. I don't fuck a broad for a week and I get all backed up. You have some girls you can send across the street for me and Jimmy?"

"Achy, huh? Kid, you ever been laid? Come on. We all have to have our first."

"Well…okay, no. Not yet. But, I've come close. Hundreds of times!"

"Yeah, okay, kid. Close, right in your own hand maybe. I got ya. Thirty minutes. I'll send over my two best. Same place that you guys always hang? That basement?"

"Yeah, how'd you know that?" asked Johnny.

"Al fuckin' knows everything, kid."

Johnny's heart was beating out of his chest.

"Oh, Al. How much?"

"Don't worry about it. It's on me this time. But you hafta treat 'em nice! Hear?"

As Johnny nodded his head yes, his nervous anticipation was getting the best of him. Would he get his dick sucked too? Oh shit, what if his balls smelled? There was nothing that a woman hated more than a set of nasty, hairy, and smelly balls. This is what Johnny had heard anyway. Walking down the stairs, Johnny explained everything to Jimmy.

"Holy shit! Whores? You did it! Shit! When?" asked Jimmy.

"Thirty minutes. Be calm. Like me. And wash your balls. I know these things. We're gonna get our dicks sucked too," smiled Johnny.

"Yeah, you know shit," cracked Jimmy.

"Listen, you want some pussy or not? Go wash your balls!"

Johnny and Jimmy washed up and tried to straighten the place up a bit. There was an old dusty, but soft couch at the far end of the basement. Johnny was calling that one. A second couch, a good distance away, a bit smaller but it would have to do for Jimmy. They'd at least have a little bit of privacy.

The waiting was the worst.

Shit, I washed my balls and now I wait. I hope they don't start stinkin' up again.

The boys both startled a bit as there was a knock at the old basement door.

"Get it," said a nervous Jimmy.

"Fuck you, you get it," said an even more nervous Johnny.

The boys, both moving simultaneously, bumped into each other.

"Watch where you're goin!" said Jimmy.

"Fuck you!"

Opening the door, the boys saw two of the most beautiful ladies they had ever lay eyes on. The one that Johnny was more drawn to was a brunette with dark, shoulder-length hair that was shining like she was in the sun. Even more importantly, she had huge tits.

"Well, hello boys. I'm Raven and my beautiful blonde friend is Sharon. Al sent us over and said to give you two handsome men an extra good time."

"Okay, uh, good," said a tongue-tied and nervous Johnny.

"Okay, fellas. Where can we go so we can get to know each other a little better?" asked Raven.

Johnny and Raven made their way over to the larger of the two couches. As Raven sat down, Johnny shut a few lights to give both he and Jimmy some more privacy.

As Johnny sat next to Raven, she wasted no time. Unbuttoning her white blouse, Raven was wearing a huge white bra.

"Care to help me with this? What was the name again?"

"Umm, John. Johnny, I mean."

Johnny fumbled with the hooks that were restraining the biggest tits he'd ever seen. Finally loosening the huge boulder holder, he slid the bra off Raven's shoulders. Turning back towards Johnny, Raven grabbed Johnny by the back of his head and pulled his face into her ample bosom.

"What's that you hidin' in your pocket, handsome?" smiled Raven.

Johnny looked down at his torn and beat up pants. His dick was half way down his leg.

"This may actually be some fun. Johnny is packin' I see."

Pulling off Johnny's pants, and his underwear, Raven went to work with her mouth. Making sucking sounds, her head bobbed up and down. Johnny couldn't believe anything could ever feel so good.

"Holy shit!" gasped Johnny, as he exploded into Raven's mouth.

Wiping what she didn't swallow from her face, Raven started to smile.

"Gentlemen warn a lady, Johnny. Now that didn't take long at all. Too bad, I was looking forward to getting on top of that monster you have between your legs."

"I'm, ready," said an out-of-breath Johnny.

"Oh my, I see you are!"

Getting on top, Raven lowered herself onto Johnny's fully erect flagpole.

"Oh, my God you're huge! That things as big as my arm!"

Raven went to work. She was enjoying herself.

"I usually take a nap, but you're special. Come on Johnny, give it to me. That's it. Harder…more…harder."

Johnny, felt it building again. It felt so good that he didn't want it to end. He tried thinking of different things, anything to distract him, even Danny's ugly face, but it was too late.

"Oh my God, oh my God…again!" yelled Johnny as he emptied his huge balls into Raven for a second time.

"That's enough, big boy. Raven is all stretched out. I'm gonna be sore in the morning! Lord, even your balls are huge."

Johnny was flushed. His head was spinning and he was still hard as a rock and ready for more. He had totally forgotten about Jimmy.

"Hey, you all done Jimmy?"

Turning a few lights back on, Johnny could see that Jimmy was all dressed and sitting on the couch.

"Okay boys, Al took care of things. Oh my God Sharon, this one here is just huge. To die for."

As the ladies left, Johnny and Jimmy just sat there in amazement.

"Shit. We can be fathers now Johnny."

"What the fuck are you talkin' about? Next time we gotta use bags. Listen, I hafta run over and see Mrs. Mangione. I'll see you later."

As Johnny climbed the dirty and hollow sounding steps, his legs trembled. What was going on? Shaking his legs a little, almost as he shook his dick after takin' a piss, Johnny started to slowly run, hoping to get the feeling back. Johnny looked down the block and saw that something wasn't right. Huge clouds of sooty smoke were billowing out of his old apartment building. As Johnny got closer, he could see a tall and lean young man, running away from the apartment building.

As Johnny got closer and closer, his heart started to flutter and his stomach felt funny.

"Vinny! What the fuck did you do? Shit! No! Mamma! She better be okay. I'll kill you! I'll kill you!" screamed Johnny.

Vinny continued to run and soon disappeared into the drifting black smoke. Running as fast as he could, and choking on smoke, Johnny made it to the fourth floor. Pulling off his white tee shirt, Johnny placed it over his face to fend off the smoke from the growing inferno.

"Mamma! Mamma! Are you in there?"

Johnny tried to push the old door in. The door was so hot that it burned Johnny's hand. Kicking and kicking, Johnny finally busted down the old door and made his way into Mamma's flame engulfed apartment.

"Mamma!"

The apartment was a blazing inferno. The heat was so intense, that Johnny had difficulty even breathing. Keeping his eyes open was a challenge. Making his way over to the tiny kitchen, Johnny took his tee-shirt and ran some cold water over it. Draping it over his head, Johnny continued his pursuit of his beloved friend.

"Mamma! Where are you?"

Making his way down the narrow corridor, Johnny entered the small bedroom. Looking frantically for her, Johnny peeked around the far side of the bed.

There she was. Momma must have been trying to get to the fourth-floor window. Blood trickled down her face. Gently shaking the older woman, Johnny tried as carefully as possible to pick her up. Tiny in stature, she was heavy, none the less.

"Come on, Mamma. Hold on! I'll get you out of this. Please don't die! I love you, Mamma!"

Making his way back to the hallway, Johnny approached the stairway. The first six or so steps, as well as the landing area were totally engulfed in flames. Johnny had no choice. Wrapping his still damp tee-shirt around mamma's face and head, Johnny just went for it.

Searing pain coursed over his chest. Johnny could smell his own flesh burning. Fleeting thoughts of the cart-man, as well as Stevie, raced across his mind. Johnny could hear sirens now. He was almost there. Exhausted, and in extreme pain, Johnny used his foot to push open the door and tumbled onto the sidewalk. As he fell, he used all of his might to protect Mamma.

"Johnny! Johnny. You okay?"

Jimmy had made his way over to see what was happening.

"Okay, son. We'll take her from here," said a man with a fireman's attire on.

"Johnny! You're hurt, Johnny. Holt shit. Your fucking chest is all burned up!"

Blood had started to form human bubbles that were full of fluid. Johnny felt faint, but tried to get up.

"No son, stay there, we'll get you in an ambulance," said a guy who looked as if he was a cop.

"No! I need to make sure Mamma is okay!"

"That's your mamma, son?"

"No, she's a friend. Please, is she okay?" Johnny cried out.

"I don't know. I don't think she was breathing."

"No! She's gotta be okay. This is all my fault!"

"Why do you say that, son?"

As Johnny's mind searched for a way to answer that, another cop approached.

"Son…I'm sorry. No. She's not gonna make it. She's gone," said the cop.

"No! That mother fucker did this!" screamed Johnny.

"Who? Who did this son?" the cop asked.

"Vinny! That fuckin' prick!"

"You have a last name for this Vinny? How do you know him?"

With that, Johnny, struggling to stay alert, passed out.

"Johnny! Come on man. Not you too!" pleaded Jimmy.

The cop splashed a bit of water on Johnny's face, and he started to come to.

"Where is she? I gotta see her. I just gotta see her one last time!" cried Johnny.

Escorted by the cop, Johnny staggered to the ambulance. Mrs. Mangione's lifeless body, soot covered, lay perfectly still. Johnny leaned over and kissed her cheek.

"Don't worry, Mamma, I'll get him. I promise. You go and meet up with your Alfredo. Oh, please mamma, give Jackie a hug. He needs that sometimes."

"Let's go son, get in the squad car. I'm takin' you to the hospital. Your chest is full of burns and blood."

Not wanting to go, the pain was searing, so Johnny gave in.

Jimmy made his way to the Rostov's. He explained what had happened to Sonia. When Anatole got home, they made their way to the hospital.

Johnny's injuries were extensive. The doctors did a skin graft, but warned Sonia and Anatole that Johnny would always have an ugly scar as a reminder of that horrific day. Johnny slept for almost a week. Sonia and Anatole both worried a lot. A week was a long time. Sonia worried that her beloved son may never wake up. Finally, Johnny showed signs of coming out of it. His eyes fluttered and he began to mumble.

"Mom? Is that you?"

"John. You wake up. Thank you. You come back to us," cried Sonia.

Johnny's chest was covered in white, cloth bandages. There was a small little table next to his hospital bed. On top of it was a small little basin filled with water and a sponge.

Johnny and his parents spoke for about five minutes. Sonia cried and Anatole was quiet. Both were ecstatic that Johnny was awake. After filling him in on all that had transpired, Johnny, feeling exhausted, drifted back asleep. Johnny would remain in the hospital for another week and after teaching Sonia how to change her son's dressings, Johnny was released to his parents.

Slowly but surely, Johnny got better. Sonia loved her son and took amazing care of him. Jimmy and Danny both came to the Ralph Street apartment to check in on their buddy. Even Leroy visited.

"Hey there. My man! Don't think they too fond of the black man all about here, but I had to check on my best worker! How you be, Mr. Johnny?"

"I'm okay, Leroy. They tell you what happened?"

"Yes, sir. You be a hero, boy! You risked your life to save that lady!"

"Yeah. But I didn't. And that's all that matters, Leroy. I fucked up."

"Boy, what in the ham sandwich you be talkin' 'bout? That wasn't Mr. Johnny's fault now. You risked your damn life! The good Lord be decidin' these matters, not Mr. Johnny."

"Leroy. I gotta come back to work. Please. I can't lose this job. I need the money. I need a car. I need money to save for college!"

"Slow down now. Whenever you parents say it's okay, we got you all lined up. No washin' dishes tho, boy. You be bussin'," said Leroy with a big grin.

Not really in the smiling mood, Johnny just nodded his head. He was sad. He was mourning the death of his friend, Mamma. He was also blaming himself. If he wasn't fucking those whores he may have been able to get there a little bit sooner. In time to see Vinny. Stop Vinny.

Anatole, Sonia, and Leroy chatted a bit, and it was decided that Johnny would need about another week to be ready for work. Physically that is. The dishwashing would be no good for a while, as the heat would be too painful. But bussing really appealed to Johnny.

Johnny waved goodbye to Leroy and said that he'd see him in a couple of days. Slowly, Johnny got out of his bed. Heading to the bathroom, Johnny slowly undid his bandages. All the bleeding and oozing had stopped. And while he still had a bit of pain, it was nothing like it had been.

After dinner, Johnny lay in bed and thought about Mamma. Vinny had shown just how dangerous he was. He had to be stopped before he hurt anyone else. Before he hurt Johnny's mom. Tossing and turning a bit all night, Johnny went over a plan. He would kill Vinny, anyway he could. But what he wanted to do is cut him up. Make him suffer, just like Mamma must have suffered.

"I'm feeling a lot better, Mom. I really wanna head over to Christopher Street and hang with the fellas."

"Let me look. I change bandages for you."

Sonia carefully pulled up her son's tee-shirt and gently changed his bandages. Johnny changed his shirt and headed out. Maybe he would talk to Jimmy or Danny about Vinny. This had to be done, but done right.

As Johnny made his way to Christopher Street, he kept looking around. He had no idea when Vinny could show up, or where he was living. Maybe he should head towards the library. After all, that's where he last saw him.

"Hey, Johnny. The hero returns! How ya feelin'?" asked Danny.

"I'm no hero," answered a sullen and stern looking Johnny.

Danny could see the discomfort in his friend's eyes…in his body language, so he left it alone.

"Where's Jimmy? You seen him?" asked Johnny.

"I hear my name? Johnny! Glad to see you."

The three boys strolled down the block and as they approached Johnny's old building, Johnny slowed to a halt. The bricks that surrounded Mamma's bedroom window were still soot and ash laden. No one said a word. They didn't need to. The silence said it all.

Johnny kept thinking. He was torn. Should he tell his friends about Vinny? He knew they would have his back. But this may be something that needed to be done alone.

"Listen. I gotta tell you guys something. But it goes no farther. Okay?"

"Yeah, what the fuck…no farther," said Danny.

Johnny spent the next forty-five minutes explaining everything. Jimmy already knew about the fire at the boy's home but he went over everything again.

"Holy fuckin' shit. That cock-sucker. Let's kill that mother fucker! I'm pissed!" yelled Danny.

"Shh. See what I mean? We gotta be real quiet like," implored Johnny.

"Maybe we should go and talk to Al?" asked Jimmy.

"I wanna cut this mother fucker up. I wanna make him suffer. There ain't nobody out there that can use a knife like I can," said Johnny.

The boys decided that the only way to find Vinny was to walk from the library and check out the streets all around it.

"Look for an old, rusted out pickup truck. Think the paint was red before it got all worn off and rusted," said Johnny.

The boys walked and walked. After about two hours, they decided to call it quits for the day and head back.

"Holy shit! Look!" yelled Danny.

As Johnny looked in the direction that Danny was pointing, sure enough, a rusted out, old pickup truck was sitting there. Parked a few car lengths away from a tiny grocery store. It looked as if Johnny may have found his man.

"Look, you two guys go in there. Buy a bottle of pop. He'll recognize me. He's pretty tall, about six feet, kinda skinny, and he talks real loud-like," said Johnny.

Danny and Jimmy walked across the street and entered the small, but very neat and orderly shop. Sure enough, unloading a cart full of cheeses and beans was a guy who fit what Johnny was describing perfectly.

Danny, looking enraged, took a few steps towards the young man.

"Hey! Where you goin'?" asked Jimmy in a hushed tone.

"I'm gonna fuck this bastard up," said Danny.

"No! Come on. Let's get some pop and go talk to Johnny. Like he said to."

"That'll be eight cents, boys," said the older woman at the counter.

The boys paid for the pop, and headed towards the door. Before exiting back to the street, Danny turned and got one more look at Vinny.

"What are you lookin' at?" said Vinny in a very angry tone.

Vinny glanced towards the front counter to see if the older woman was looking.

"Come on, come on!" said Jimmy.

Now Danny really had it in for Vinny.

"That fucker is a punk, I'm gonna kill him," said a pissed off Danny.

"It's him alright. And he's a piece of fuckin' shit!" said Danny.

"I seen the sign on the front door, Johnny. They close in an hour. How 'bout we wait and cut the bastard up then as he's leavin'?" asked Jimmy.

Johnny was in a trance. He couldn't get Mamma from his thoughts. It was as if a picture was etched in his mind and it wasn't leaving.

"Yeah, that's what we do. But he's mine. You guys wait off to the side. In case I need you's."

Johnny felt for his knife. It was there. It was sharp. He was ready. Still feeling a little weakened from his ordeal, it didn't matter. He just couldn't wait.

The boys all waited, as the sun set. Brownsville, despite all its filth, had a special type of pretty during a summer sunset.

It was now pretty dark out. Outside of the occasional horn honking, all seemed calm.

"There he is!" said Danny.

Cigarette dangling from his mouth, the tall lanky teen walked out of the store.

Johnny made his move. Quickly, he pounced. Reaching for his knife, he came from behind Vinny and raised the knife to strike down on the taller opponent's neck.

As Vinny reached for the door handle, he saw Johnny's reflection in the old trucks window. Vinny ducked down as Johnny missed and tumbled forward. The knife fell to the street and slid under the pick-up.

"You little, useless piece of shit! You can't take me down. I'm gonna fuck you up! I told you, I'm the real deal," yelled Vinny.

Danny and Jimmy charged from the side alley.

"He's all mine," yelled Johnny.

As Vinny laughed, the two boys squared up. Even in his weakened condition, Johnny had no doubts.

With much longer arms, Vinny was popping Johnny's head back with vicious jabs. Getting inside and tying up his taller foe, Johnny pounded Vinny's ribs as he winced in pain. Shot after shot, Johnny was really getting the best of him now. With every last ounce of his might, Johnny reared back and landed a crushing left hook to Vinny's ribs. Doubled over in pain, Vinny

Knowing the inevitable, Vinny reached into his pocket, felt for his knife and came out swinging. The blade came close to Johnny's face. Jumping back, Danny and Jimmy moved forward.

"Better stay back or I'll slit his throat! Now I butcher you up, real good, tough guy!" yelled Vinny.

Vinny was coming very close to hurting their friend. Johnny was exhausted, as he wasn't fully recovered yet. The two were in a locked-up position, Vinny struggled to extend his arm and end it all for Johnny. Suddenly, Johnny fell to the ground. Jumping on top of him, Vinny had him. As he prepared to come down on Johnny's face and neck with his weapon, Danny leapt and reached under the pick-up. Getting Johnny's knife, he quickly got up as Vinny's arm was coming down.

"Ahh...shit!" yelled Vinny.

Danny had plunged the sharp instrument right into the base of Vinny's skull. Blood spurted out, and soon covered the sidewalk.

Getting to his feet, Johnny pulled the knife out from Vinny's head. In a rage like he's never felt before, Johnny slit his throat. Again, and again, he plunged the knife into Vinny's lifeless body.

"Come on Johnny, put that knife away and take off that shirt. Danny, help me load this asshole into the pick-up. Now!"

Johnny pulled off the blood-soaked shirt and helped his two friends put Vinny's shredded body into the front bench seat of the pick-up. Putting his shirt over Vinny's face, he pulled the lifeless body to the floor.

"Fuck you, asshole! Yeah, I won't forget. You're the real deal alright. Burn in hell, mother fucker!" said Johnny.

The boys started to nervously walk away. Sweating now, they agreed not to run, as this would just garner more attention. As the boys got back to Christopher Street, they all agreed that they would never speak of this day again. Ever.

"You guys gotta promise. Okay? Lemme hear it," implored Johnny.

"I promise," said Jimmy.

"Me too. I promise," added Danny.

This promise meant everything to Johnny. He could put up with a lot of things, but lying from people he cared for, that was just wrong. Friends just didn't lie to each other.

As Jimmy took off for home, Danny asked Johnny to stop at his place to wash up a bit.

"No one's home. Come on. We'll get you washed up and I'll give you a shirt to wear."

Danny's apartment was nice. Nicer than the one Johnny had grown up in. Danny had two siblings, an older sister, Melissa, and a younger brother, Billy.

"What's up, Johnny?"

"Hey, Billy. What's up?

"You got blood all over you. You guys get in a fight?" asked Billy.

"Nahh, we just were runnin' from some niggers. They outnumbered us. You know how they are. They won't fight you one on one. Tripped and fell," explained Johnny.

"Fell on your face, huh?"

"Just wiped the sweat off my face, musta got some blood on it," said Johnny.

Billy was a twelve-year-old smart-ass. He had to have taken courses in school, to get this good. Danny loved his brother, but he sure did get on his nerves. Awhile back, Danny had a real looker in his room. They were making out and Danny was making progress. Lifting this beauties sweater over her head, she started to scream. Danny hadn't a clue what was going on but Billy had hidden in the closet, timed it and reached out and squeezed both of this girl's ample tits. Johnny had always wanted a little brother, a tit mauler or not.

"Thanks, Danny. Appreciate it."

"Come on…no problem. We're brother's, Johnny."

"No, you're not. I'm your brother, Danny. Asshole."

With that, Billy ran out of the apartment and into the long, dark hallway. Well, one thing was for sure now, and that was there'd be no looking over anyone's shoulder for Vinny. Ever.

Chapter Thirty-One

JOHNNY WAS QUIET when he got back to his Ralph Avenue apartment. He seemed to have a strange calmness that just took over his mind and body. Johnny felt no guilt. He had never looked for trouble, but if trouble came looking for him, Johnny would always be ready. And he took care of business. No one would ever hurt him again. Or anyone that he cared about, or loved. Pretty much fully healed now, Johnny would have some nasty scarring across his chest. Hoping that the scars would fade, he was somewhat self-conscious about anyone seeing them. Jimmy and Danny had, but he'd make sure to always have a shirt on now.

The Rostov's new apartment certainly wasn't brand new, but it was a big step up for them. Anatole had never even used his latest invention, the paint roller. Well, besides the hideous home-made green paint that Johnny and he used at the Christopher Street dwelling. The walls were all an off-white color and Sonia had been asking for some different colors to liven up the place a bit. The living room was a bit smaller but as far as Sonia was concerned, a good trade-off. Her new kitchen was close to double the size now. Johnny's bedroom was still small but had a window and at night, with even the smallest of breezes, brought in a welcome, cooling relief from the oppressive summer heat. Lying in bed that night, Johnny kept thinking of the whores. Raven sure was amazing, and now that Johnny had officially become a man, he had big plans. Mrs. Williams would just have to fuck him. After all, an experienced whore like Raven had said he had a huge cock. Johnny rubbed one out, thinking of that blowjob. Then he whacked off again, remembering Raven on top of him, grinding her pussy into him. Johnny couldn't get Raven's huge tits out of his mind either so he jerked off for a third time.

Shit, something is fuckin' wrong with me. I could jerk-off ten times a day. Man, do I love pussy, he thought.

Finally drifting off, Johnny had put his nemesis, Vinny, totally out of his mind. Besides, pussy had complete control over him, there wasn't any room for anything else. His mind was full.

"John! Wake up! We leave in ten more minutes!" yelled Anatole.

"What? Leave for where? I'm tired…"

"Get up. I leave for work and so do you. I not be late. Ever! Always get to job early."

"Okay, Dad. I forgot. I'll be ready."

Johnny moved quickly and got himself into the bathroom. He had grabbed a clean tee-shirt to change into. As Johnny stood in front of the bathroom mirror, he slowly raised his shirt over his head. His wounds weren't completely healed and scabs were sticking to the shirt. The scarring was hideous.

"Let's go, John!"

Johnny was frozen as he stared at himself. How would girls still want him, with such a horrendous scar on his chest? Putting on the new tee-shirt, washing his face, and brushing his teeth, Johnny was now ready.

The subway was empty and barely a word was spoken. It was just his father's way, Johnny figured.

Exiting the train, Johnny and his dad walked the few blocks to the museum.

"Okay, Dad, see you later. You want me to make you a sandwich?"

"No, son. Your mother make food. I no afford more. She always leave to me a little note. Make me happy."

Johnny knew better than to offer his father a free sandwich. Anatole Rostov paid his own way.

"Well, my man! You miss your boss, 'Ol Mr. Leroy? How you be, Mr. Johnny? The pain all gone? Workin' with a hero! That's right!"

"I'm no hero, Leroy," responded Johnny in a very subdued tone.

"Okay, Mr. Johnny. I'm sorry. I just be proud. Listen, we gonna have you do some bussin', okay?"

"No, I'm okay. I can get back to the dishes."

"We gots someone doin' 'em for now. A week or two and we switch you guys up. No one can replace Mr. Johnny, don't you worry 'bout that! It's all good. Leroy likes to have everyone doin' everything."

Johnny went into the room behind the back counter. Steam was already billowing up from the long double sink.

"Holy shit!" said Johnny.

Turning around, the new dishwasher had a pretty little smirk on her face.

"I mean...I'm sorry for cursing," said Johnny.

Wearing the usual white tee-shirt and slacks, the newcomer also had a black apron on.

Damn. I can't see her tits! thought Johnny.

"Mr. Johnny, this be Darla right here."

"Hi, Johnny! Don't get too used to bussin'. I want that job back!" said Darla.

Standing about five-foot-tall, Darla was tiny. Johnny had always been attracted to tiny, petite girls. If they had big tits, he was a happy man. As Johnny worked the angles, he could see that Darla, while very cute, was lacking in the titty department.

She wants me. When she sees my big cock, she'll wanna fuck me every day. Maybe more. I really should just pull it out.

But Darla did have something that he had never really paid attention to before. An ass. For as slight as her tiny body was, she was blessed with the most beautiful, round, and curvy ass that Johnny had ever seen.

Oh yeah, I gotta have that ass! he thought.

"Okay, Mr. Johnny, stop your trippin' over your tongue now, and let's get to bussin'," said a smiling Leroy.

Work went by quickly. Johnny learned how to bus the tables easily. He did however, find every excuse in the books to make his way back to talk to, and stare at Darla. That ass was driving him crazy, and Darla knew it.

She's gotta be about my age. I wonder if she's ever gotten fucked. I mean, with all of my experience, and my huge cock, she'll never want anyone else again! She's got that look. I know she's tasted a few dicks too. Damn, I hope my balls don't smell.

Business was slow. Johnny really liked his boss. Whenever things slowed down, Johnny would always find work to do. The floors needed to be mopped, counters and chairs wiped down, food rotated forward, and more. That's one of the things that Leroy liked about Johnny. He never had to say a word to him.

"How you feel, boy?"

"I'm okay, Leroy. The burns on my chest still sting a bit. Especially when I sweat."

"You don't have bandages on there?" asked Leroy.

"Well, I did, but I stopped puttin' em back. They're annoying."

"What happened, Johnny? Did you get hurt?" asked a concerned Darla.

Johnny just stared at the wall. Mamma Mangione was a tough but very sweet and caring woman. That bastard Vinny. This was all Johnny's fault. If he hadn't set that fire, and he hadn't met Vinny, Mamma would still be alive! Johnny blamed himself for Mamma's death.

"I don't wanna talk about it!"

"Okay, I'm sorry. Don't be mad, okay?"

Darla was a sweet girl. She could see the pain on Johnny's face.

"No, it's okay, Darla. You'd have no way of knowing, right? I'm sorry for yelling."

"You have some folks just sat their behinds down. You okay there, Mr. Johnny?" asked Leroy.

"Yeah, I'm sorry, Leroy. I got it."

"All good, Mr. Johnny."

Johnny took the orders. They were a nice, young, wealthy looking couple. They had a young boy with them. He must have been about four.

"I wanna pop, Mommy. With ice."

Johnny turned back around and approached the mom.

"That okay, ma'am?"

Johnny waited but the young lady just kept staring at him.

"Umm, yes. That would be fine. A small one please. But no ice."

What the fuck was she staring at? Fuckin' people are rude. She probably wants some of what I have between my legs. Her old man ain't given' it to her right. You could tell in a woman's eyes. If she was starin' at your balls, she wanted it. Also, the way that they walked. A woman that was getting' it, walked different. Her hips moved around different.

Johnny just knew all of this. At least he thought he did. Handing the order slip to Leroy, Leroy was also looking funny at Johnny.

"Mr. Johnny. Go on back to the closet and get you another shirt. Put that one in the hamper and clean off that chest a bit. Okay?"

So that was it, thought Johnny.

Johnny's burns were oozing again. He probably wasn't ready for all of this, but he was hard headed. Walking back to the storage closet, and with his back to Darla, Johnny lifted his shirt, up and off.

"My oh my. Look at the muscles on your back!" said a giddy Darla.

Johnny turned around while slipping on the new shirt.

"Eww! That's disgusting! I can't even look at you. Gross!" said Darla.

Johnny was hurt. But he didn't say a word. Maybe this wasn't going to work out.

"I can't work with him, Leroy. That's disgusting!" said Darla.

"Excuse me, young lady? What you be sayin'?"

"It's gross. His chest has all burn marks and scabs on it! I should not have to work with someone like that!"

"Well no one told you to be lookin' at the man's damn chest now!"

"But…"

"No, you get your little chicken ass outta here. Get! Go on now!"

"You owe me my pay. Three days!" said Darla

"Go on now. We'll mail it to you. Go on before you get Leroy really pissed off at your big fat ass! Got an ass the size of Brooklyn. Fat little bitch."

Leroy said all of this to himself. For even though he was in charge, a black man just couldn't talk to a white girl like that. He would get fired. Or worse.

"Food's ready, Mr. Johnny! Here you go," said Leroy.

Darla took off her black apron and hustled on by Johnny.

"Disgusting!" she added on her way out of the cafeteria.

Johnny, shaken a bit, tried to act as if everything was okay. But Leroy knew better.

"Okay now, I gots this one. Here now, you let old Leroy handle this," said the understanding boss.

Leroy served the food, and went back to start on the dishes.

"I got this, Leroy. I have to do something. Maybe I shouldn't have come back so soon. I need the money and, well, I like working here with you."

"That steam is just gonna make it worse. Don't get that new shirt all wet now. You fine. Bus them tables and Leroy gots the cookin' and dishes."

Johnny worked the rest of the day in a daze. How could someone be so mean? Just before the end of his shift, Johnny thanked Leroy once again. He meant it. Here was a man that Johnny barely knew, his boss, and he was treating him like family.

"Okay, Leroy. Be back tomorrow. That is if you want me."

"What? Boy, you best be here. You's the best that Leroy has. Or ever has."

Johnny took off and met his dad outside.

"How work today, John?"

"It was okay."

"What is it that wrong?"

"Well, nothing really. Just that people can really be mean. Some girl saw my scars and said I was disgusting."

As Johnny and his dad walked to the subway, Anatole could see how upset his son was.

"Some people. They have no hearts. I have known many such people. What they do to me and my friend in Russia is something my mind never lets go of. I learn that these people, you must not hold what they say in your heart. It just hurts you and never them."

Johnny just nodded. His father was a wise man. Talking to Johnny was never easy for him. It didn't come naturally at all. But he tried. Johnny may have acted tough on the outside but his father saw more than that.

"Dad, what would you think if I became a writer? I mean, I love to read. All type of things. I was thinking that I would also like to write."

Anatole stiffened as he glared at Johnny. He had that look.

"You need to get job that you can take care of family. I no do good job with this. I want better for you."

The subway was crowded. Johnny and his father stood so that woman and children could sit. After thinking about it for a while, Johnny decided not to pursue this conversation with his dad. He certainly couldn't bring it up with the boys, no way they would understand. The ball busting would just go on and on. Maybe his mom. Mom was a writer and she adored her son and understood him. Johnny had always loved his mom, but now he really felt loved. Yeah, he was gonna talk to his mom about his writing.

"John. We go. John. You no want go home?" barked his dad.

Johnny had been day dreaming. Usually it was about sex, but this was different. The idea of someday becoming a writer really appealed to Johnny.

"Oh, yeah, Dad. Wait up."

Johnny and his dad walked down the stairs to the street. The heat was stifling, like a blast from a furnace, just smacking them in the face. Johnny's chest hurt. He could feel the perspiration sting his wounds.

"I hate the heat. Why can't we move somewhere cold?"

"You want move Russia? I think no," said his dad with a rare smile.

"Dad, you never really talk about Russia. Why?"

"If no talk about, then leave alone! Stay in my past!"

Johnny slowed his pace, his heart beginning to race. He still got a bit nervous when he saw that look. That look of anger. He would always remember what his father was capable of.

"Sorry, Dad."

By the time the father and son had reached their Ralph Avenue apartment, they were both saturated in sweat.

"You want ice cream or cold drink?"

"Who, me?" asked a startled Johnny.

"No, President Truman," said his dad with a slight smile.

Hortons Ice Cream and Fountain drinks, had the best ice cream around. Not that Johnny had been there much. Ice cream was expensive and it was a rare treat. Besides, any money that he and the boys got was going straight to paying for whores now.

Johnny and his dad opened the door to the sweets shop. A small little bell jingled as the door opened. Johnny followed as his father took a seat on a bar stool at the counter.

"Okay, gentlemen, what will you have?" asked the pretty waitress.

"I have the egg cream," answered Anatole.

"Me too. And a vanilla fudge sundae," said Johnny.

Johnny's dad just looked at his son and nodded.

The two sat quietly and finished off their treats quickly. Feeling refreshed, they both made their way home.

Chapter Thirty-Two

TIRED, JOHNNY WENT to sleep early that evening. His mom even wanted to talk about poetry, and his dad was playing opera on the old phonograph they had, but nothing interested Johnny. Not even jerking off.

Tired, but not yet sleepy, Johnny worried. What would girls say when they saw that scar? True, he had a huge dick, but girls were funny like that. He hoped that someday he'd meet someone. Someone special. Someone who would love him, no matter what. Scars or no scars. That they would have a true love affair. Forever. And maybe even lots of kids. Just like his father had met his mother.

The boys worked a lot that summer. They also got into their fair share of trouble as well. After all, this was the last summer of their lives. When school started up again, they would be seniors. Johnny really wanted to go to college. He may have to go at night. That way he could work during the days. Johnny's mind, finally putting the brakes on his run-away thoughts, let him drift off and finally, fall asleep.

Johnny woke up with his dick as hard as a rock. What a waste! By the time he hit the streets, his balls would smell. It just didn't seem fair. Laughing, Johnny got up and headed to the bathroom.

"Your father try wake you, John."

"For what, Mom? Oh, I know. I forgot to tell him. This chick, Darla, she quit, so Leroy hired two new people as backups. He let me have off today. No work."

"You have plans?"

"Not really. I was thinkin' I'd hang out with the fella's."

"Okay then."

"Why Mom? You need my help with somethin'?"

"I think to maybe talk to you about your future."

Oh no. I love my mom, but I hate these kinda talks.

"Okay, sure, Mom. I always like to talk to you. Especially when Dad isn't around. I mean…"

"It okay, John. I understand."

"Mom, when did you first start to love reading? And what about your writing?"

"Many questions, John. That okay. I look at you and many things like your father. You're strong like him. You are determined. I no worry too much about you making life for yourself because you are tough. You grow in Brownsville, so you can live everywhere. But you have passion. The passion to read. Read much, John. I feel you can, if want, write the stories of life as well. I long time no say nothing for this as I want you to choose own pathway to life. But now I say to you. I know my boy and you no want friends to know."

"Wait, how'd you know that?"

"Ahh, I am mother, I know many things. I no say many things, but I know them," said Sonia with a wide but gentle smile.

"I love talking to you, Mom. I love you."

Johnny was feeling emotional. His mother had always been an amazing woman, an amazing mother, but her timing was totally perfect today. If ever Johnny needed a boost, emotionally, it was today.

"So, this college. What is it you think?"

"Well, I want to still live at home. This way I can work and help you and dad as well. The only place would really be Brooklyn College. It's pretty close, on Bedford Avenue."

"How to pay, John? I feel so important for you to do, but your father and I no have that money. We try but no have. I feel badly."

"No, don't, Ma. I'm gonna keep working and after high school, I'll get a full-time job and go to school. I'll make it work, you'll see."

"I have no doubts for my boy. I love you so much, John Rostov."

"So, Mom. How is it that you write? I mean, how do you think of the things. I have so many things that are always moving within my mind, how do I put them on paper?"

"I take deep breath and clear mind. Then I picture myself in some place and I write down on paper what my mind sees. You try someday and let me read. You want, I will help."

"Thanks, Mom. You made me feel so much better today. Okay, I think I'm gonna go hang with the fellas now? I mean, if you really want, I'll stay here with you."

"No, of course. I am too much busy today. Many things to do. You go with friends. Have fun but no trouble. Remember…mothers know many things."

Johnny gave his mother an extra big hug and kiss. He had really gotten lucky to have such an amazing mother. He hoped to someday have a wife of his own. Just like his own mom.

Johnny made his way to Brownsville and ran in to Jimmy and Danny.

"Where's Mickey?" asked Johnny.

"Who the fuck knows. We haven't seen him too much. I think his dad lost his job and he's gotta work a lot so they don't lose their apartment," said Danny.

"Hey, kid!"

A beautiful, shiny red Cadillac had pulled up to the curb.

"I remember you. What happened? My dad finished all six of your paintings. You have his money?" Johnny asked Mr. Donegan.

"Sure kid. Slow down now. It's my fault. I was supposed to come back in ten days or so and…"

"Yeah, he worked his ass off and then…"

"I know, son. I was trying to say, yes, I got called away on business and haven't been to this part of the country for a while now. Is your dad around?"

"No. Well, I'm not sure. We live about fifteen minutes away now. Over on Ralph Avenue."

"Hop in. I'll take you home. Okay?"

"Okay. Listen fellas, I'll see you guys tomorrow. Maybe some whores?"

"Always some whores," laughed Danny.

Johnny got into the passenger side of this beautiful and luxurious vehicle. It even smelled amazing. Like woman's perfume.

"So Mr., How'd you…"

"It's Harry. Just call me Harry."

"Okay. Harry, how'd you get rich enough to get a car like this?"

"Well, Johnny, I got pretty lucky. Spent a few years riding the rails. Met an old timer who told me about the life. From the first time I heard his words, I knew it was for me. I actually fell in love with the romanticism of it all. I can't imagine that a tough kid like you would understand that type of thing though."

"What? Actually, Harry, I would. Or, I'm kinda startin' to. I just used to like school for the broads. You know, watchin' the tits pop. But I'm fallin' in love with books now. English Literature, poetry, the classics. I don't let too many people know."

"I understand, Johnny. It was tough, but I met a great friend. And he helped me out a lot. It's a long story but...I also met my wonderful wife, Helen, on the road."

"Make a left here. Okay, pull over...on the right. Lemme run up and see if my dad's home. If not, you pay me first and I'll get you the six paintings."

"Okay, Johnny, thanks."

Johnny ran up the stairs. He always made note of just how much more solid they sounded than Brownsville.

"Hey, Mom! Dad! You guys home?"

Not seeing or hearing anyone, Johnny returned to the luxurious vehicle.

"Nah, no one's home. Gimme three hundred and I'll bring you the six paintings. You'll be happy. My father's the best."

"That he is," as Harry unzipped a leather pouch and counted out sixteen twenty dollar bills, handing them to Johnny.

"Wait a sec...you gave me twenty too much."

"Very good. That's for you, Johnny."

Johnny hustled back to the apartment and retrieved the paintings. Damn, they were good. He also got the photos that his dad had neatly kept next to the finished pieces.

"Here you go, Harry. Where's the missus?"

"She's in Manhattan. Shopping. She'll be very happy to see these. Your father is a very talented man. Go with your passions, Johnny."

"Thanks."

"Take care. Who knows, maybe we'll meet again someday."

"Maybe."

Johnny headed right back upstairs and left the three hundred dollars in a box in his parent's room. Standing there for a few seconds, Johnny added the extra twenty.

They need it more than me. Besides, what I can't make, I'll hustle.

Johnny was feeling restless. He sometimes felt this way, almost a nervous energy within his legs. There was always one solution to this…walk! Johnny loved to walk. Now, Brooklyn wasn't exactly scenic, it still had its points of interest.

Johnny bounded down the hallway staircase and re-entered the world of Brooklyn. Heading south on Ralph Avenue, he wasn't really in a talkative mood and planned on just keeping to himself. He checked his pocket, just to make sure he had his trusted buddy, Mr. Knife. Man, the broads were out today. The sun was on the verge of setting, but the heat was still stifling. All the brick and concrete, plus the asphalt from the streets, held in the oppressive reminder of the sun's daytime visit. Johnny was sweating. His burns stung. Was this pain ever going to go away? Would he someday meet a girl who wouldn't cringe, or be disgusted?

"Hey good lookin'. Wanna a date?"

Johnny looked up and saw an ugly, middle-aged woman. She almost looked nervous. She was definitely a whore.

"No, I don't think so. Thanks though," replied Johnny.

He almost felt sorry for her. Johnny had eyes for the woman always, but was strangely subdued today. Perhaps the scarring on his chest was bothering him even more than he was aware of. Maybe he'd swear off woman for a while. Taking his walk down some side streets that he wasn't familiar with, Johnny kept his head on a swivel. This wasn't Christopher Street, but you still had to be careful.

Now sweating profusely, Johnny thought of taking off his tee-shirt. But he was in pain and figured he'd just do that when he got home. Plus, no one could say anything about the way his scars looked. It was starting to get dark and Johnny was completely lost. Retracing his steps, Johnny headed back towards Ralph Avenue.

"Hey you. You look lost?"

She was stunning. Just about seventeen, she had long, dark hair, and the most beautiful brown eyes that Johnny had ever seen. He even loved her voice. It was sweet, but she sounded smart. Maybe there were more to girls than just tits. Brains were starting to become important as well.

"Is it that obvious?" laughed Johnny.

"Just a little. What's your name?" she asked.

"Johnny. Johnny Rostov. And you?"

"Anne. Anne Shafer."

A Jew, huh? I've always liked Jewish girls. I heard they fuck really good.

"Nice to meet you, Anne. Do you live around here?"

"No, Johnny. I live in Florida," she said sarcastically.

"Okay, okay. We gotta wise one here. Beauty, and a sense of humor. You'll do,"

"Oh I will, huh? A girl have a say in this at all?"

"Oh, absolutely. Not!" laughed Johnny.

Johnny liked this girl. He felt at ease with her.

I hope that the first time I fuck her, she don't mind the scars.

"Where do you live, Johnny? What you doin' around here?"

"Just out walkin'. Needed to move. Things on my mind I guess. I live over on Ralph Avenue."

"Okay, anything you wanna talk over? I'm a great listener."

Is this girl serious? She really wants to know how I feel?

"There's a small park, down the road. You wanna go, sit and just talk?" asked Anne.

"Umm, okay. For a little bit maybe. Then I gotta get goin'. Don't want my mom to worry. She's the greatest. Always worries about me. I sure do love her. My mom."

Yeah that's it, Johnny. They always go for the guys that love their mothers. And then when she sees my huge cock, she'll wanna marry me!

Anne led Johnny to the park. Finding the bench, they both sat together.

"So, what's bothering you so much?"

"I dunno. Maybe I just don't know what I'm gonna do with my life. I have all this stuff inside of me. And it like, wants to come out. I don't talk it out so good though."

"Well, did you ever think about writing?"

"Yeah. That's it. I wanna. But I just can't let the fellas know. They'll never understand."

"What say's they hafta? I mean, if it's important, there's only one person that matters, and that's you."

This girl is makin' sense. Plus, her tits are lookin' awful good to me and that's makin' even more sense.

Johnny looked into her eyes. He leaned over and kissed her.

"Wait! What are you doing? I said talk! Talk only!"

Genuinely surprised, Johnny pulled back. This never had happened before.

"Umm, I'm sorry. I just thought…I mean…you know," Johnny stammered.

"Yeah, I know. Well, okay. I'm a nice girl. If you wanna talk, that's great. Anything else? We'll see. But not right away. Okay, Johnny? Got it?"

Johnny nodded as they both stood up. Starting to walk away, Anne assured him that she wasn't mad. He was just a little fast. For her at least.

"Follow your passions, Johnny. Come by and see me tomorrow?"

"Sure. I can't wait. I love it here in Florida. Want me to walk you home, Anne?"

"No. Thanks for asking, but I'm a big girl. But, that's so sweet."

Johnny watched Anne walk away. He kept watching until she faded into the urban darkness.

I'm in love. Look at that ass.

For the next week or so, it was pretty much the same routine. Johnny would work at the cafeteria with Leroy. The two new guys that Leroy had hired, were okay. Johnny had hoped they'd be girls, but it was probably better this way. After getting home, Johnny would kiss his mother, grab something to eat and take off. Walking. To Florida.

"Hey. Hi, Johnny. What's the matter? You look sad."

"Hi, Anne. I don't know. Summers half way over and I still don't know what I'm gonna do after graduation."

"There's plenty of time. You know, I noticed you in school last year. You used to be a skinny little kid, but you're so handsome now. I can't wait for everyone to see that we're together now."

"Wait. We are? Well, you wanna take a walk? To the park, maybe?"

"Why, Johnny? What exactly do you have in mind?"

It was dusk and the park was pretty empty. Finding a place behind some large evergreen trees, Johnny steered Anne towards a soft patch of pillow like grass. Helping Anne down, they lie side by side. Johnny reached over and but his hands, on Anne's tits.

"No kiss first?"

"Well, that didn't get me anywhere last time," laughed Johnny.

"You're so bad!"

Johnny went back to work, feeling Anne's tits and was kissing her passionately. Reaching down towards the bottom of her plaid skirt, Johnny ran his hands slowly up her thighs.

If my cock gets any harder, it's gonna explode!

Rubbing his fingers between Anne's legs, he felt her wetness. Johnny wasted no time and started to pull down her panties.

"Wait. Not here, Johnny!"

"There's no one here," whispered Johnny.

"I've never gone all the way before Johnny. I'm scared."

"Don't be. I'm really good at it. Here. Put your hand here."

Johnny loosened his belt buckle and unzipped his pants. His huge cock sprang to attention.

"Oh, my God! That thing is too big! No way…it's gonna hurt."

"No. No, it won't. Watch. I'll just go real easy like."

With that, Johnny pulled his pants all the way off. Getting on top of Anne, Johnny positioned his manhood between Anne's legs. He pushed forward about an inch. Then another.

"Is that it? It hurts!"

Johnny couldn't control himself and pushed forward as Anne cried.

"It hurts, Johnny."

"Should I stop? I mean...does it feel good at least?"

"Well, yeah, it does kinda. Just go slow."

Johnny tried his best to slow down. And he did. For about thirty seconds. Not being able to control himself any longer, Johnny plunged forward and pumped as fast as he could. It would only be seconds longer and he exploded.

"How was that?" asked Johnny.

"It was...okay. It stopped hurting, but that thing is so big. It's like a foot long!"

"Wanna do it again?"

"When? Now? No! I'm sore."

"Oh, okay. Maybe in five minutes?"

"Get dressed Johnny. Please hand me my panties. Get dressed before we get caught."

"I can't zip up my pants. I'm still hard. You know, it's really bad for a guy to be like this. You sure we can't..."

"No, Johnny. You're too much. Take that big thing and go home. We can talk tomorrow. If I can even walk," said Anne as she stood up.

Johnny kissed Anne goodbye and made plans to meet her again the next evening. Walking home, Johnny was finally able to zip up and close his belt. He did keep his eyes open for any more pretty girls.

Johnny slept well that night. That is, after he jerked off two times.

When he woke up, Johnny's balls ached. Washing his face with cold water, the cobwebs started to clear. He missed his boys.

"Good morning, John."

"Hi, Mom. I love you so much!"

"You in very good mood. This makes me so happy."

Johnny had a bite to eat and kissed his mom on the cheek. Running down the stairs, he exited his apartment and hit Ralph Avenue. It was a long walk to Christopher Street, and while he would occasionally make that walk, his balls ached. Johnny decided to take the subway. Walking up the metal steps to reach the platform, Johnny paid his nickel, and took a seat. The subway was pretty empty. He'd usually let a woman or kid sit, as his father had taught him to do that, but with achy balls, he was glad to just sit.

Johnny hit Christopher Street and started to walk. It was a cool morning. At least he wasn't sweating yet. Every time he did, his chest wounds would sting.

"Hey. Is that a Rostov? A Johnny boy sighting? What the fuck? You married?"

"Shut the fuck up, you ball buster. Been busy, that's all. No one's called me Johnny boy in a long time now."

"Yeah, well I was the inventor. Remember? A long time ago," said Jimmy.

The sun was just starting to peek out from behind the greyish urban clouds. Johnny had walked to Christopher Street to see his boys. No work today, and Johnny really missed the fellas.

"Listen Jimmy, you wanna try and get everyone together today? I miss the boys."

"It's gonna get too hot for a ballgame. Wanna get some whores?" asked Jimmy.

"Nah, I don't feel like whores today."

"What? Are you not feelin' too good?"

"I'm okay. I was thinkin' of walkin' to the library."

"What? Huh? The library? What the fuck? You get in trouble or somethin'?"

"No, I just promised my mom. She likes to read, and gets lonely goin' by herself. You know."

"Yeah, I know. And I know that your mom ain't here with you now."

"No shit. I figured that I'd hang with you geniuses for a while and take the subway back to Ralph Avenue, and then walk with my mom to the library. There's another one close to our apartment."

"You sure are spending a lotta time at the Library. You sure you ain't getting' all queer on us?"

"What the fuck did you just say, Jimmy?"

"Hey! Johnny...what's up?"

Danny and Mickey had just walked up, and Johnny forced himself to smile.

"Hey, what, are you shavin' now? Look it, Johnny is officially a man now. Probably still has a two-inch pecker though. About time,

Rostov. Thought you were gonna have that peachy face forever," cracked Danny.

"Look at your face in the mirror some time. Your face looks like a baby's ass. A nice, smooth, and shiny one," answered back Johnny.

"Come on, both of you fucks are baby faced pussies," said Mickey.

Mickey was probably the only one of the boys that had ever used a razor. He was really growing, now standing at least six feet tall. Shoulders much broader than the rest of them, Mickey was becoming an intimidating kinda guy.

"Let's get some beers. It's gonna be hot. It's early, but pussy boy here has to run back to his mommy to go read at the library, so let's get some now," said a sarcastic Jimmy.

"What the fuck is wrong with you Jimmy? I mean, you gotta start some shit over this? You wanna man up and swing? I'm getting' sick of you. Let's go! Right now."

"Whoa, whoa… come on now, Johnny. He was just bustin' your balls. What happened to family? We watch out for each other, not beat up on each other…right?" asked Danny.

Jimmy extended his hand towards Johnny. As Johnny started to shake it, Jimmy let loosed a monster of a fart.

"Damn! Holy shit, that fucker smells like a dog's asshole," said Mickey.

"Let's go, boys. A few blocks down. We can try to score some beers at Bay River Liquors. Who's got some money? Come on now, don't all you fuckers answer at once," said Danny.

The boys walked the few miles to Bay River. There were times that they'd pay a wino or a bum a little extra and they'd go in and buy the beers. Johnny always felt badly for these lost souls, but beer was beer.

"Mickey, since you shave now, why don't you go in and try? Two six packs?" said Johnny.

"Get Pabst. That's all I drink. Well, that's what my dad drinks, plus, it goes down smooth. Just like the broads we get," said Danny.

The boys all pitched in and Mickey walked into Bay River. The doorbell chimed as he opened the front door and the guy behind the counter glanced in Mickey's direction. The guy had on a white apron, looking sort of like a butcher. Square jaw, he looked like he could fight. Plus, he probably had a gun.

"Can I help you there, son?"

"Yeah, two six packs Pabst. Umm, please," asked Mickey.

The large man opened the glass doors to the cooler. Pulling out two six packs, he placed them on the counter, placing them in a large brown paper bag.

"That's a buck-fifty. Hey, how old are you?"

"Eighteen. Can't you tell? Look...I shave."

"A buck-fifty. I ain't got all day now."

Mickey counted out a dollar and fifty cents and put it on the counter.

"Fuck. What's this shit…all pennies?"

Mickey stood still for a moment as they guy counted his change.

"Okay, have a nice day now," said a nervous Mickey.

As he turned and headed for the exit, Mickey could hear the guy mumbling to himself.

"You got it? Holy shit, Mickey," said a surprised Danny.

Mickey carried the large brown paper bag under his arm, and headed towards the hangout. It had gotten warmer, and Johnny's clean white tee shirt started to stick to his wounds.

"Damn! This shit ain't ever gonna heal," complained Johnny.

"Ahh, quit bitchin'. Makes you look tough. Ain't no nigger gonna try and flush your head down the toilet while you're lookin' like this," said Danny.

"Yeah, well I really hope it's gonna by the time school starts up again," said Johnny.

"Aww, balls. Damn…we ain't got a can opener!" said Mickey.

"Gimme that. We don't need no can opener," said Danny.

Danny took one of the Pabst's and put the metal cap in the door latch. Quickly pulling the bottle, the top popped off.

"Damn, you got skills. Take a few more," said Mickey.

Mickey opened a few more beers and the boys sat around the dingy hangout. Johnny turned on all the lights and put on an old radio.

With some Frank Sinatra playing in the back- round, the boys sat there drinking their beers.

Johnny wasn't a big drinker, but he was extra thirsty. He downed a few and felt a buzz.

"I'm gonna get outta here someday. Gonna go to college, become a writer maybe. I'm gonna meet the girl of my dreams. The best broad anyone could ever find. She's gonna be real special like," said a slightly drunk Johnny.

"Ahh, that's the fuckin' beers talkin'. Slow down, Johnny. Maybe we shoulda built our hangout in the fuckin'' library?" laughed Jimmy.

Johnny didn't care what the boys thought. Yeah, it was the beers, but also what Mrs. Mangione had said. Not to care what his friends thought. He needed to follow his passions. And no one was gonna stop him. Not now. Not ever.

"I'm just sayin', it ain't wrong to want things."

"I want things too. I wanna fuck you in your ass," said Danny.

Total silence. Danny's eyes darted around the hangout. Jimmy and Mickey had a serious look, and Johnny was looking down. After a moment, Johnny raised his head.

"Hell no. No way! I wanna meal, not a fuckin' snack!"

The rest of the boys exploded in laughter. Big, robust belly laughs.

Everything was good again. The library could wait for another time. For today, this is where Johnny wanted to be. This is really where he belonged.

Chapter Thirty-Three

"WAKE UP, YOU dickhead. You got so drunk, you fell asleep. Johnny! It's late. You better get your ass home," yelled Danny.

Johnny started to stir. Slowly, he escaped his sleep induced fog.

"Oh shit! I was supposed to meet Anne. I'm fucked now. What time is it?"

"Eight-thirty. You passed the fuck out," added Mickey.

"Who's Anne?" asked Jimmy.

"You getting' some pussy, and you ain't tellin' us? You prick," said Danny.

"She's just a friend. I still have time. Lemme get my ass to the subway. She's gonna be pissed."

Johnny shook his head side to side, trying to wake himself up a little more. It was more than getting laid. He thought that he really connected with Anne.

"I'll see you fellas. I gotta go."

Johnny made his way up the dingy basement steps and out onto the hustle and noise of Christopher Street. Johnny got the first subway he could and as fast as he could, made his way to the park where he had fucked Anne.

Looking all around, Johnny was all alone. Johnny started to leave, and saw a figure in the darkness. It had to be her, look at that ass!

"Anne! Hey, wait up!"

As Johnny started jogging towards what he hoped was Anne, he realized it was in fact her. Turning around, he could see that she wasn't looking very happy.

"Well, I didn't think you were gonna show. I waited and waited."

"I'm sorry, Anne. I hadn't seen my boys in a while and we got a few beers, and I fell asleep. I got here as fast as I could. I'm sorry."

"A few beers. Johnny, your breath stinks. No kisses for you tonight."

"Would sucking my dick be out of the question?"

"What did you say? How could you talk to me like that?"

"I'm sorry, Anne. See what happens when I start to hand out with my boys. I just get used to talkin' like that. I'm sorry."

"Well, okay. Just don't let it happen again. And who knows…maybe I would have done that. But, you're all smelly. Plus, that thing's too big. I couldn't fit it in my mouth."

Johnny had a million responses lined up, but decided to show some restraint. After all, this girl had let him fuck her after just meeting him. That was fantastic of her.

"Nothing to say? I was sure you'd have a line."

"Nope, when you're right, you're right. I wouldn't let you do that anyway. It's hot, and I'm all sweaty. I can't blame you."

Maybe that will get her. Girls like sweet talk like that. Maybe she'll suck my dick. I heard Jewish girls gave the best blowjobs.

Anne grabbed Johnny's hand and led him to their special spot. Taking Johnny's hand, she put it on her breast. Johnny squeezed and didn't wanna let go. Anne's hand traveled down to Johnny's zipper and she worked his pants open. Pulling them down a bit, his dick popped up.

"This thing is just too big. I could barely walk today. But, lemme try," said Anne with a sexy smile.

She barely fit her mouth over the head, but Anne did her best, bobbing her head up and down. Using her hand to help her mouth, she pumped Johnny's huge cock, over and over. Johnny wasn't sure whether to warn her as the end was near. Some girls were okay with it going in their mouths, but some wanted no part of it. The right thing was to ask, he reasoned.

"Johnny! Ew, you came in my mouth! You wanna kiss me now?"

"Umm, no. That ain't right. I ain't no queer."

"You're supposed to ask a girl...or at least warn her!"

"I know, I know. It's just that it felt so good. I couldn't stop myself. Best ever. You're amazing. Incredible."

"Really? Why, thank you," said Anne.

Anne was totally smiling. She had only done that to one other guy. He had at least warned her.

"You ready?"

"Ready, for what? Oh no, you're not gonna stick that big thing in me, two days in a row! You'll kill me!"

"Really? You don't wanna?"

"Oh, Johnny. Don't start your sad eyes. Maybe tomorrow. I really do still hurt."

"Okay. Umm, maybe I can just pit a little bit in?"

"No! You're so bad!"

Anne was right. Johnny was bad. He was interested in sex, any kinda sex, almost every second, of every day. Pulling up, and zipping his pants, Johnny stood up and offered his hand to Anne. Helping her up, he walked hand in hand, to the bench that was close by.

"So, Johnny. Are some of the same things bothering you tonight? Did you think about what I told you? You know, follow your passions. Dreams are just dreams when you don't act on them."

Fucking Anne was incredible, and having his dick sucked was amazing, but Johnny was really drawn to Anne's way of listening to him. She made him feel special. Maybe it would, and maybe it wouldn't be her, but whoever Johnny would wind up marrying someday, she'd have to want to listen to him.

"So, what do you wanna be? You know, after high school. For a living?"

"I wanna be an actress. I wanna be famous. The movies. Maybe plays. But, I'm gonna follow my passions. Just like you should."

"Yeah. That helped me, thanks for telling me that. Hey, Anne. You wanna go on a date sometime? You know, like getting a burger, and a pop? Maybe a movie?"

"Sure. I'd love to. I gotta go. My parents worry when I stay out too late. Kiss me, Johnny?"

"Sure."

Johnny reached forward and kissed Anne, on her cheek.

"Want me to walk you home?"

"Nice kiss. No, I'm okay. See you soon?"

"Yeah, what's your address? I mean, don't you wanna let me see where you live? You don't always want to meet me in the dark, in the park, do you?"

"For now, that's okay."

Anne walked away and just like the previous night, disappeared into the darkness. What was wrong with Johnny? He wanted to fuck her, maybe even twice, but he also wanted to talk. And have Anne listen.

Johnny made his way back home. Climbing the stairs to his Ralph Avenue apartment, Johnny was afraid that his father would be mad. It was after ten. Putting the key into his apartment door, Johnny turned the lock and pushed the door open.

"Well, look who is. He come visit his mother and his father," said Anatole, with a smile.

Johnny exhaled. Things were okay.

"Hi, Dad. Where's Mom?"

"Mother in bathroom. Bathing, I think. I go sleep. We go work tomorrow. You have work John?"

"Yes, Dad, I'll be ready. I'm gonna get some sleep also. I just wanna wait for Mom. Wanna kiss her goodnight."

"Good boy. Goodnight, John. See you in morning."

Johnny sat and waited for his mom. After giving her a hug and a kiss, Johnny hit the sack. Normally, Johnny would think of girls, tits, ass, and getting laid. But tonight, was different. Johnny hoped that he would someday meet a very special woman. Someone who really loved him the way his mother loved him. Was she out there? Could there even be another woman who was that sweet, that loving, and that special? Or had his dad found the only one? Johnny always had one eye open for the woman. But things would be different now. Now the other eye would be open as well. For the perfect woman. He'd find her. He'd know it. Someday.

Anatole and Johnny walked sleepily down the stairs to Ralph Avenue. Opening the door, you could feel the humidity in the air.

"I think rain today, John."

"No way, Dad."

"Maybe we go back to get the umbrella?"

"No, we're good, no rain, Dad. I know these things."

As Johnny and his father reached the metal stairs that would bring them to the subway, the skies opened. A torrential rain poured down through the urban heavens. Johnny loved the smell of rain. It washed the dirty city of Brooklyn, and it really needed the bath.

"What I tell to you? Hurry up. We are soaked."

Sitting in the empty subway car, Johnny shivered. It sure wasn't cold out, but the rain gave him the shakes. With his shirt now soaking wet, he became even more self-conscious about his wounds.

"I sure hope Leroy has a shirt to change into. Maybe I can even wear one of those white aprons."

"I am lucky. We have locker, and I change to security guard shirt."

The rain was coming down even harder now. Johnny and his dad, getting off the subway, ran for it. As they approached the museum, Johnny was slightly out of breath. Surprised that not only had his dad kept up, but he wasn't even breathing hard.

"Nothing ever bad compared to winter in Russia," said Anatole with a smile.

"Okay, Dad. See you later.

Johnny made his way to the cafeteria, and was met by Leroy.

"My man! Mr. Johnny is all wet. Look like a rat!"

Leroy was really laughing now and Johnny wasn't finding anything too funny.

"What's the matter, my man? A little rain gonna melt, Mr. Johnny?"

"No. You wouldn't understand, Leroy."

"Well try me. Leroy been through lots of things in all his years. I done heard most of what you can hear."

"Look. My shirt! It's all wet, and now people can see my scars. It's disgusting looking Leroy. I don't even wanna take off my shirt. People will stare."

"Okay, son. Now, what I don't understand is, Mr. Johnny seems to me to be a pretty tough customer. Why this be bothering you so much?"

"I don't know. I just wanna find that special woman someday, Leroy. I'm afraid that when she sees my chest, she'll want nothing to do with me."

"Listen here, Mr. Johnny. A woman who sees your chest, and runs? Let her ass go on. She ain't worth shit. If she be the right one, nothin' like that gonna make any difference to her."

"How do I know when I meet the right one, Leroy?"

"Well, for one thing…she sees that chest, she won't bat an eyelash. She the right one? She ain't gonna care about nothin' but you, Mr. Johnny."

Johnny had no response. But Leroy's words hit him harder than the rain outside had. Now he knew.

"Thanks, Leroy. Let's get to work."

The morning was slow, so Johnny worked on other things. Stools needed to be cleaned, the bathrooms cleaned and more. Johnny never minded doing the dirty work. He figured that he was getting paid, and he was supposed to do anything that had to be done. He heard those words within his mind. In his father's voice.

"This be the last high school year for you?"

"Yeah, I can't wait to get the fuck out. Leroy, I'm gonna fuck every girl I see this last year. They all want it. I know they do."

Leroy laughed and laughed. He genuinely liked Johnny. Lunchtime was really busy and the time flew by.

"Okay, Mr. Johnny. Be seeing you tomorrow. Don't be tearing up too much of that ass out there now. Need to have your legs strong to work, that pussy be dangerous sometimes. Tear a man's legs up!" laughed Leroy.

Johnny nodded his head and laughed as well. As he made his way down to meet his father, Johnny kept thinking of Leroy's words. He wondered if Anne was that special one. Would she react when she saw all his scars?

Johnny met up with his father. He looked tired.

"No more rain. This is good. Let us go to subway. When get home, I want to paint. Before dark."

"Okay, Dad. You look tired. Are you okay?"

Anatole looked surprised, but touched.

"I am good. Yes, tired a bit. I walk much today. What for you, John? I know you have things bother to you."

"No, I'm okay. Leroy taught me something important."

"What is this?

"That if someone is really worth it, they won't care about things like scars. They just care about the person."

"Your boss very smart man."

"Dad? Do you think I could ever find someone, you know…like Mom? Someone so wonderful, someone that cares so much about me, that we almost become one?"

"I hope for you, yes. She wonderful woman. Sweet, and very smart. And talent for her, too. She write like beautiful painting. I am very lucky man. This, I know."

"Thanks, Dad. I hope I find someone like her."

Johnny spent most of the summer, his last before college, working as many hours as he could. He didn't quite retire his shoe-shine box, as when he could, he'd be out there hustling up a few bucks. Time spent with his boys was always hard to find, as they all became busier and busier. Danny and Jimmy found jobs for the summer, and Mickey seemed to fall in love every week. Johnny continued to see Anne, and had plenty of sex, always in the park. He met her parents and had dinner over there a few times. Johnny still kept his shirt on though. No matter how intimate things became, he hadn't let Anne see his scars. Not yet anyway. Johnny tried to save as much money as possible. He was becoming more and more confident as far as his ability to learn about so many things, all by reading. Reading became an immense passion for him. He also started to write a bit. Sonia was very supportive of this, although Anatole worried. He wanted Johnny to have tangible skills, so that he could take care of his own family someday.

"Hey, Anne. Sorry I didn't make it over last night. I went to the library and actually fell asleep. The cafeteria has been so busy lately…I've just been exhausted."

"That's okay. I understand. Now that you come to my apartment, I don't feel scared waiting here in the park."

"Two more weeks and we're back to school. I can't believe it's so close. And we'll be seniors," said Johnny.

"I know. I think I'm gonna go to secretarial school. There are jobs out there and I could always change my mind. Johnny…when we, you know…we need to be more careful. I thought I was pregnant. I was so scared. It's okay though, I'm not."

Johnny was speechless. How could he have been so stupid? So, irresponsible? There was just no way, at seventeen, he was ready to become a father. There was college, and work, and… well, he hadn't even thought about settling down. He had been steady with Anne, but he still looked at and thought about sex with other girls. Pretty much every single woman that he laid eyes on. Seventeen or not, Johnny still peeked in Mrs. Williams' window. Man, the older she got, the nicer those tits became. Someday, Johnny was going to fuck her. Her husband was just gonna have to understand. Plus, this guy was probably old anyway. He couldn't possibly be giving it to her the way that Johnny could. After all, Johnny was carrying around a third leg in the crotch of his pants.

"Whew, that's good. I definitely wanna go to Brooklyn College. I'm so interested in literature. Deep down inside, I wanna write books someday. Maybe even try acting a bit. I'd be a bit scared, but… I might try it. And you wanna be a secretary and that's great. Okay, I'll get some bags."

"Bags? That's what you call them? Bags?

"Okay, I'm sorry. Rubbers? Is that better?"

"A little. I guess."

"Umm, I don't have one now, but do you wanna…you know. I'll just pull out."

"No! You say that all the time!"

"Okay, well I oughta be going anyway. I have work tomorrow and my mom wants me to get my clothes organized for school. You know, sew up all the holes."

Johnny offered to walk Anne home, and she said yes. Upon getting to her apartment, he reached over and gave her a quick kiss.

"Goodnight, Anne. See you tomorrow?"

"Well, we'll see. I might be busy," she replied.

She might be busy? What the fuck kinda shit is that? Maybe I'm gonna have to start getting closer to Mrs. Williams and those torpedo tits.

Before Johnny knew it, it was the night before his senior year of high school. He found it almost unbelievable. It seemed like just yesterday that he was hopping down that staircase in Brownsville, the hallway echoing with each step. That large and oh-so-heavy old, wooden door that he could barely open. Johnny remembered crossing Christopher Street, and meeting Jimmy. He liked Jimmy right away. After all, Jimmy even changed his name. Johnny boy. Man, that was such a long time ago. Nights on the roof, stealing tires. All the trouble, the laughs. Where had it all gone?

Johnny was really having a hard time accepting the fact that he was a year away from college, and Jackie was…dead. He'd gone back and forth about that day. Over and over. Was it his fault? Jackie trusted him, listened to him. Followed him. But then Johnny would think of the vision…the voice…Jackie's voice. He had made it clear that it wasn't Johnny's fault, that he was not only okay, but happy. Johnny hoped that he would see Jackie again someday. Johnny was ready. He had confidence. Confidence in his ability with his studies, confidence with the woman, and with all those pushups he'd done, confidence in kicking ass. Anyone fucked with him or his boys? They'd get an old-fashioned Brownsville beat down. After all, no matter where Johnny went from here, he'd always be from Brownsville…he'd always be Johnny boy.

"Wake up, John. School for you now."

Johnny loved his mother dearly, but her voice, probably anyone's voice, that early in the morning, just drove him nuts!

"Okay, Mom…I'm getting up."

Shit, why the fuck can't I just stay home? This shit sucks. I just wanna jerk-off all day.

"John, need to move. Listen to you mother," yelled Anatole.

On his way to school, Johnny thought of all that this year would be. He guessed that he'd have to hold hands with Anne in the hallway. Shit, that would take him off the market. He'd have to figure that one out.

"Hey! Rostov! This is it, man. Our last year. We gonna get tons of pussy!" said Jimmy.

"Well, make sure you use tons of bags," said Anne.

Anne had walked up behind Jimmy and Johnny. Oh shit. What a way to start the new school year off.

"We was just jokin,'" said Jimmy.

"Hey, what's up fella's? Ready to take this school over?" said Danny.

"Where's that big fuck, Mickey? That boy gets any bigger and he won't fit down the hallway," said Jimmy.

"Wait up, Anne! Don't be mad," asked Johnny.

"Aww, let her go Johnny. You know woman. Besides, look at the ass on that one over there!" said Mickey.

Johnny glanced towards a beautiful blonde. She wanted him. He just knew it. Johnny undressed this blonde beauty, with his eyes. In two seconds he had her naked and his dick in her mouth.

I'm gonna go over, introduce myself to her, tell her how big my dick is, and she's gonna wanna fuck. Right now, probably.

"Hold up, Anne! Wait! Don't be like that," said Johnny.

Johnny ran up the stairs and caught up to Anne. Putting his hand gently on her shoulder, she slowly turned around. Facing Johnny, he could see that she had been crying.

"What? Why are you crying? It was just a stupid joke…guy stuff. You know how we can be."

"Do you love me, Johnny?"

Holy shit. Love? What the fuck! I love my mother, and some days, my father, but… I kinda just love fucking this girl. And her sucking my big sausage.

"Well sure. I think you're swell, Anne."

"But do you love me?"

"Love? Swell? Johnny, what happened to you over the summer?" asked Jimmy.

Anne had enough. Glaring at Johnny, she turned and took off, ponytail bouncing up and down as she walked briskly away.

"Now, why'd you have to fuckin' do that, Jimmy?"

"Damn Johnny, I was just fuckin' around," Jimmy responded.

Johnny attended homeroom, where they handed out the schedules. Senior year would be a breeze, he thought. Advanced English Literature. Wow. Who would have thought than Johnny Rostov would have such a passion for literature? Johnny had been thinking more and more about college, and possibly writing a book. His dad had always advised him to write about something he knew about. He had also told him to get a job that made sure he could care for a family. Not like he had done. Johnny sometimes felt that he took care of his parents, not the other way around.

Johnny was a hustler. Shining shoes, stealing things, running errands for gangsters, he was resourceful. He'd always find a way to care for a wife and kids. A wife…Johnny could see her. In his mind's eye, she was on the shorter side. This would make Johnny feel taller. He liked that idea. Almost six-foot-tall now, he still felt like that little boy that took such a bad beating from his father. She would also have to be beautiful. As good looking as he was, she'd obviously have to be pretty, but the beauty would need to start on the inside. With a soul, as amazing as any ever created. With a heart that was like no other. Well, no one except his own mom that is. Yes, she would be a shorter version of his mom. Johnny just knew that he'd find her. Eventually.

Chapter Thirty-Four

SENIOR YEAR WAS going by quickly. Anne and Johnny were on and off. Johnny was starting to feel closer to Anne. He thought long and hard about it. Johnny decided to ask Anne to go steady. He had never felt this way about anyone before. That was it. Tomorrow, at school, in front of everyone, he was going to ask her. Of course, she'd say yes. Johnny already knew that.

Johnny woke up the next morning, with a smile on his face. That never happened. Yes, this was going to be a great day. As he left his room his mother was surprised to see him awake already.

"John. You are awake? Go brush your teeth and wash you face, keep that smile nice and white for the girls," laughed Sonia.

Johnny washed up, grabbed an apple and was on his way. Well, that's after he kissed his mom goodbye.

"Mom, today is gonna be a great day!"

"Yes, John. For this we want. All good days."

Now, late October, Johnny was comfortable on the normally steamy subway. Arriving at school, he set search for Anne. Walking towards her homeroom class, he saw her leaning up against her locker talking to someone. Suddenly, this guy that she was talking to, reached over and kissed her. And she was kissing him back!

"What the fuck? Anne, what are you doing?"

Startled, Anne suddenly pulled away.

"Mickey? Wait, how the fuck could you be kissin' on my girl? And you! What the fuck are you doin' with my friend?"

"Look, Johnny, she said you guys broke up. I didn't know."

"You don't talk to me first? You're fucked up! I oughtta beat your ass!"

Mickey took a step towards Johnny. He now towered over his slender friend, and must have outweighed him by fifty pounds.

"Look, Johnny, you don't want none of this. Just walk away. We're friends. Don't make me hurt you. And don't try none of that baby, knife shit. I'm on to you."

Johnny stood up to Mickey, his face barely reaching Mickey's neck. Quick as lightening, Johnny took the inside heel of his hand and rammed it into Mickey's neck. Gagging and choking, Mickey was reeling. As he staggered backwards, Johnny was on him. Bringing his elbow across the end of Mickey's nose, blood gushed, as it made a snapping sound. Johnny felt for his knife and started to pull it out. Mickey, now desperate, used the only thing he had left…brute strength. Putting Johnny in a bear hug, he squeezed as hard as he could. Johnny was having trouble breathing, and his strength was slowly leaving him. Suddenly, Mickey let up on his powerful grip, and Johnny started to slip downwards.

A crowd of students and teachers had started to gather. The teachers seemed too afraid to get involved. As Johnny slid down Mickey's massive torso, Mickey grabbed Johnny by his throat.

"That's it, mother-fucker! There ain't no such thing as friends now!" yelled Mickey as he literally tried to force the life from Johnny's body.

Johnny could feel himself starting to lose awareness. He was now the desperate one. With every ounce of possible resolve, Johnny reached into his pocket. Almost in slow motion, he pulled out his friend, Mr. Knife. Johnny hesitated but then thrust the knife, deeply into Mickey's thigh.

The scream was bloodcurdling. Blood gushed out, quickly pooling on the high school's hallway floor. Even the crowd of niggers that were watching, and cheering, looked away, cringing.

"Break it up! Get outta the way, before we lock you all up!"

The police had been called, and they grabbed Johnny and knocked the knife from his hand. One of the cops picked up the bloody weapon and stuck it in his pocket. The school nurse and a cop, tied a tourniquet around Mickey's upper thigh, and tended to his broken nose.

"Come on, you little bastard," said the burly cop.

"Fuck you!" replied Johnny.

Reaching back, the cop punched Johnny in his face, with a brutal force so great, that he almost lost consciousness. Dragging

Johnny through the halls and out the school's front doors, the cops threw his bleeding body into the backseat of the squad car.

"So, you think you're a real tough guy, huh? What the fuck is wrong with you? You're goin' to the slammer, and for a long time."

"There ain't no such things as friends. He was fuckin' around with my girl. We've been friends since we was kids. It ain't right."

The cop, driving slowly, suddenly pulled abruptly to the side of the road. Johnny had gotten his attention, and he softened a bit.

"He was fuckin' around with your girl? That ain't right. But, you can't be usin' a fuckin' knife. You gotta use your hands."

"He was chokin' me. I felt like I was gonna die."

Johnny sat bleeding, as the cop told him that he'd been in a similar situation, that his best friend had done him wrong also.

"One thing you're wrong about, kid, and that's that there are friends. People will do you wrong, but there's good ones out there."

"No, fuck that. There's no such thing as a friend. Just family. That's it. Fuck everyone else! Fuck 'em all!"

"Look, if I don't lock you up, you two are gonna go at it again, and this time, someone's gonna get killed. And what, over some broad?"

"She's a damn whore. We was getting' serious. He was my friend? Friends don't do that shit! I'm tellin' you, there's no such thing as a friend in this world."

The cop pulled back on the road and asked Johnny where he lived. Johnny knew that he was going to expelled from school, but jail? That he didn't want. He wanted to go to college, meet someone incredible, someone amazing and sweet, just like his mom. He couldn't go to jail.

"Look officer, I know I did wrong. Can't you just let me go? I'll stay outta trouble. I wanna go to college next year. Plus, I don't wanna disappoint my mom. It'll really hurt her."

"You don't think your buddy is gonna let this go, do you? You know he's gonna come back at you. I gotta lock you up."

"He ain't gonna do shit. He knew he was wrong. He won't have a friend left. He's probably gonna just get outta town. His parents wanna move to New Jersey anyway. It'll be okay. There won't be no trouble."

"Look, I should never do this, but I'm gonna go to the hospital and see what's up with this guy. Look, I gotta put the cuffs on you."

The cop drove to the hospital. As he pulled into the parking lot, he exited the driver's door and opened the back door where Johnny was sitting.

"Look, I'm gonna cuff you. You sit here. You fuckin' try to take off and I'll find you and fuckin' waste you. Understood?"

"Yes, sir."

Johnny sat there for what seemed like forever. Partly in shock, as well as angry, confused, and in shock, Johnny thought about what would happen.

Jackie. I don't know if you can hear me or not, but if you could pull some strings with the big guy up there, I'd sure appreciate it.

"Son…Son!"

Johnny snapped out of his dream like trance and looked up towards the menacing looking cop.

"Look, he's gonna be fine. His leg is gonna be fucked up, but his mom was there, and you're right. She wants out. Your parents at home? And no bullshit."

"I don't know. My dad is a security guard at the museum. My mom is a writer, so sometimes she's at home, sometimes she's out."

"The museum? He the guy with the accent? German or something?"

"Russian, yeah. Why?"

"He an artist?"

"Yeah. What's goin' on?"

"Your father's okay. He did a painting for my wife. He's good. Look, I'll bring you home. But if there's any trouble with this kid, your friend, I'm gonna lock your ass up. And that's after I beat the shit outta you! You understand me?"

"Yeah. 'cept, he ain't no friend. Cause there ain't no such thing as friends!"

"Okay, okay. You'll learn someday."

Johnny asked the cop to let him off a few blocks from home. He'd just tell his parents that he got into a fight. Pulling over, the cop opened the rear passenger door and took off Johnny's handcuffs.

"Look, can you gimme back my knife? I don't go lookin' for trouble, but these streets ain't safe. Gotta have my protection."

The cop reached into his pocket and pulled out the bloody blade. Tossing it to Johnny, he was full of doubt. Normally, he'd just beat the snot out of a punk, and throw his ass in the slammer. Johnny was lucky. Very lucky.

Mickey did move away, and Johnny never heard from him again. He actually wished that he had stayed. Payback was a bitch, and fucking one of Mickey's girlfriends would have been great. Jimmy and Danny couldn't believe what had happened, but had Johnny's back, all the way. They all agreed that something had happened to Mickey over that last summer. He grew like a weed, and got huge. Something went wrong with the kid. Johnny's parents were mad. But, kids in Brooklyn, especially those who grew up in Brownsville, got into lots of fights. The week that Johnny got suspended from school, his father put him to work. Up at six, he was cleaning and fixing things all day. That is, until he left for his own job at the cafeteria.

Leroy was very understanding. But he did warn him to stay on the lookout. Johnny knew this. He had gone through it with Vinny. That was one thing that worried Johnny. *The promise*. Mickey was in on what happened to Vinny. He had made the promise, and along with Danny and Jimmy, had sworn to never mention what happened to anyone. For the rest of their lives. Johnny reasoned that Mickey would shut up. After all, he was part of it as well.

Johnny got through the time away from school, and when he went back, no one said a word. There was a lot to catch up on however. Johnny truly missed his English literature class. And he really needed to get good grades, as he wanted to go to college. He had it all figured out. He would of course still be living at home. He started to consider night classes. This would surely work out great. He truly enjoyed working at the cafeteria, with Leroy, but he would need a "real" job. His parents needed the money, and Johnny would gladly help out. He'd done that most of his life anyway. He'd figure out some time to study, and of course, there was the never-ending search for new pussy. Johnny decided that, in addition to there not being such a thing as a real friend in this world, that until he found the right one, the true love of his life, he was just going to fuck girls and get his foot-long hammer, sucked on.

Johnny had been spending more and more time in the library, and while he still felt funny about them knowing, Jimmy and Danny never said a word about it anymore. They spent less and less time hanging out together and Johnny was starting to miss it.

"Hey, Mom. I'm gonna head over to Christopher Street and hang out with the boys. I'll be back tonight. Not too late, don't worry. And yes, I washed my face and brushed my teeth. And…I'll bring a jacket and even zip it up if it starts to get cool," said Johnny, with a smile.

"Yes. Okay."

Sonia didn't sound okay. Something wasn't right. In fact, as Johnny thought about it, Sonia hadn't seemed okay for a while now. She was always tired and was just not herself.

"What's wrong, Mom? Are you okay?"

"I am good, John. You go. Have fun with friends."

"No, Mom. I'm gonna stay here with you. I can always have plenty of friends, but I only have one mom. I just happened to get the best one ever."

Sonia looked very touched and even a little bit emotional.

"Thank you, John, but I am okay. Perhaps just little tired. You go. Friends important."

"Moms are more important. Besides, I would rather stay here and talk to you."

Johnny spent that evening talking to his mom. He did a lot of listening as well. Sometimes, Johnny took his mother's amazing love for granted. After all, it was all he'd ever known. He pretty much assumed that all moms were that way. But, the older he got, the more he realized just how lucky he was.

As his senior year moved along, Johnny started to prepare, and plan for his future. He really was feeling good about becoming a writer. It made sense. His dad was an amazing painter, his mom, a very talented writer and poet. Johnny had so much to say. He was starting to realize, that paper and pencil was the way to express himself.

One evening, Johnny couldn't sleep. Instead of tossing and turning, he got up, and went into the kitchen. There wasn't much to eat. Johnny was restless. He found a writing tablet and a pencil, and just started to write. He had no idea what he was doing, but after a while, the words, the feelings, and the passion started to flow from his mind, to his fingers.

While Johnny certainly was a horny guy, he was really a romantic at heart. He wanted a love affair. He wanted to meet someone and have a lifelong love affair. He could see her. They would be just perfect for each other. Johnny was a good looking and talented guy, a guy who wanted to take care of someone. She would be stunning, but need him. Johnny wanted to take care of someone, someone who needed to be taken care of. Johnny had pain, pain inside. Deeply inside of himself. He never got over how his father had hurt him. Sure, the physical pain had healed, but his dad was his hero, and the emotional scars were deep. He just knew that there was a wonderful soul out there somewhere. She'd have suffered as well. They would fit like the last pieces of a complex puzzle. And everything would then be complete. Life would always have its challenges, but together, they could deal with anything. Whatever problems that life presented, by themselves, they would fail. But together? There would be nothing that they couldn't overcome. They'd have lots of kids together, they'd grow old together. She'd be the woman of his dreams.

"What wrong, John? No sleep?"

"I'm okay, Dad. Yeah, just was tossing and turning. Decided to do some writing. You know, just like you paint visual pictures…I take my feelings and paint them with words."

"Yes, I see this. Like you mother. Wonderful."

"You mean, you understand?"

"Yes, John. I do. I just want you make good job. Take care of family."

"I know, Dad. And I will. I promise."

When Johnny was younger, he was angry at his dad. Angry at the beating he had gotten, but also angry that, in his mind, his father had never taken care of him. Not like other dads did. Johnny's perception was that most dads worked full time jobs, and made lots of money. Their families wanted for nothing. Johnny was starting to learn that this, of course, was not true. But, it was becoming more and more clear, that Anatole felt guilty. His own father had always provided for him, but he had not done so for his family. He wanted to make certain that Johnny would always be able to take care of his own family.

For as much as Johnny wanted to attend college, he knew it would have to be Brooklyn College. It was close, and would be the least expensive, overall. In speaking with his English Literature teacher, Mrs. Collins, she suggested that he take a test for entry. If he scored high enough, school would be free. He would of course, need to pay for books and labs. Mrs. Collins suggested that Johnny always tried to get used books. In fact, when he was done with the course, he could then sell the books back, thus saving even more money.

As graduation got closer and closer, Johnny spent more and more time reading, and studying. Just as he had wanted to always be the best at everything he did, he put all he had, into becoming well read. He had also been spending most evenings in his bedroom, writing. He wasn't yet sure about the title of his work, but the working title was *The Woman of My Dreams*. Partly a story of his own search for that perfect woman, someone who was like his mom, and the story of the family he envisioned having one day. Only eighteen, Johnny just knew that he wanted to have kids. And, a lot of them. But no matter what, he'd wait. For that perfect woman. The one he dreamed of.

Chapter Thirty-Five

"DAD, DO YOU have a minute?"

"Yes, John, for you, yes, I do."

"Is Mom okay? I mean, she's not sick, but I'm worried about her. She seems okay, but then she keeps getting out of breath."

"I see this sometimes, too. I don't know. Maybe she should see doctor?"

"I think so, Dad. It can't hurt."

"But problem is that she take care of you and me, but she no does for herself."

"Well, just tell her she has to. I'm worried."

"Yes. This, I will do."

"Oh, and Dad. I decided I want to go to college. Brooklyn College. I'll stay at home and go to school. This way, I can work. Probably get a full-time job and go to school at night. Well, you know, I'll pay for books and labs, and well, I have to still figure it out."

"Good, John. I am sorry, we cannot pay."

"It's okay, Dad. I understand."

The conversation was a bit strained, but Johnny wanted to talk about his future, with his dad. For all the studying, and maturing that Johnny had done during his senior year, he still wanted to hang with his boys. The Money Boys.

"I'm gonna ahead over to Brownsville, Dad. Gonna hang out with Jimmy and Danny. Haven't seen them too much lately."

"Yes, you see in school though, no?"

"Yeah, but we all have different classes."

"Okay, John."

Johnny took off and headed for the subway. Taking a seat, he felt for his knife. He may have been maturing, but he still wasn't going to take any shit. From anyone.

"Hi there."

"Hi. How are you?"

Johnny, glancing to his right, saw the most beautiful, angelic face. Ethnic looking, but having soft features, she had the most beautiful brown eyes.

"I'm Johnny. What's your name?"

"Janet. I'm just on my way to visit my friends. I've been working so much that I never see them anymore it seems."

"Where do you work, Janet?"

"Bechtel Group. It's in Manhattan. It's a nice place to work, it's one of the biggest companies in the world."

"Really? What do you do there?" asked Johnny.

"I'm a secretary. Why?"

"Was just curious. I'm a senior this year…"

"College? Where do you go, Johnny?"

"Ummm, no, high school actually."

"High school? Oh, you look much older."

Johnny knew that he didn't look old enough to be a college senior. Some people were just strange. She did have a nice rack, but Johnny was really interested in getting a job. Bechtel sounded good.

"Yeah, I'm gonna be lookin' for work soon. I gotta work full time, and then I'll take night courses. Are they hiring? Can I mention your name?"

The subway screeched as it came to a sudden halt. Janet grabbed her small bags and started to leave.

"Wait! What's your last name?"

It was too late. Janet mouthed something, but the noise of the loud subway, taking off again made it impossible to hear.

Bechtel, huh? Manhattan? Not too bad. Hey, it's money. I'll find out what they do there. I can do anything.

Johnny got off at the Brownsville stop. Walking down the green metal steps, he was feeling funny. Memories of being just a little kid, came flooding back to him. That little kid, tough as nails, filthy and grimy, covered in black shoe shine polish, had worked this area. Johnny was going to make it. He had been through too much. He was still tough, but now, as he matured, he was getting focus. He would escape Brownsville. It would take a while, but he'd do it. He'd find the girl of his dreams, marry her and have children. Maybe even buy a house. No one he knew had ever bought a house. He'd be the first. He'd do it. With his perfect partner, nothing could stop them. They would be perfect together.

"Johnny! He's back. All you virgins…lock up your pussy's! The pussy destroyer is here!"

Jimmy still had a sick sense of humor. Now eighteen, he still could act like he was eleven.

"Shut the fuck up, man. What the fuck is wrong with you?" laughed Johnny as he slapped Jimmy on his back.

"Where's Danny? Probably in church, huh?"

"Yeah, fuckin' the priest up his ass," laughed Jimmy.

"Life's goin' by too fast, Jimmy. I still can't believe that Jackie is gone. I miss that kid."

"Yeah, me too. Not that prick Mickey though."

"Don't even mention that cock sucker's name," said Johnny.

"Okay…sorry!"

"Listen Jimmy, I love Danny like a brother. He's one of us. But not tonight. It started out, you and me. Just us. Remember? I was like five, came running out. Didn't know what the fuck was goin' on. You called me Johnny boy."

"What's wrong Johnny? You seem weird. Tell me."

"I don't know. My mom. I'm worried about her Jimmy. She's not the same. She's always tired. She keeps coughing. My dad knows, but he hasn't taken her to the doctor. Not yet anyhow."

"She in pain? Your mom is one of a kind, Johnny. They don't make 'em like her, much."

"I know. If they do, I'm gonna find one though. My own, perfect woman."

"Ahh, you just wanna fuck 'em all!"

"Well, yeah. That too. I mean, when you have a dick that big, you just gotta share it!"

"Whatever. Fuck you!"

Johnny was really going through a strange phase. Part little boy still, traveling on a journey to become a man. On the lookout for someone perfect. He knew that he just had to go to college and get a good job. He'd have lots of kids. But he'd take care of his kids. He'd work. Always. A real job. No painting for him. Painting doesn't fill a kid's stomach or buy them clothes. Johnny knew that his father tried. He probably was doing his best. But Johnny would do better. He had to.

The two friends walked the streets of Brownsville as the sun was setting. A marvelous, bright ball of fire, expiring as it cast its head downwards. Its fury heated an entire city by day, but now, almost depleted, was an urban art form.

"Ya know, even these filthy fuckin' streets can look pretty. You can find anything on these streets, Jimmy. Your past, and if you look hard enough, even your future."

"I think the water over on Ralph Street is makin' your brain all fucked up!"

Both boys just glanced at each other. After mere seconds, they exploded in laughter.

"What the fuck you lookin' at? Get the fuck off my street," a voice called out.

Johnny didn't look up, but instinctively felt for his knife. Safe and sound, it was just a split second away from action. If someone was foolish enough to invite him out.

"What? Hey, Johnny. Look at this little bitch. Hey, little bitch. How old are you? Twelve? You a badass? Show me what you got," said Jimmy.

"Leave the kid alone. He's just like we used to be," said Johnny.

"I ain't twelve. I'm fourteen. And yeah, I'm a badass. You guys are lucky. I'm not in a fightin' mood."

"Haha, haha, haha. Listen to this kid, Johnny. Okay, kid. You're a bad ass. Boo! Let's keep movin', Johnny. We might get our asses kicked."

Johnny and Jimmy walked the streets of Brownsville that night. The sky still had a reddish hue. Over the city rooftops, was a concrete reflected beauty. Even the rumbling of the old cars that passed by, couldn't rob the streets of this moment. It fell on deaf ears. As the sun continued to set, Johnny realized that his life in Brownsville was on the verge of vanishing as well.

Johnny got home a little later than usual that night. A little nervous that his father would be mad, Johnny's mind raced, trying to think of reasons.

"Where have you been? You mother is sick. We need to take to hospital, I think," said Anatole.

"I didn't know. Mom, what's wrong? What can I do?"

Johnny helped his parents down the stairs and to the subway.

"We go to Jewish Hospital. They are good. Not too far. You help me talk to doctors, John?"

"Yes, of course, Dad. Mom, you're gonna be okay."

"I am fine. All this fuss. For nothing. I am just tired. Little bit," assured Sonia.

After a short subway ride, Johnny walked with his parents to the hospital.

They just let Jews in here? I hope my dad knows what he's doin'.

Johnny held the door open as his father steadied his mother. Looking around and looking nervous, Anatole wasn't sure what to do.

"Doctor? Can someone tell me where we should bring my mom? She doesn't feel well," asked Johnny.

A tall and slender nurse motioned to Johnny to bring his parents to a small room, located behind the nurse's desk.

"What's wrong, dear?"

Sonia looked at the nurse, but seemed confused.

"She has pain. Her chest. Also, she breathe very hard. This for many months now," said Anatole.

"Many months? Okay, well, at least you brought her in. You are her husband?"

"Yes, I am."

"Okay, I'm going to get the doctor. Son, you can wait outside."

"No, I can stay. This is my mom!"

"It is okay. Your father with me. Just wait outside. I will be okay. I love you."

"I love you, Mom."

With that, Johnny stepped outside. In a few moments, a stern looking man, wearing a long white jacket and carrying a notebook, entered the small room where his mother was. Johnny paced back and forth. Johnny and his friends had smoked cigarettes before, but Johnny never really liked them much. Tonight, he needed one.

"You got a smoke?"

The large man looked like a cop. But he wasn't. Maybe a hospital guard.

"Sure, here you go."

Taking a drag on his own cigarette to light Johnny's, he nodded and walked away.

Johnny stepped outside into the brisk fall evening. Taking drag after drag, he soon flicked the butt into the street and walked back into the hospital.

"Can I go in yet? What's taking so long?"

"Calm down, son. The doctor is in there with your parents. Just have a seat," replied the helpful nurse.

Johnny was thinking of all the things that could go wrong, when the doctor emerged from checking on his mom.

"How is she? How's my mom?"

"She's okay. She just needs some rest. She is fine. Calm down now."

"All this worry, over nothing. I told the both of you…I am fine," said Sonia.

Johnny and his dad both helped Sonia to her feet and slowly walked out of the hospital.

"I don't fill out papers or nothing. Am I supposed to go back?" asked Anatole.

"No, Dad, let's just go. Let's just get Mom home."

Johnny was worried. He didn't trust this doctor. He didn't trust anyone. Anyone but family. And maybe Jimmy. Doctors only cared about one thing, and that was getting paid.

The subway was pretty empty and Johnny made sure that both of his parents took their time and walked slowly. Something still wasn't right, and Johnny knew it. This was his mom, after all. He was certain. He would make sure that she was okay. Johnny may have been a few weeks short of eighteen still, but when it came to his mother, he would do anything. Anything to make sure that she was okay. Johnny was worried that night. After his parents went to sleep, he tossed and turned. He even got up a few times and pressed his ear against their bedroom door. All seemed quiet. Quiet was good.

In the morning, Johnny was groggy, and didn't want to get up. He almost had forgotten the events of the previous night when there was a knock at his door.

"John. Wake up. We eat. Wash your face, brush you teeth, now."

Johnny smiled. Maybe Mom was going to be okay. She just had to be. Johnny washed up and joined his parents. He just had some toast and a little bit of milk. He wasn't very hungry.

"Today Sunday, Anatole. No work?"

"No, they cut back extra hours a bit. But it is okay. I still have regular hours."

"And you, John?"

"Monday, Wednesday, and Friday, Mom. Leroy is trying to get me more hours, but I was thinkin' about it, and with all the time I need to study at the library, that's about all I can do. I have to take the test, right after the holidays, and I just hafta get in. College is my way out. A good job. Oh yeah, I met this girl on the subway…"

"You meet many girls, I hear," said a smiling Anatole.

"No, ain't like that. We was talkin', and she told me about a company she works for, in Manhattan, Bechtel Group. I am gonna get a job there. Right after graduation."

"This big company, John. I hear of them too. What you will do for them?"

"I don't know, Dad. I'll do anything. I just need the work. For books, for labs, and of course to help out here, at home."

"This my job. I take care of family."

Johnny knew that tone. He also knew that this was a sensitive subject with his father. He figured he'd just leave it alone.

"I know, Dad. Of course."

"When you go for interview, John, always remember…there be many people. They are also smart people and work hard. You need to make them remember you more. When you have appointment, get there early. Even too early. This is always good thing. My father teach this to me, when I was young man. Good to learn this."

"Okay, Dad. I will. Thank you."

Johnny settled back into high school. Things were going well. The fight with Mickey was almost never brought up, and even the niggers were leaving him alone. Jimmy was even talking about his future. He wanted to learn to be a mechanic. He was good with his hands, and he was smart. They weren't totally convinced that maturity was the way to go though.

"Hey, Jimmy. It's been a while. Let's get Danny and get some whore down to the hangout. We gotta the perfect setup. A hangout with no pussy, is no hangout. Plus, they need what I wanna give 'em," bragged Johnny.

"Yeah, okay. Mister Needle dick, himself."

"Suck my needle dick, cock sucker!"

Both boys laughed.

"Better get to class. This girl Beatrice. Oh my God, the fuckin' tits. Her face ain't all that, but the tits and ass. I know she wants me," said Jimmy.

"Like I said, suck my needle dick!"

Johnny slapped Jimmy on his back and was on his way to his favorite class. English Literature. Mrs. Collins.

"Good morning, John. Have you thought about the test yet?"

"Yes, Mrs. Collins. Right after Thanksgiving. And I'll be early too."

"Early? That's good, John. You'll do very well. You've turned into one of my better students. You've surprised some people around here, Mr. Rostov."

Mrs. Collins was smiling. Not the type to pass out compliments easily, this made Johnny feel good. And boosted his confidence. As tough as they come, Johnny was still getting used to his intellectual side. There were days when it was a natural fit, as well as those that it felt as uncomfortable as a hot Brownsville rooftop.

After school, Johnny decided not to go to work. Johnny never let an opportunity to work go by. But he was stressed. He was worried. Mostly about his mom. And college. When Johnny felt cornered, he usually felt for his friend, Mr. Knife. But a knife was not going to help him now. Johnny felt helpless, and he didn't like the feeling. Not at all. And, as far as college, he was just going to have to do his best. Not that many kids made it out of Brownsville. The tough, mean streets would eat you up. Some never made it out alive, and others never quite shook the brutality, violence, and criminal ways of the dirty, concrete prison system.

"John, you no have work today?" his mom asked, interrupting his thoughts.

"No, Mom. Leroy gave me today off. I need that money, but I just felt like…like I just need to study for that test. You know, just to make sure. Work tomorrow for sure. Leroy told me."

Johnny was lying. In fact, he never even got word to Leroy. That he should have done.

"Mom, I'm gonna hit the library for a while. Are you okay?"

"No worry for me, John. I am okay. Feel better."

Okay, I think I'll hit the library now. You sure you're okay? Can I get you anything?"

"You go. You do study. John…I love you."

"I love you too, Mom"

Johnny figured that he owed Leroy an explanation. He would stop at the museum, talk to Leroy, and then go over to the library, and study.

Johnny entered the museum and made his way to the cafeteria. As he approached the wooden double doors, he heard a buzz. The place was busy. Very busy.

"Mr. Johnny! You is late. Hurry on up, now! Get them dishes goin' and help with these tables. Then I'll get my ass back to cookin'"

"Umm, okay. Sorry, Leroy."

Johnny simply had no choice. The library would have to wait. Johnny suddenly heard his father's voice.

Never be late, John. Always be early to job. Protect you job. Important to take care of you family.

Johnny hustled to the back and threw on his white apron. The blasts of steam hit him directly on his chest. Apron or not, it still stung.

"Mr. Johnny. Get yo' ass out here, now!"

Johnny had never seen Leroy mad, before. He knew he was late, but he was there at least.

"Hurry on up, boy! Don't be pissin' me off now."

Johnny tensed up. He didn't like anyone to talk to him that way. What the fuck was going on? Johnny did his beat, taking orders, running them back to Leroy, serving food, cleaning tables, and trying like crazy to catch up with the dishes. After about two hours, things slowed down, and slowly, Johnny and Leroy caught up.

Johnny sized Leroy up. He really liked his boss. Something must be wrong though.

"Look, Leroy, I'm sorry, man. I know I was late but…"

"Late nothin'. This ain't be your fault, Mr. Johnny. This 'Ol Leroy's fault. I ain't nothin' but a stupid, old black nigger anyway, right?"

"What are you talkin' about Leroy?"

Leroy sat on a stool at the now empty counter. Sweat rolled down his aged and cracked face.

"I was takin' this white man's order, and I repeats it back and he says 'Yeah, that's right. You want me to say it again, nigger? You apes are all morons!' Guess he be right."

Leroy was breathing hard. Parts anger, frustration and shame, he was very upset.

"Where is this mother fucker? I'll cut him up! I'll slice him like an apple!"

Johnny reached for his trusty friend, Mr. Knife. Pulling it out, he showed it to Leroy.

"Put that the fuck back in yo' pocket now, Mr. Johnny! That's all I be needin' 'bout now. I worked this job for ten years before I got made cook and boss-man. I can't lose it now. They look for any 'scuse to get ridda old Leroy."

"I'm sorry, Leroy. I just don't want you to be all upset. Why would that asshole talk to you like that? You didn't do anything to him."

"Some peoples just be born that way, Mr. Johnny. Hate in their hearts. No good reason for it. I'm a black man. I can'ts be sayin' nothin' or doin' nothin'. Specially to no white man. They hang my ass up. Just like that poor man you done seen when you was little. Thank you though, Mr. Johnny. And Leroy be sorry for yellin' at you."

"No problem. I have your back, boss-man. Always."

Without saying a word, the two friends got up and started to wipe down tables. Ketchups and mustards were filled, as well as the salt and pepper shakers. As Johnny was finishing the last of the dishes, he could hear the loud clicks as sections of the cafeteria lighting were shut down. One by one.

Johnny and Leroy once more sat down on the counter stools. All was quiet.

"You ever worry about something…or someone, so much, that your head hurt?"

"Course I have. Leroy has a wife, two kids. Well, they ain't kids no more, but they was mine. Almost never be a day whens we don't worry about somethin'. Why, Mr. Johnny? What be troublin' my man?"

"Worried. About my mom. She's been having pain. Her chest, and she's always tired. We brought her to the hospital. They said she was fine, but I don't trust doctors. Something is just wrong. I can feel it. I mean, she's just unbelievable, Mr. Leroy. She always takes care of me, always makes sure I'm warm in the winter, makes sure my jacket is zipped. I can feel her love from a mile away. I just can't lose her."

"Wait, now, you ain't gots no reasons to be worried like that! Mr. Johnny, them doctors done told you that she be fine. You gots to trust somebody in this life. I gots your back too, Mr. Johnny. Always. For sure."

Johnny shook hands with his boss, and they both made their way outside. Taking off in different directions, they said they'd see each other the following day. A very somber Johnny made his way to the subway. Subways were a strange thing. You knew that at certain times they'd be busy, but sometimes you just couldn't figure it out.

The train was packed. And it smelled. It's a good thing that it was cold out. When it was hot, the heat held onto the smells. Body odor, urine and garbage, were just a few of the smells that were the normal, on the Brooklyn subways. The wheels on this car screeched like no others ever had. Johnny stood. There were a few seats, but his father had always told him to let woman and children sit. As Johnny listened to the sounds of the subway, the murmur of voices, the coughing and sneezing, the whoosh of the wind outside, it sounded like a symphony. A symphony buried deep within a concrete jungle. Johnny was tired. His head was starting to nod. But he couldn't let himself sleep. That was a good way to get hurt. Or worse. Two more stops. Johnny shook his head, as if trying to clear it.

As Johnny's stop approached, the normally very energetic teen, struggled to move. Willing himself to put one foot in front of the other, he made his way to the open doors.

Slowly walking down the metal steps, Johnny hit the streets. He felt something. As if someone was watching him. Turning around, Johnny saw two people. They kept coming towards him, long strides eating up the dirty streets, like a homeless person would, a free meal. Johnny held his ground and felt for his knife. He was too tired for this. Too worried about his mom. He just didn't have the fight in him tonight. As the strangers got closer and closer, Johnny thought about just how much he wanted out of Brooklyn. He was ready.

Focusing clearly now, Johnny pulled his knife from his pants. He may be tired, but he wasn't going down like this.

"Come on, baby. You know I love you. I'll just put it in for a minute."

Giggles and hushed laughter filled Johnny's ears as a young couple made their way past him. The guy just nodded towards Johnny. Johnny nodded back. Maybe Brooklyn wasn't all bad.

Chapter Thirty-Six

JOHNNY SPENT AS much time as possible studying for the entrance exam to Brooklyn College. As the big day arrived, he felt a sense of calm. After he finished, he felt confident that he had done well. The next few months were pretty uneventful, and as spring approached, Johnny was anxious to find out the test results.

Johnny sat in his English Literature class. It was one of the first warm days of spring, and he was sweating. His chest wounds had finally started to heal, but he was left with horrible scarring. As class ended, Mrs. Collins motioned for Johnny to come to the front of the classroom.

"Mr. Rostov, I have the results of your entrance exam."

"So? How'd I do, Mrs. Collins?"

"Well, how do you think you did?"

"I'm not sure. Pretty well, I guess. I hope."

"Well, Mr. Rostov, you did exceptionally well. In fact, you scored in the high nineties. I'm very proud of you."

"So, that means that I'm in?"

"Well, you were always in. Brooklyn College is a free college, but your labs and books will be discounted now. Used books are still the way to go."

Johnny was a bit confused. Thinking that Mrs. Collins was just getting him to apply himself more, Johnny understood.

"Thank you, Mrs. Collins. I appreciate all of your help."

Johnny met up with Jimmy and Danny after school.

"You guys remember the promise, right?

"What promise?" asked Danny.

"Yeah, we remember. No worries, Johnny. What happened that night, stays between us. Forever. And don't fuckin' worry about Mickey. That prick. He'd have as much to lose as any of us. He'll keep his trap shut, "said Jimmy.

"I'm just gonna head home. Work today, and then I'm gonna do some writing," offered Johnny.

"Writing? Schools over, shit-head. What the fuck are you writing about?"

"Just shit. You know, it makes me feel relaxed. I'm writing about us. All us guys, and what it was like growing up in this fuckin' armpit of a place. I can't wait to get out. And I will. I'm gonna fight my way out. My family's always been like that. M dad did it. They were gonna kill him in Russia. The commies. But he outsmarted them, and escaped. Came all the way here," explained Johnny.

"He shoulda stayed in Russia. This place just gotta be worse," said Danny.

Work was a bit uncomfortable that day. Johnny didn't say much. Leroy was also quiet. After making his way home, Johnny said hello to his father, and kissed his mom.

"Sit, John. Wash you face, and brush you teeth first. Then we eat."

"No, Mom. I ain't hungry. Ate at work today," lied, Johnny.

Johnny went to his bedroom, and lay on his narrow, stiff mattress. Johnny liked this room much more than his steamy and tiny room in Brownsville. At least, here, he had a window. Although the room was tiny, Anatole had made Johnny a small desk that fit in the corner perfectly. Hopping up off his bed, Johnny took a seat at his desk. The chair was a bit wobbly, but it'd do. Johnny opened the one draw that he had, and pulled out a stack of papers. *The Woman of My Dreams.* Johnny had played around with the title, over and over. He knew that he'd most likely change it several more times still. Having over two hundred pages written so far, Johnny was telling the story of growing up in Brownsville. His hardships, his passions, and his dreams. That was the main thing. His dreams. He wanted to get out of the filth, the crime, and the poverty of Brooklyn. He lived on Ralph Avenue now, but it was still hell. But most of all was his search for that perfect woman. He'd know it when he finally found her. She'd be perfect. He dreamed of her every night. He had already fallen in love with her. He just hadn't met her yet. She'd love him as well. She'd just have to. She'd have his mother's sweetness and caring, and they would connect in every way possible. Johnny was a happy kid, but he hurt inside. Deep inside. He may not have even been aware of it at a conscious level. The woman of his dreams would understand this. She'd have that same pain, that same hurt soul, deep within.

I don't know...maybe there's no such woman. Maybe I shouldn't even look. If I ain't gonna find her, what's the point?

Johnny stayed up almost all that night, writing, and writing. It was strange...by his writing, he was becoming more and more aware of his true feelings. Johnny wrote until his hand cramped. He flexed it a bit and continued to write. He couldn't stop. Finally, he fell asleep. Pencil in hand, he simply nodded off.

Johnny's senior year continued to be a transition for him. Before he knew it, it was graduation time. Johnny was happy, but scared. Scared of the future, scared that his mom hadn't been getting better, and scared that the woman that he'd already fallen in love with, may not even exist. One more week, and high school was over. Johnny walked down the hall, his eyes trying to memorize everything. Not only would this be his last few days in Brooklyn High School, but soon, he'd be out of Brooklyn...forever. Something was missing. Johnny was missing his boys. They didn't Always get along, but they always had his back.

"You know somethin', Johnny? We gotta hang out more. When's the last time we even got in trouble? I mean, we don't even bang whores down in the basement anymore. What the fuck? We ain't old men yet!" said Jimmy.

"You're right! Let's go get in some trouble! Let's steal something. Wait…oh man, I can't. I can't take a chance. I need to get into college and with all the shit I've gotten away with over the years, why take a chance now?"

"Okay, well at least, let's get a few bottles, and all of us should get shit faced. Just for old times' sake," said Jimmy.

"Yeah, that sounds good, Jimmy. I miss that. But shit, our lives don't end soon. I'm gonna go to college, but I'm right here in Brooklyn still. I'm gonna work, and then do home study. I'll be using the college library a lot, but there'll still be time for the Money Boys! Always!"

"I hope so. My uncle is getting' me a job at his garage. I'm good with cars already, but he's gonna teach me, and I'll be set. Who knows, maybe I'll get my own place someday."

"Let's meet up after school. We'll get some beers. You see Danny, you tell him, okay?"

Johnny took the subway back to Ralph Avenue. It was the beginning of the month; the relief check had come and the Rostov's had money. Johnny's mom was cooking dinner.

"John, wash face. I make the macaroni cheese. I know you like."

"Umm, okay, Mom. Thank you. I was gonna go see the boys. But sure, I'll eat first. Where's Dad?"

"Still work. He be here late. Okay, we eat now."

"Mom?

"Yes, John. What is?"

"Are you okay? I mean, really, okay? I worry. I worry always. Can I do more, so that you can rest?"

"Rest does no good for people. Need to work. I am fine, son. Just tired. Sometime. Do not worry for your mother. You have great future. You take care of yourself. Study, go to college. Have family with many children. Maybe five," said Sonia with a huge smile.

"Five? No way! Never! I can't imagine even having one. But, I do know one thing, Mom. I want to find the woman of my dreams. Like Dad did. The perfect woman."

"John, you make me cry. You so sweet. I love you so much."

"I love you too, Mom. I always will."

Johnny ate quickly. Before his mother had a chance to remind him, he put his plate in the sink and washed up and brushed his teeth.

"I hope the woman you dream for can cook. And clean. Because, I teach you nothing. John Rostov, you like little baby. Strong, smart, handsome man. But you always need a mom. Or your dreams," said Sonia, her smile growing even bigger.

She was right. Johnny was self-sufficient. On the streets, at least. He could take care of himself. He was smart, and tough. But as far as anything else? Not a chance. He never made a bed, folded a single piece of clothing, did any wash, and forget about cooking! Johnny's experience in the kitchen consisted of pouring a glass of water, or eating a piece of government cheese. After that, he was helpless.

The subway was empty, and it was a good thing. Because it stunk. Like armpits, and death. Johnny made his way to Christopher Street, and decided to go see Al. Crossing the street, he opened the door and heard the familiar sound of the chime.

"Al here? Johnny here to see him."

"Johnny who?"

This was a new guy. He didn't realize that Johnny was family. Near, a regular in the candy store. In fact, he pretty much grew up there.

"Just tell him Johnny!"

Things were different now. Johnny wasn't Johnny boy, the little wise-assed kid. He was almost six-foot tall, and will he was lean, all those push-ups had paid off. His wiry arms popped with muscles.

"What's the fuckin' racket out here? Hey…Johnny! How are you, kid? Look, Vito…this guy walks in here, he goes right by. Capisce?"

"Yeah. Whatever. Okay, Al. You the boss."

"Sorry kid. What's up? What can your Goomba, do for you today?"

"Nothin', Al. I just wanted to stop by. Few more days and I'm all done with high school."

"Ahh, okay. Al gets it now. Okay, kid. You finish up and you come see me. I'll set you up. We'll start with collections, and then…well, we'll see where we go. Okay, kid?"

Johnny knew well enough to not interrupt Al. He also knew that to say no, would be to insult him. Al was a good guy, but a bad-man.

"Okay, I'll come see you. I was thinkin' that maybe I should go to college. You know?"

"What? College? Lemme tell you somethin', kid. That's a great move. Forget collections. It's money, but you gotta have a strong neck to survive. You know...always lookin' over your shoulder. You're a tough kid. Always was slick. Even as a little fucker, rippin' off your pal, Al."

"I never did that..."

"Shut the fuck up! Come on back. Stop lookin' nervous. I ain't gonna shoot you...yet," Al laughed and laughed.

The two went back to Al's small office. Johnny remembered his first time in that office. So many years ago. Al had the same furniture. Shit, it looked like the same papers on the desk even.

"You need help with this college shit? You know...scharole? Money?"

"Well...I was gonna get a job...full time at Bechtel. You know, in Manhattan. Then go to class at night. Maybe do most of the work from home even. You know, help take care of my parents."

"Bechtel? Are you kiddin' me? Listen. You go down and ask to see Mr. Cairone. His name is Vincenzo, but you call him Mr. Cairone. And 'sir.' You got that? You tell him that Al sent you. Al from

Brownsville, okay? You say this real quiet-like. Capisce? You understand what I'm sayin', and how I'm sayin' it?"

"Yeah. Yes. I understand. And thank you, Al. I appreciate that."

"Okay, kid. You remember one thing…anyone, and I mean anyone fucks with you? You let Al know. I'll have their knees shattered, and their fuckin'' brains blown out. Especially the fuckin'' eggplants! I hate those niggers!"

Johnny knew that Al meant well, but he saw no colors. His friendship with Leroy had taught him to be color-blind.

"I will, Al."

Al opened his office door and walked Johnny to the front.

"Who the fuck you lookin' at now? You eggplant," said Johnny, barely able to hold back his laughter.

Vito just waved him off. He knew the deal.

"Hey, kid. You want some candy? Or are you just gonna steal it? You know. Like you always used to, when you was little! Hahaha. You don't think Al knew?"

Al gave Johnny a slap on the back and a half-hug as Johnny walked back onto Christopher Street. The blare of the horns was like music to his ears. Happy times. Bad ones also. But it was his home. Not much longer though. He was leaving. Brownsville and Brooklyn. The place didn't smell much better than the armpits and death smell of the subway.

Johnny crossed the street. He still refused to look both ways. A car was coming? Fuck it. He walked those streets like he owned them.

"Hey, you little fuck!"

The car's driver had to swerve a bit to avoid hitting Johnny. He let him know just how unhappy he was. Looking across the street, the driver saw Al.

"Never mind, kid. Sorry," as he took off quickly, never looking back.

Al just winked, and Johnny nodded. Johnny made his way to the alley. As he walked down the familiar, narrow road, he couldn't help himself. Mrs. Williams' bathroom light was on. Johnny didn't have to stand on his toes any longer. In fact, he needed to crouch down a bit. There she was. Reaching behind herself, she undid her huge bra. Johnny had seen those beautiful tits before, but he could never get enough. Next came the panties. That ass was almost as nice as those monster- melons. Mrs. Williams turned towards the window. Johnny froze. The window was partially fogged up from the bath water. Could she see him? Johnny wasn't sure, but he knew one thing. He could see everything that there was to see. And his dick was as hard as the car that almost hit him.

Mrs. Williams took the few steps left that separated her from the steamy window. Using a single finger to motion Johnny closer, she lifted the window upwards.

"Like what you see? You've been looking at me since you were a little boy. And by the looks of that bulge in your pants, there's nothing little about you anymore. No one's home."

As she slowly lowered the window, Johnny could feel his heart start to beat faster and faster. If it beat any faster, it would fall right out into the traffic on Christopher Street. Johnny raced around to the front of the building. The front door handle slowly turned, and Johnny pushed it open. Looking straight ahead, Johnny could see the sweeping motion of a large white towel, as it made its way into apartment 1C. It's what was under that towel, that Johnny just had to have. As the apartment's door started to close, Johnny put his foot in the way, bringing the closure to a halt.

"Have a seat. It's John, right?"

"Well, Johnny. I mean, yea, that's okay too. John," Johnny stammered.

Mrs. Williams looked amazing. Red lipstick had just been applied. Johnny wanted her lips wrapped around his cock. Sitting down next to him, her towel loosened a bit, her beautiful tits started to spill out. Leaning over, the blonde beauty whispered in Johnny's ear. Just the warmth of her breath made him even harder.

"No one will be home all night. I want you to fuck me, and I want it hard. And fast. Take your pants off. Now."

Johnny had his ragged pants off in mere seconds. The shorts followed, and Mrs. Williams' beautiful red lipstick was all over

Johnny's mammoth cock. She sucked and sucked, and has happened before, he lasted about thirty-seconds, exploding inside of her mouth.

"I'm sorry. I know I should warn a lady. But, umm…you are so good."

"But, I really wanted that inside of me. I wanted to fuck."

Johnny, now having some experience, and still hard as a rock, put his hands on the blonde beauty's shoulders and pushed her backwards onto the couch. Not saying a word, he guided his missile between her legs and started to push. Evidently, Mr. Williams must not have had much size, as Johnny had a hard time entering.

"Oh, my God…Johnny, it's so big. Fuck me. Come on, fuck me!"

Not needing to hear it again, Johnny started to fuck Mrs. Williams furiously. Faster and faster, harder and harder. His back was hurting, but he kept going.

"More…more. I coming!"

Just as Johnny exploded for a second time, Mrs. Williams pulled back.

"What the fuck are you doing to my wife? Come here, you skinny little fuck. I'm gonna kill you, you little bitch!"

"No! Doug…leave him be. It's my fault. Don't kill him!"

Mr. Williams was a huge man. The thing was, that Johnny had never seen him before. Standing well over six-foot, he must have weighed three-hundred pounds. His forearms were thicker than Johnny's thighs.

Seeing that she was distracting him, Mrs. Williams made eye contact with Johnny. Nodding slightly towards her front door, a panicked Johnny picked up his pants and shoes, and ran for his life. Out the front door, down the short hallway and onto a now dark Christopher Street, Johnny ran for his life. Jimmy, Danny, and the drinking would just have to wait.

Johnny never looked back. Not until he bounded up the green metal subway steps, did he slow and look behind him. Reaching for his knife, Johnny felt an overwhelming sense of panic, as it wasn't there! It must have slipped out, as his pants slid to Mrs. Williams' floor.

Oh, my God. That was close. I don't think that he saw my face. He sure as shit saw my ass though. Shit! Damn, that was good! That was the best piece of ass, I've ever had. Man, I've wanted to fuck her since I was seven years old. Maybe even before that. I musta jerked off to her, five-hundred times! I should go back! He didn't look so tough!

Johnny wondered if he could ever go back to Christopher Street. He surely could never peek into Mrs. Williams' window again…but then again, he wouldn't have to. He had gotten the real thing. Johnny loved woman. He loved sex, and there was no changing that. Not any time soon though. But he knew that for as much as he loved sex, he wanted more. He longed for the woman of his dreams.

Chapter Thirty-Seven

THE BIG DAY was finally here. Johnny, Jimmy, and Danny were finally graduating from the Brooklyn Slum. Johnny was happy, but not excited. He was focused. He was all set for Brooklyn College. The big thing was getting that full-time job. He had let Leroy know that he could work another week or so, but after that, he'd have to leave. He'd be forever grateful to Leroy, for giving him a job and even more than that, for teaching him so much about life. He would stop by and see Leroy, until he escaped the filth of Brooklyn, once and for all.

Anatole and Sonia were excited for the big day. Anatole, especially. It had been a long, and difficult journey for him. Things had not gone as planned, as he had hoped they would, but his son would now be graduating from an American High School. And he would be going to college. He reflected to his youth, the wealthy and trouble free days in Russia. How quickly that all changed. He had forbid himself to think about the horrors. Of the pit, the gunshot blast that killed his best friend. Today he thought of Christopher. How ironic that they would move to a street called Christopher. When he let himself, he could still feel the bodies squirming, the taste of the blood that seeped from above, the moans. Yes, life had not gone as planned, and he had made many a mistake. He regretted the day that he lost his temper, and his son's trust. He wished that he had done a better job taking care of his family. But his son would do better. A high school graduate! College bound. Yes, he was proud.

Johnny was early for the ceremony. He was already heeding his father's advice.

"Hey, you prick. Nice dress! Where's Jimmy?" asked Johnny.

"I hate these gowns. What the fuck? I can't wait for this shit to be over. Let's find Jimmy. I think we can all sit together," said Danny.

The boys found their friend and took their seats. They were supposed to sit with the groups that had the same first letter of their last names, but no one was listening.

Johnny listened as they started to call names to the front of the auditorium. He gazed around the large and plain looking room. He saw Al, and Mrs. Collins. Anatole and Sonia sat there beaming with pride. But Johnny's mind finally succumbed. Succumbed to what was really bothering him. Jackie. Jackie should be there. Ina strange way, he was there. Johnny could sense his presence.

"What are you waiting for? Go, you rat fuck! You are John Rostov, right?" said Jimmy.

Johnny popped up and made his way to the front stage. Shaking hands with the principal, he said thank you.

What the fuck am I thanking him for? I'm the one who went through all the shit. Fucking asshole.

Johnny returned to his seat. Danny and Jimmy took their turns as well. It was over. A new chapter was about to begin, and Johnny was ready. Ready for Bechtel, ready for college. Ready to begin. Begin his escape. His fight. To get out of this hellhole.

"I love you so, my son. I proud to you. I want only good for my son," said Sonia.

"Good job, John. You do well. Now, get job, take care of family. That is, when you meet her," said Anatole, with the slightest trace of a smile.

"Oh, I love her already. I haven't met her, but I love her."

"I know you say. I understand, John," said Anatole.

Johnny worked the next few weeks at the cafeteria. Now that school was over, he rode the subway each morning with his father.

His time with Leroy had ended. Johnny finished his last day and thanked Leroy.

"You taught me so much, Leroy. How to be a good worker, how to look at people, that everyone is the same. Black or white. It doesn't matter. We're all the same. Thanks for never giving up on me, boss."

"What in the damn ham sandwich is you talkin' 'bout, Mr. Johnny? You done teached me! Now I know. All you white folks isn't too bad. Now, you do your boss proud. Do up that 'ol college, and meet that dream girl. Just don't forget about 'ol Leroy, now."

"Never."

Johnny and Leroy gave each other a big hug. For the last time, Johnny heard the clicks of the lights going off, section by section. Walking out to the streets, Johnny headed for the subway. And Bechtel.

Johnny slept well that night. A knock at his bedroom door startled him a bit.

"John? You wake for now?"

"Yes, Mom. I'm up. Come in."

Sonia opened the old door and brought in a large brown bad. Inside, folded neatly were a new pair of slacks, a white shirt, a tie, a belt and a pair of black, shiny shoes.

"What's this, Mom?"

"You father work extra hard for you to get. You need for interview to job. Try on. If no fit, I fix."

Johnny had never had new clothes. His mother taught him how to make a knot for the blue tie. Everything fit perfectly.

"I hope you wash face, brush teeth before you put on, John."

"Oh yeah, sure. I mean, I did, yes," lied Johnny.

This was the day that Johnny had thought so much about. What was this guy's name? He should have written it down. Vincenzo? No, Mr. Cairone. That was it. Johnny would remember. Giving his mother a hug, and a kiss, Johnny headed for the apartment's front door.

"You okay, Mom?"

"Yes, John. Forget for me. Do good."

Johnny headed for the subway. He knew his way around Manhattan, well. The subway was crowded. The smell was, as usual, putrid. Johnny got off at his stop and walked the streets of the big city. Finding his destination, and full of confidence, Johnny pulled open the large heavy front door.

"The Bechtel Group."

Johnny walked around the lobby for a while. Looking for signs that may help direct him, he asked a sweet looking woman behind a large desk.

"Sign in. The offices are on the third floor. But they ain't hiring," she said.

Maybe she wasn't all that sweet. Johnny took to the staircase and made his way to floor number three. This was easy. Johnny had been climbing stairs, his entire life.

Knocking on a door marked "employees only", Johnny turned the doorknob and let himself in. Looking around, there must have been ten different desks. All with ugly woman sitting behind them.

"Can I help you, son? Do you work here?"

"No. But I will."

"Did you see the sign on the door? The one that said, 'employees only?'"

"Yes, and I will be one. Very soon in fact. Has anyone ever told you what a beautiful speaking voice you have?"

Johnny watched as the grimace turned to a big, wide smile.

"Why, aren't you the charmer. Okay, son. What can I help you with?"

"Vincenzo. I mean, Mr. Cairone, please."

Looking a bit stunned, the now, very pleasant lady directed Johnny to the fifth floor.

Johnny opened the door from the staircase, and wondered around until he saw the thin stenciled name "Mr. V. Cairone" on the translucent front glass, of an office door.

Johnny knocked a few times.

"Come in."

Johnny opened the door and walked into the office. Short, balding and chubby, Mr. Cairone was not at all what Johnny had pictured him to be

"How can I help you?"

"I need a job," answered a confident Johnny.

"You and the rest of the city. We're not hiring."

"I understand that sir. But, that would be for everyone else. My name is Johnny Rostov, sir. I can do any job that you need me to do. Just give me a chance, and I'll do it."

"We're not hiring, I said. Now, if you don't mind..."

"Al. Al from Brownsville, sir. He asked me to say hello to you."

Suddenly speechless, Mr. Cairone just stared at Johnny.

"You know Al?"

"Yes sir. Grew up across the street from…well, from where he works."

"You ever operate a press? A printing press, that is?"

"Yes sir. I can do anything. You give me a chance and I can do it."

"Okay, then. Go outside and see Lucy. She's my secretary. She will give you some forms to fill out. You can start next week."

"I can start today, sir. I mean, if that's okay. Sir."

"You are anxious, huh. Okay, well, fill out that paperwork, and go back down to the second floor. Look for a door that says "Printing." See Murphy. He's the supervisor."

"Thank you, sir. I appreciate it. Very much."

"Okay, son. And you tell Al, that I said hello."

"I will, sir."

Johnny found Lucy. She wasn't quite as ugly as all of the others. Plus, she had a big rack. As she leaned across her desk to hand Johnny the forms to be completed, Johnny stole a quick glance down the top of her blouse. This was a skilled move. Years and tears of practice led to moments like this.

"I saw that," said a stern sounding Lucy.

After finishing the paperwork, Johnny made his way to the printing room. Johnny had never even seen a printing press, let alone used one.

As he put his hand on the doorknob, Johnny could feel the vibrations of what lie on the other side. Opening the door, the noise was deafening.

A huge room, almost as big as the auditorium that he just attended graduation in, was filled with various sized presses. Workers worked quickly, moving from one end of a machine to the other. Paper was loaded at the top, higher end, and as the copies stacked up, they scurried around to the bottom, straightened and stacked the finished product on rolling carts.

I can do this shit. I survived Brownsville. Nothing scares me. Shit, I banged Mrs. Williams. Right in front of her husband!

A supervisor was walking around, checking samples at random.

"Yea! What?"

"Umm, Johnny. Johnny Rostov. Mr. Cairone sent me down. Told me to find Murph."

"Ahh jeez. Another fucking rookie. Just what I need. Okay, rookie, follow me. Take off that tie! You wanna get the life choked outta you?"

Johnny struggled to remove the unfamiliar neck-piece. It was special to him, none the less. His beloved mother had given it to him after all.

Soon, Johnny realized just what Murph had meant. Standing on a wooden crate, Johnny had to feed large pieces of paper into a fast-moving set of rollers. After that, he had to check the ink levels and add as needed. Quickly, he needed to get to the bottom of the press, where he would organize and stack the finished product on a cart with four large wheels. Johnny watched the worker move rapidly. This looked simple.

"Are you crazy? A white shirt? You'll learn. Hey, my name is Louie. Yours?"

"Johnny. I can barely hear in here!"

"You'll get used to it. You smoke?"

"A little. Sometimes, why?"

"No smokin' on the press. The cleaning fluids are explosive. Okay? Serious."

"Okay. You got it."

Within minutes, Johnny was soaked in sweat. He could deal with it. It couldn't be any worse than those hot summers nights in Brownsville. Johnny had started at about ten am. By the time lunch rolled around, he was dying of thirst.

"There's a cooler over there. You bring lunch?" asked Louie.

"No, I'm good. I will tomorrow."

Johnny made it through the day. And then a week. After about a month, there was no press that he couldn't run. And faster and better than anyone else there. Even the older guys that had been there for years, and years. Johnny would start at $1.10 an hour. He knew he could make much more money, hustling on the streets of Brownsville. Hell, he could make many times that as a worker for Al. But, Johnny wanted to do this the right way. This was the first step. Then college, and along the way, the woman of his dreams.

After about a month, Murph approached Johnny as he walked through the door. Early, as usual, he knew that he was doing a good job. What was this about?

"Hey, Johnny. Got word from Vinny, upstairs, there's a position opening. Upstairs. You're gonna work in the supply room. Much better work. You can go back to that white shirt. Even that tie. I don't know more than that though. Go on up. See Norma. Good job, kid. You never did any of this shit before, did you? Vinny said you had experience, but I knew you were fulla shit. Come see us sometime."

Johnny shook Murph's hand and started towards the fourth floor.

"Oh, Murph! I'm okay dressed like this?"

"Yea, they know the deal. Just wear that fancy shit tomorrow."

Bounding up the stairs, Johnny found Norma. The starting pay would be $1.25 an hour. He's be responsible for putting orders together as they came in. There was an employee leaving in two weeks. He would take the orders, mostly office supplies, and bring them all over the building. Pencils, paper, typewriters, empty folders, and more. Johnny would be taking his place.

Johnny trained, over those two weeks and had it down pat. He could find his way around Brooklyn, so finding his way around Bechtel would be easy.

"Johnny. Here you go. Cart is loaded and you're ready to go. Take the cart to the service elevators and then on to the destination written on the tags. Be nice. Smile."

Johnny did as he was told. He delivered pencils and pens, folders and staples. The cart was almost empty now. There was one item left and then he'd go back to the storage room and re-fill the cart. He was good at this. He made people laugh, and smile, and he was fast.

Okay, typewriter to the Chief Engineer's office. Mr. Kobalt. Let's go.

Knocking as he opened the door, Johnny approached the secretary. Pushing his cart with the typewriter, he came up quickly on the petite brunette.

"Oh! You startled me!"

Johnny froze. She was the most beautiful woman that he had ever seen. Her voice was as sweet as any he had ever heard.

"Hello? Hello? Can I help you?" she asked.

"Hi. How are you? I'm Johnny. I have your typewriter?"

"Is that a question?"

"No. But, what's your name?" asked Johnny.

Looking directly into her beautiful eyes, Johnny also noticed the small sign on her desk.

"Grace? I'm Johnny."

"I know that. You've told me twice now. Well, Johnny, we need that new typewriter. I'm afraid it's a little too heavy for me though."

Grace stood up, and Johnny could see that she was tiny. Her hair was dark, almost black and everything about her was perfect. She even smelled amazing.

"I'll take care of everything. Here, lemme take that old one from you, and set up the new one."

Johnny lifted the heavy typewriter and put it on the bottom cart of the shelf. He then replaced it with the new one.

"Okay, thank you. Back to work now."

"But, make sure it works okay, Grace. I mean, make sure it's perfect for you."

"It's fine. Thank you again. Now, I have a lot of work to get back to."

"Grace? Would you like to go out with me?" said Johnny with the most charming of smiles that he could muster up.

"Well, no. I don't even know you. I really do need to work now. Thanks."

"Okay, well I'll be back tomorrow."

"How do you know that I'll need anything?"

Johnny was back pedaling, and had to think quickly.

"Loneliness! I'll bring you another typewriter…in case that one gets lonely!"

Grace couldn't help herself. She laughed. And smiled. Then laughed and giggled some more. She actually had to put her hand over her mouth, to soften her laughter.

Johnny was totally taken. Her laughter was amazing and her smile lit up the entire room. He felt so amazing, just meeting her. Talking to her.

"Tomorrow!" laughed Johnny, as he opened the office door and disappeared.

When Johnny went home later, he couldn't get Grace out of his mind. As he made his way back to Ralph Avenue, he made his way up the stairs as if he was floating.

"Hi, Mom! I love you!"

"What wrong, John? You no get job, no more?"

"No, I not only still have my job, but I got a promotion. More money too. But that's not it, Mom. I met her!"

"Who this you meet?"

"Grace. The woman of my dreams, Mom."

"Be careful, John. Many woman in this world."

"I know, Mom. But she's the one. I already asked her out."

"No good, John. If she say yes, she wrong for my John," said a worried looking Sonia.

"No, Mom. She said no! She's perfect. I won't give up though. Look at this face. How could a woman resist me?"

Sonia started to laugh and laugh. Johnny was the happiest he'd ever been. Johnny went to wash his face and brush his teeth. Sonia, putting a cloth over her mouth, started to cough. Her chest felt funny. But she didn't want Johnny to know.

Johnny made sure that his good clothes were clean. Well, he asked his mom to make sure. Johnny would make sure he looked and even smelled his best in the morning.

I wonder where she lives? Does she live alone? She's just adorable. Beautiful. Perfect. I'm in love!

Johnny woke up early. He bathed, shaved and even splashed some aftershave on. Probably a little too much. Full of energy, Johnny made his way to Manhattan.

"Any orders for Mr. Kobalts office? I mean, I brought her…I mean, Mr. Kobalt, a typewriter yesterday. Do they need pencils or pens?"

"Whoa, slow down," said Norma.

"I'm just ready to work!"

"You're ready, alright," smiled Norma.

Any carts ready?" asked Johnny.

"You just got here. Let's take inventory. You're doing very well. There may even be another position for you…"

"No! I like this one, fine. I want to make those deliveries."

"Yes, but becoming a purchasing agent pays $1.50 an hour."

Johnny really needed the money. But he wanted to continue to see Grace. Well, one thing at a time. Johnny took a deep breath and listened to Norma as she walked him through the inventory process.

The day went along smoothly, and Johnny made his deliveries. With every cart-full of supplies, came the hopes of a Mr. Kobalt's office delivery.

"Johnny, there's a cart over there for Mr. Kobalt," said Norma.

Johnny's heart skipped a beat. Grace! But Johnny only saw an empty cart.

"The cart's empty," said Johnny.

"Look again."

Looking more closely, Johnny could see that there was a single pencil sitting on top of the cart. Norma winked, and Johnny took off. Excitedly, Johnny made his way to Mr. Kobalt's office. Again, knocking as he opened the door, he saw her. She was even more stunning than he remembered. Johnny had never even seen Mr. Kobalt, and Grace was alone again.

"I heard that you needed a pencil?" smiled Johnny.

Grace lifted her head up. She had been typing a mile a minute and was intense in the way she went about her work.

Doing a double-take, Grace slowly smiled and then shook her head, while letting out a cute little laugh.

"You are so funny. Yes, I really needed that pencil. Thank you."

"I know you remember my name. Come on, what is it?" asked Johnny.

"Umm, umm…I don't remember. Okay, I must get back to work now. I'm busy."

Grace couldn't help but shake her head and smile. All of the sudden, she started to laugh.

"You see? I knew you couldn't resist my charm. And my good looks!"

"Go away!" said Grace, in a hushed tone.

"Not until you go out with me."

"No. I don't know you. Besides, I'm very busy."

"Busy at home? Where is home? Do you live by yourself?"

Grace looked around and shook her head back and forth. This charming, and handsome guy sure was persistent.

"I live in Queens. With my mother and my sister Rose. I have plenty of other brothers and sisters, but they've all moved out. Okay? Now let me work!"

"Grace, will you go out with me?"

"No." Grace was still smiling.

"Grace? What's your last name?"

"If I tell you, will you go?"

"Yes!"

"Mannello. Grace Mannello, okay?"

"Okay, Grace Mannello. Someday you're gonna be Grace Rostov. Mrs. Grace Rostov!"

Johnny had struck out two times, but he wasn't the quitting type. This was the girl of his dreams. One in a million. He loved her before he ever met her. He loved her even more now, after meeting her. She was the one. He'd love her forever.

Chapter Thirty-Eight

JOHNNY WAS SO consumed with Grace, that he had neglected to stay on top of his getting things in order, for college. Everything took a backseat to Grace. Johnny was determined to convince Grace to go out with him. He decided to turn the Rostov charm on, full tilt. Johnny decided to buy Grace two roses. He brought them to work with him, and at the first opportunity, made his way to Mr. Kobalt's office. As had become his custom, Johnny knocked as he entered the office.

"Well, hello Mrs. Rostov…"

"And how exactly can I help you, son?"

Johnny was taken aback by the booming, and very deep voice. What was Mr. Kobalt doing, interfering with his time with Grace?

"Hello, sir. I'm from the supply room. Johnny, Johnny Rostov. I was just checking up on the new typewriter that I brought your lovely secretary, Grace."

"Oh, I can see that. I think perhaps that maybe you were just checking up on my lovely secretary?"

Johnny was silent. Suddenly, he saw a slight smile on Mr. Kobalt's weathered face.

"I sure hope that rose isn't for me. I wouldn't want my wife getting jealous," added the boss.

Johnny smiled. Mr. Kobalt was an okay guy.

"Grace, do you have those reports ready?"

"They're already on your desk, sir."

Mr. Kobalt thanked Grace and entered his office, closing the opaque glass door behind him.

"What are you doing? I told you, that I'm busy here. You're so funny though," said Grace with a school-girl's smile.

"Here, this is for you," said Johnny, as he handed Grace a single red rose.

"Thank you! But not here. Thank you, but go! I have a pile of paperwork to get through," said Grace, in a hushed tone.

"Okay, but, now will you go out with me?" asked Johnny.

"No! Shhh, he'll hear you."

"Okay, but you'll see. You'll love me. Soon enough. How could you possibly resist me?" smiled Johnny.

Johnny blew Grace a kiss and left. Seconds later, he reappeared and gave Grace the second rose.

"In case the first one gets lonely!"

"You are something else. Maybe you should date my sister. After all, her name is Rose," said Grace with a huge smile.

Grace was not the type to laugh at her own jokes. But laugh she did.

Johnny wasn't the only one who worked the rest of that day while distracted. Grace was quite taken with Johnny, but she was a professional. After all, being the secretary for The Chief engineer for Bechtel Group was a very prestigious position. Grace needed this job and had worked very hard to get it. A quiet, but fun loving student at Newtown High School in Queens, Grace had earned a scholarship to the prestigious Katherine Gibbs Academy. In fact, she won the even more prestigious "White Glove" tier division, as one of the highest scoring applicants on record. Yes, Johnny would have to be on his toes with this one. Grace was his equal in every single way. Except with handling knives, of course.

Johnny had found out that Grace left at five, the same as he did. He asked Norma if he could please leave a few minutes early.

"Gotta catch her before she gets on the subway, huh Johnny?"

"You know it!" said Johnny.

Johnny was waiting out front for Grace. It was five o'clock and had just started to rain.

"I don't have an umbrella, but here, let me offer my jacket, so you can keep your beautiful face, nice and dry," said Johnny, the gentleman.

"You again? Oh my! You really don't give up, do you?"

"Right here…right in front of all these fine New Yorkers, Grace Mannello, will you please go out with me?"

Grace was smitten. She was weakening. She barely knew this tall, good looking, funny and charming stranger. But she liked him. A lot. Grace was starting to see beyond Johnny's charm and handsome, good looks. There was something else. Something that Grace was drawn to.

"Okay! Okay! Yes!" she giggled.

"I knew it! I knew it! You've always been crazy about me! You just never knew it! Come on, let's get a cup of coffee," said Johnny as he held his light jacket over Grace's head.

"What, now? No. I have to go home. I need to make dinner for my brother. And my mother. My brother Joe, he's moved out, but he's always there for a meal. A meal made by me! Some other time!"

Johnny genuinely looked devastated.

"I don't think I can survive another day, without your company. Come on, Grace. Just a cup of coffee. Then I'll walk you to the subway. Heck, I'll go with you to your home. Just to make sure you get back ok. And stay dry!"

"Boy, I've never in all my life, met anyone like you. Okay. Just a cup of coffee. One!"

Grace was once again overwhelmed by that strange feeling. She was starting to feel safe around Johnny Rostov.

Grace's father. Ignazio Mannello, was a tailor by trade. He and his wife, Maria had longed to come to America. Living in Calabria, Italy, a beautiful area in Sothern Italy, was tough. It was a very clean and tidy, but extremely poor area. The Mannello's barely could feed their children. So, with a pregnant Maria, Ignazio, after saving every penny he could, took off for America.

They reasoned that Ignazio could find work in New York City. After all, there would always be a need for tailors in the big city. Ignazio worked and worked, saving every penny to bring over his family. He missed them so. After two years, Maria and the kids were on their way. Ignazio had saved enough money to get a nice two-bedroom apartment in the Jackson heights section of Queens. The family was soon reunited and Ignazio continued to work hard. The Mannelo's soon added two more members to their large family: There was Rose, and then finally, Grace. Grace was a lovely child. The apple of her father's eye, they became extremely close. Grace loved her daddy. When she was about two years old, she and her daddy were walking down the street when Grace saw a little girl holding a doll. Ignazio slowed down a bit, and observed his daughter. Grace watched closely as this little girl kissed her doll, and put her in a tiny little carriage. The look on Grace's face, told the whole story, and Ignazio understood. Soon thereafter, Ignazio gave his beautiful daughter a very special present. Ignazio brought Grace into the large living room. Grace worked on removing the wrapping paper.

"A doll! Oh daddy, thank you. I love you."

"There's more, Grace. Look!"

Ignazio rolled into the room a tiny baby carriage.

"For me? And my own baby?"

"Yes, Grace. Just for you. Daddy loves you, and will always be there to take care of you.

Over the next year, Grace was a very happy little girl. She had her doll, which she named Dorothy, as well as her carriage. She felt special. And she felt loved.

That weekend, the Mannello house was very quiet. Everyone was sad. Rose was crying, as was grace's mom, Maria.

"What is wrong?" asked Grace.

"I'm scared. Where's my daddy? I need my daddy."

It was soon explained to Grace, that her beloved daddy had fallen ill. He had passed away. Grace was almost three years old, and this concept was hard for her to understand. Grace missed her daddy. Who would take care of her now? Daddy had said that he would. Where was her daddy?

Johnny and Grace walked down the streets of Manhattan, Johnny holding his jacket over Grace. Suddenly, someone inadvertently bumped into Grace. Johnny's Brownsville instincts took over.

"Hey, pal. You have something to say?"

"Huh? Like what?"

"Like, saying you're sorry, to my girl here!"

Johnny locked eyed eyes with the rude, but harmless stranger. Slowly, he moved his free hand towards his pocket. Pausing for effect, Johnny held his glare.

"Okay, okay. Look, I'm sorry."

"Are you okay, Grace?"

"Yes! I'm fine! I can take care of myself, thank you!"

Yes, she could. But deep inside, that meant a lot to Grace. She liked this new friend, and liked the way he took care of her. She was starting to really have feelings for this Brownsville charmer. But Grace, at that moment, realized something. She hadn't felt protected like that, since she was a very little girl. Since her daddy took care of her.

"Lexington Candy Shop, right here," as Johnny steered his girl to the front door.

"Candy store? You said a cup of coffee. One cup of coffee," said a puzzled Grace.

"That's right. The coffee here is amazing. Come on in. You didn't get wet, did you? Let's sit at the front counter, okay?"

Johnny reached for Grace's hand. As he held it, he could just feel the most amazing feeling come over him. This was so right. They were just meant to be together. As Grace gazed at Johnny, he just knew that she felt the same way.

I know she's gonna tell me she loves me!

"Johnny…I can't get on this stool. I'm not tall enough!" giggled Grace.

Johnny laughed. Sure, she could. Maybe she couldn't. She was that tiny. But to Johnny, that made her all the more adorable.

"I tower over my mother!" she smiled.

Johnny gazed at the tables, until he saw an empty one.

"Here we go. Even better. I always sit here."

"Have you even been here before, Johnny?"

"Of course not!"

The two, laughed, and laughed. The waitress approached, and Johnny ordered for them both.

"My girl here will have coffee. Black, no sugar. I'll have an egg cream. Then we'll have two pieces of…coffee cake."

Johnny looked at Grace and her eyes were just melting into his gaze.

"How did you know?"

"I told you. I've always loved you. I've just had to wait to finally meet you."

"You're crazy!"

"Grace, you don't know the half of it. I am. Crazy about you, that is."

Johnny and Grace enjoyed their light meal. The laughs never stopped, but Johnny felt something he'd never felt before. Trust. He could tell her anything. Anything! And he wanted to know everything about her. It was difficult, getting her to open up. Perhaps that was because Johnny never stopped talking. And all of it was about himself. But he was charming. And she was sold. Grace was finally letting herself feel secure again. She felt safe with Johnny. He'd always take care of her.

Johnny had a lot of feelings. They were locked up inside. Some were deeply hidden, but Grace was his key. Everything was safe with her next to him. They were a team. He just knew that this was right.

When they finished, Johnny paid the bill, and they left. It had stopped raining, but the summer's sun had started its descent. A slight chill had taken hold of the big, bold streets of the city.

"Let's go. I wanna make sure that you get home okay. Plus, I wanna meet your, so very tall mother. Johnny suddenly thought of Mrs. Mangione. Italian mothers were extra special, and Johnny couldn't wait to meet Grace's.

"I'm fine! I'm a big girl. I'll see you tomorrow."

"No, I'll go with you."

"Really. I'm okay!"

With that, Grace almost kicked the pavement with her high heels.

"Did you just stomp your feet?" asked Johnny with an adoring look.

Grace just nodded. Okay, she was a bit tougher than he had thought. But, he even loved *that* about her.

Johnny walked Grace to her subway. As the train pulled up, he thanked her for spending time with him, and that he looked forward to seeing her at work tomorrow.

"Bye!" said a cheery looking Grace.

"Grace!"

Johnny stepped forward. Leaning down, he gently put his right hand around the nape of Grace's neck. Gently caressing her dark, beautiful hair, he kissed her. And kept kissing her. The subway doors closed, and the train took off. Johnny slowly pulled away, and then gave Grace another, small kiss.

"Your train just left."

"I know. They'll be another."

Sitting on a platform bench, Johnny felt as if this was all a dream. It had been a dream. He had dreamed of this moment, of this woman, for all his life. It was such a strange and surreal feeling, finally meeting someone that he had long been in love with. Johnny was born to love Grace. Grace Mannello was all that he wanted, all that he ever could have wanted.

Before he knew it, the next subway train approached. The bench shook, the vibrations felt, all throughout the platform.

"Johnny, I really must go now. This was wonderful," said Grace.

"Okay, be careful now. Are you sure that…"

"Yes! Johnny Rostov, do I need to stomp my feet again?" smiled Grace.

Holding hands, Grace slowly backed away. Not wanting to let go, they barely held on, fingers locked together. Their fingers let go of each other and Grace looked one last time into Johnny's eyes. She then disappeared into the subway train, and into the night.

Chapter Thirty-Nine

JOHNNY COULD BARELY sleep that night. Between working full time, preparing for college, and finding the love of his life, his mind was racing. Johnny had to put his feelings down on paper. He decided to resume his writing. Sitting at his small desk, Johnny brought his story up to date. Writing his feelings down, Johnny realized just how much this was meant to be.

As he continued to write, Johnny heard something outside of his bedroom. It was Sonia, and she was coughing.

"Mom? Are you okay?"

"John. Why you wake? Go sleep. You work in morning. I am good. Just have cough."

"Mom, maybe we need to go back to the hospital. Let me talk to Dad about it."

"No, your father worry too much now. I am okay."

Johnny didn't believe that. And was worried. Very worried.

Eventually, Johnny drifted off.

In the morning, tired, Johnny made his way into Manhattan.

"Hi! I missed you!" said Grace.

"Hi."

"What's wrong, Johnny? Tell me. Please."

"Nothing. I'm okay. Just some things on my mind."

Johnny knew that Grace was busy. Work was work, after all.

"Can we talk after work? Maybe have a cup of coffee?"

This was a side of Johnny, that Grace hadn't seen before. He was subdued, and distant. Worried.

"Sure, I was hoping that we could do that anyhow."

Work dragged on, and on. Johnny stayed busy, but he couldn't stop worrying about his mother. At five o'clock. Johnny stood outside again, and waited for Grace.

"What's wrong, Johnny?"

As they walked together, Johnny explained his concerns, as well as his fears. Johnny was a tough, young man, and he could never talk to his boys like this, but Grace was different. His feelings just flowed freely. From deep within his soul, they easily came to the surface, and Grace was an amazing listener. Never having a lot to say, she listened in a way that Johnny just knew that she cared. Deeply. Passionately. Completely.

"You really love her, don't you?"

"Yes. Grace, I love her so much. She's such a wonderful person. Sweet, smart, and caring. I'm a grown man, but she still worries that my jacket may not be buttoned up, that I'll get a chill. Every single one of my friends that met her, fell in love with her, they all wished that she was their mom. I've been very lucky. And now, you. Now I have you. I'm a lucky man. Grace, I'd love to meet your family. That is, if you want me to."

"Sure, Johnny. Whenever you want. My brothers…well, they can be…difficult at times."

"Your father lets them be that way? Mine never would."

"My father died when I was almost three years old. My brother, Joe…he's the oldest. He pretty much runs everything. My other brother, Al, he was in the war. He started to drink, and…well, it causes some problems. My sisters, Rose, Yolanda, and Frances are all wonderful. Especially Rose. We're close in age and we've always been close. Come today. It may take your mind off of things."

"Okay. I can't stay too long. My mom…I need to make sure that she's okay."

"Another time?" asked Grace.

"No, today is fine."

Johnny and Grace made their way to Queens. Jackson Heights. As they walked the streets, Johnny realized something.

Man, I haven't seen so many Italians since I was little and hung out at the candy store every day.

Opening the front door, Johnny and Grace walked up the dark flight of stairs. Grace fumbled through her pocketbook, and found her keys. Letting herself in, she yelled out.

"Mom? We have company."

Right there in front of Johnny, sat the sweetest looking soul.

"Grace, you're late. Where's my dinner?"

"Johnny, this is my brother, Joe."

"Hi, Joe. Nice to meet you."

Johnny extended his hand, to show respect.

"So, what are your intentions with my sister?"

Johnny stiffened. He didn't like this Joe guy, already.

I hope I don't have to cut this fucker up in his own fucking house.

"Intentions?"

"Joe! Don't say things like that. He's drunk, Johnny. Ignore him."

"No, that's okay, Grace. My intentions, Joe? To take care of her. Every day. From here forward, that's my life. To take care of her. And to make sure no one, and I do mean no one, ever harms her. In any way. Understood?"

Grace was worried, but Joe just shook his head and walked away. Grace was overcome with emotions. Emotions and memories from when she was a little girl.

Right here, in this very room, I remember my daddy. He took care of me, protected me. Now, I have my new protector. I feel so safe with Johnny.

Johnny walked over to Grace's mom. Looking so comfortable, sitting in her chair, Johnny reached down and gave her a gentle hug. Grace was right. As short as she was, her mother was even tinier.

"Nice to meet you." said Johnny.

"Ciao."

The Italian started to flow, and Grace and her mom were talking and smiling, back and forth. Finally, Grace's mom nodded towards Johnny and said, "Nice. Lui è bello."

Grace giggled, as did her mother.

Johnny looked at Grace with an expression that was saying *"What? What are you guys laughing about?"*

"She likes you. She said you're handsome," smiled Grace.

"Well, of course I am!"

Grace had been right. Doing something different had taken his mind off his worries. A little bit at least.

"Come into the kitchen. I'll pour you something to drink," said Grace.

"Come downstairs to the bar. Drink like a real man. Can your skinny ass even drink?" asked Joe, as he suddenly reappeared.

"Joe! Stop it!"

Johnny glared at Joe. He sensed that if he wasn't there, that Joe may have really yelled at Grace. Or worse. But he didn't. He wouldn't. He knew better.

A fast learner. Good for you. You fuck. You don't know who you're messing with here. I'd die for this woman.

"No, I'm fine, Joe. Sure, Grace. I'll have whatever you'd like to have." Johnny followed Grace into the tiny, little kitchen. As he crossed paths with Joe, he stared at him. Joe, once again, looked away.

"Sit down, Johnny. Would you like some lemonade? Maybe a beer?"

"Water. Water is fine. Really."

Johnny sat there, and just gazed at Grace. Grace's mother walked into the kitchen. As tiny as these two ladies were, this kitchen was getting crowded.

"Lui è Innamorato di te," giggled Grace's mom.

"Mamma! Stop that," smiled Grace.

Johnny didn't say a word. He knew it was good though, as Grace's laughter was a give-away.

"She said that you're in love with me," whispered Grace, after leaning over towards Johnny.

"I think I love her, as well," said Johnny.

"Cos'ha detto?"

"Mamma. English. He loves you too," smiled Grace.

Johnny was totally loving Grace's mom. He stayed for about an hour more and then realized that he better be heading back to Brooklyn. He was still concerned about his mom.

Johnny gently hugged Grace's mom and said goodbye.

"I'll walk with you to the train," said Grace.

"No. You stay here. You're nice and safe. I don't want to have to kill anyone who may bump into you," laughed Johnny.

While Johnny was indeed joking, Grace appreciated his protectiveness. She had barely had a father, after all. Besides Johnny's good looks and charm, his caring and protective soul, may have appealed to grace even more. They walked together, down the stairs and outside to the streets of Queens.

"Bye, Grace. Thank you for having me over. You know something?"

"What, Johnny?"

"I love you."

"But, we barely know each other, Johnny."

"Tell me you don't love me," asked Johnny.

Grace just stood there. She knew that she was falling for this wonderful, and caring man, from Brooklyn, but love?

"Stop. I don't know. I think so. Maybe!" she smiled.

Johnny reached over and kissed Grace. They continued to kiss until a voice from above interrupted them.

"Bambina!"

Grace's mother had opened their second story window. She was reminding Johnny that, that was *her* baby.

Johnny and Grace both started to laugh. Johnny blew Grace's mom a kiss, and backing away, waved once more to Grace. Johnny mouthed "I love you!" and turned, disappearing into the streets of Queens.

Grace went back inside. She needed to think. Think about her past. The pain that she felt when she was just a little girl. Maybe she had blocked out many of the emotions that she had felt.

"Your boyfriend is a smart ass. He's lucky…"

"Oh Joe, stop it. You're the one who's lucky."

Grace needed to get away. She started to cry. Grabbing her pocketbook, she started to take off. Opening the door, she looked back at her mom. She had tears in her eyes.

"Mamma, it's okay. I'm just going to take a walk. I love you."

Grace walked back in and gave her mother a kiss. She loved her so much.

Walking through the streets of Queens, Grace couldn't stop thinking of her daddy. She barely remembered his face, but she vividly remembered that feeling…the feeling of safety. As a little girl she knew that no harm could her come to her, as long as she had her Daddy. Grace decided to do something that she never did. She decided to visit her father's grave.

It was a long bus ride, but when Grace got to the cemetery, she had no idea where to go. Looking around, she could see that there were signs that showed locations based on the alphabet. Grace looked for the "M's". Walking up and down the rows, she finally saw the tombstone. "Mannello". It was a large marker, set under large shade trees. Grace started to feel even more emotional.

Daddy. I miss you. I've missed you so. I'm still your little girl and I always will be. I love you daddy.

Grace sobbed quietly. She felt her father's presence. And she felt his approval.

The subway ride went quickly, and Johnny was soon bounding up the stairs to his Ralph Avenue apartment. Opening the door, Johnny was faced with his worst nightmare.

"John. Help me. Your mother, she is very sick. Pains in chest."

The Rostov's had never gotten a phone, so Johnny thought quickly.

"Hold on. I'm gonna go down the street to the grocer's, and use their phone. An ambulance will be here soon. I'll tell them to hurry."

Johnny flew down the block and begged the grocer to use their phone. He called the hospital and pleaded with them to send an ambulance. It was too far to walk, and Sonia was too ill to get to a subway.

It took about twenty minutes, but they finally got there. Anatole was very nervous and Johnny, seeing the need, stepped up. He gave them all her information, and made certain they were gentle when putting her on the stretcher. Following them out to the ambulance, Johnny held the rear door open, and made certain that they were careful when loading her into her ride.

"Come on, Dad, let's get the subway, and we'll meet them at the hospital…Dad?"

Anatole was in a daze. He had been through so much in his life, and had shown so much bravery, but now, he was almost frozen.

"Dad! Let's go!" yelled Johnny.

"Yes, okay. We go," replied a somber Anatole.

It took about thirty minutes, but Johnny and Anatole finally arrived at the hospital.

"Sonia. Sonia Rostov. Her son, and husband here."

Johnny had advised the nurse behind the long front desk. Doctors and nurses flurried about. Patients on stretchers were brought behind two large swinging type doors.

"Okay. I know you're here. As soon as the doctors say anything, I will let you know," replied an older, kind looking nurse.

"But…that's my mom! I need to see her!"

"I understand. And I promise you that I will get you as soon as I hear a word. Let the doctors do their jobs, please."

Johnny led his shaken father to the waiting area. Johnny had work tomorrow, but he knew that he wouldn't be able to make it. Bechtel was a huge company and he was hoping that he could get through and leave a message for Norma.

"May I please use your phone? Please? I need to call my job," asked Johnny.

The nurse looked side to side, and then pushed the phone across the desktop, towards Johnny. Johnny was able to contact someone, and they promised to leave a written note on Norma's desk.

Johnny so wanted to talk to Grace. He needed her.

Johnny and his dad waited impatiently. Anatole was a big smoker, and was outside puffing away, when a nurse approached a tired, Johnny.

"Son. This is Dr. Everett. He will speak with you and your father."

"Okay, lemme get him. He's right outside."

Johnny darted outside and grabbed his father. As he came back in, he noticed the downcast look on the doctor's face. This wasn't good.

"Mr. Rostov? Your wife had a major heart attack. I'm very sorry, we did everything we could, but she's gone."

"What is he say? What?" asked Anatole, as he looked directly at his son.

"Doctor, can't you do something else? Please! Please try something else!"

"Again. I'm so sorry. She most likely had a heart condition for many years. It was just too far gone. I am so sorry."

And just like that, he walked away. Johnny and Anatole just stood there in stunned disbelief. This couldn't be happening. This was Johnny's mom.

No! This isn't real. Mom! I love you, Mom...

Anatole could barely speak. He did however, approach a nurse and ask to see his wife.

"Come, John. We say goodbye."

Johnny, steadying his father, walked with him behind the double doors. A nurse motioned to them, and led them to a hospital bed that had a screen wrapped around it. Pulling open the screen, there she was.

She just looks like she's sleeping. Mom! No! Please! Wake up. I love you...

Anatole approached the bed. He pulled up a chair and sat besides his wife.

"My Sonia. I love you so. We be through so much. You leave me soon. Too soon. I am sorry that I no better husband and man for you."

Leaning over, he kissed his beloved wife. Johnny felt sick. Sick to his stomach, and sick that he wasn't home earlier. Maybe, he could have done something. This was his fault. Just like it was his fault that Jackie died!

"I'm sorry, Mom. I let you down. I should have been there, I should have been home more. I wanted you to meet her. She's like you, Mom. She's wonderful, just like you. I love you."

Johnny and his father stood there for a while and just stared. Anatole was quiet. Johnny was worried about him. A life spent together, and then it's just gone. It wasn't fair. He had just spoken to his mom, earlier that very day. He just wanted to talk to her once more. He needed Grace. He needed the only woman, other than his mother, that he truly loved.

It was the quietest train ride of his life. The screeching rails, fell suddenly silent. The rumble of the passengers, a hushed whisper. Anatole was unsteady, and Johnny was there for him. Climbing the stairs to their empty apartment, the two men opened the apartment door. The door creaked, but all else was silent. Sonia's apron sat, folded across a kitchen chair. This couldn't be happening. Johnny had never experienced such pain. Nothing could ever be good again. Who would take care of him? How would his father get by? Sonia took care of both of them. Anatole, avoiding going to his and Sonia's bedroom, lay down on the couch and cried. Johnny went to his room, and did the same. Getting up to use the bathroom, Johnny saw that his father had finally fallen asleep.

In the morning, Anatole asked Johnny if he could handle the arrangements. This was very difficult for Johnny. He had no experience with this, but it was what it was. Someone had to do it, and it was him. As Johnny started to splash some water on his face, and wash up, he heard his dad talking to someone. Johnny patted himself dry, and went to the front door.

"Grace? What in the world are you doing here? This area isn't safe. Wait...how did you even know where I lived?"

"I worried when you weren't in this morning. I spoke to Norma and she told me that you were in the hospital with your mom. Your father just explained that she passed. I'm so sorry, Johnny."

Tears rolled down Grace's face. As she spoke, her voice cracked. She was genuinely emotional and sad.

Johnny put his arms around Grace. They held each other. As Johnny led Grace into the small apartment, they sat down at the kitchen table.

"I'll help you, Johnny. Don't worry. We'll do this together. I actually grew up across the street from a funeral home, Costa's. I'm not afraid of those places. In fact, if you want, I'll take care of everything for you. You stay here with your father."

"No, we'll go together. Thank you. I don't know what I'd do without you. I love you, Grace."

"I love you too, Johnny."

"Are you okay, Mr. Rostov?"

"Me, no. But yes. Okay. I miss my Sonia."

"Of course, you do. It will be okay. She's in heaven now."

"I hope for this, that true."

Grace gave Anatole a hug. Looking around the apartment, Grace asked if there was anything else she could do.

"Would you like me to make you breakfast, Mr. Rostov?"

"No hungry. Thank you much."

"Okay, but let me know if you need anything, okay?"

"Okay, thanks to you."

"Grace, don't you have to get back to work? Mr. Kobalt seems like he needs you there," asked Johnny.

"He's a big pussy cat. I told him it was a family emergency."

"You shouldn't take a chance like that, and lie to him, Grace."

"What lie? It is family. I'm your family now, Johnny Rostov. And you're never getting rid of me. Never."

Johnny told his father that he and Grace would leave and take care of all the arrangements. Johnny hugged his father, took Grace by the hand, and let themselves out. Walking down Ralph Avenue, Johnny thought of the only funeral home that he knew of. English Brothers' Funeral Home.

"About three blocks down, there's a place," said Johnny.

Johnny and Grace walked into English Brothers' and looked around for someone. Johnny took charge, he acted strong, but Grace knew better. She could see right through him. His heart was broken and his eyes were windows to his soul. And the windows were shattered.

"May I help you?"

Johnny just stared at the soft-spoken man.

"Yes, we need to make arrangements for my boyfriend's mother," said Grace.

"My deepest condolences on your loss, my name is Mr. Todd."

Mr. Todd led Johnny and Grace to a back room. It was eerily quiet, and the whole place had a funny smell to it. Johnny was very uncomfortable, and almost felt numb. They went over all of the costs, and Grace was wonderful. She picked out the casket, the flowers, and set up the viewing times.

"What will that come to?" asked grace.

"Well, with the burial…a hundred and fifty dollars."

"I don't have that much with me," said Johnny.

"That's okay. I have my checkbook. Here, a check for one hundred and fifty dollars," said Grace as she handed the check to Mr. Todd.

"I will pay you…" started Johnny.

"Shh, no. My money is your money. We're a team. We're inseparable," said Grace.

Johnny just started to sob. With all that he had been through—the fire at the boy's home, the beating by his dad on the roof, Jackie dying—this was the most painful. By far. But as he looked at Grace, he realized that for all he'd lost, he also gained so much. This was a woman like no other. Besides his mom, there were just no other perfect souls like this.

Grace stood up and gently rubbed Johnny's back. They shook Mr. Todd's hand, and said goodbye.

The main chapter in Johnny's life had just ended. But a new one had also, just begun.

Chapter Forty

FOR AS PAINFUL as the funeral was, Johnny made it through. Without Grace though, he could never have survived it all. His love for his mother was immense.

Work was good. Johnny did well, and received another promotion, as well as a raise. He was now head of the purchasing department. Slowly but surely, and with Grace's help, his sense of humor and wit started to return. Johnny still couldn't shake the feeling that his mother's death was somehow his fault. The same as with Jackie. Try as she might, Grace found out just how stubborn he was, as she tried to explain that he bore absolutely no responsibility at all for anyone's death. That people die. Being Italian, Grace was brought up in a religious family. She was Roman Catholic, and had a strong belief in God, as well as heaven. Johnny was another story. He really wasn't quite sure, but leaned towards not believing. He had seen too many terrible things to believe that there was a God, done too many things that were wrong, to believe that any God would accept him.

College had started, and Johnny did well. He worked hard all day, studied when he could, and went to the library and clinicals in the evening. Most of his course work was done from home, after work. Grace was wonderful. She supported Johnny and had his back. No matter what.

"Grace, you know that you're everything to me. Nothing else matters. But…my friends Jimmy, and Danny. I haven't seen them in forever it seems. Would you mind if I got together with them tonight? I'll take you home and then take the subway back to Brownsville. We're just gonna hang-out for a while, talk, maybe have a few beers."

"Of course not. But no girls! I know you!" said Grace with a huge laugh.

Johnny knew that Grace was joking. She understood him and knew that he had that boyish charm still. In fact, she loved his sense of humor. He was the most mature "child" she'd ever known.

After dropping Grace off safely at her apartment, Johnny headed back to Brownsville to meet up with Danny and Jimmy.

"The married college man! What an honor. Johnny boy, the big shot!" yelled Jimmy.

"What are you talking about?" asked Johnny.

"Huh?" asked Danny.

"I mean…fuck you, you cock suckin' motha fucker. Suck my big tool, you faggot!"

"Now, that's my Johnny! Welcome back, ya prick!" said Jimmy.

"The hangout? Been a long time. Let's go, the Money Boys roll!" said Danny.

Walking down the alley, Johnny couldn't resist. Mrs. Williams' bathroom. And the light was on. It was a cool October evening, and was already, pretty much dark.

"Oh, my God, this bitch could really suck a cock, fellas. But two minutes later, I was hosin' her good. Made her cry, I fucked her so good. Then her faggot old man shows up. He's one big, retarded looking mother fucker. Imagine that? I fucked his old lady good, throttled her ass and blew a load down her throat, and walked right out. Right in front of him."

"You talk pretty tough, for a skinny punk. The old lady gotta good laugh outta your skinny little prick. We both laughed real hard at you, your knees knockin' as you stumbled and fell out my front door!"

The voice was booming, and echoed throughout the entire alley. Johnny turned around quickly. It was him alright.

"We got your back, Johnny," said Jimmy.

"Listen, you big fuck. Take off, before I tag your old lady's asshole, too. You know what's good for you, you'll leave," said a boastful Jimmy.

Mr. Williams took two large steps towards Johnny. Johnny started to reach for his knife, but it was too late. The man was immense. And powerful. Before he knew it, he had a hand around Johnny's throat. Danny approached and cocked his right arm, ready to let fly, when he was laid out by one shot from the monster's one free hand. Jimmy went next, and didn't fare much better. Getting slapped with a backhand, Jimmy reeled backwards. But in doing so, the large man lost his grip on Johnny's throat. Johnny jumped, as he was startled by a huge blast. And then another. The large man, slumped down to the gravel of the alley. Johnny looked up. It was Al. His handgun was still smoking.

"You ever gonna stay outta trouble, kid? You okay? This fat fuck had it coming. Owed me money, too. He'd beat his wife all the time. What'd you climb on top of her too? I think the whole neighborhood has. Look, clear outta hear before the cops get here. I got this. My boys, well, they know how to take care of these situations."

"Thanks, Al. I owe you," said Johnny.

"You's owed me since you was seven," laughed Al.

Danny and Jimmy slowly got to their feet. The boys walked away, but no longer towards the alley. Walking down Christopher Street, they headed towards Mrs. Mangione's window. No longer soot covered, Johnny, staring at that window, made a decision.

"I'm done. With the filth. The garbage, the noise, the guns, the knives, all the danger. It's enough. I lost my mom, but I found the love of my life. I want out, boys. It's enough. I wanna get married. I'll take care of my dad, but I wanna take Grace, buy a house, and have some kids."

"Sorry about your mom, Johnny. We didn't know what to say," said Danny.

"Yeah, sorry. She was swell," added Jimmy.

"My father always talks about the suburbs. That when he escaped from Russia, to this hell-hole, that he always wanted to make it to the suburbs. You know. New Jersey. The houses are all new, and everything is pretty much perfect, you know?"

"New Jersey? There's all faggots in New Jersey, Johnny. Fruits. Say you ain't serious," said Danny.

"No boys, I'm serious, all right. And, the sooner, the better. It's like it's my destiny. My family's been running forever it seems. The running stops here. My father had to run from the Red Army, and I've been running, into and outta trouble, my whole life. With you two pricks, also. I'm gonna finish college, marry Grace, and I'm gone. And I ain't lookin' back neither."

Johnny, Danny, and Jimmy, stood there and talked for a long while. The moonlight cast a strange and mysterious glow over them. It was almost as if someone above had lit the way for Johnny. Maybe it was Jackie. Maybe it was Sonia.

Johnny shook hands with his boys. He'd see very little of them from that night out. Making his way back to Ralph Avenue, Johnny checked on his father before hitting the sheets, himself.

In the morning, Johnny was helping to clean the apartment, when his father approached.

"For you, John. Your mother's. She want you to have. For to give, Grace. You know, to marry with her."

"What? That's Mom's wedding ring. I can't take that, Dad. I can't."

"No, she want this. We speak of this for many times. Please, John. I am old man. Make for me to be happy."

It was a Saturday morning. Johnny took the ring, and went for a walk. He had both, his gun, and his knife with him. No one was going to fuck with him, or his mother's ring. No way. Johnny made his way to the local jewelry store, Goldstein's Jewelers.

"Hi, I'd like to have this stone made into several tiny ones, and then mounted back onto that same band. How much?"

The old man walked with a cane. Putting an eyepiece in, he carefully examined the stone, mumbling the whole time.

"Let's see. For you? Fifty dollars."

"How about forty?" asked Johnny.

"Get out! Leave."

"Okay, okay. Fifty it is," agreed Johnny.

"I should make it fifty-five now, but…"

"How long? I need it now."

"Everyone needs it now. You have the money? Pay now. I'll have it by closing. Most places would tell you two weeks. Pay up."

Johnny knew better. He'd seen his father make this mistake, time after time. He would pay. After the job was done!

"Okay, here's the fifty. What time can I pick it up?" asked Johnny.

"Nine o'clock. It will be beautiful."

"Okay. Thank you. She's sure beautiful. I hope she likes it. It was my mom's ring."

"You just love her. Rings? Nice. But the love. The hearts. Two becoming one. Stay as one. Two people. One heart."

Johnny just walked a step or two away…thought for a moment, and turned back towards the old man. But he was gone. But his words weren't.

Two people, One heart.

That was perfect. Johnny spent most of the day walking. He still had a little bit of "Johnny boy" left in him. He loved to walk. It cleared his mind. But now when he walked, he wasn't looking for trouble. He would teach his kids…

Walk on the other side of the street. Avoid a fight. Only fight to protect your family!

And they would all listen to him. Of course, they would. Look at all he knew, all that he had been through. Johnny made his way home. He wished that they had a phone. He wanted to call Grace. But, he'd see her. Tomorrow. He'd visit with her, and her mom. Hopefully Rose would be there. Hopefully, Joe would not.

Johnny checked on his dad. He was concerned as he was losing weight. Neither one of them could cook, or really knew anything about taking care of themselves. Johnny was so lost without his mother. Maybe there was a God. Who else could have made such a perfect creature, such as Grace?

At eight forty-five, Johnny opened the front door to Goldstein's Jewelers. The old man hobbled to the front counter.

"Sixty dollars."

Johnny just stared blankly. Not saying a word, a look of disappointment spread across his face.

"Ahhh, good boy. Okay, this ring is the right one for you. You have a kind heart. If you yell at an old man, I take the ring and shove it up your ass. But, you have a good soul. Go. Be happy."

"Thank you, sir."

Johnny stepped outside the front door. He hadn't even looked at the ring. Taking a peek inside of the brown bag, there was a small jewelry box. Popping it open, the light from the street light, illuminated the beautiful, and sparkling stone. It shone so brightly that those in heaven, who cared, just must be able to see this beautiful light. It was amazing. Johnny thought and thought for the perfect words. But he realized, he loved Grace so much because he could be himself. Silly or serious, happy or sad, she understood him. No matter what, they would be one. One heart.

Johnny woke early and bathed. Once again, he borrowed his father's aftershave and splashed it on, quite liberally. Johnny made sure that he had the ring. He only had so many pockets, so something would have to be left behind. The gun would just have to stay. Never the knife. He'd have the knife on his wedding day. Johnny sat with his father for a while. Still getting thinner and thinner, he told him of his plans.

"I know this to happen. So I give to you mother's ring."

"Thank you, Dad."

Johnny took off for the subway. Getting off at Jackson Heights, he walked the few blocks to Grace's apartment. As he approached her building, there she was. Grace's mom, at the bedroom window, yelling something in Italian at the smartass kids. They were yelling back, so Johnny tapped one on the shoulder. Speaking softly, he motioned for the biggest kid to step towards him.

"You want me to cut you up like a sausage, you little fuck? Say you're sorry to my mother. Or I'll put you on an Italian roll and serve you for dinner. You deaf?"

"We're sorry. We didn't mean nuthin'."

With that, they all took off, not looking back at all.

Maria Mannello just laughed. And laughed. She waved to Johnny to come on up. Walking very deliberately, Johnny made his way up the stairs and knocked two times.

"Who is it? Oh, you? You ready for some beers? Shots?"

Joe was his usual, charming self.

"Johnny? Joe! Get out of the way. Johnny! Hi!" said Grace. She had the biggest grin on her face, and happiness was just overflowing from her tiny frame.

Johnny side stepped Joe and entered the apartment. Not showing disrespect, Johnny also didn't react well to bullies.

Johnny wasn't going to wait. But he wanted to do this right.

"Joe, I realize that you're the man of this house. I love your sister. So, I want to ask both you, and your beautiful mother, for permission to ask Grace to marry me."

"Grace! Did you hear that? Hi, I'm Rose. I'm Grace's favorite sister. Just ask her!"

"He's talkin' to me. That's the right way to do it, Johnny. Respect. And yes. Let me talk to Mamma," said Joe.

"Mamma, vuole sposarla," explained Joe.

"Ohhhh! Yes!" replied Maria.

Grace's mom was ecstatic. Not only did she think that Johnny was handsome, strong, and funny, but she just knew that he would take care of her baby.

Johnny took both of Grace's hands, and led her to right in front of the chair, where her mother was sitting. Dropping to one knee, he started…

"Grace, I've only loved one woman in my life, and that has been my own mother. That is until now. The love I feel for you, is a love that is meant to be. Grace, I've loved you before I ever laid eyes on you, I've loved you forever. And I'll love you forever more. I'll always take care of you, always protect you, and be the best husband that I can possibly be. I will respect you, for you are your own person, but we will share. Share a life together, children together, and a heart. Two people in love. One heart. Grace, please marry me."

Silence. Johnny expected tears of joy. It had gone perfectly. He thought it had. He was wonderful, if he didn't think so himself.

"Say yes, Grace! Say yes!" said a giddy Rose.

"It's just that I have it so good here!" she smiled. Pausing for just a moment or two, she then answered. "Yes, of course I'll marry you. Together, we're complete. I don't know what else to say. You have all the words, but, I love you. Yes. I'll marry you!"

"So, now will you have a few shots?" said Joe.

Johnny laughed and after he kissed Grace, Maria, and even Rose, he and Joe went and had their shots. Life would be good now. They could do anything together; they could overcome all odds together.

It had been a long, hard journey. The Rostov family was a tough one. They never gave up. But they persevered. From the bloody pit, and cold fields of Russia, to the filth, and dangers of Brownsville, the family had come a long way. Poverty, hardships, and even death may have slowed them down, but they still moved forward. Johnny and Grace would escape New York and make their way to the suburbs of New Jersey. There would be many more obstacles in their future. But as long as Johnny had Grace, they'd be okay. And as long as Grace had Johnny. Her protector. Grace just knew that her daddy was smiling down from heaven. They were two individuals. Two hearts, but one soul. Their love would be eternal. The woman of his dreams… she had always been there, but Johnny had finally met her.

THE END

About the Author

Christopher Morosoff Sr. was born in Manhattan, New York, to parents of Russian and Italian heritage. He married his high school sweetheart, Theresa, and started a family. Christopher has worked in many different fields and it is just very recently that Christopher's father, Andre, began to encourage him to give writing a try. His first novel, *The Boxcar Traveler*, was based on a memory that Christopher had from his youth. Always finding the thought of 'riding the rails' to be an interesting and romantic notion, he simply started to write. His style has been all stream of consciousness and the book has been very well reviewed and submitted for Pulitzer prize consideration. Christopher and Theresa have three adult children, as well as a grandson and granddaughter.

Books by Christopher Morosoff

The Boxcar Traveler
Johnny and Grace

www.ingramcontent.com/pod-product-compliance
Lightning Source LLC
Chambersburg PA
CBHW051430260626
47162CB00001B/22